She couldn't have be

"What exactly are you accusing me of?"

Caught off guard by Marcus Van Buren's anger, Daisy stammered, "You...you kissed me." The incident suddenly blurred in her mind, taking on a surreal quality. "I...I think."

"Believe me, Ms. Malone," he said in a dangerous tone, "if I ever kiss you, you'll damn well know you've been kissed."

In the downstairs foyer, huddled around an open leather suitcase, stood the Van Buren ghosts. James leaned against the front door, knocking his fedora against his thigh and raking his other hand impatiently through his hair. He watched as his sister, wearing an ornery grin, buffed her red-polished nails while Jonas shrugged out of a modern, pin-striped suit jacket and hurried to replace it onto a padded hanger.

It had always been like this when they were alive. Jonas and Izzy instigating, him playing catch up. Just like old times. Unable to contain his curiosity, he pushed off the door and advanced on them, hands on hips. "All right, you two. What are you up to?"

This book is dedicated to our mentors and champions. Colleen Admirand, Stephanie Bond, Terri Brisbin, Terri Castoro, Sandra Chastain, Kathryn Falk, Jo Ann Ferguson, Sandy Ferguson, Shirley Hailstock, Linda Kichline, Jim & Nikoo McGoldrick, Debra Mullins, Julie Templeton, Mary Stella, Jennifer Wagner, Lyn Wagner, and NJRW.

Cynthia especially thanks her Dad, Bill Klimback, for letting her read his books, and Ken Valero, who knows why. Beth especially thanks her husband (and true-life hero), Steve, and her circle of incredible friends.

Scandalous Spirits

***

CB Scott

SCANDALOUS SPIRITS
Published by ImaJinn Books, a division of ImaJinn

ISBN: 1-893896-23-4

10 9 8 7 6 5 4 3 2 1

PUBLISHER'S NOTE:
This book is a work of fiction. Names, characters, places and incidents are products of the author's imagination or are used fictitiously. Any resemblance to actual events or locales or persons, living or dead, is entirely coincidental.

Books are available at quantity discounts when used to promote products or services. For information please write to: Marketing Division, ImaJinn Books, P.O. Box 162, Hickory Corners, MI 49060-0162, or call toll free 1-877-625-3592.

Cover design by Patricia Lazarus

ImaJinn Books, a division of ImaJinn
P.O. Box 162, Hickory Corners, MI 49060-0162
Toll Free: 1-877-625-3592
http://www.imajinnbooks.com

Prologue

"I'm dying of boredom."

"Keen trick, Izzy, considering you've been dead for the last seventy years."

Cigarette holder poised between two slender fingers, Isadora Van Buren-Valentine-Mueller-Tadmucker-Carr slicked her bobbed hair behind one diamond-studded ear, blew out a lazy stream of smoke, then snipped, "Go chase yourself, Jimmy."

"Vamp."

"Goof."

Jonas Van Buren shook his head as his cantankerous younger siblings launched into yet another verbal tussle. In confounding "hereafter limbo" since 1928 and they were still at it. Some things never changed. "Lay off, you two. Bickering won't solve our plight. In fact, it's what got us into this mess in the first place. Or have you forgotten?"

"If memory serves," Isadora drawled, flicking her ashes into an etched blue crystal bowl, "Jimmy's lousy driving got us into this mess. He's the one who steered the Pierce-Arrow off the bridge and into the drink."

"I was distracted," James snapped in self-defense, plunking down the deck of cards he'd been fanning and shuffling on the table before them. But when he palmed up the snap-brim of his brown felt fedora, guilt plagued his handsome, boyish features.

"I know you were, sweetie," Isadora quickly amended, her cupie-bowed lips drawing into a contrite frown. "I'm sorry." Suddenly morose, she added, "If anyone's to blame, it's me. I'm the one who talked you and Jonas into staying late at the speak-easy."

"You didn't talk us into anything, angel," Jonas said, sorry he'd introduced the subject of their physical demise in the first place. "It was a collective decision, remember? All for one and one for all."

James' mouth slid into a lopsided grin upon hearing their childhood oath. "You said it!"

"And how!" Isadora exclaimed, her ruby red lips curving back into a smile.

Grateful for their easily restored humor, Jonas smiled as well. Smoothing the shawl collar of his double-breasted vest, he returned then to his usual post: the arched glass window of the secluded west tower of Laguna Vista, the infamous Van Buren Estate. Or as they'd come to refer to it as of late, the Van Buren Prison.

He braced his palms on either side of the sash and looked out in disgust over the unkempt grounds. Gnarled brambles and rampant sea grass thrived in place of sculptured hedges and exotic roses. The once immaculate lawn of the Spanish-style mansion was no longer green but brown, and littered with rocks and empty liquor bottles. Or as Isadora so colorfully referred to them, dead soldiers.

The former summer home of their parents, the powerful and wealthy department store tycoon Jonathan Bernard Van Buren and his socialite wife Ella, Laguna Vista had been the high-society playground for some of America's most popular celebrities, not to mention occasional politicians and assorted European dignitaries.

Up until 1928, anyhow.

That tragic year James accidentally drove the family's luxury automobile off a bridge, ending his fast-lane life along with that of his sister's and brother's. Of course it had been foggy and he'd been speeding, but as Isadora had said, the fact that they ended up in the bottom of the bay swimming with the fishes wasn't entirely their little brother's fault. They'd all been blotto, hopped up on hooch compliments of Isadora's favorite gin mill. And they'd been bickering. Not that *that* was unusual. The Van Buren siblings were famous for their caustic, though mostly harmless, tiffs. They loved each other dearly. They just didn't happen to agree on everything. Strike that, Jonas thought with an amused grunt, they didn't agree on a lot of things. Like who were the cat's pajamas? The Yanks or the Dodgers?

The details revolving around the fatal crash and the moments thereafter remained a mystery to the three siblings. One moment they'd been arguing over who would take the World Series in '29. The next they were free-floating twenty feet over the murky water, looking on as a fleet of gumshoes fished the dented Pierce-Arrow out of the bay. Seeing their lifeless bodies being pulled from the car was a bit of a shock, to say the least. *How could they be dead when they felt so alive?* And if they *were* dead, shouldn't they be in heaven or hell or . . . something?

"Maybe we're hallucinating," James had offered. "That's what we get for drinking coffin varnish."

"Don't be a sap," Isadora snapped, watching as two meds hoisted her limp, slender form onto a gurney. Pointing a translucent finger at her raccoon-ring-eyed, lipstick-smeared face a short distance beyond, she said, "I've been corked on bootleg whiskey more times than I can count, and I've never looked as bad as that."

To which Jonas replied, "Says you."

Then it occurred to them. They weren't kickin' in the physical sense, but spiritually . . .

Jonas recalled Isadora and James launching into a heated debate over the subtle differences between ghosts and spirits, then lapsing into a fit of snorting laughter while plotting the swell tricks they'd get over on their cousins. He even remembered tossing in a few choice pranks of his own. But his most vivid recollection was the heart-wrenching moment they'd sobered up, simultaneously realizing the impact their deaths would have on those they'd left behind. It crushed their fanciful mindset and landed them within the grieving walls of Laguna Vista in the blink of a snake's eye.

And here they'd been stuck ever since. A problem Jonas had spent the last seventy years trying to rectify. Ghostly limbo wasn't all it was cracked up to be. Unlike Isadora and James, he'd never reveled in the novelty of being a disembodied spirit. He'd merely tolerated their fate, as he seemed to have no choice. He longed to cross over, to join friends and family members in heaven, or at least to graduate to a higher non-physical plane. However, for reasons that eluded him, the Powers-That-Be turned a consistently deaf ear to his simple request. It was as if he was being punished, but for what? *What?*

Isadora watched as Jonas' shoulders sagged in familiar defeat. He was mulling over their fate again. She hated when he did that. It tended to depress him, and she hated anything sad. Sighing dramatically, since it was one of her better talents, she snuffed out her fag after one last drag then rose from the settee to join him. The high spiked heels of her patent leather pumps clicked on the polished marble floor, filling the same silence that had worked her into a lather moments before.

Izzy Van Buren-Valentine-Mueller-Tadmucker-Carr, scandalous heiress-cum-flapper extraordinaire, detested silence—oh, and anything sad.

"You know," she cooed, sidling in beside him, "haunting Laguna Vista was fun for the first sixty years or so, but these last ten years, well, sheesh. I had more fun at my own wake."

"I know you're bored, angel," Jonas replied without cracking the smile she'd hoped for. "Believe me, if I could figure a way to spring us from this joint, I would."

His brows cut down into a stern vee, the reason as clear as moonshine to Izzy. It baffled him that they could permeate every wall within the seventeen-room mansion like kites through a cloud, but they couldn't pass through the outer walls to gain freedom to the outside world. She grinned, recalling the time James had tried to escape by jumping out a window while she shimmied up the chimney. Of course, stick-in-the-mud Jonas had taken the mortal route by trying to walk out the front door. All three had hit invisible barriers.

"This is the longest Laguna Vista has remained vacant," she thought aloud. "And for the death of me, I don't understand why."

"No doubt because of us," Jonas replied, distracted by a late-seventies vehicle rolling to a stop just inside the front gate of the mansion.

"Yeah, Izzy," James taunted, coming up behind them. "You scared everyone away."

"Did not!"

"Did so!"

"Dry up, you two." Jonas snapped his fingers to gain their attention then motioned them to peer out the window. "Looks like we didn't scare *everyone* away." Gazing past the bug-splattered windshield of the four-wheeled junker, he pinpointed the willowy broad sitting in the driver's seat. The one with the pert-nose, freckled face, and long blond hair swept up in a playful, bobby-soxer ponytail. He let loose a soft, appreciative whistle. "Lordy, that blonde's a looker."

"She's sweet and all," James agreed, leering from his third-story vantage point, "but fix your blinkers on the tomato sitting next to her. The one in the short skirt." He snapped his suspenders and hooted. "Now that's a choice bit of calico!"

"She's also a choice bit of jailbait," Izzy noted. "I'm with Jonas. The blonde is definitely more interesting. Look at how she's giving this place the once over. She's moving in. I can feel it! Oh, I do hope she turns Laguna Vista back into a disco. I so loved the music." She broke into the "Hustle" with an imaginary partner while belting out the chorus of "I Will Survive."

James rolled his eyes before training them on the blonde. "Nah, she looks more like the bed-and-breakfast type to me. What do you think, Jonas?"

Jonas peered closer, noticing for the first time the logo emblazoned across the long-dented door of the ancient hippie-mobile. *Society of Parapsychological Sleuths.* An uneasy feeling wound through his gut, the same daunting feeling that tied him in knots whenever he'd had dealings with the IRS. Rocking back on his oxfords, he palmed his hand over his slicked-back hair and sighed. "I think we're in big trouble."

One

"What a dump! You're actually going to *sleep* here?"

Daisy Malone ignored her sister and the deserted mansion she'd spent nearly half her life trying to avoid. She was too busy gripping the steering wheel so as not to lunge for the glove compartment. Its broken door hung wide open like a beer belly out of a ratty tee-shirt. She knew the cigarette lay buried beneath the jumble of expired insurance cards and matchbook covers scribbled with unwanted phone numbers. She'd put it there herself. Just in case. For emergencies.

Surely this qualified as an emergency.

"What if we have to pee?" Jill asked.

Definitely an emergency.

When Jill Malone had planted herself in the passenger seat, arms crossed, demanding a first-hand glimpse inside Atlantic City's most notorious residence, Daisy should've pushed her right out of the van. Sometimes she wished sibling rules didn't change as you got older. Sometimes it was just easier to wrestle than to be polite and ignored. Of course, on any other day, at any other place, she'd be delighted with her sister's company. But today, here, now, her stomach twisted with the threat of failing her family. And with Jill here, of failing *in front* of her family. That reality wasted no time in showing its ugly face. Of course there'd be no running water in the house, let alone a toilet in which you'd even think to chuck a cigarette.

I want that cigarette. She gripped the wheel tighter.

Where *would* she go to the bathroom? Four days was a long time to have to sneak into the overgrown bushes behind the mansion. She'd already been hauled away from Laguna

Vista once by Atlantic City's finest.

"There's the fast food joint down the road," Daisy finally answered with a sigh, knowing she couldn't smoke that cigarette in front of her younger sister, even if that younger sister had the mind and body of the wiliest Bond girl. Besides, time was running out. Eventually, she'd have to face the fact that she had a job to do. That, or Jill would have to walk to that fast food joint to call the white coats to come pry her sister out of the driver's seat.

"You can't use their restrooms unless you buy food."

"So I'll be eating a lot of French fries," Daisy mumbled, staring idly at the broken odometer, wondering exactly when her relatively normal life had taken the leap into the absurd.

"You know, there's nothing wrong with being a waitress, Daisy."

That snapped her head up. She looked at her sister, who now chomped on the cigarette Daisy had been agonizing over. She snatched the cigarette from Jill's mouth, only to be rewarded with sulky, drooping lips. "You're only seventeen. You're too young to smoke."

"You're only twenty-seven. You're too young for a mid-life crisis." Jill fumbled with the lighter built into the van's ashtray. "You should really get this thing fixed."

Daisy's palms began to sweat as she clutched the cigarette in one hand, the wheel in the other. "What do you mean, a mid-life crisis?"

"Oh, come on." Jill ran her fingers through her prom-queen hair before jabbing her thumb toward the back of the van. "You blew your savings on a boatload of ghostbusting equipment you barely know how to use. Most women take a lover or go on a diet when they're feeling inadequate."

Daisy peered over her shoulder at the dust swirling above cases of antiquated ghost*hunting* equipment, dulled further by the pale morning sun.

Inadequate. Is that what she was feeling?

It didn't matter. Inadequate or not, right now she needed to be the super hero. Dazzling in her good intentions. Chest swelled with confidence. Cape snapping, teeth gleaming.

Rushing in just in time to save the day...

Fear clutched her belly. What if she couldn't do it? What if she couldn't save the day? She chucked the cigarette onto the dashboard. What if Pop hadn't gambled away his money? What if she hadn't been selfish and blown hers on a silly dream?

Questions raced around her mind, as futile to chase as a greyhound after the mechanical rabbit. The urge to pack it in and turn tail before she made a worse mess of things nearly overwhelmed her. Then again, how could she possibly make things worse? Her family teetered on the brink of financial ruin. She had the opportunity to bail them out. An opportunity afforded to a *parapsychologist*, a title she'd only recently acquired through a string of community college courses. So what if she hadn't aced the technical exams? She had a gift. The telepathic gift of a "sensitive," according to Cliff and Randall, her professors. And she was counting on that gift a hell of a lot more than the ghosthunting gadgets and gizmos piled up behind her.

Drawing a deep breath, she turned back to Jill. "The Society of Parapsychological Sleuths has disproved 95% of all investigated hauntings," she recited over-confidently. "That's why Mr. Sinclair hired us."

"There is no more *us*," Jill pointed out. "Clyde and Rathbone—"

"Cliff and Randall," Daisy grumbled.

"—moved to California, taking their expertise with them. All you've got is their junky equipment—a rip-off if you ask me—and the Society's name. Though I guess the reputation's worth something considering you got this job your first time out. Oh, and by the way, technically it was Marcus Van Buren who hired you. According to you, Sinclair was just his peon mouthpiece."

"More like a thug in a suit, on second thought. And I'm well aware of who's footing the bill," Daisy said. She was bought and paid for, just like yesterday's newspaper. And like yesterday's newspaper, Sinclair had read her as if he already knew what was printed. Easy mark. Sucker. Desperate. Sign a paper stating Laguna Vista 100% ghost free, he'd said, and we'll pay you ten grand. An astronomical amount considering most institutes were non-profit and most reputable societies conducted studies for a pittance and a write-up in a paranormal journal. Refusing to analyze Sinclair's motives, she'd endorsed the thousand-dollar bonus incentive check knowing she was not only signing the check, but signing over her integrity as well. She'd agreed to verify Laguna Vista ghost free, despite the results of her investigation. Lying came as easily to Daisy Malone as tap dancing across a high wire.

However, when it came to her family's well-being, she'd make any sacrifice.

"Yeah, well, Marcus Van Buren won't lose any sleep over *that* bill," Jill added. She whipped out the copy of the tabloid she'd purchased when they'd stopped to pick up a six pack of soda at the convenience store. "Did you see the size of his new yacht in *The Tattletale*?"

Daisy glanced at the cover story and frowned. "That's why I'm more than thrilled to take his money," she replied, not thrilled at all.

"Check out the hooters on his twin bimbos!" Jill whistled. "I wonder how much they paid for those."

Daisy shook her head in disgust. No wonder the man's fiancée had dumped him. The photo featured Marcus Van Buren snuggling with identical twin babes. *This* was not the behavior of a one-woman man. But then why should she be surprised? The man had never had to work for a thing in his life. Want something? Go buy it. Lose something? Get another.

The sight of such blatant frivolity sickened her, and when she turned away from it to force her attention to the house, she felt even worse. The mansion, once touted as the jewel of the Eastern Seaboard, now looked as rundown as her life. Boarded windows, broken roof tiles, overgrown shrubs. The house had been left abandoned for over a decade, forgotten like a worn-out shoe on the side of the highway. As expected, she felt an urge to cry as she studied the defeated structure. It looked as if it had struggled long and hard against the elements and neglect, then finally, tired of fighting a losing battle, just sank down in the sand and gave up. Disheartened. Nothing but a memory.

How could Marcus Van Buren spend such an obscene amount of money on a stupid boat when right down the shore his family's heritage deteriorated into oblivion?

No, scratch that. She didn't care. Wouldn't care. She was being paid a ridiculous sum not to . . . which reminded her of the reason she was here.

The money.

Forcing herself out of the van, she kicked aside an empty beer bottle with a long-faded label.

"Marcus Van Buren should be flogged for allowing this place to go to pot," she complained despite herself, continuing to direct her angst in his direction because, truthfully, it felt good.

"Maybe he's tired of trying." Jill slid open the van's heavy cargo door, which screeched hideously on rusted gliders. She started unloading, piling cardboard boxes and red milk crates onto the dead lawn. "I mean, how many failed restaurants and nightclubs does it take before you start to look like an idiot?" Jill leaned against the equipment. "Face it, Daze. There's a reason no one comes here. Laguna Vista is haunted."

"Presumably haunted," Daisy corrected, hauling out two hard cases of assorted camera gear. "It's all just rumors, and I'm going to prove it."

Her sister snorted. "Rumors? Did you fall out of bed and crack your head again? You're the one who swore she saw a ghost in that window."

Daisy lifted her gaze to Laguna Vista's west tower. The true source of her dilemma. She'd been avoiding it since she'd put the van in park, but now its arched window seemed to loom over her, gaping dark and empty like the splayed jaws of a shark.

She had been ten years old the night she'd seen the man in the window. A seeming trick of the moonlight. But what touched her in that ripple of time went far beyond simple explanation.

She'd stood frozen, paralyzed, as she stared at the man,

as something stronger than her own will pinned her where she'd stood. After watching that horror-flick festival after school that Halloween, she should have been terrified. Her imagination should have run screaming into the night, wishing she'd never left the safety of her popcorn-ridden couch. But just when she might have done that, an incredible sadness rammed into her chest, hard and heavy as a linebacker, knocking wind and sensibilities clear from her young body.

Only a compulsive need to comfort remained. To help. But this man was a complete stranger. She a child. How could she know this?

She'd stood wringing her yellow softball shirt between clenched fists, when suddenly, like the shadow of a cloud, his gaze drifted over her. He saw her. Any breath left in her lungs deserted her as loneliness—a deep hole of emptiness—swallowed her being. Then, just as it became unbearable, he was gone, and the feeling with him.

That was the first and last time Daisy Malone had laid eyes on the infamous Jonas Van Buren.

Today, like every other day she'd come as a child to stare up at that arched window, she saw nothing but a pitted, bleary pane.

Today, for the first time ever, she was glad.

Daisy shivered but remained neutral as she deflected the truth. "I was ten years old. It was Halloween. We'd been telling ghost stories. I thought I saw something, but I was wrong. My imagination got the better of me."

"You're so full of it. You don't believe it was your imagination anymore than I do," Jill said, calling Daisy's bluff. "You're not the only one who claims to have seen a Van Buren ghost. Stories have been circulating about this place for years."

She'd heard them all. Jonas, Isadora, and James Van Buren … three siblings who'd lived and loved in the fast lane. Rich, reckless, and inseparable—even in death. Too scandalous for heaven, too pure of heart for hell. Legend had it the Van Burens were tied to Laguna Vista in ghostly limbo, serving some sort of penance for countless, shocking indiscretions.

Because it was all she could do, Daisy wore the mask of

skeptic as she grabbed the last of the equipment. "There is no substantiated proof that Laguna Vista is haunted," she said in her most professional voice.

Jill tucked a tripod under her arm, preparing to set off for the house. "How are you going to get substantiated proof that Laguna Vista *isn't* haunted? What if you *can't* get it? Then we'll be in the same jam we were in before."

Daisy winced but turned away before Jill could see.

I will not fail. I cannot fail.

Reaching the shadowed alcove of the front entry, she pulled out the key given to her by Sinclair. Despite her misgivings about the job, her excitement began to mount. How many times had she dreamed of getting inside this place? Of finding out for herself if Jonas Van Buren really existed?

As if she could read her thoughts, Jill asked, "Are you prepared for this? I mean, you spent a good chunk of your childhood obsessing over this guy. Are you prepared for the truth, whatever it may be?"

Daisy smiled and unlocked the door. "There's nothing to prepare for. Like I said, it was my imagination."

Jill twisted her lips. "Whatever you say."

Daisy pushed open the door and took a shaky breath. How many times would she have to lie to her family, even if it was for their own good? If they knew she planned to lie, they'd demand she quit on the spot. Not to mention the negative impression she'd make on her younger siblings. Maybe Jill knew she was full of it, but Daisy would never admit it aloud.

She stepped inside the foyer.

For an instant she forget everything else.

Finally I'm here.

As she stood in the house for the first time, she closed her eyes and tried to quiet her nerves. *Is anyone here? Jonas? Isadora? James?* She waited for a feeling, any feeling, that might alert her to another presence. But after a few moments, she dismissed the churning anxiety as her own, as well as the ridiculous disappointment.

She drew a settling breath, expecting the air to be musty, clogged with a decade's worth of dust and faded dreams.

Instead a potent lemon scent teased her nose. She opened her eyes. The colorful, mosaic-tiled floor gleamed as if freshly washed. The twenty-four-foot-high ceiling of the grand hall sported not a single cobweb. Odd.

"I guess we don't have to worry about where to pee so much as who's watching," Jill said drolly.

Daisy ignored her as she looked around in awe, feeling as if an elusive dream was finally coming to light. "Cary Grant and J.F.K. crossed over this very threshold, or so legend has it. Imagine the flirtations and steamy affairs that flared up under this old terra-cotta roof." She winked and wiggled her brows. "Imagine if these walls could talk."

Jill dropped her boxes to the floor. "Well, according to you they can't, so we'll never know what really happened, will we?"

Daisy forced herself to remain calm. How could she argue with her sister, who was suspicious by nature? Not that her suspicions were unfounded. Growing up, the would-be lawyer had heard countless retellings of her big sister's adventures at the spooky old mansion. How many times must she have heard Daisy ramble on about Jonas? How many times must she have passed the picture of him that Daisy had photocopied from the newspaper archive at the library and tacked to her wall?

None of that mattered now. She had a job to do, and despite the farce it might be, her family's future depended on her ability to function as a scientist rather than a wistful girl chasing childhood fantasies.

Mentally shrugging into a lab coat, she told her sister, "Laguna Vista is nothing more than a deserted mansion with a colorful history. Speaking of which, I read somewhere that Clark Gable and Betty Hutton shared a lusty one-night fling here." She pursed her lips. "Or was it Gable and *Barbara* Hutton?"

Jill grunted with annoyance. "Maybe it was both."

"My point is," Daisy continued, "this house may be a *stuccoed lemon*, but it's a lemon of notorious historical interest—an interest which Marcus Van Buren reportedly doesn't have. Rumor has it he's never set foot in the house lived in by his father, grandfather, and great-grandfather before him. Well," she snorted as if that said it all, "let's just say that I venture our local casino moguls possess more sentimentality in their manicured pinkies than Marcus Van Buren, President and CEO of VB Enterprises, does in his whole Christen Dior-suited body." Daisy's opinion of the country's most elusive bachelor millionaire withered further. "What do you want to bet that financial-wizard, deal-spinning workaholic makes love with a cell phone in one hand and the Dow Jones report in the other?"

"I'll take your word for it, Daze," Jill said, rolling her eyes. Making her way out of the foyer, she added over her shoulder, "I thought you didn't like him."

"I don't."

"Then why are you imagining him naked?"

Daisy stopped short. "What? Naked? Get real." Despite her denial, her cheeks burned with the mortifying realization that she'd done just that. Imagined Marcus Van Buren naked. For a split-second at least. Well, who could blame her when every time she set foot in the food store, his picture was splashed across at least three of the rag journals at the checkout counter. He was a handsome man, for crying out loud. He gave those *Soap Opera Diary* hunks a run for their money. Just because she didn't like him didn't mean—

"This is so cool!" Jill's whistle echoed through the first floor of the cavernous mansion. "You could fit the entire senior class in this room."

Daisy stepped into the main living area behind her. "Don't even think about it."

"I can't believe how clean it is. No mess, no muss, no dust. Weird."

"I know. Maybe Sinclair hired a cleaning service."

"That, or the ghosts are clean-freaks," Jill cracked.

Daisy scanned the living area, compelled by its immensity and subtle charm. Her gaze traveled up the wrought-iron, spiral staircase to a balcony edging the south and east walls. According to her research, the arches beyond that balcony led to three large bedrooms, two baths, and a library. Or what was once a library anyway. Laguna Vista had been converted and redecorated so many times over the decades, she'd be surprised if the contemporary layout resembled any of the original 1923 floor plan. Although, sans furniture, the living room looked much the same as in an early photo—spiral staircase, grand fireplace, and all.

Jill spun around. "Now what?"

Daisy set down her own cases and propped the tripods in the corner. "I guess I'll do a little exploring, get a feel for the place before I set up the equipment."

"Then what?"

"Then I'll disprove the rumors."

"What if you can't?"

Daisy shrugged and started in the direction of the kitchen, hoping to escape the dark cloud circling over her head. "I will," she said irritably.

"Humor me," Jill asked. "What if the ghosts are here? Then what?"

Daisy sighed. "Then I'll have to try to reason with them."

"You mean ask them to leave?"

"Help them to leave," Daisy amended over her shoulder. Quoting a research book, she added, "Oft times disembodied spirits are unaware that they can cross over simply by..."

"Simply by what?" Jill called.

"Holy moly," Daisy exclaimed, redirecting the conversation. "Haul your butt in here and check out this state-of-the-art kitchen! Mom would freak!"

"*Simply by what?*" Jonas demanded, anxiously circling the kitchen chandelier.

"*They're on another subject now, Jonas.*" James sat cross-legged atop the super-deluxe refrigerator. "*Don't cast a kitten. They'll get back to it.*"

"*Yeah, sweetie,*" Isadora piped in, stretched out languorously atop the kitchen's wall-to-wall cabinets. "*They just got here. And you want to leave? Didn't you hear the part about Marcus? Aren't you curious about him? He's your grandson, you know.*"

"*Of course I heard,*" Jonas snapped. "*I'm dead, not deaf.*"

"Well, I for one want to know why your grandson is so anxious to write us off, so to speak. Our own flesh and blood. He never comes around. He's let Laguna Vista sit empty for ten years, leaving us bored and lonely. And now he wants to deny our existence officially? Frankly, Jonas, I consider it the ultimate snub."

The fact that Marcus avoided Laguna Vista didn't strike Jonas as a snub so much as a relief. They'd seen few family members since their parents closed down the house after their deaths, and those rare times had been bad enough. Who needed that kind of misery? Who needed to feel like a goldfish in a tank, watching the family through an invisible barrier, not being able to say or do anything? *"If that dame has our ticket out, Izzy, I want it."*

Isadora flew across the room, squaring off with Jonas at the crystal chandelier. *"I'm not so sure I want 'out.' What's 'out' there anyway? Heaven? Hell? We hardly lived the lives of angels, you know."*

"Hell couldn't be much worse than this," Jonas bellowed.

"This isn't hell, you brooding jackass. It's home!"

"Lay off, you two," James shouted. *"You're scarin' my sweetheart."*

"What's up with the chandelier, Daisy?" Jill asked.

Daisy looked up at the tinkling chandelier and frowned. From the moment she'd stepped into the kitchen, her anxiety had lunged and strained like a dog against a choke chain. Though she'd managed to hold her temper in check since arriving, her dander was suddenly up and ready for battle. She stalked over to a partially opened window and closed it. "The wind," she snapped. "Didn't you feel how cool it was in here? Sheesh, you'd make a rotten parapsychologist."

Jill cocked a haughty brow. "Excuse me for living."

Daisy drew a deep breath and rested her hand on her sister's arm. "I'm sorry, Jill. It's this room. It feels ...I feel...I don't know."

Jill chimed the theme to the *Twilight Zone.*

"Cut it out. It's not that. Maybe . . . I guess everything happening with Pop is getting to me." Finally, the partial truth.

Her family's uncertain future weighed on her shoulders, though she'd never admit it to Jill or to any of her four siblings. A lot was riding on this case. Her pride the least of it. On the "important-things-in-life" list, family ranked number one.

Again her thoughts turned to Marcus Van Buren. They'd never met face to face, but she'd seen him often enough on various profile news shows and read about him plenty in those rag journals while waiting at the checkout. From what she'd read and heard, he was a loner. No wife, no kids, no family. Well, a mother who lived in southern Florida and a slew of cousins and other assorted distant relatives, but no one you saw him cozying up with for feel-good promo shots.

The thought struck Daisy as sad and...odd. Especially since he descended from a flock of Van Burens who were notoriously devoted to one another. *All for one and one for all.*

Her eyes flicked back up to the ornate chandelier.

What if?

No. She couldn't afford to go there. Couldn't afford to give in to her imagination. From this moment on she needed to think logically, rationally. She needed to collect fact-based data, proving Laguna Vista irrefutably, undeniably ghost-free.

It didn't matter that she thought him the lowest of the low. She needed Marcus Van Buren's money.

Two

"I've got three different women holding on three different lines, Mr. Van Buren. All three with bulletproof charm. All three insisting on speaking with you personally. Just like the two dozen others who've called so far today. Are you in or out, sir?"

Marcus set aside the Laguna Vista contract with a sigh. He had never despised anyone in his life. But tabloid reporter Joe Rush was lobbying hard to become the first.

His secretary had buzzed in with calls every ten minutes for the last two hours. He knew without asking what those three women wanted. A date. Thanks to this morning's edition of *The Tattletale*, he was suddenly the most popular man in Manhattan. So far he'd turned down several luncheon invitations, four dinner parties, a night at the opera, a weekend in Paris, and an afternoon of hot sex at The Waldorf. He was fresh out of polite refusals. He pressed the button on the intercom. "Out."

"Yes, sir. Uh, Mr. Van Buren, sir?"

"Yes, Ms. Bishop?"

"I know it's only ten a.m., but I'm thinking you may want to be 'out' for the rest of the day. Where these ladies are concerned, I mean. Given the article and all, that is. Sir."

"Good point, Ms. Bishop. I'll trust you to make the proper apologies. And you can stop calling me sir. We're not all that formal around here."

"Yes, sir. Thank you, sir. Good-bye, Mr. Van Buren."

Marcus smiled. Fresh out of school and eager to please. He remembered those days well. "Good-bye, Ms. Bishop." He released the intercom button and took up this morning's edition of *The Tattletale*. He wished for a match, overwhelmed by an urge to watch the unrepentant tabloid flare up in flames right there on his desk. Of course, he ignored the impulse and simply glared at the headline for the hundredth time.

Marcus Van Buren. America's Most Eligible Bachelor Lookin' for Love.

He cursed Joe Rush, not for the first time in his life.

Rush. The star reporter who flashed rabid teeth just before sinking them into your life and ripping it to shreds. The reporter who'd become that star and built a lucrative career by reporting the trials and tribulations, personally and professionally, of Marcus Van Buren, CEO of VB Enterprises, heir to the Van Buren fortune.

Two months ago Rush had glamorized Marcus' engagement to socialite Kimberly Langford. Last month he'd gloried in exploiting the details of their breakup. This month, *this morning*, Rush had splashed across the front page photos of Marcus enjoying a rare weekend away on his yacht. A weekend he'd planned to spend alone. Relaxing. Reflecting. The blonde twins in skin-tight leather had been Rufus' idea. Funny how Rush had snapped the photo just *after* Marcus' dog of an assistant had gone below for more champagne, leaving Marcus the focus of the twins' amorous affections.

Hence the headline, the cover shot, and the tagline, 'MVB shows KL that there are plenty of fish in the sea ... and he's reeling 'em in two at a time!' Hence the flood of phone calls this morning from some of the city's most ambitious single fish. Uh, females.

Marcus tossed back three aspirins and washed them down with a swig of spring water. The headline blared in his memory, adding to the headache that had started with his review of the Laguna Vista contract.

America's Most Eligible Bachelor.

Why him?

What was Rush's fascination with him? Or the country's for that matter? He was a businessman, plain and simple. A very successful, very wealthy businessman perhaps, but certainly not royal-family-intrigue or nude-beach-frolicking material. But maybe that was it. He *was* fresh blood, seemingly untainted, but still Van Buren blood. Maybe Rush believed the apple didn't fall far from the tree. Maybe Rush believed it was only a matter of time before another Van Buren provided the scoop of a lifetime.

Hence Rush lurking in the shadows, waiting for anything fit, or even better, unfit to print.

Scandal. The curse of a Van Buren.

A blast of impatience ripped through Marcus. *God, he couldn't wait to be rid of that house.* Speaking of which...*Buzzzz.* "Ms. Bishop, when Mr. Sinclair gets here—"

"I'm here." Rufus Sinclair skidded into the room, wiping what suspiciously resembled crimson lipstick from his chiseled cheek. He smiled as a lock of rumpled dark hair fell across his forehead. "What's up, Chief?"

"Thank you, Ms. Bishop." Marcus lifted his finger off the speakerphone to wag it at his friend. "You have this annoying habit of romancing my secretaries, only to break their hearts and cause them to resign. Ms. Bishop is my third secretary in six months. She's sweet and efficient. I don't want—"

"I get the point," Rufus interrupted. He snatched the tabloid off Marcus' desk then plopped down in the opposing leather high back. "Kelly—"

Marcus raised a brow.

"That is, *Ms. Bishop*, said the phone's been ringing off the hook. Women admirers. Ready and willing admirers. Christ, Marc, you're one lucky son of a bitch. You're the last of an American dynasty, an icon with a hot bod and no wife. And now this. *America's Most Eligible Bachelor.*" He perused the additional photos on page two. "That Rush is no dummy, I'll tell you that. Your mug plus a buck-twenty-five...as long as you stay single, millions of American women still have a chance." He shook his head ruefully. "Millions."

Marcus suppressed a smile. "This from someone who's restless unless knee-deep in some sort of lewd conduct. And for the record, I'm not interested in millions. I'm not interested in anyone."

Rufus eyed him over the top of the paper. "Sure you are.

You're interested in Miss Right. Miss Perfect. An apple-pie, pure soap, all-American girl. A cross between Meg Ryan and Doris Day. Gidget." He yawned loudly. "That's who *you're* interested in."

Marcus ignored the sarcasm. More than his right hand, Rufus Sinclair was as close to a best friend as Marcus allowed. Hence, Rufus being the lone soul privy to Marcus' ideal of the perfect woman. An ideal recently blown to unidentifiable bits. "Women like that exist only in film and household product commercials. Not in real life. Not in *my* life." He'd once envisioned Kimberly Langford as the Polly Purebred wife of his dreams. Unfortunately, things were not always as they seemed.

Rufus cast aside the tabloid, his expression intense. "I know I poke fun at you, Marc, but don't let Kimberly poison you. She's not worth it. Somewhere out there is a good woman. A woman who won't care squat about your money."

Marcus grunted, dismissing the topic and returning his attention to the legal document that had initiated his migraine. "How'd your meeting go with Ms. Malone?"

"Who?"

"The parapsychologist."

"Oh, her." Rufus's face sagged with disinterest, then suddenly his brows shot up. "Oh, *her*. Great."

"When can I expect it?"

"The signed document? Four to five days."

"That long?"

Rufus shrugged. "She's a professional, Marc. Besides, she has to conduct some semblance of an investigation before declaring Laguna Vista ghost-free. What if Zigfreid shows up at the mansion unannounced? I wouldn't put it past the old geezer."

"Point taken. I've waited this long. I suppose another week won't kill me." Marcus returned his attention to the contract. He flipped to page four of the fifteen-page document. "So long as I get that document."

"You'll get it." Rufus thoughtfully stroked his dimpled chin. "You know, Marc, if you're so bent on getting rid of the place, you could make it a hell of a lot easier on yourself. You could turn it over to a historical society in a heartbeat."

Marcus sniffed. "The first thing they'd want to do is restore it, which means fundraisers. Which means pleas to the media. Which means dragging the Van Buren name through the mud because I dumped a rotting albatross in their laps and won't shell out a penny to help them. And besides the horror of my ancestors' dirty laundry being aired on the network news, the last thing I need is some overeager tour guide with lipstick on her teeth rehashing my grandfather's indiscretions in sordid detail. No thanks. I want that mansion and its memories wiped off the planet."

"I can't understand why you hate that house so much. You've never even been there."

Marcus pressed his fingers to his throbbing temple. "Let's just say nothing good ever came from it."

"So why haven't you knocked it down yourself?"

His head pounded harder, his palm sweating as he gripped his pen. "I can't," he admitted. "For some godforsaken reason, I can't pull the plug."

Rufus grinned. "So you'll let Zigfreid do the dirty work. It's okay, Marc, I won't tell anybody you're really a soft, fuzzy pussycat on the inside."

"Gee, thanks."

Rufus shrugged. "It'd be a waste of time anyway. Once you start collecting your share in Zigfreid's latest gambling monstrosity, you'll be known as the Shark of the Atlantic. Have I told you lately that you're my hero?"

Marcus suppressed another smile. "Have I told you lately that you're a royal pain in my—"

Buzzzz.

He pressed the intercom button while thumbing to page five. "What is it, Ms. Bishop?"

"Your mother is holding on line one. Ms. Langford is on line two. I told her you were out, but she doesn't believe me."

"Tell my mother I'll call her back. Tell Kim—"

"Tell Ms. Langford," Rufus interrupted, voice raised, "that Mr. Van Buren is being attended by his personal masseuse...Lola, and can't pick up the phone. His hands are full. I mean *hers*."

Marcus rolled his eyes. "Just tell her I'm in a meeting, Ms. Bishop."

Ms. Bishop giggled. "Yes, sir. Goodbye, sir."

"You can't avoid her forever," Rufus said.

"Kim and I have said all there is to say."

"I was talking about your mother."

"Oh." Marcus frowned, the image of his meddlesome, will-I-ever-have-grandchildren-before-I-die mother springing full to mind. "Luckily, forever isn't necessary. She's been nagging me for years to sell Laguna Vista. In four days, she'll be dancing a jig when I tell her it's done. Then maybe she'll forget about this damn article. Even better, maybe she'll be distracted enough to forget the daughter of some country club crone she was about to fix me up with. You did say four days, didn't you?"

"Five at the most," Rufus said easily, as if it were all in the bag.

Marcus shook his head. "I can't believe I've actually hired a ghostbuster." He looked back to the document. "I can't believe Zigfreid, a businessman of supposed sound mind, insisted that I do so."

Rufus waved an impatient hand at the document. "You've been over that thing a hundred times. So have I. So has your lawyer. The contract is pretty standard outside of that one screwball stipulation. Provide Vladimir Zigfreid with reputable verification that Laguna Vista is absent of any and all apparitions, poltergeists, and hauntings, and you've got a sale. Reading it again won't change the content, Marc. You're dealing with a nut."

"A rich nut," Marcus clarified, still amazed that a multi-million-dollar deal hinged on a peculiar billionaire's spectral phobia.

Rufus leaned forward, resting his forearms on his knees. "A good percentage of the Earth's population believes in unearthly specters. Angels, guardian spirits, ghosts. Zigfreid not only believes in ghosts, he fears them."

Marcus snatched a pencil and absently tapped it on the blotter of the antique desk that had once belonged to his great-grandfather. "Zigfreid is eccentric. That's for sure."

"Worse. He's superstitious. He consults a damned astrologer before he takes a piss in the morning."

Marcus raised a lone brow.

"All right. I'm exaggerating. But not much. His closest advisor is a psychic. A psychic who likens discontented spirits to bad luck charms. Zigfreid's not about to build a casino on a property believed to be inhabited by your dead ancestors!"

Marcus tapped harder, snapping the sharpened end off the pencil. "You're referring to decades-old rumors. Romanticized ghost stories. Nonsense."

Rufus cocked his head. "The same stories that have caused you to shun Laguna Vista for the last thirty-six years?"

Suddenly restless, Marcus stood. He jammed his hands into the pockets of his pleated trousers and turned to face his floor-to-ceiling windows. He stared at the horizontal blinds in a neighboring skyscraper, careful not to look down. "Your assumption is flawed, Rufus, considering I don't believe in ghosts." He could name a hundred and one reasons for never visiting Laguna Vista. Fear of meeting up with a dead relative was not among them.

"Zigfreid believes differently. My advice? Spend a couple of nights under Laguna Vista's roof. You could use some R & R."

Marcus looked over his shoulder at Rufus, who smiled like a hood about to score his lunch money. Marcus raised a brow in pointed accusation. "You mean like the R & R I *tried* to get this past weekend?"

"Forget it, Marc. I refuse to feel guilty for trying to cheer you up." He rose to leave. "Like I said, you could use some R & R. Time away from the Kimberly Langford fiasco. What can it hurt? Then you can sign your John Hancock right alongside that of your hired parapsychologist's and put Zigfreid's concerns to bed. Make the sale, Marc. You'll be happier for it."

"If I were any happier," Marcus said, his gut uneasy with

Rufus' sudden enthusiasm, "I'd be whistling "Zippety-Do-Dah" out my—"

"I get the point. Mind my own business." Rufus made his way toward the door. "But I was serious about spending some time at Laguna Vista. My crystal ball assures me it'll make a favorable impression on Zigfreid."

Marcus sniffed at that. "I'll take your suggestion under advisement." He waited for the door to close then massaged his throbbing temples.

Migraines. Laguna Vista never failed to spur one on. The mansion and its dubious history had been a thorn in his backside since the day he was born. A financial white elephant, he should've sold the jinxed mansion years ago, but the vast shoreline estate was worth a fortune few could afford, and its distance from the heart of the city hadn't exactly enticed buyers to beat down his door.

Marcus was no fool though. Despite his mother's nagging and his own animosity toward the house, he wasn't about to give away the property for a song and dance. J.B. would roll over in his grave. His great-grandfather, the only Van Buren who had Marcus' respect, had built that home with dreams of his children's futures. A place where either grandchildren could roam or a Senate nominee could announce his campaign. But J.B. hadn't founded and driven VB Enterprises into the mighty corporation it was today on sheer sentimentality. He'd been shrewd, cutthroat, and realistic. It would've been the utmost disrespect if Marcus didn't make an attempt at turning a profit on the fallow land.

Unfortunately, the buyer was a ghost-a-phobic. Though Marcus had quipped about the illogical fear with Rufus, inwardly he commiserated with Zigfreid. Marcus had his own personal phobia to deal with. A debilitating phobia that kept him from looking down on Madison Avenue, on the hordes of people milling about the sidewalks, on the gridlocked traffic that mucked up one intersection after another. If he glanced down for so much as three seconds, he'd suffer a bout of vertigo that'd put Hitchcock's Jimmy Stewart to shame.

Acrophobia. The only thing in his life he'd been unable

to conquer.

Feeling anxious, he steered his attention from the window to his desk. Piles of financial reports cried out to him. Stacks of impending contracts demanded review. His laptop jingled with incoming mail. His beeper went off. His cell phone rang.

His head pounded.

Then, in the midst of it all, a blonde, bubbly Gidget danced into his thoughts to the theme of "Ghostbusters."

That did it.

He leaned forward and buzzed Ms. Bishop.

"Yes, Mr. Van Buren?"

"Cancel my upcoming appointments." Mind still reeling from the "Kimberly Langford fiasco," as Rufus so often referred to it, he wasn't about to entrust his future to yet another female. Especially not some crystal-wearing psychic with a spirit-seeking radar detector.

"Sir?"

"Ready the helicopter."

"I'll need to inform the pilot of your destination, sir."

"Atlantic City. Have a limo waiting to take me from Bader Field to Laguna Vista. Oh, and locate Mr. Sinclair. I need—"

"When do we leave?" Rufus sailed into the room, wiping the same crimson lipstick from his *other* cheek.

"Thank you, Ms. Bishop." Marcus shook his head at his assistant. "You're hopeless."

Rufus smiled. "I'm irresistible. I'm also glad you've decided to take my advice. About Laguna Vista, that is."

Marcus opened his briefcase and proceeded to pack it with only his most urgent business, chucking in a bottle of aspirin out of habit. "I'm going to spend a couple of nights there. I'll need you to make the place livable. But keep it low profile. I don't want the media catching wind of this. I've had all the press I can stomach."

"Like you need to remind me." Rufus jabbed his finger at the tiny scab on his forehead, his already impossible Brooklyn accent thickening with sarcasm. "My badge of honor for tackling Rush before he attached his zoom lens."

"You tripped over his camera bag."

Rufus shook his head, dramatically woeful. "Not the point," he muttered. "This baby's going to scar. Just you wait and see."

"Like the twins haven't given you enough sympathy already." Marcus gave up and smiled. "Just keep it—"

"Low profile. I know." Rufus plucked his top-of-the-line cellular out of his jacket pocket and placed the appropriate call. He relayed his instructions in three minutes flat, snapped the receiver shut and reported, "The place will be furnished and stocked with groceries, booze, and cigars by the time we get there."

Marcus scooped up his laptop and briefcase and strode toward the door. "You're coming?"

Rufus fell in behind him. "Marcus Van Buren, President and CEO of VB Enterprises, and Gidget the Ghostbuster together? Under Laguna Vista's infamous roof? I wouldn't miss this for the world."

***

"*She doesn't look very happy,*" Isadora said, elbowing her way in between Jonas and James.

The trio watched from the tower window as Daisy stood, arms folded over her chest, foot tapping, waiting impatiently for the last of the moving vans to amscray. Jill stood nearby filing her nails and chomping on her gum, looking more bored than annoyed. Which was amazing since Laguna Vista had been a hotbed of activity for the past couple of hours. Movers, caterers, cleaning crews. Izzy didn't understand either girls' reaction. *She* was ecstatic. Someone was moving in! "*Please, God, don't let them be holy rollers.*" She quickly looked up. "*No offense, Chief, but the entertainment's gettin' pretty dull down here.*"

"*Who cares about her?*" James said, dismissing Daisy in favor of her younger sister. "*Oh, Jill,*" he crooned, wiggling his tawny brows, "*say you will.*" Then he sighed and whistled. "*That dame's a knockout.*"

"*So you've said twice or forty times.*" Isadora twirled her cigarette holder in the air. "*Give it up, Jimmy. She's out of your league. She's mortal.*"

James shrugged. "*Semantics. She's a skirt, isn't she?*"

Isadora nudged Jonas in the ribs. "*Rudy Valentino here plans on romancing the redheaded tomato there, even though he's deader than the Charleston. Ain't that a kick?*"

Jonas shushed his sister, suddenly pushing her and James away from the window. He stepped back into the folds of the tattered velvet curtains. "*She's looking our way.*"

"*Who? Daisy? For crying out loud, Jonas.*" Isadora lit up another cigarette. "*It's not as if she can see us.*"

"*I'm not so sure,*" Jonas said with a thoughtful frown. "*I think maybe she can. I think maybe she did before.*"

"*Before when?*" James asked, pushing his fedora onto the back of his head. "*Before downstairs?*"

Jonas waited until he heard the front door close then let out a pent up breath. "*Before, years ago. I'm not sure, but I think she's that little girl. Remember the one I told you about? Except now she's all grown up.*"

Isadora widened her kohl-lined eyes. "*The one you swore saw you.*"

Jonas nodded. "*I think she's one of 'them.'*"

Isadora and James sucked in a collective breath. *Them* was the term they used to describe those few mortals who could actually see their ghostly bodies, or at least a fuzzy, transparent image of their current selves. In seventy years they'd encountered fewer than a dozen of *them*. Mostly they scurried away like scared ninnies. One, the little girl in the yellow shirt, hadn't looked scared at all, according to Jonas. In fact, she'd scared *him*. He'd sensed a connection with her. A connection he hadn't felt before or since. Then, of course, there'd been that one unfortunate boy. But they weren't allowed to talk about what Isadora had labeled as "*the incident.*"

Jonas forbade it.

"*Wait a minute,*" James said. "*If she's one of 'them,' how come she didn't spy us when we were hovering about the kitchen earlier?*"

Isadora blew out a long stream of smoke. "*Wise up, goof. Has it been that long? The circumstances have to be just so, remember?*"

James quirked a boyish grin, his blue eyes wide in sudden recollection. "*Ooooh, yeahhhh.*"

Jonas rolled his eyes. As if they honestly knew what the "just-so circumstances" were. They only knew two things for sure. One, for some reason they were more visible in the west tower than anywhere else in the mansion. Two, the Van Buren ghosts became visible to *them* when the ghosts had the opportunity to slip into mortal clothing. Izzy had had a field day with that little trick. But the phenomena only lasted for a few minutes, then for reasons beyond their knowledge, they faded like invisible ink right before *them's* very eyes. That's when *them* usually ran screaming into the night, never to return.

"*Mmm,*" Isadora purred. "*A chance to mess with one of 'them's' minds. This day just gets better and better.*"

"*Back off, angel,*" Jonas warned. "*She's mine. She's my ticket out of here.*"

"*That's just great,*" Isadora complained. "*You've got blondie. Jimmy has dibs on the tomato, and I've got bupkes. Just great!*"

"*Whine, whine, whine,*" James said. "*You really gripe my cookies, Izzy. You've been married three times—*"

"*Four,*" Jonas said, moving back to the window.

"*Four times. And you've had more affairs than Wetzel's Catering Hall. Dry up, dumbdora, you're giving me a pain.*"

"*Zip it, you two.*" Jonas peered down on the grounds and motioned James and Isadora to join him. "*The plot thickens.*"

A sleek limousine rolled to a stop inside the rusted gates. The rear door opened. A man climbed out. He straightened and turned, hands in pockets, to examine the house. Isadora's face lit up like a kid's in a candy store. "*Hellooo, tall, dark, and handsome,*" she purred.

"*He's mortal,*" James singsonged, gleefully flinging her words back at her.

But Isadora was too smitten to care. *Oh, look!*" she squealed, fanning herself like a poolside starlet, "*another one's stepping out. Mmmm. Snappy dresser. Confident air...*"

She let out a low whistle as the dark-haired Adonis came full into view. "*Good lord, Jonas. That man is the spitting image of—"*

"*Me.*" Jonas stood frozen, speechless as he stared down at none other than Marcus Jonathan-Bernard Van Buren. His grandson.

***

"Are you all right, Marc?" Rufus nudged Marcus in the side. "Yo, sport."

"What?"

"Are you all right? You're looking a little green around the gills."

Marcus diverted his attention from the rundown mansion and reached back into the limo for his briefcase. "My head is splitting." He dug deep into a zippered pocket and fished out his bottle of aspirin. "Must've been the bumpy flight," he grumbled, popping off the lid. He hated to fly. "Remind me never to use that chopper pilot again."

Rufus produced a bottle of spring water seemingly out of nowhere and handed it to Marcus. "The ride was bumpy? I didn't notice."

"I'm not surprised." Marcus popped back two aspirin and washed them down with a quick swig. "You were practically sitting in our pilot's lap. It's a wonder she could see over your head as you quizzed her on the proper use of flotation devices."

The beatific smile on Rufus' lips was surely rooted in evil. Marcus tossed the water bottle to his friend, who caught it one handed. "I'm having a hard time believing my regular pilot, my never-been-sick-a-day-in-his-life pilot, *Joe,* was suddenly stricken with the Hong Kong flu."

"A relapse from his Army days."

"Mmm. And there wasn't a competent male replacement to be found in all of the five boroughs of New York?"

"Don't be a sexist pig, Marc. Ms. Flanders had excellent credentials."

Marcus rolled his eyes. "And I'm sure you checked them thoroughly."

Rufus employed the impish dimple that had once driven a supermodel to spout ridiculous love poems on his answering machine for two weeks straight. "Of course. One never knows what he might miss if he doesn't look closely."

Marcus shook his head, the throbbing easing with their banter. He hadn't wanted to come here, had always avoided it with the same precision he avoided women wearing red spandex and blue eye shadow, but he had to admit that, despite his headache, the knot in his tie had begun to ease its stranglehold. "One day some woman's going to knock you on your ass and set you straight, Rufus. And I want a front row seat."

Rufus wiggled his brows. "I'm meeting our pilot later for drinks. I'll see what we can do."

Marcus' lips twitched despite himself. "I swear you get laid more than a rock star."

Rufus beamed, delivering no change on the highest paid compliment. "Seduction is indeed my art."

"And you're a Master. Yeah, yeah. I get it."

"You have to loosen up."

"Why, because I don't rub up against everything that moves?"

Rufus laughed. "You should try it sometime. Gives you a whole new perspective on things."

"I'll pass."

"You know, Marc, I've been thinking. What you need is an honest-to-goodness, wet-and-wild, hot-and-heavy fling."

"Excuse me?"

"You've been buttoned up so tight ever since the Kimberly Langerford fiasco, I'm afraid you're going to explode like that chick in *Willy Wonka's Chocolate Factory*. You know the one who ate all the candy..."

Marcus raised his brow. "Your point?"

"Well, let's just say your sex life has been, um, dead."

Marcus nearly choked. "Dead? It's only been a month!"

"My point exactly. A whole month gone by, and still you sit home alone in that penthouse every Saturday night like some poor slob who can't even get cable."

Marcus slammed the door, lowering his voice as the limo driver popped the trunk. "I can't believe we're talking about this."

Rufus waved his hand at the house. "Don't waste this opportunity, Marc."

"*What* are you talking about?"

"Gidget. Daisy Malone. Your ghostbuster. I've found your dream woman, my friend, and you're going to be sleeping under the same roof."

Marcus cocked his head. "Excuse me?"

"Forget those social climbers, Marc. Why don't you challenge yourself for once? See if you can't get into this sweet thing's pants."

"I don't believe this."

"I didn't hear a no."

"Because this doesn't even bear consideration. First of all, I've never met the woman. Second, I've just endured a nightmare with someone I thought was my so-called 'dream woman.' I don't need to tempt another media debacle, nor do I need to seduce some unsuspecting girl just because *you* think my masculinity is at stake. I have nothing to prove."

"Maybe not to me, but to yourself."

"What the hell are you babbling about, Rufus? I'm not the one who has to prove it every second of the day."

Rufus rubbed his throat. "Ouch. Damn. I hope you brushed those teeth before you ripped out my jugular." Then his voice turned serious. "I deserved that," he admitted, "but I'm really worried about you, Marc. You've always been uptight, but ever since this Kimberly Langford fiasco, you've been downright unbearable. Your confidence is shaken. You're questioning whether she faked the big O all along. You've been dumped for another man, for chrissake. An *older* man with a shorter yacht. Don't tell me it doesn't bother you. I'll know you're full of crap."

Marcus felt as if Rufus had sliced open his belly and held up his guts for all the world to see. How did his friend know so much? Was he that transparent? Marcus had known how wily and sly Rufus could be, but he'd never realized just how much so until this moment. "If you were anyone else," Marcus began with a hint of danger in his voice, "you'd be flat on your back right now crying for your mother."

Rufus grinned. "Yeah, but you love me, and you know I'm right."

Marcus eyed his friend who'd grown up on the tough streets of Brooklyn and realized Rufus only said and did these things because he cared. But damn if he couldn't pick a better way to go about it.

Not admitting to anything his friend said, but his curiosity piqued, he asked, "Are you deliberately trying to insult me, or are you just worried you might get bored without the Spice Channel this weekend? If I'm so pathetic, what do you recommend I do, King Stud of the Jungle?"

"Forget who you are for the weekend. I called in a few markers, planted a few red herrings. The media, including that a-hole Rush, think you're out of the country on business. Ten to one, he's on a plane for Paris this minute. For God's sake, Marc, give yourself a break. Have some fun. You're only human, though you try like hell to aspire above and beyond. Stop trying to behave like the perfect man and just behave like, well, a man. You'll be amazed at how much better you feel."

He wasn't trying to be perfect, Marcus wanted to say. He was trying not to be a "Van Buren."

Despite the fact that he should be pissed as hell at Rufus, he wouldn't trade their friendship for the world. Rufus reminded him of those grammar school days, when you could beat the crap out of each other at recess, split lips, dirty shirts, then share your box of Cracker Jacks while calling each other names.

"So what do you think?" Rufus asked.

"We'll see," Marcus answered, perturbed and noncommittal.

"No, I mean about the infamous Laguna Vista?"

Marcus had avoided taking the mansion into full view, and thereby consideration, since they'd arrived. Finally he allowed his gaze to skate over broken roof tiles, dangling shutters, and rusted trellises framing boarded-up windows. Well, not all of the windows were boarded, but enough were to make it look as conspicuous as a hockey player's mouth.

He tried to conjure the grandeur of its heyday, but all he saw was a bedraggled money pit.

The back of his neck prickled as his gaze skimmed over the tall, dark tower window. Something uncomfortable tugged at him, like an itch he couldn't quite scratch.

His headache worsened. He did not want to be here. "I can't wait to get rid of the place."

Seeing enough, he moved to the rear of the limo, slipped the chauffeur a generous tip then waved him away from the leather suitcases he'd just hauled from the trunk. "We'll handle it from here, O'Brien. I'll call you when I need you. Thanks for coming on short notice."

O'Brien tucked away the bills, thanked Marcus, then hopped into the stretch limousine and hauled butt as if racing away from Amityville's horror house itself.

"Did you notice how he kept eyeing the place?" Rufus asked, hefting two cases. "I was afraid he'd jump out of his old skin if he actually had to tote our bags inside."

"An image only you could conjure, Rufus." Marcus grabbed the remaining bags and dragged himself toward the house like a man condemned to the gallows.

"Marc?"

"Mmm?"

"I know you blew it off back at the office, but *do* you believe Laguna Vista is haunted?"

"No."

"Do you believe in ghosts?"

"No. You?"

Rufus thought about it then shook his head. "Nah."

Marcus' lips twitched. Rufus didn't seem one-hundred-percent sure of his spectral denial. "Don't worry, my friend, there are no such things as ghosts. Our stay here will be quick and painless."

The chorus of Springsteen's "Glory Days" suddenly belted from the house.

Rufus smiled wickedly. The voice was unmistakably feminine.

Marcus' glare would have withered a lesser man.

The heavy mahogany door stood ajar, and as Marcus slipped through it without knocking, he couldn't stifle the echo of his mother's reproach as he committed another social infraction. Ridiculous, considering he owned the place. It made no difference that he'd never set foot on Laguna Vista property in his life.

"I can't believe we're here," he grumbled as he dropped the bags inside the door, his emotions suddenly jumbling and twisting into an anxious knot. "J.B. better appreciate this."

Rufus drifted toward the voice of the slightly out-of-tune rock and roller. Marcus followed.

Two things impressed him as he leaned quietly against the foyer wall. Rufus' ability to furnish the place so quickly. And the derriere of the shapely electrician he'd hired. Busy unfurling some kind of wire, the blonde crawled backwards toward them on her knees, unaware that she was being watched. Intently.

Marcus shook his head. How did Rufus do it?

Marcus' regular chopper pilot had been replaced by a buxom redhead who hadn't worn a stitch of clothing beneath a flight suit with a conveniently broken zipper. And now this. This one wore little brown hiking boots, a white ribbed tank top that showed off her toned, creamy arms, and a pair of faded, skin-tight jeans that were worn and frayed in some very interesting places. Her teeny-bopper pony tail swung in time to her song as she shuffled over the floor. Watching the curvaceous electrician rig up his house, he wondered just when Rufus had sold his soul to the devil.

Abruptly, she stopped singing. "Damn! Not long enough." She dropped the cord and swiped her forearm across her brow. He hadn't seen her face yet, but if her killer body and sweet voice were any indication...

It dawned on him then. That voice. Sweet. Pure. *A cross between Meg Ryan and Doris Day.* The woman he'd been admiring wasn't a hand-picked electrician, but his newly hired ghostbuster. However, with the genetic mix Rufus had concocted, Marcus had expected a cutesy bob hairdo and a long, printed dress like a mattress tag, 'Illegal to Remove.'

"This is all Marcus Van Buren's fault," she railed to the thin air about her. "I would've had the video cams rigged by now if it wasn't for him. His moving thugs set me back three hours and disrupted the entire vibe of the place. And that cleaning crew! They whizzed through here like Mary-friggin-Poppins. Who's moving in? The Pope? I can't believe he doesn't trust me enough to leave me here alone!" She swiped her hand on the back pocket of her jeans as if he were the grime. "He's paying me to do a job. I'll do the job. It's not like I can run off with the money. That SOB is holding it back until I sign the paper!"

Marcus turned a suspect eye towards Rufus. This was the woman he should seduce?

Rufus shrugged his shoulders, smile widening.

Suddenly the kitchen door swung open. On the other side, balancing a weighted down plate of food on one hand while brandishing an uncorked champagne bottle and two glasses in the other, stood the common man's naughtiest fantasy. A teenaged, Catholic school girl. Or at least a trendy version of one. Dressed in a short plaid skirt, knee-high socks, and a clingy white sweater, red hair brushed to a high gloss, the uncommonly pretty girl oozed blatant sexuality.

Marcus' hand shot up, warning Rufus to silence the wolf whistle he was about to let loose.

The girl's green eyes widened when she spotted them, but the unlit Cuban import pressed between her pink-glossed lips kept her from immediately speaking.

"Who the hell does he think he is?" the infuriated ghostbuster demanded, rising to her feet to check a monitor on the archaic-looking equipment before her.

The redheaded woman-child perched her culinary booty on the mantle of the oversized fireplace then plucked the cigar from her mouth. Her lips crooked up in an ornery grin as she assessed Marcus and Rufus from head to toe in one sweeping glance. Just as Marcus was sure *she* was about to let loose with a whistle herself, she said, "Um, Daze?"

Daze was frantically turning knobs and checking tangled wires for a short. The monitor registered blank. "Have you heard a word I said?" she raged on, whacking the screen with the flat of her hand. "I can't believe the elephant-sized balls on that man."

"Daze!"

"What!"

Grinning from ear to ear, the redhead waited for her friend to look up before pointing the cigar at their unexpected guests.

The blonde turned. Outside of the slight blush fanning across her freckled cheeks, she seemed unfazed by their presence.

His gaze drifted down to a luscious mouth—naturally pink yet unnaturally sweet—that had spoken of his most intimate of areas. Entranced, he could do nothing but watch as she nabbed a long-sleeved, blue and green flannel shirt from a nearby chair and pulled it on, knotting it at her small waist. Without another word, she confiscated the cigar from the younger girl, broke it in half, then chucked it into the fireplace. *Then* she started across the room.

Marcus wondered if he sported a target on his head today as she approached them with all the poise of a White House aide amidst a dirty Presidential scandal. He couldn't help admiring the stubborn tilt of her chin as she advanced on them, hands on hips. "Mr. Sinclair."

"Ms. Malone," Rufus greeted, not even attempting to hide his smile.

Her gaze flicked to Marcus. "And you must be..."

"The elephant-sized SOB himself," he finished, extending his hand out of habit. "Marcus Van Buren. A pleasure to meet you, Ms. Malone."

Ignoring his hand, Daisy Malone stiffened her spine and offered a condescending smile instead. "Trust me, Van Buren. The pleasure is all yours."

Three

Thank God the family bar of soap was home, along with her mother. Daisy had let her mouth get away from her. She hadn't intended to insult Marcus Van Buren. As a matter of fact, while setting up her equipment, she'd given herself a dozen lectures on how his business was none of hers and how she was here for the sake of *her* family, not his. But her emotions had been out of whack ever since she'd crossed Laguna Vista's threshold, and when she saw him standing in that same doorway, all cool confidence and regal air, the acid level in her body could've melted the bumpers off a Buick. His blimp-sized ego flashed "shoot me down." What was that suave play he tried to pull on her? *A pleasure to meet you.*

Was Marcus Van Buren mocking her?

Daisy recalled her mother's words, the ones that had been pumped into her through high school like cartons of milk and cardboard meatloaf on the cafeteria line. *Don't sink to their level. You'll be the bigger person for it. If you can't say anything nice, don't say anything at all.* Hmmph. Sometimes easier said than done.

She glanced at him with distaste, simmering in her juices all over again. He was everything she despised in a man. Handsome, arrogant, rich.

Looking glossy and perfect, as if he'd just stepped off the cover of a men's fashion magazine, he wore a deep blue, chalked-striped suit (no doubt Armani or Versace), a starched white shirt with tiny indigo stripes, and an indigo silk tie frenetic with gray and white geometrical shapes. Daisy smirked. If she mixed stripes and patterns together like that, she'd look like she'd dressed in the dark. Van Buren looked as if he'd been dressed by Ralph Lauren himself. To add insult to injury, his lean, impressive build screamed personal trainer. And since his thick, dark hair was the perfect length and cut for his long, angular face, it was safe to assume he frequented a $300-an-hour stylist to the stars.

In short, Marcus Van Buren needed a statue in Central Park where all the wallflowers of the world could come to mourn their inferiority. Of course, Daisy preferred to imagine just how the pigeons would pay homage. She had learned long ago the consequences of acquiring a Picasso when your nature was better suited to an Elvis on black velvet.

As her haughty inspection continued, Marcus Van Buren's eyes hardened like packed, winter earth. "Ms. Malone, there's no need to be hostile. I'll be more than happy to compensate you for any delay."

He might as well have been a talking mannequin for all the emotion behind his words. Direct yet detached. Stiff but polite. He was just like...oh my, God...he was just like Jonas.

She'd already known he resembled his grandfather, but, in that moment, he was his very essence. How many nights had she studied the faded photocopy of the deceased millionaire's handsome face, only to be left with the sad impression that he'd never really lived. As she looked into his grandson's remote eyes, she saw that same bleak landscape. However, for some reason, she'd never imagined Jonas this remote.

"Ms. Malone?"

"Your pictures don't do you justice, Mr. Van Buren," she said, referring to his latest featuring role in *The Tattletale*. "I can't imagine what your ex was thinking, except...how does the saying go?" Her audacity amazed even her, but she couldn't seem to help herself. "Ah, yes. Beauty is only skin deep. Though I'm sure that couldn't possibly be the case with you." She feigned a sugar-sweet smile and gestured to the newly delivered furniture. "So, who's my appointed baby sitter? You? Pretty-boy? Or an absent third party?"

Seemingly unscathed by her remarks, the poker-faced CEO cast his assistant a sideways glance. "Would you excuse us for a moment, Rufus?"

Rufus, who seemed to have mixed feelings in regards to being referred to as *pretty boy*, moved forward and held out his arm to Jill.

"She's only seventeen," Daisy warned.

Rufus snatched back his arm as if from a trap.

"Eighteen in July," Jill countered moodily.

"Yeah, *next* July."

Jill rolled her eyes. "Give it a rest, Daisy. He's too old for my taste, anyway."

"Hey! Ease up," he said, looking positively stricken, "I am standing right here, you know."

Jill ignored him and focused her attention on Marcus. "Don't mess with Daisy, Van Buren. I know people."

"Jill!" Daisy screeched.

"Just want to make sure we understand each other," she said, her eyes leveled on Marcus.

Rufus nabbed Jill's elbow, leading her into the kitchen. "Did you spy the roast beef? I specifically requested roast beef. You haven't lived until you've tasted one of my special-ingredient hoagies."

"It seems we've taken you and your friend by surprise," Marcus said after they were gone.

"Jill's my sister." Hand on hip, she waited for him to chastise her for inviting a family member along on the job. Or to rebuke her for her earlier comments or to scold her about Jill raiding his refrigerator.

Instead he gestured to the contemporary black leather couch that clashed with the retro charm of Laguna Vista. "Shall we sit?"

The last thing she wanted to do was sit around and powwow with "America's Most Eligible Bachelor." And she was smart enough to know it had nothing to do with the canyon-sized gap in their social statuses. He was a man accustomed to getting his own way and obviously resorting to any means to do it. Worse, unlike Rufus Sinclair, who flaunted his cocky charm and determined nature like the lead story in *The Tattletale*, Marcus Van Buren was a closed book.

She couldn't read him. Just to make herself feel better, she grumbled, "I have a lot of work to do, you know."

"And I put you three hours behind schedule." He shrugged. "I couldn't help overhearing."

"How long were you standing there?"

"Long enough to know that you resent the prospect of being watched over while you work. Long enough to know that you consider me an SOB." He cocked his head. "I'm curious, Ms. Malone, just when did I grow elephant-sized balls?"

Again his directness caught her off guard. Though it shouldn't have. He headed a major corporation with an iron fist. Beating around the bush probably played into his average day once every six months. "Didn't your mother ever tell you that it's rude to eavesdrop?"

"I'm sure at some point or another she mentioned it."

The lack of animosity in his response burned her buns. She was primed for a fight, and he seemed determined not to give her one. "Listen, Mr. Van Buren. You hired me to prove Laguna Vista ghost-free. Either you trust me to do the job or you don't."

A chill wind blew across the frozen earth of his eyes. "Ms. Malone, I know nothing about you and, frankly after meeting you, I prefer to keep it that way. However, I have no doubt you will prove Laguna Vista ghost-free."

Bitterness stung like bile in her throat. "I'm sure you don't."

He crossed his arms as he leaned against the wall. "If you have an issue with your employment, Ms. Malone, take it up with Mr. Sinclair. He is the one who negotiated your contract."

She smirked. "In other words, voice my complaints through the proper channel. So Sinclair can come off the heavy if need be. Good cop, bad cop? How typical." She clutched the back of the couch and leaned forward, itching to pierce that over-inflated ego. "Just so I have this straight. Does that go for my day-to-day observances as well? Say, for instance, I get a curious EMF reading on the Tri Field Meter? Or catch an anomalous energy on film with my Polaroid? What if your ancestors *are* here as rumored? You'd rather me go to Sinclair than come to you? Even about something as personal as that. I mean, they *are* family."

He didn't even blink. "That won't be an issue. No disrespect for your profession, Ms. Malone, but ghosts do not exist."

"If you're so confident, why are you here?"

He cocked a brow. "I wasn't aware that I had to explain my presence, considering I own Laguna Vista."

She plowed on. "You realize, of course, that I'll be spending the next few nights here. Despite your feelings about my investigation, you obviously need me to conduct a semblance of one, and it would be helpful to know your schedule. Ghosts are different from you and me, Mr. Van Buren. They don't operate on a strict nine to five."

"As I said, I don't believe they operate at all." He pushed off from the wall, circled her video cam, then indicated the monitor and a nearby crate of audio recorders and journals with a disinterested jerk of his thumb. "But if your investigation consists of a twenty-four-hour watch on your part, so be it. Whatever it takes."

"Whatever it takes." Daisy couldn't agree more. She'd do anything to bail her father out of financial ruin, even put up with the disdain of a spoiled rich boy who needed a swift kick in the pants. He didn't take her seriously at all. She was like the token clown at a birthday party, or worse, the donkey that was led around in a circle in the front yard. In comparison to sleeping under the same roof as Van Buren, falsifying a document suddenly seemed of little consequence. Unfortunately, she couldn't count on her pop or her brother to agree. The Malone men were an old-fashioned lot. They'd have a thing or two to say about her sharing accommodations with an unmarried man. They'd worry about her reputation, even though her reputation wasn't worth worrying over, God love 'em. Speaking of which...

"I hope you don't plan on having any of your chippies over for a slumber party. I'm sure being 'America's Most Eligible Bachelor' has its advantages, but Jill will be in and out of the house all weekend. She's very impressionable."

He sunk his hands into his pockets. "Chippies?"

"You know floozies, mistresses, *twins.* Men tend to go a little hog wild when they're on the rebound, if you know what I mean."

His eyes widened, but he quickly disguised it. Instead, he smoldered at her as if posing for an underwear ad. *No! Not underwear!*

"Don't worry, Ms. Malone, I'm sure you'll be a handful all by yourself."

A warm tingle spread through her stomach as his heated gaze roamed over her. He was mocking her again. She knew it, but it didn't matter. She felt herself defrosting like a TV dinner under his artificial heat. Dammit, she knew better than to feel this feeling. She feared this feeling. She'd felt it before, first with Mitchell Pierce, then with Brad Worthington.

Brad. As always the thought of him stirred up a nasty concoction of shame and regret. She felt suddenly and absurdly suffocated, as if the walls of the cavernous room had shrunk inward, forcing her and Marcus Van Buren together in a way that squeezed the breath right out of her.

Her heart pounded as she stood mesmerized, achingly aware of the scent of his expensive cologne, of the blatant perfection of his dark, chiseled features. She flushed, shivered, and broke out in a sweat all at once. "Oh, God," she moaned, disgusted with herself. How could fate be so cruel? How could *she* be so shallow?

Concern etched Marcus Van Buren's expression as he moved toward her. The first sign that he wasn't an unfeeling robot. "What is it?" he asked softly, which only made things worse.

Run. Run fast and far, Daisy. Screw the money. But her feet ignored her brain. She stood frozen, all but her knees. Her knees fairly wobbled as a storm of emotions pelted her.

Marcus captured her forearms and held her steady. He peered into her eyes, searching. She hated the concern she saw there. "Are you ill?"

"No," she managed to squeak. His touch only complicated

matters. For with it came a sense of loneliness and of...guilt? She bonded with Marcus Van Buren, if only for an instant. For in that lone instant she learned that they had at least two things in common. It knocked a hole in the wall she'd erected between them and scared her to death. How could she empathize with a man she despised? He thought she was a joke. To feel anything other than contempt for him was simply unforgivable.

A phone rang, breaking the spell and spurring Daisy into action. She side-stepped his touch, nearly tipping over a steel-based halogen floor lamp in the process. She steadied it while he plucked a cellular from an inner pocket of his Armani jacket. "Van Buren here." His gaze flicked to Daisy. "Ms. Malone, hold up. Ms. Bishop? I'll call you back. In two seconds. Just tell him...Ms. Malone..."

But Daisy was already backing out of the room. She tripped twice before making it to the hall. "I have to...I need to...the ladies room. Excuse me."

Marcus stood perplexed, his secretary yammering in his ear as Daisy Malone slipped around the corner and out of sight. Her transformation from a belligerent wise-ass into a babbling, doe-eyed girl intrigued him to say the least. One minute she was cursing at him, the next she—

"Where's Gidget?"

Startled, Marcus jerked around. "Jesus! Don't sneak up on me like that." A feminine voice cried in his right ear. "Not you, Ms. Bishop. Ms. Bishop...tell Webster I'll get back to him tomorrow. *Tomorrow*. Good-bye, Ms. Bishop." He slipped the phone back into his pocket and regarded Rufus with a frown.

"What?"

"For the record," Marcus told his friend, "Gidget was a sweet, cheerful innocent. Ms. Malone has shown herself to be neither sweet nor cheerful. And with a mouth like hers, I highly doubt she's all that innocent."

Rufus grinned. "Makes for a more interesting challenge, don't you think?"

"Forget it. Despite the fact that I have no intention of

pursuing our ankle-biting ghostbuster, said pursuit would be fruitless. She dislikes me. Intensely, though God knows why. Don't tell me that escaped your notice?"

"I have to admit I don't remember her being so...outspoken. Not that it's a bad thing. Imagine if she's that feisty in the sack." Rufus' eyes took on a dreamy light. "Ahhh, the thrill of the hunt. I envy you, Marc. I can't remember the last time I had to actually *work* at getting a woman into bed."

Marcus shook his head. "I'm worried about you. Truly I am."

"So where is she?"

"Powdering her nose. Where's her sister?"

"Still in the kitchen. I came out to see if either of you wanted a sandwich. Since I was making one for Jill...it's probably because of her job," Rufus said, switching subjects mid-sentence.

"Come again?"

"Gidget's colorful language." Rufus crossed to the rectangular, plate glass coffee table and plucked a cigar from the wooden box due center. "She probably picked it up at work. So she curses a little. So what? I think it's sort of refreshing next to Kimmy's *oh, pooh's* and *darn you's.*"

"Leave Kim out of this," Marcus warned as Rufus lit up an illegal Cuban import. The mere mention of his ex-fiancée's name initiated a dull throbbing behind his left temple. He hadn't even realized his former headache had disappeared. "Despite my better judgment, please explain to me how Ms. Malone picked up her colorful language at work. She's a parapsychologist. Not a bartender."

"Close but no cigar," Rufus twanged, blowing out a stream of smoke. "She's a waitress in her father's pub."

Marcus held up his hand. "I specifically asked you to hire a reputable parapsychologist."

"I did. A parapsychologist who also doubles as a waitress. Don't be obtuse, Marc. There are those who need to work two jobs to pay the bills. Not all of us were born into money."

It was a side of Rufus Marcus rarely saw. A side that reflected his difficult childhood. "I didn't mean it like that,"

Marcus said, treading lightly. "It's just that a lot is riding on Ms. Malone's reputation. No offense, but most of her equipment looks as if it dates back to the Seventies. I know her van does. I swear to God, if you hired her just because—"

"What difference does it make so long as you get the desired result? A signed document from a reputable parapsychologist stating Laguna Vista one-hundred percent ghost-free. I made the proper inquiries, Marc. The S.P.S. has disproved ninety-five percent of all investigated hauntings. You'll hand the document over to Zigfreid. Zigfreid will pass you back a check. And you'll be rid of this stuccoed menace once and for all. It's a done deal. Relax."

"Only if she signs."

Rufus snuffed out the cigar. "She'll sign."

"Where's Daze?"

The two men spun around to find Jill pushing through the kitchen's swinging door.

"Ladies room," Rufus answered.

"Figures. It's all that stupid soda she drinks. Pure poison."

Jill Malone strutted over to the coffee table and plucked a cigar from the box. Without a please or thank you, she lit and inhaled the stogie with such expertise that Marcus wondered how many times she'd done it before. Blowing out a lazy stream of smoke, she leveled him with those eyes again. "Look, Marc, let's cut to the chase. You're going to be shacked up here alone with my sister. We don't know anything about you except you're disgustingly rich and refuse to pose nude in *Hot Male*. Now that may give you credibility with some people, but don't expect some sort of free-for-all just because my sister is sleeping in the same house as you."

What was it with these Malone women? "I can assure you, Jill, that hell would freeze ten times over before *that* would ever happen."

Her lips, the kind photographers loaded up with strawberry lip gloss and shot with a zoom lens, twisted in suspicion. "Well, since Daisy can't stand you and Rufus seems to have his own date tonight, I guess there's nothing I can do. But remember what I said about those friends of mine. They don't discriminate about whose legs they break."

Marcus tried not to laugh. "I'll keep that in mind." He wondered again about the cantankerous Daisy Malone, a woman whose mouth should be registered as a lethal weapon. Her sister displayed such an unfailing loyalty to her. Obviously there were two sides to this very tarnished coin.

"See that you do," Jill warned. She ground the barely smoked stogie into the ashtray. "Which bathroom is Daisy in? We've gotta fly. Danielle has a dress rehearsal at five, and Daisy promised to drive her."

Marcus looked at Rufus, then back to Jill. "Danielle?"

Jill rolled her eyes as if she were dealing with complete idiots. "Our little sister. She's got the lead role in *Romeo and Juliet* over at the high school."

"But what about..." Marcus gestured to the ghostbusting equipment.

"Get over it," Jill said. "Daisy'll get the job done. The S.P.S. has disproved ninety-five percent of all investigated hauntings, you know."

"So I've heard." Marcus glanced again at Rufus.

Jill moved toward the hall. "Which way to the can? We've really gotta fly. Danielle will have a cow if we're late."

Rather than risk insulting Rufus again by questioning his choice of parapsychologists, Marcus motioned Jill to wait. "I'll get her."

Jill raised a suspicious brow. "You've never even been here. How is it you know your way around?"

"Christ, does everyone know my business?" Marcus shook his head, recalling that the she-devil before him was still only in high school. Besides, this was Rush's fault, not Jill's.

Her brow arched higher. "Well?"

"He's seen blueprints."

It was as if Rufus had flicked on a switch. Full-blown visions of the mansion's rooms erupted in Marcus' mind. Full-colored, detailed visions.

He shivered. His heart raced. His temples pulsed.

The moment was intense but short-lived. Bewildered, he

took a calming breath and adjusted his tie. So what if he knew Laguna Vista like the back of his hand. There must be a logical reason. "Yes, blueprints," he mumbled, then set off in search of the bathroom.

Jill shouted after him. "Tell Daisy to get a move on!"

Marcus' surreal episode took a temporary backseat to the very real Malones. As he stalked up the stairs, he couldn't help wondering when he'd stepped into a bizarre episode of "The Waltons," a fictional phenomena where siblings were staunchly devoted to one another. Being an only child, it was beyond his comprehension. In his life, work came first. The fact that Ms. Malone would shirk her responsibilities her first day on the job to attend a dress rehearsal of a high school play blew his mind. As he searched for her, his mood worsened.

First the disturbing visions and now...now without the distraction of barbed conversation, he felt suddenly and anxiously adrift, like a man caught between two worlds. In a sense, of course, he was. J.B. had walked these very halls, as had Jonas, as had his father, Regis. The Van Buren men. His predecessors. For a fleeting moment, he was a boy again, squeezing his eyes shut and wishing them back, because if he wished hard enough, it just might be so.

Startled, he opened his eyes. What the hell was wrong with him? Overcome by a weak moment of sentiment? He frowned. Not likely. Those same men, with the exception of J.B., had deserted their wives and sons for self-indulgent, thrill-seeking nights of gambling and sex. As if that hadn't been bad enough, his own father had been the worst card player in Atlantic City. He'd set himself up nicely with a penthouse and a floozy and never bothered to call home. He was always "hot on the tail of a lucky streak," and the remaining Van Burens were damn lucky he didn't lose the business.

But it was Jonas who had set the tone, along with Isadora and James. Though he supposedly loved his wife, Jonas' pecker had had a mind of its own, landing the rakish tycoon in more beds than a French whore. Like Rufus, he'd thrilled in the hunt, but once snared, interest ceased.

And Isadora. She'd been married how many times? Four?

Which didn't count the random passel of lovers in between. As for James, beauty queens with more ambition than brains had been his game of choice. He never liked work much.

Marcus sighed. If only his ancestors had stayed in their pants and out of the booze, maybe so many people wouldn't have been hurt. "Idiots."

A sudden chill swept over him. He fought the urge to look over his shoulder. There was nothing there. The only thing lurking in this house was neglect. Not his fault. He wasn't the one who'd blown off his son's birthday party in favor of the one on the other side of town...the one where he could get laid and then so drunk that he plowed over a bridge.

Yeah, this place was haunted all right. By selfishness and reckless behavior. Mentally cursing his dysfunctional ancestors, he stalked farther down the hall, taking two wrong turns before remembering a third and remote bathroom located on the second floor.

Meanwhile, Daisy paced in what used to be the library, from the looks of the floor-to-ceiling shelves, chastising herself for her less-than-professional behavior. How did she expect to pull her family out of their financial mud pit when she was insulting the only man with a rope? She leaned back against the wall, bunching the hem of her shirt in her hands. It was over. If Van Buren didn't fire her for insubordination, he'd fire her for being a kook. Tears pricked at her eyes. She'd just let her family down. Again.

Too jittery to stand still, she began to pace the garish orange and yellow shag carpet, an obvious décor leftover from Laguna Vista's disco days. She'd broken one of Cliff and Randall's golden rules. She'd let her personal feelings interfere. As a result she'd purposely insulted her employer. Not just rude, she'd been downright hostile. The girl whose mother once said her sweetness could rot teeth stood in this lonely, vacant room wondering just what had come over her. Sure, she cursed in traffic and laughed at dirty jokes, but she also held the door for strangers and tucked those unwanted matchbook-cover phone numbers in her pocket with a smile. Not only did she loathe confrontation, but she also never did anything before thinking it through. Of course, as proven time and again, forethought didn't always make a difference.

Then, as if the carnage of her attack wasn't horror enough, she'd acted like a smitten groupie and raced away from him as if she'd seen a ghost. Which in a way, she had. Marcus Van Buren was not only a dead ringer for Jonas, he was also Brad Worthington all over again, ten years later. A rich boy with more money than mettle. And yet...and yet...

Someone touched her shoulder.

Daisy whirled around and found herself face-to-face with her new tormentor. Marcus Van Buren. Her breath stalled in her lungs as she struggled to find the right words. As much as she hated to beg, she needed this job. She could control her mutant hormones and runaway mouth. *She could.* "Mr. Van Buren...I...that is to say..." Nameless emotions clogged her throat.

He pressed a single finger to her lips, compassion swirling in the depths of his eyes. It was as if he understood her misery, as if some connection flowed between them. In the next moment, his arms were about her.

She closed her eyes and leaned into him. He brushed his lips across hers, surprising her. She knew he'd meant to comfort her, but instead the kiss slammed into her like a crashing wave, overwhelming her. Loneliness, guilt, sadness. Emotions heavier than those she'd sensed before. She swooned, the intensity of the moment distorting her consciousness.

Just when she feared she might crumple to the floor, she felt a strong set of hands about her waist. "Ms. Malone?"

Daisy's eyes flew open. Before her, just as he should be, stood Marcus Van Buren. Only gone was the compassion that had shone in his eyes brief seconds before. Instead confusion reigned. Censure.

His skeptical regard was as good as being doused with iced water. Daisy stiffened and swung out, slapping her employer across the face. "You bought my word, Mr. Van Buren. Not my body."

Marcus's eyes narrowed to slits. His cheek turned pink,

then red, but he didn't lift a finger to soothe it. Instead he clenched his jaw and advanced, causing her to retreat until her back was up against a barren, splintered shelf built into the wall. "I've endured your hostility, Ms. Malone, your insults, and if I may be so bold as to point out, your out-and-out rudeness. This, however, is where I draw the line." He braced both hands on either side of her head and leaned in menacingly close. "What exactly are you accusing me of?"

Caught off guard by his anger, Daisy stammered, "You...you kissed me." The incident suddenly blurred in her mind, taking on a surreal quality. "I...I think."

"Believe me, Ms. Malone," he said in a dangerous tone, "if I ever kiss you, you'll damn well know you've been kissed."

In the downstairs foyer, huddled around an open leather suitcase, stood the Van Buren ghosts. James leaned against the front door, knocking his fedora against his thigh and raking his other hand impatiently through his hair. He watched as his sister, wearing an ornery grin, buffed her red-polished nails while Jonas shrugged out of a modern, pin-striped suit jacket and hurried to replace it onto a padded hanger.

It had always been like this when they were alive. Jonas and Izzy instigating, him playing catch up. Just like old times. Unable to contain his curiosity, he pushed off the door and advanced on them, hands on hips. "*All right, you two. What are you up to?*"

Four

"What did you think?"

"I thought you were great, Danielle. Perfect."

Danielle crossed her arms over the jeweled bodice of her costume. "What about the part where I shot myself?"

"Very dramatic," Daisy said, her gaze locked on the balcony window on stage left. She imagined Jonas Van Buren standing in that window as he'd stood in the tower window all those years ago. He looked so much like his grandson. Or rather his grandson looked so much like him. The resemblance disturbed her to the point of obsessed distraction. No matter how hard she tried, she couldn't shake it.

Danielle huffed then slapped her hands to her sides. "I didn't shoot myself. I stabbed myself. It's Shakespeare, Daisy. *Romeo and Juliet*. Not *Die Hard III*. You weren't paying attention at all!"

Daisy flinched at her sister's hurt tone. "What? Of course I was," she said, quickly focusing on Danielle instead of the stage. A telling rash burned at the base of Daisy's throat. She'd been thinking about Laguna Vista, about Marcus Van Buren and his ghostly ancestors for the better part of the night. But she wasn't about to admit that to Danielle. "I was paying attention, honey. Honest." The rash burned hotter.

Danielle pursed her lips and narrowed her eyes. "The gown I wore in the first act. What color was it?"

"It was …" Daisy looked to Jill who stood just beyond Danielle's shoulder. "I recall it being..." Jill held her breath, puffed out her cheeks and pointed to her face. "Red!" Daisy said with a bright smile.

Danielle's face fell.

Jill smacked her forehead.

The rest of the family groaned, including little Sean.

"Mom," Danielle whined, turning into her mother's outstretched arms. "Was it that boring? Oh, God. We're going to flop tomorrow night. I can't flop in front of my friends. I think I'm sick. Maybe I'm coming down with malaria."

"You're not coming down with malaria. And you're not going to flop," Angie Malone assured her youngest daughter as she ushered her backstage. "Come on, let's get you out of this gown." She turned and cocked a disappointed brow at Daisy. "We'll meet you all out front."

"Nice going," Jill said after their mother and Danielle had gone. "Blue. The gown was blue."

Daisy felt awful. "You held your breath, Jill."

"Duh. And what color does your face turn when you hold your breath?"

"Red," Daisy insisted as they exited the theater.

"Blue."

"Red." Daisy looked to her brother, Mickey, and his wife, Candie, for help.

They smiled apologetically and shook their heads. "Blue."

"Hold your breath until your face turns blue," Sean reminded her.

Daisy groaned as they piled into the S.P.S. van. Her mother's station wagon was on the blink, so she'd volunteered to act as family chauffeur tonight.

"What's up with you, anyway?" Mickey asked from the rear bench seat. "You've been out of it all night."

"Laguna Vista," Jill singsonged, hopping into the passenger seat.

"That creepy old mansion on Route 40?" he asked. "What about it?"

"It's haunted," Sean said, making a scary face.

Mickey reached forward and ruffled their kid brother's hair. "Common knowledge, Mouth." He then directed his attention to Daisy. "Does this have something to do with all that ghostbusting equipment you bought from Clem and Raymond?"

"Cliff and Randall. And it's ghost*hunting* equipment. Not ghostbusting. It's a reputable occupation, Parapsychology. You can even earn a degree in it."

"All right. All right," Mickey said, holding up his callused hand in surrender. "Don't get your panties in a bunch. So, you're using your ghost*hunting* equipment at Laguna Vista. Finally gonna track down the infamous Van Burens?" he joked.

"She's been hired to prove that the ghosts aren't real," Jill volunteered.

"Of course they're *real*," Sean said. "Tell 'em, Daisy. Tell 'em about how you saw Jonas!"

Daisy flicked on the overhead light and blinked at her youngest brother. "How do you know about Jonas?"

Sean pointed behind him. "Mickey told me. He told me and my friends all sorts of spooky stories last Halloween. He told us about how you saw a ghost standing in the tower window when you were a little girl." Sean's face lit up as he squinted his eyes and leaned forward. "Was Jonas really holding his head in his hands?"

Daisy flinched. "What?"

"Mickey said Jonas' head got chopped off in the car accident, so he had to hold it in his hands so he wouldn't lose it. So was blood and icky stuff oozing out of his neck?" Sean pantomimed slicing his jugular. "Or was it a clean cut?"

Candie and Jill screwed up their faces. "Ewww."

Mickey laughed.

Daisy shot Mickey a chastising frown, then told Sean, "Jonas' head did not get chopped off. When I saw him, his head was right where it belonged. On his shoulders."

Jill clapped her hands together, hooted, then pointed at Daisy. "Busted!"

Crap. "I thought I saw him," Daisy backpedaled. "More than likely it was my imagination. When people are scared or stressed, their imaginations can play all sorts of tricks on them." She thought about the incident in the library. About the kiss she'd *imagined* Marcus Van Buren had placed on her lips. She'd definitely been stressed at the time.

"You know, Daisy," Sean said thoughtfully, "if you take a

picture of one of the ghosts and it comes out, you can sell it to a magazine for lots of money, and then maybe Mom won't have to use up all of Jill's college fund."

Daisy and Mickey nearly came out of their cracked vinyl seats. "What!"

Jill Malone was the pride and joy of the entire family. Her sassy mouth aside, she was an honor student who'd amassed a boatload of scholarships and was probably going to graduate Valedictorian. A title Daisy herself had nearly earned until she'd committed the royal screw up. If one Malone was bound to escape the blue-collar ranks of her ancestors, it would be Jill. "Who told you that, Sean?"

"No one told me," he said, shrugging his little shoulders. "I overheard Mom and Jill talking."

"Mouth!" Jill reached back to whack her brother. Anticipating her move, Sean ducked.

Daisy rubbed her hand across her face. She suddenly felt a hundred-and-two years old. "Does Pop know about this?"

"No way," Mickey insisted. "I would've heard that argument over the jackhammers at the construction site. You know how badly Pop wants Jill to go to college. Christ, he took out a second mortgage on the house rather than touch that money."

Daisy cringed at the bitterness in her brother's voice.

"It was my idea," Jill piped in. "I've got my scholarships. I'll make up the difference myself."

"How?" Mickey bellowed. "By getting a job? Do you have any idea what kind of money we're talking?"

Jill shrugged. "Exotic dancers make *beaucoup* bucks."

Candie groaned.

Mickey's right eye twitched with barely contained fury. "Over my dead body."

Daisy blew out an exasperated breath. When it came to his sisters' virtues, Michael Malone's fuse was as short as an army recruit's hair. And to bring up his wife's past occupation...Jill was really pushing it. "She's kidding, Mickey. Cut it out, Jill."

"Then again, swimsuit models make a pretty penny." Jill

fished a cigarette from her yuppie backpack. "Bernie Polanski has been after me to pose for a calendar for six months now."

Mickey jerked forward. "That skirt-chasing bas—"

"Relax," Daisy snapped. "She's not going to pose for Bernie or anyone else."

Bernard Polanski. A second-rate photographer with a whispered fetish for young girls. To add insult to injury, the smooth-talking slime was married to Daisy's high school rival, a vile woman who held onto grudges like the Coppertone puppy held onto swimsuit bottoms. Daisy nabbed the cancer stick out of Jill's hands, broke it in half, then chucked it out the window. "What's wrong with you? You know better than to tease Mickey about stuff like that."

"I just want him to back off," Jill said, folding her arms over her chest. "It's my college fund. If I want to use it to help bail out Mom and Pop, then that's my business. You took a second job. Mickey took a second job. Why should you be the only two to sacrifice?"

"It's not a sacrifice," Mickey grumbled.

"You're the co-manager of Malone's Pub," Jill said. "That's a full-time job. One that keeps you busy until three a.m. six days a week. And now, in addition, you're working on the city's newest casino, breaking ground and laying concrete from seven a.m. 'til three. When do you sleep, Mickey? When do you see your wife? You're telling me that's not a sacrifice?

"And what about Daisy?" she ranted on. "Talk about pressure. She's got to do the impossible. She has to collect scientific data proving Laguna Vista isn't haunted when she knows damn well it is! Which probably means, though she wouldn't admit it in a thousand years, that she's willing to lie."

"Jill," Daisy shrieked, horrified she suspected the truth.

"We all know how Daisy feels about lying," Jill continued. "So I go to college a few years later than planned. So what? We *need* the money!"

Daisy, Mickey, and Jill launched into a heated argument, neither leaving room for the other to get a word in edgewise.

Amidst the tirade Sean's innocent voice rang out. "Are we gonna get kicked out of our house?"

The elder Malone siblings fell silent. Daisy flicked off the overhead light to hide her stricken features. Again it occurred to her that her family was falling apart. Sure they argued now and again. But not like this. And never in front of the children. At least not on matters as serious as repossession. Yet in the past two days Sean had gotten an earful. The kid was nine years old, and he knew more about grown-up life than most kids twice his age. Of course, a lot of that was due to his obnoxious penchant toward eavesdropping. Still, he shouldn't be worrying over things like eviction.

Suddenly she understood Mickey's bitterness. In this moment, it was very hard *not* to resent her father. She'd been telling herself for two days that it wasn't his fault he'd gambled away the mortgage on their home and the pub. He had a weakness for gambling, just like an alcoholic has a weakness for liquor. He couldn't help himself. She'd immediately placed the blame on those who perpetuate gambling. The casinos. It was easier that way. Less painful. This was her father after all, the light of her life. It wasn't as if he wasn't suffering. The shame was such that he hadn't been able to look one of his five kids in the eye since Wednesday morning. The morning he'd called the family meeting. The morning he'd admitted he'd screwed up. Big time.

"No, honey," Daisy assured Sean. "We're not going to get kicked out of our house. Everything'll be right as rain in a few days."

"Plan on winning the lottery?" Mickey snapped.

"No. I plan on proving Laguna Vista ghost-free. As luck would have it, someone's willing to pay dearly for that verification." That she still had the job amazed her. Thank God Sinclair and Jill had interrupted them before Van Buren had a chance to fire her. After she'd accused him of kissing her, he'd advised her on the penalties of filing a fraudulent sexual harassment suit, if that's what she was cooking up. After which she'd called him a paranoid tight-ass. If Jill hadn't whisked her out of the mansion that moment, undoubtedly

Marcus Van Buren would've sent her packing.

"Here come Mom and Danielle," Sean said.

Daisy smoothed stray hairs back up into her ponytail and switched on the ignition. The van sputtered and backfired twice before settling into an uneven idle. "About Laguna Vista," she said to her sisters and brothers, "let me break it to Mom and Pop."

"What's the big deal?" Mickey asked, his ire on the wane.

"The big deal," Jill said, climbing into the back to free up the passenger seat for their mother, "is that she plans to conduct a three-day, twenty-four-hour investigation, which means she'll be sleeping at Laguna Vista."

Sean giggled. "Cool."

"So it's a little creepy," Mickey said. "So what? I guess that's what ghostbusters, excuse me, ghosthunters, do. I'll peek in on you, Daze, if you're worried about being alone."

"Oh, she won't be alone," Jill said, barely containing a derisive snort.

"Jill," Daisy warned.

"Marcus Van Buren, and his assistant, Rufus Sinclair, are down for the weekend. They'll also be sleeping at Laguna Vista. Two men," Jill pointed out. "Two *single*, hunk-o-rama men."

Daisy shot Jill a withering glare. She'd wanted to break the news to the family herself. In her own way. Especially to Mickey and her father. Luckily for her, her mother swung open the passenger door and climbed in before Mickey had the chance to blow a gasket.

Danielle squeezed in between Sean and Jill. "Hey," she said in cautious greeting, breaking the uncomfortable silence.

"Hey," the siblings muttered back.

Daisy anxiously shifted the van into first.

"All right," Angie Malone said, before they'd gone two feet. "What's going on?"

*** *** ***

Marcus stared at the screen of his laptop. He'd read the same page four times now. He may as well have been reading Greek for all the sense he was making of Websters' financial report. His mind was fixed on another set of numbers.

34-24-36.

Daisy Malone's admirable breakdown, compliments of Rufus. The image of her in those tight jeans, sun-kissed ponytail swinging like a pendulum over his self-control, would not quit. Rufus was right. She easily resembled Doris Day and Meg Ryan rolled into one. Good-girl cute. Short, spiky bangs. Pert, little nose. Peaches-and-cream skin humbled by a sweet sprinkling of tawny freckles.

Wide, blue eyes to trap a man.

Dress her in a tight sweater and a short, pleated skirt, slap a couple of pom-poms in her hands, and she'd make the perfect cheerleader. The all-American girl. His dream girl.

Unfortunately, the fantasy died every time she opened her mouth.

He fiddled with the computer mouse, trying to remember if anyone had ever insulted him so blatantly to his face. A moment's reflection told him no. Absolutely not. Not his staunchest competitors. Not...anyone. *Paranoid tight ass*, she'd called him. And she was his *employee*. If anyone had elephant-sized balls, he thought dryly, it was Daisy Malone. Pumping him full of insults from that double-barrel mouth, and then before the smoke cleared, accusing him of sexual misconduct. An accusation to which he took great offense. He should've terminated her on the spot. But he hadn't. Fool. Curiosity had curbed his natural inclination. That, and Rufus and Jill's timely intervention. What had Daisy meant, *"You bought my word?"*

Marcus growled, pushing her cryptic words from his mind as he removed his tie and loosened the top four buttons of his shirt. If he wanted answers, he need only ask Rufus. He'd been the one to make the deal. He'd know what was burning the defiant Ms. Malone's cute buns. But Marcus wouldn't ask. He didn't want to know. Not really. Knowing the particulars of the deal more than likely involved knowing the particulars on Ms. Malone's life or, at the very least, her financial status and why Rufus was so sure "she'd sign." If she had three children who needed new shoes or a grandmother who needed surgery, he didn't want to know. If she'd blown her life savings on a non-existent time-share in the Poconos, he didn't want to know. If he didn't know, he couldn't care. He wouldn't feel compelled to set things right or to get involved. Emotional distance, the only thing that kept him sane in a world gone mad.

Before he had a chance to feel the ultimate insensitive clod, Marcus reminded himself that whatever her story, Daisy Malone would benefit from this deal. Whatever her financial difficulties, they would disappear or at least lessen considerably after she collected her ten grand. All this for the simple task of signing her name to a document that stated the truth—there are no such things as ghosts.

As if sensing they didn't stand a chance of regaining his attention, Webster's figures disappeared. The screen saver popped up, and colorful, three-dimensional shapes danced before his eyes. One. Two. Three minutes slipped by. Still he sat, staring at those wiggling shapes and thinking about Daisy. The woman he, or rather Rufus, had hired to conduct a paranormal investigation. She didn't look like a parapsychologist. Then again, what did a parapsychologist really look like? What had he expected? A woman in flowing scarves, maybe one wrapped around her head, a bunch of jangly bracelets, and a giant crystal to read the future? His old college roommate, Thaddeus Bookman, a man constantly bumbling around in safari khaki and with his nose in a textbook, certainly hadn't looked like a ghostbuster.

Again Marcus thought that perhaps he should have contacted Thaddeus for this job, but the Princeton history professor, author of two bestseller books and head of a North Jersey paranormal institute, attracted more media than Marcus himself. He was the Geraldo Rivera of the ghostbusting world. A man who wanted to share his explorations with the public, even if it meant stumbling along the way. And although Thaddeus Bookman did not have ego, he did have high profile. The last thing Marcus wanted.

So long as she knew her stuff, Daisy Malone served his purpose. *So long as she knew her stuff.* Marcus frowned, thinking back on the way she'd smacked her hand against the video equipment, like banging a television with bad reception. An image of her struggling to program a VCR formed in his mind. Suddenly curious about the technical aspects of ghostbusting, Marcus signed on to the Internet and typed "parapsychology" into the search engine.

He clicked on one of the thirty-two sites that came up.

After a lengthy delay, a white screen greeted him with the bold words, Host Unreachable.

The next four links lead to the same dead end. Two more sites came up as Moved and another four as Error. Then the screen froze.

Whistling the theme to the *Twilight Zone*, he shut down his computer. He shoved the stack of reports back into his briefcase, stood, then stretched. He paused, arms mid-air as the room came back into focus. He dropped his arms with a quick, sinking feeling. He'd forgotten he was still here.

He'd buried himself in work three hours ago, trying to keep his mind off the mansion and the strange feelings it invoked in him. He'd finally found some relief when he'd rationalized the odd visions from that afternoon. Throughout his life, he'd heard so many stories about Laguna Vista that it made sense to feel as though he'd been here before, as though he knew every room and most of what had happened within these walls. Jonas, Isadora, and James had died long before he'd been born. Yet he felt as though he knew them. The feeling that they were with him now made him want to look over his shoulder again. He didn't.

Instead he shook his head. Maybe the power lines hung too close to the house. Something was messing with his head. He hadn't felt right since he'd stepped foot into the place. He needed to take a walk. Get outdoors for awhile, clear his head in the tangy salt air. But the thought of encountering an overanxious reporter kept him inside. The same reason he hadn't ordered the boards off the windows. Privacy. At least for now. Rufus had bought him some time, and with it, peace and anonymity. He planned to enjoy it.

His cell phone rang. *So much for the peace.* He plucked the phone from the corner of the desk. "Van Buren here."

"Marc!"

"Rufus?" Loud music and a burst of applause competed with his friend's slurred voice. "Where are you?"

"In one of the casinos," he shouted over a rousing rendition of "Hound Dog." "I forget which one. I'm in the showroom. You should be here. They've got this Elvis impersonator, Marc, he's unfriggin-believable. He's got Barbie worked up and ready to throw her bra at the stage, even though she's not wearing one."

"Barbie?"

"Our chopper pilot, Ms. Flanders. You remember."

The horrendous helicopter flight from New York to A.C. was firmly entrenched in his mind, as was Barbie's seemingly perpetual braless state. "How could I forget?" he said. "You're on a date and in the middle of a live show. Why are you calling me, Rufus?"

There was a pause. Sloppy kissing noises and a muffled "yeah, baby" from Rufus. "Hound Dog" blared on in the background. How appropriate.

"Sinclair!" Marcus shouted into the receiver.

"Yeah? Oh. I called to let you know I won't be coming home tonight."

"I never thought for a moment you would be."

"I just didn't want you to worry."

Marcus rolled his eyes. "I appreciate your thoughtfulness. I'd also appreciate your remaining sober enough to remember to practice safe sex. The world's not ready for a Rufus, Jr., and neither are you."

Rufus snorted. "I've gotten drunk off my ass and done a lot of stupid things. But I've never done anything as stupid as to forget to slap a slicker on Peter!" A woman, presumably Barbie, giggled into the phone. "Just a minute, baby. Marc!"

"Still here." *Though God knows why.*

"I won't be home until sometime tomorrow morning. Sometime *late* tomorrow morning."

"So I gathered."

"Which means you and Gidget will be alone tonight. *All* night."

"Goodbye Rufus."

"But—"

Marcus clicked off the phone and tossed it into the desk drawer. Rufus' sudden penchant for matchmaking made him uncomfortable. Especially since he and the targeted woman were so obviously *mismatched.* He wondered if he'd worked Rufus too hard this year. "Once I dump this old place," he told his absent friend, "I'm sending you on a month's vaca to Tahiti. Like it or not."

A heartbeat later, something hit him in the back of the head. Startled he spun around, one hand rubbing the base of his skull. "What the..." He glanced down and saw a teardrop shaped Austrian crystal lying on the floor. Glancing up, he pinpointed the chandelier from which it had fallen. Though the crystals sparkled and the gilded brass gleamed as if newly polished, the base appeared rusted and ever-so-slightly detached from the cracked ceiling. Peering harder, it appeared as though the entire fixture was hanging by a single, exposed wire. Frowning, he scooped up the crystal and slipped it into his pocket. "I guess I'm lucky the whole damn thing didn't fall on my head."

"Maybe you'd be more comfortable at a hotel."

Ruminating his brush with disaster, he hadn't heard her come in. Her voice was unmistakable, though. Her tone predictable. The comment hadn't come out as polite suggestion so much as sarcastic crack. Given her track record, he'd not have expected otherwise. He looked up and saw his belligerent 'dream girl' walking toward him, a backpack slung over one shoulder, a sleeping bag hanging from the other. Gone were the jeans, replaced by a short, blue and green plaid skirt. The scrunched-up socks and hiking boots remained as did the *I Dream of Jeannie* ponytail. A green, cropped angora sweater revealed a good portion of her midriff as well as a pierced belly button. Gidget meets Madonna. Against his will, but beyond his control, Marcus felt himself harden.

"Didn't your mother ever tell you that it's rude to eavesdrop?" He moved quickly forward to relieve her of her baggage. Thankful for the props, he held her backpack at crotch level to hide his ill-timed arousal.

"I'm sure she mentioned it at one point or another." She surprised him by crooking a nervous smile. "Talking to yourself or to your ancestors?"

"Myself, of course." He'd never seen her smile, outside of that one acidic smirk earlier on. The fact that she did so now tweaked his suspicions.

"Of course. Because your ancestors are dead and the dead don't talk unless, of course, they're ghosts and you, by your own admission, don't believe in ghosts." Her tone was as tight as her smile.

"That's right." *She wanted something.*

They fell silent for one, two, three awkward beats, then spoke at the same time.

"About before..."

"I apologize if..."

Daisy pressed her lips together and waved Marcus on.

He shook his head. "Ladies first."

"Oh, well...thanks. I guess." She cleared her throat then took a deep breath. He'd swear he actually saw her swallow her pride. "About before. I don't know. It's just that I was so sure..."

Marcus lifted a suspect brow.

"At any rate, I'm sorry if I mistook you for someone else. I'd appreciate it if you didn't hold it against me. I sort of...I desperately need this...I'm damn good at my job." She let out a pent-up breath then sank down on the arm of the leather couch, seemingly drained. "Your turn."

Her job. She wanted assurance that she still had a job. Marcus grinned, despite the fact that she'd failed to amply explain her accusation that he'd kissed her. Her apology, if that's what it was, had apparently been a bitch to get out. Her shoulders sagged. Her mouth drooped. Even her ponytail had lost some of its former perkiness. *I'm sorry if I mistook you for someone else.* Who? Rufus? He wouldn't blame his friend for stealing a kiss from the leggy Ms. Malone. Wouldn't put it past him. And Rufus did resemble him somewhat. Tall, dark hair. But Rufus had been downstairs. Hadn't he?

"I apologize if I overreacted," he offered. "My former female assistant accused me of sexual misconduct two years back. In reality, she made the pass. I declined."

Daisy nodded. "Hell hath no fury."

"No kidding." The suit had cost him a fortune to keep out of the tabloids. "Suffice it to say, my next assistant was a man."

"Sinclair."

"A pain in my ass, but as loyal as they come. And damn good at his job. He assures me that you're the man, sorry, woman for the job. I trust his judgment."

She rose cautiously to her feet. "You're not going to fire me?"

He gave her archaic equipment a cursory glance. "Are you capable of providing me with the document that I need?"

"Capable and willing."

Her strangled words yanked his gaze back to her. "Then you're not fired."

Instead of looking relieved or, God forbid, grateful, she looked...resentful. What was it with this woman? Strike that. He didn't want to know.

She straightened her shoulders, primped her ponytail higher, then brushed by him. Fishing a notebook and pen from one of the crates, she asked, "So what happened?"

"Excuse me?"

"You said, 'I guess I'm lucky the whole damn thing didn't fall on my head.' I assume you're referring to the chandelier. So what *did* fall on your head?"

Marcus dropped the sleeping bag on the couch then plucked the crystal from his pocket. "This." He held the sparkling trinket in the palm of his hand for her inspection. "No bigger than an acorn. Amazing, considering the little sucker smarted like hell."

She jotted a note in her book. "Where were you standing when this incident occurred?"

He slipped the crystal back into his pocket and moved to his left. "Here."

She looked at him, up at the chandelier, then back to him, brows scrunched. "Are you sure?"

"Give or take an inch either way, yes, I'm sure."

Frowning, she looked back down at the book and scribbled away. "Odd."

"What's odd?"

"What happened in the moment before the crystal fell? What were you doing?"

"Is this really necessary?"

She glanced up. "It's important that I document all peculiar events," she said, serious as an undertaker. "If you want me to do my job, yes, it's necessary."

"But it's not."

"What?"

"A peculiar event. In fact, it's understandable."

She snorted.

He pointed to the precariously hanging fixture. "It's falling apart."

"Whose fault is that?" She waved away her own terse words. "Never mind. Clearly your explanation is a logical one, and possibly the correct one. It is not, however, conclusive. Besides, I have to put something in my report. That is if you want it to look in any way legitimate."

He bristled at her implied meaning. "You're trying my patience, Ms. Malone."

Pen poised, she repeated, "So what occurred in the moments before the crystal fell and hit you on your head?"

Dropping into a chair with the backpack on his lap, he recited at breakneck speed the events as he remembered them. "I was talking to Rufus on my cellular. He's out on the town with the helicopter pilot who flew us down from New York. He was calling from some casino, some showroom. Whichever showroom is featuring an Elvis impersonator."

"Uh huh." Focused on her notepad, she scribbled to catch up with his monotone dictation. Apparently shorthand wasn't taught in Ghostbusting 101.

"He was calling to explain that he won't be home tonight."

She scribbled some more. "Mmm hmm."

Marcus's gaze fell to the tiny red gem adorning Daisy Malone's belly button. He never would've thought it, but he actually found the decoration incredibly sexy. He shifted the backpack over his crotch. *Dammit.* There was something undeniably twisted about being attracted to a woman who despised him. Again Rufus' words rang in his ears. *"Your confidence is shaken. Challenge yourself. See if you can get in this sweet thing's pants."*

Sex. Rufus' cure-all for everything from the common cold to a bad mood. Marcus thought back on Rufus' references to his broken engagement and damaged ego. About Rufus' lame-insinuating comments regarding Marcus' recent celibacy. Casual sex. Rufus' style, not Marcus'. While Sinclair reveled in boffing every other beautiful model, actress, and singer in Manhattan, Marcus preferred sleeping with a select few. Before Kimberly he'd dated divorced professional women. Women as adverse to an emotional entanglement as he was. Women who eagerly engaged in a night of hot sex and considered it just that. No lingering for breakfast in the morning. Not even an indent in the pillow from his head. A blind man could see Daisy didn't fit that mold. Yet Rufus had been suggesting, prodding, pushing, and encouraging Marcus to indulge in a weekend fling with her since before they'd left New York this morning. Why?

He was up to something.

Marcus gave himself a mental shake. Maybe Rufus wasn't up to anything at all, other than the obvious. Maybe this *was* a simple matchmaking effort on his part. A code-blue zap in what he thought to be Marcus' dead love life. A diversion from the Kimberly fiasco. A noble gesture—in Rufus' mind, anyway.

And he'd gone all out. Marcus had to applaud his friend for finding what must be the most incredible needle in a haystack. A parapsychologist who just happened to resemble his self-professed dream girl. Remarkable. Resourceful. Then again, that was Rufus.

"He won't be coming home tonight," Daisy repeated engrossed in her notebook. "Got it. Go on."

He hated to admit it, but Rufus was on to something. Marcus hadn't given the office much thought since arriving at Laguna Vista. He'd given Kimberly even less thought. The women before her no thought at all. Still, he and Daisy Malone were about as compatible as rattler and mongoose. A weekend fling screamed disaster. So why was he actually contemplating one?

"Which means we'll be alone," Marcus heard himself saying. "You and me. Tonight. All night."

"You and me tonight . . ." Her pen stilled. She looked up from her pad and locked gazes with him. The big, blue trap of her eyes widened. Her cheeks flushed. Her succulent lips parted, and he marveled at the dark space just inside.

The silence pulsed around them. Each waited for the other to break it.

At last a voice sounded. "You've got mail!"

They both started and turned to the laptop across the room.

Daisy jumped up to busy herself with her video cam.

Marcus approached the laptop with furrowed brows.

He'd shut the computer down less than twenty minutes before.

Five

Daisy shivered as she approached the coffin-sized freezer. She'd definitely seen too many mobster movies. Images of hacked-up body parts stored like chuck beef flashed through her mind. You don't have to open it, she told herself. *Yeah, right.* Curiosity killed the cat, her mind warned. *Shut up.*

With a trembling hand she clasped the door handle. This was it.

She held her breath.

Lifted.

Empty.

She sagged with relief, letting the lid drop with a thud.

Ghosts were one thing, but dead bodies? She shook herself. Yikes, but they gave her the willies.

The cold metal of the freezer seeped through her sweatshirt, reminding her she was snooping around in a dark and damp garage. Directing her flashlight towards the stairs, she ran none-too-slowly back up into the kitchen and shut the door.

She'd been prowling the house the entire night, hopped up on cola and half a box of fluff-inflated cupcakes. Granted the sugar and caffeine had kept her awake, but her nerves were as jangled as a hippie at a barber convention. With the aid of her flashlight, she made her way back to the living room, her sister's Cookie Monster slippers sliding like ice skates over the hardwood floor. Afraid she'd get cold and lonely, Danielle had insisted her big sister borrow her favorite bedtime companions. Daisy grinned as she checked her equipment for the umpteenth time. God, she loved her family.

Running her flashlight across the monitors, her smile

faded.

Nothing.

Not a blip, not a vibe, not a single drop in temperature. Was this for real? Or had she plugged everything in wrong? And if it was for real, then that meant there was absolutely no paranormal activity.

She sagged against the back of the couch. So what was her problem? She should be ecstatic. She should be doing Tom Cruise's *Risky Business* dance every time her equipment registered nothing but thin air. She wouldn't have to lie.

Oh, please. Who was she trying to fool? Deep in her heart, she knew the truth. She wanted Jonas Van Buren. Needed him. Needed to know she wasn't crazy. Needed to know why he was in such pain. Needed to help him. She'd known it from the moment she'd set eyes on him. It was why she'd come back time and time again. To help him. As she'd stood there in her little yellow softball shirt, she'd known, even in her child's heart, that she wanted to be the one to save him.

Now, staring at the lifeless monitors, she should be happy that he didn't exist. Happy to be let off the hook. Happy to know that his pain had only been a figment of her imagination. But something inside her tapped like the fingers of a cynical juror. One night did not prove anything. Maybe Jonas was shy...

Visions of this afternoon's kiss sprang full-blown to mind for the hundredth time. A gentle brush of the lips. Compassionate eyes. A warm embrace. Loneliness, guilt, sadness. A kiss and a hug shouldn't evoke such desperate emotions. And why had Marcus stared at her as if she'd flicked a fly off his nose with a forked tongue?

Because it wasn't Marcus, you idiot. He said so himself. Think, woman. Think.

Loneliness, guilt, sadness...that same black hole of depression she'd felt when she'd first seen Jonas. But it couldn't be...a ghost couldn't kiss a mortal woman...wouldn't she have known it? And how did he get into Marcus' clothes? Had they been wearing the same tie? She couldn't remember! Her thoughts spun wildly until they finally collapsed on themselves. Clicking off the flashlight, she flopped down on Marcus' leather couch. Two gallons of artificially-flavored syrup and a pound of puffed-up sugar could really mess with your mind. Not to mention revving in high gear for almost twenty-four hours straight. She was thinking crazy. She had to get a hold of herself.

Leaning her head back, she stroked her fingers over the cool, silky leather. Dark and decadent as Black Forest cake and twice as sinful. The testosterone-driven couch screamed sex, and because she wasn't in her right mind, she let her bare legs rest against its debauchery. Suddenly, images of a different nature sprang to mind. Hot, disturbing images. Hands splayed through hair. Head thrown back. Neck exposed. Mouth on skin.

Daisy leaped from the couch. Abstinence and leather did *not* mix.

At first, she'd dismissed the couch as a poor judgment call by Van Buren. Now she realized he knew exactly what he was doing. If a leather couch alone was that hot, she dared not imagine it with Van Buren!

She bolted up the stairs. She needed a shower. A *cold* shower, a toothbrushing, and a fresh set of clothes. Anything to get her mind back to normal. Which it hadn't been since the first moment she'd stepped into the mansion. As she rounded the corner to the east corridor, the first rays of dawn stabbed her eyes through the stained glass window. She squinted, watching the dust of countless years swirl in the shafts of pale light, like the silent snow of a Christmas globe filled with watered-down Kool-Aid. She stepped into the warm little rainbow world, wrapping herself in its timeless serenity. Drawn to the window, she pressed her forehead to the heated glass, allowing its warmth to seep through her after a long, lonely night.

Van Buren slept soundly in the room to her left. Not a peep out of him the whole night. She wondered what he thought of her. She hadn't exactly given him reason to like her. Not that she wanted him to. What would have happened if he hadn't received that email? Would he have kissed her? God knows she'd wanted him to. Again.

No, not again. It was Jonas.

Was it? she argued with herself. How could she be sure? Kissed by a ghost. It was...it was ludicrous.

Then kiss Marcus. Either the kiss will burn like your thoughts on the leather couch or tear you apart with its maddening sadness like this afternoon.

Everything inside her stilled.

That was it. That was the answer. Kiss Van Buren. If she still felt those heavy emotions, then it was him the first time. If the feelings were different, then maybe, just maybe it was...

What was she thinking? Her mind had this disgusting habit of skipping off the trail and into the woods to pick flowers. Plotting to kiss Van Buren. Bad enough she'd be the one to fry in the end … what about her family?

Daisy stiffened her spine. It was time she got her head back on straight. She had to forget her heart, forget Van Buren's family. She had her own family to save.

Hadn't her past mistakes taught her anything at all? Hadn't the lessons been hard enough? She'd let herself be swept away by Brad Worthington's kisses, his words, his promises. And where had it gotten her? He'd left her with more than just regrets. She'd ignored her family, acted on her own whimsy. Well, they'd all paid dearly for that. They would not again.

Then just like that, her bravado faded. The hair on the back of her neck prickled.

Something cool brushed her skin.

Guilt, loneliness, sadness.

Oh, my God.

She spun around, thought she saw him, then nothing. No one. *Nothing* was there.

The feeling, like a drifting cloud, pulled away.

She followed. "No, don't go," she whispered. "Stay. Show me. Show me...something."

It drifted farther, faster.

Before she knew it, she was running into the west corridor. "Wait!"

She ran into a wall.

The feeling disappeared.

"No, dammit!" She pressed her palms to the flower-papered wall. "Don't leave me again." Tears filled her eyes as she slid to the floor. Despite her earlier conviction, she mumbled, "I just want to help."

Closing her eyes, her senses reeled into blackness, but not before she smelled smoke.

***

Marcus woke up with a crick in his neck and a twinge in his lower back. Just one more thing to add to his "Bawl Out Rufus List." His assistant had been so revved to get out of the house last night for his date with Chopper Chick that he hadn't even double-checked the delivery from the warehouse. As Marcus tried to turn to his side, his heels touched the cold springs of the king-sized bed, the twin mattress lost in the massive frame like a raft at sea. He crossed his arms, once again forced to lie supine and still as a board. It was undoubtedly the worst night's sleep of his life. That is, what little sleep he'd managed to get.

At first he'd tossed and turned and cursed Rufus' name for a solid fifteen minutes. Then he'd switched the light back on and lain awake for the next hour reviewing a pending contract, another half hour contemplating his mysterious email, and another half hour (give or take five minutes) finishing off *The New York Times* crossword puzzle—all the while listening to Gidget the Ghostbuster putter up and down the stairs, in and out of rooms, doing whatever ghostbusters do at one a.m. Add to that another forty-five minutes trying to talk himself out of his insane attraction to the mercurial Ms. Malone, two minutes wondering whether or not Rufus had gotten luckier tonight than he had, thirteen minutes cursing Rufus for getting luckier tonight than he had, then another hour organizing his next day's schedule while staring up at the cracked ceiling and waiting for a portion of the chipped, yellowed plaster to fall square in his face.

All in all, four hours of insomnia hell, followed by three hours of tormented sleep. Oh, and of course, the two times he'd awoken in a cold sweat plagued by a nightmare that now eluded him.

He massaged his throbbing temples, craving a handful of aspirin and a bucket of coffee. He'd gone to sleep with a headache and now woke with a migraine. "A weekend of R & R, my ass," he muttered. Tired and cranky, Marcus glared up at the same cracked plaster he'd been staring at before he'd fallen into that fitful slumber. In the light of day, the ceiling looked even worse. He whipped aside the silk sheets and swung out of the Tom Thumb bed before the sky came tumbling down.

Stepping into his slippers, he begrudgingly awarded Rufus one merit point for the superhuman cleaning crew he'd hired. There wasn't a cobweb or dust clump in sight. The solid mahogany door frames, marred though they were, glowed like warm mulled wine. Brass fixtures gleamed, though some hung crookedly or precariously, like the grand chandelier in the living room. And most importantly, for a place that had been deserted for ten years or better, mold, mildew, and rodent droppings were conspicuously non-existent.

He grabbed his pants and headed into the adjoining bathroom, thankful he didn't have to watch where he stepped. As he tossed one of the thick, stocked towels to the floor, he noted the tile was pitted and scarred, though he imagined he could eat off the black-and-white-checkered squares should he so choose. Everywhere the tangy aroma of lemon polish mingled with the woodsy scent of pine disinfectant, producing an air of cleanliness sure to please the most fastidious mother.

Marcus drew back a spanking new shower curtain and twisted the hot and cold faucets. The left knob came off in his hand. Scalding water spritzed skyward. Cursing, he hurriedly replaced the metal dial, making a mental note to call a plumber *and* an electrician after breakfast. Stepping out of his monogrammed pajama bottoms and into the deep tub, he realized the absurdity of initiating repairs on a house slated for destruction. If all went as planned, bulldozers and wrecking balls would be on the grounds by month's end. Still, he had to make the place livable for the next few days. The former mansion, former restaurant, former disco, former bed and breakfast was a far cry from his impeccably furnished penthouse, and the last thing he needed was a fifty-pound chandelier falling on someone's head. Regardless of the whirlwind surface cleaning, Laguna Vista was falling apart.

"*Whose fault is that?*" Daisy Malone's chastisement rang in his throbbing brain. He moved directly under the showerhead, allowing the pulsating water to pelt his head and drown out her words.

"At least the water pressure's decent." Grateful for the simple luxury, he rolled his head in a full circle, anxious to ease the persistent pains in his neck, each of which had a name. Laguna Vista. Rufus Sinclair. Daisy Malone.

Nabbing a new bar of soap, he scrubbed his body, shampooed his hair, and battled an early morning hard-on inspired by the image of his enigmatic ghostbuster and her exotic belly ring.

He'd been two seconds from asking her out for a late supper when that email had voiced its arrival, shattering their sexual tension like a sledgehammer through a vase. *She'd* darted for her video camera. *He'd* made a beeline for his computer. Thereafter they'd spent the next three hours avoiding each other. *She* trying to figure out what was wrong with her antiquated equipment. *He* trying to figure out what was wrong with his state-of-the-art computer.

He'd shut it down. He was sure he'd shut it down. Apparently he hadn't. Apparently he'd only thought he'd shut it down. It was the only logical explanation. As for the message, he had no clue who Louise Brooks was. Obviously she'd emailed to the wrong address. It was pure coincidence that the phantom message hit home at the precise moment he'd have asked out Daisy.

Nevertheless, he thanked Louise Brooks.

Although Rufus' matchmaking scam was as obvious as a red dress at a funeral, Marcus had nearly fallen prey to Daisy Malone's unwitting charms. She'd softened before his eyes, something he'd have bet his yacht never to see. Twisting her sweater in her fingers as she'd waited for the verdict on her job. Smiling as if maybe it would help her case. Hunching over her bare knees as she wrote industriously in her notebook, jotting down details as if it would make some kind of difference.

He dropped the soap in its dish. Any sane man would have reacted the same way. Dark, lonely night. Cold, empty house. Luckily, that angel of mercy had interrupted them before he'd completely lost his head. *Dinner*? Was he out of his mind? Table for two. Soft candlelight. Intimate talk. Sharing life stories. Finishing each other's desserts.

Thank God he'd been spared. He could imagine the deer in the headlight look on his face when she'd naturally lean forward, her eyes sparkling in the candlelight, to ask, "So, what were you like as a child?" or "What do you do to have fun?"

He'd nearly slipped. It wouldn't happen again. His attraction to Daisy Malone could be controlled. For good measure, he doused himself with a shot of freezing water before climbing out of the shower.

"Only a couple of more days," he reminded himself. "This house will be out of my life forever and so will Daisy Malone."

Wrapping the towel about his waist, he pulled a razor from his toiletry bag and approached the sink. He dropped the razor, however, upon reaching the gilded mirror hanging crookedly over the basin. Written across the face of the steamed-over glass, the same message that had greeted him via email the night before.

You should be ashamed.

Six

Barefooted, bare chested, hair dripping wet, Marcus barreled out of his bedroom, zipping the fly of his trousers and muttering dockside expletives. Pranks. He loathed them. Rufus knew his views on practical jokes. And still he dared to indulge?

He strode down the hall to the room Rufus had claimed the previous day. He must've gotten home early, must've crept into the bathroom when Marcus was showering, and used his finger to scrawl that asinine message on the steamy mirror. As for the email, he'd probably sweet-talked one of the casino's female employees into letting him use her computer.

You should be ashamed.

He congratulated Rufus on his uncanny timing at any rate. He'd been thinking about sex, about Ms. Malone, about having *sex* with Ms. Malone seconds before each message appeared. The fact that Rufus was chastising him for thinking of seducing Gidget when it was he himself who'd suggested he seduce Gidget, struck Marcus as warped. Not funny. Warped.

The only logical explanation, the only forgivable one, was that Rufus had been drunk as a skunk when he'd sent the email. A distinct probability considering his slurred speech during the "Hound Dog" episode. As for this morning...well, wanting to give Rufus the benefit of the doubt, he decided the alcohol must still be fogging his brain.

He intended to question Rufus pronto on this adolescent behavior—that is, if he hadn't already passed out. Marcus barged into his assistant's room without knocking.

"Rufus?" His voice echoed off the faded pink walls. Rufus was nowhere in sight. The bed, the nice *doublewide* bed, was still made, though barely visible under the mountain of trousers, dress shirts, and short-sleeved crew necks. Apparently, lover boy had wrestled with his wardrobe when deciding how best to impress Helipad Barbie.

Marcus retreated and headed down the hall in the opposite direction. The sudden smell of sizzling bacon made his stomach growl. Rufus loved bacon. Marcus clenched and unclenched his fist. So, his assistant was celebrating his wily tactics over eggs, bacon, and coffee, was he? If Rufus knew what was good for him, he'd keep that frying pan close at hand.

As Marcus rounded the corner to the staircase landing, he spotted a curled-up form propped against the wall. He rolled his eyes. Carrying his intoxicated friend back to his room and tucking him into bed wasn't exactly the retribution he'd had in mind. Stepping through the hazy stream of early morning sunlight, he found not Rufus but Daisy. Right cheek pressed against the wallpapered wall. Sound asleep.

She must be cold, he thought, as his gaze traveled down her long, bare legs. He knew he should scoop her up and carry her to her bed, but the coward in him preferred to throw a blanket over her and run down the stairs. He didn't want to go anywhere near her. She was corrosive to his self-control, and he'd be downright stupid to touch her with his bare hands.

She shifted, pressing closer to the wall and wrapping her arms around herself.

Figures. She was cold.

He crouched down, surveying her chosen attire with undeniable interest. An oversized sweatshirt advertising Malone's Pub, plaid flannel boxers, and fuzzy blue slippers displaying the head of some golf-ball-eyed monster.

The official SPS ghostbusting uniform? With her clean, scrubbed face and simple ponytail, she looked more like a victim of an all-night slumber party. Either way, a far cry from anything Kimberly would've been caught dead in. Then again, Kimberly wouldn't have been caught dead sleeping under Laguna Vista's roof. Period. Whereas the spunky Ms. Malone, however, seemed oddly at home.

Spunky. When was the last time he'd used that word to describe anything in his life? Especially a woman? He breathed a sigh of relief as his fascination with the ghostbuster started to make sense. Daisy Malone was nothing more than simple intrigue.

He'd never met anyone like her. Everything about her was new. Her walk. Her talk. Her style. Her profession. Her life. Everything. He'd never spent any measurable time with someone who didn't have to do with his business or his mother or, as Rufus so crudely pointed out, his big-O-faking social climbers. Daisy Malone was simple human interest.

He rolled back his shoulders and relaxed.

He should carry her to bed now.

He didn't move.

You're thirty-six years old, for crying out loud. Head of a Fortune 500 company. You can bench-press two-hundred-fifty pounds. Think of her as a ball. Whisk her up, race to her room, and dump her in the end zone.

Reaching out to slide his arm around her neck, his fingers accidentally brushed her cheek. He froze. Though she slept on, his heart raced and his fingers tingled. He'd never felt a more intimate contact in his life. Yes, he'd had sex, and even made love once or twice, but caressing a woman's cheek? It was so...personal. Granted, it had been an accident, but somehow he felt as if he'd just taken advantage of her.

Why did she have to look so vulnerable and innocent? He almost wished she'd wake up, utter something snide, and shatter the illusion. Instead she turned her face into the palm of his hand...and moaned.

Damn. He had to get out of here.

Her lashes fluttered, then raised ever so slightly. "Jonas?"

Her voice was husky with sleep. She must still be dreaming, or waking from a dream, her mind still fuzzy with faces and images of her subconscious. She must've been dreaming about her work. About ghosts.

She'd mistaken him for his dead grandfather.

"Daisy." He lightly tapped her flushed cheek. "Daisy."

Her lids drifted shut. She snuggled closer against him.

"Hold me."

He swallowed hard. He'd hold her, all right, for the thirty seconds it took him to carry her to her room and deposit her on her bed.

Again the smell of bacon wafted up the stairway, mingling with the rich aroma of freshly brewed coffee. Rufus. Had he walked right by Daisy? Left her sleeping on the floor while he played his prank then returned downstairs to scramble his eggs? Marcus furrowed his brows. Highly unlikely. True, Rufus was a dog. But he was also a gentleman. A combination that confounded Marcus to this day. No, Rufus would've scooped up the sleeping ghostbuster and toted her to her bed. Which is exactly what Marcus rushed ahead to do.

He expected her to wake. She didn't. He'd heard her shuffling around at about three a.m. when he'd finally drifted off. She must've worked through the night. Why she conked out in the corner of the hall instead of the comfort of her bed, he had no idea.

Padding down the hall, sleeping girl in his arms, Marcus sought out her room. He quickly found it, one door down from Rufus'. After finagling with the knob, he eased through the doorway to find a double bed loaded down with crates of cords, film, and audio and video tapes. Research books lay open at the foot of the sagging mattress. Glancing right he noticed her sleeping bag unfurled against the wall, a pillow ready and waiting.

It wasn't even an option.

Marcus bypassed Rufus' room and stepped into his own. Setting her on his bed, he removed her slippers then pulled the blue satin sheets to her chin, along with the thick down comforter. Damn, it was cold in this room. He checked the windows for a draft. Finding them firmly shut, he located the heating vent and opened the shutter, allowing a warm rush of air to flow into the room.

Daisy sighed, and he moved back to the foot of the bed. He watched her, reminding himself it was only *intrigue* that kept him standing there the extra moment. Intrigue that made it difficult to keep his thoughts professional. She sighed again and snuggled deeper under the covers. This time, his imagination burned rubber over his line of careful distance. Deciding she was safely tucked away, he followed the hot trail of his thoughts.

He imagined her naked beneath those sheets, her skin as smooth and soft as the silk threads sliding against her. He wanted to touch her. Badly. Sleeping as she was, she was picture perfect, his dream girl. He smirked. It seemed the only thing able to douse the flames of this insane attraction was her sassy mouth. If only she'd wake up and put him out of his misery.

In the next instant, the hairs on the back of his neck prickled. He spun around, certain someone was looking over his shoulder.

But no one was there.

Shaking off a chill, he reached for a shirt in his closet. His hand froze.

Someone had tampered with his clothes. Hanging amidst his trousers, his favorite blue dress shirt. When it came to his closet, he was admittedly fussy. Trousers with trousers, shirts with shirts, jackets with jackets, each section arranged by color.

He pulled the renegade shirt from the hanger. His nostrils flared at the scent of another man. He sniffed the material. Cigars. The spicy scent of an expensive, pre-embargo Cuban.

Scanning the clothes rod once more, he spied his gray pin-striped, single-breasted Armani squeezed in between his navy Lauren and indigo Versace jackets.

He growled Rufus' name as his fist tightened around the sullied shirt. Deciding the face-off with his prankster assistant had waited long enough, he left Daisy Malone to her ghostly dreams and headed for the stairs.

***

"He looks madder than Father the day I told him I married Buddy Valentine." Isadora flicked her ash as her grand-nephew stormed right through her and out the door.

"Which husband was that?" James asked.

"Husband Number One," Jonas reminded him, tucking his Cuban into his inner pocket while mentally noting his

grandson's closet obsession for future reference. *"The saxophone player."*

"If he takes a poke at Rufus, I hope he punches something other than that pretty face." She clasped her hands to her heart and fluttered thick lashes caked with Twenties-fashionable mascara. *"He's sooo handsome. Maybe his stomach. Marcus couldn't do much damage there. Not with all of those rippled muscles in his way."*

"I don't know what he sees in her," James said. He hovered over Daisy, stretched out on his stomach mid-air, his chin resting in the palm of his hand. *"Or you either, Jonas. She's sort of plain. Grouchy, too."*

Isadora nodded. *"You said it. That poor little bunny's closed up tighter than a spinster's legs. She needs to loosen up if there's to be any chance of a romance. I can't remember the last time this place worked up a good sweat."*

"The disco manager and that cocktail waitress in the magenta hot pants," James reminded her.

Isadora snapped her fingers. *"That's right! Karl and Ginger. All legs, that dame. Remember when they did it on the balcony? Talk about limber."*

"I wonder if I could get Jill on that balcony," James said. *"Now she's the snake's hips."*

Isadora rubbed her hands together. *"Oh, the things I'd like to do to Rufus."*

James sighed. *"Oh, to be seventy years younger."*

"Oh, to be alive," Isadora cooed.

"Oh, can it," Jonas snapped.

Isadora cocked a haughty brow. *"What's eating you?"*

"What's eating me? What's eating me?"

She looked from Jonas to James, cupie-lips curled up in a smirk. *"Is there an echo in here?"*

"I'll tell you what's eating me," Jonas growled. He leveled his brother and sister with a disappointed glare. *"Your adolescent behavior."*

James and Isadora blinked at Jonas then at each other. *"Moi?"*

Jonas raised his eyebrows at James. *"Chasing after a*

twinkie who's barely out of diapers."

James floated over to stand toe to toe with Jonas. *"Don't call my babe a twinkie."*

"She's not your babe," Jonas exploded. *"You don't stand a chance with her! Take a look at yourself, Jimmy. You're dead!"*

Isadora looped her arm about her younger brother's shoulder. *"So he's a little pasty-faced. No need to get nasty, Jonas. So she's young. So he's dead. Who says Jimmy can't romance the vamp? Since when does love know boundaries?"*

"Jimmy wouldn't know true love if it bit him on the butt. And you," he said, pointing a finger at Isadora. *"What's the big idea pitching that crystal at my grandson's head?"*

"He was badmouthing our home. Dump this old place...as if Laguna Vista had no more value than a dented Pierce-Arrow."

"You should be ashamed?" Jonas continued.

"You bet your wing tips Marcus should be ashamed. Frankly, Jonas, if you ask me, your grandson has an attitude problem, not to mention he threatened to send my Rufus to Tahiti."

Jonas rolled his eyes. *"My babe. My Rufus. We're in serious trouble here. And you two are acting like besotted college kids."*

"Look who's talking," James snapped. *"You kissed the grouchy tomato! Not only that, you tempted fate and appeared to her. If anyone's besotted, brother, it's you."*

"That's why you're trying to rain on my matchmaking parade." Isadora crossed her arms. *"You want Daisy for yourself!"*

"I'm trying to get us out of here!"

James hooted, jerking a thumb over his shoulder. *"By seducing blondie?"*

Jonas jammed his hands into the pockets of his wool trousers and regarded his little brother with a frown. *"Unlike you, I'm in search of information, not a paranormal fling. Aside from being one of them, Daisy's an expert on ghosts. She can help us cross over. I'm sure of it."*

Isadora huffed an exasperated breath. *"Again with the*

crossing-over hooey. Really, Jonas. You're beginning to sound like a broken record, not to mention a drip." She turned to James. *"I don't know about you, but after ten years of cooling my heels, I'm ready to twirl my pearls. There's a living, breathing Van Buren in this house again, and I say it's high time he started acting like one. Are you with me?"*

James looked from Isadora to Jonas. *"Well...I..."* He hooked his thumbs behind his suspenders. *"Give me a minute here."*

Jonas shook his head. *"You're way off on this, angel. We should be uniting our efforts, not dividing them. Besides, you're barking up the wrong tree. Marcus prefers the meek and mild."*

Isadora snorted. *"That's a load of bushwa, Jonas. You married a prim and priss, a respectable woman. Can you stand there and honestly tell me Sara lit your fire?"* She folded her arms and smirked when he didn't reply. *"I didn't think so. Trust me, I'm right on this one. Marcus has met his match in Daisy. Her combative edge turns him on. And I have nothing to do with that. He gets it from you."*

Now Jonas snorted.

Isadora raised a sleek brow. *"Deny it all you want. He's got it bad. It's only a matter of time."*

James nudged him. *"You gotta admit, when it comes to men, Izzy knows her onions."*

Jonas threw up his hands. *"Fine. Have your fun. But hear this. I won't spend another seventy years in this house. I'm crossing over, with or without you."*

Isadora hooked her arm through James' and grinned. *"Like you'd go anywhere without us."*

Jonas faded from the room. *"Watch me."*

***

Marcus burst into the kitchen. "I'm gonna kick your ass!"

"I can make pancakes if you prefer."

An attractive woman wearing a chestnut bob and a frilly apron stepped back from the stove, greasy spatula in hand. Marcus blinked at her. Jesus, Rufus had traded up from Barbie chopper-chick to Suzy homemaker. And he'd brought her home. He glanced behind the kitchen door, certain Rufus was hiding behind it and getting a hearty chuckle out of Marcus' misdirected threat. But Rufus wasn't behind the door, or anywhere else in sight.

He looked back to the woman, one brow raised. "And you are?"

She closed the space between them, brandishing the spatula in her right hand. "I'm Angie Malone."

Oh, God, Marcus thought. No, Rufus. Not Daisy's sister!

"Daisy's mother."

Jesus!

She switched the utensil to her left hand and offered her right in greeting. "And you're either Mr. Van Buren or Mr. Sinclair."

She didn't know Rufus. Ridiculously relieved, Marcus dredged up a pleasant smile and shook her hand. "Mr. Van Buren. Marcus Van Buren. Please, call me Marcus." Her enduring beauty stunned him. Daisy's mother? She looked forty, if a day.

She eyed him up and down, withdrew her hand from his grasp, then returned to the stove. "Figures."

He hadn't missed the hint of disapproval in her appraising gaze or in her tone. Open disdain from yet another female Malone. What was it with these women? He glanced down at his bare chest and winced. Remembering the balled-up shirt clenched in his fist, he hurriedly shrugged into it. The lingering cigar smoke taunted him as he buttoned all but the top three buttons. "So you haven't met Rufus? That is, Mr. Sinclair?"

"No." She glanced around the room then refocused on the frying pan. "Nice kitchen."

"Thank you." Not that he'd had anything to do with it. The spacious layout had been J.B.'s doing. Rufus ordered in the state-of-the-art appliances. "Excuse me for asking...how did you get in?"

"Daisy made me a spare key. In case of an emergency." She moved the skillet to the back burner and wiped her hands on the apron. "So do you prefer pancakes?"

"Excuse me?"

"I'd hate to get my ass kicked over something as

ridiculous as breakfast. If you hate eggs that much..."

He waved his hands before him. "No, I like eggs. Eggs are fine. I..." He blushed and jammed his hands into his pockets. "That is to say, it wasn't your ass I was threatening to kick."

"Well," she said, loading a plate with three eggs over easy, two slices of toast, and a heap of bacon, "since my ass is the only ass here, you can see my confusion." She set the plate on the large kitchen table and motioned him to take a seat. "Eat up before it gets cold."

Spoken like a true mother, Marcus thought, taking his appointed chair. Except for the 'ass' part.

He stared at his plate for a full minute, contemplating the kindest way to say, "Thank you, but no thank you. Do you mind leaving my house?" Nothing came to mind. Instead he asked, "Aren't you going to join me?"

"I've already eaten, thank you." She poured two cups of coffee, set one before him then took a seat at the opposite end of the table. "I'll join you for coffee, though." She smiled tightly. "So?"

Marcus' fork paused mid-air, his senses on full alert. "So?"

"Where's my daughter?"

"Sleeping." *In my bed.*

She regarded him coolly over the rim of her steaming coffee. "It's nine-thirty."

"She was up all night. Investigating."

"Investigating."

"Which is what I hired her to do."

"I know." She pointed to his plate. "Your food, Mr. Van Buren."

"Right." He forced the steaming eggs into his mouth. It was a hell of a lot better than arguing with the woman, or God forbid, insulting her. He had the distinct feeling that beneath that Brady Bunch mom facade beat the heart of a drill sergeant. Angie Malone had an air of authority about her. Like she was used to ordering people around and used to getting her way. He realized, begrudgingly, that he liked her. He shoveled in three more mouthfuls. "This is good."

"Thank you."

Her reply was polite. Automatic. But he'd meant what he'd said. The food was delicious. Nothing fancy. Still, there was something about a mom's home cooking. Not that his own mother had ever cooked for him. "That's what hired chefs are for, darling," she'd once said.

Angie Malone sipped her coffee and continued to study him as he finished off the country-style breakfast. At one point, she idly fiddled with a steak knife. Shifting in his seat, uncomfortable with what she might be thinking, Marcus sought to break the tension. "So," he said, nibbling on his butter-slathered toast, "to what do I owe this honor?"

"Actually, I'd hoped to patch things up with my daughter by cooking her favorite breakfast."

Marcus swallowed, feeling somewhat guilty for cleaning his plate. "I'm sorry. This was meant for Daisy."

At last she flashed a sincere smile, laying the knife safely to the right of her cup. "Relax, Mr. Van Buren. There's plenty." She gestured to a platter on the counter piled high with bacon, toast, and scrambled eggs. "I'm used to cooking for seven."

"Seven?"

She nodded. "I have five children."

"Five!"

"Two boys. Three girls."

He took in her perfect shape as she stood and moved to the counter to refill their cups. "Five children." He whistled under his breath. "Wow."

Coffee sloshed over the sides of his cup as she set it, a little too hard, in front of him. Something told him she hadn't appreciated the whistle. He'd meant no disrespect. He'd simply been astonished that a woman who looked like, well, like Gidget's older sister, could have five children. He started to explain, then thought better of it, certain it would only worsen the already uncomfortable situation.

He sighed in relief when she moved to the sink to fill it with steaming water and dishwashing soap. Cleaning up. She was cleaning up. And...going home? He could only hope. Wanting to expedite her departure, he stood, cleared the table, and deposited the dirty dishes in the sudsy water. Another new experience since the Malones had burst into his life.

"Well?" she asked, scrubbing the dried yolk from his plate.

"Well, what?" He grabbed the skillet from the stove. Grease had caked in its black bottom. Marcus frowned. Good God. What had he allowed this woman to do to him? Fried eggs and bacon and white toast soaked with real butter. He could feel his arteries clogging this very moment.

"Aren't you going to ask what Daisy and I argued about?"

"No." He scraped the congealed grease into the trash bin then dropped the skillet into the water as if it was a smoking gun.

Brows scrunched, Angie scrubbed the frying pan with skilled zeal. "You're not even curious?"

"It's none of my business."

"That's true, I suppose," she said bearing down and scrubbing the blackened pan harder. "After all, you don't know us. You don't know anything about us. Us, as in the Malones."

"No I don't." And he liked it that way.

"You know nothing of our background. Nothing about my kids. Nothing about their devotion to family..."

"Mrs. Malone..."

"They'd do anything...any one of them would do anything to help another out of a bind. Especially Daisy. She...she..."

"Mrs. Malone." Marcus reached into the soapy water and stilled her hand. At this rate she'd scrub a hole clean through the cast-iron bottom. He'd meant to stop her chattering. Meant to stop her from revealing whatever problem was plaguing her. He'd meant to suggest family counseling. He wasn't a damned therapist or a priest. But then she looked up at him through teary eyes. "What did you and Daisy fight about, Mrs. Malone?"

"You."

"Me?" Why wasn't he surprised?

"My daughter is a sensitive soul, Mr. Van Buren. Generous, protective, and kind to a fault."

Daisy?

"She'd do anything for her family. *Anything*. She has no

pride where we're concerned. She's totally unselfish. And that," she said, looking suddenly like a lioness protecting her young, "worries me."

"I'm not following you, Mrs. Malone."

"Why did you hire my daughter, Mr. Van Buren?"

Marcus released the woman's wrist, turning off his compassion as easily as the faucet. He had no intention of discussing the potential sale of Laguna Vista. "I required the services of a reputable parapsychologist," he said simply.

She stared at him. "I repeat, why did you hire Daisy?"

Marcus dried his hands on a nearby dishtowel. "Are you saying she's *not* a reputable parapsychologist?"

"Did she say she was?"

He narrowed his eyes. "It's what I was told."

She turned away from him to rinse the skillet in the opposing basin. "You're a rich man, Mr. Van Buren. You could hire a world-renowned expert..."

"I'm not interested in attracting the media."

She plucked the towel from the counter and furiously dried the pan. "On the East Coast alone—"

"Daisy was geographically desirable...and recommended to me by a trusted friend."

Rufus. Marcus frowned, the reality of the situation becoming clear. Rufus had risked a multi-million-dollar deal for a weekend fling. *Your confidence is shaken. You've been dumped for another man.* Rufus might have meant well, but whatever his intentions, Marcus was pissed. He hated being lied to.

"Are you telling me your daughter is a fraud?"

She slammed the skillet onto the counter. "Absolutely not. My daughter knows more about ghosts than Baryshnikov knows about dancing. She's always been obsessed with them. She's read countless books on them. She took that course at the community college. Cliff and Randall declared her their star pupil—"

"Cliff and Randall?"

"Daisy's professors. The founders of the Society of Parapsychological Sleuths." She tilted her prideful chin. "They disproved ninety-five percent of their investigated hauntings, you know."

"*They* proved," Marcus repeated, feeling the rumblings of a migraine.

"She's gifted," Angie plowed on. "What did Cliff and Randall call her?" She snapped her fingers, searching the air for an answer. "A medium? A channeler?" She pounded her small fist into her other palm. "A sensitive!"

Marcus reined his temper, choosing instead to direct it at Rufus or Daisy or both, not at an overprotective mother. He massaged his throbbing temples. "Is she or is she not a member of the Society of Parapsychological Sleuths?"

"She's the owner. Cliff and Randall sold her the business."

"Is she or is she not a reputable parapsychologist?"

She thought about it a moment. "The society is extremely reputable."

"I wasn't asking about the society. I was asking about Daisy. Is she or is she not a parapsychologist?"

"I suppose that depends on your definition of a parapsychologist. If being able to connect with the dead counts, then yes."

"Mary, Mother of—"

"It's not her fault she failed the technical exam. Who can understand all those sophisticated gadgets and gizmos anyway? Besides she doesn't need them, not really. Cliff and Randall said so. If there's a ghost on the premises, she'll feel it. She's a sensitive."

"So you said," Marcus grumbled.

She grabbed his forearms. "I came over here to patch things up with my daughter. I have a terrible feeling that I just made it worse."

Marcus worked to digest this new information and to ignore the desperation in Angie Malone's touch.

"I don't suppose you'd be willing to forget this conversation?"

If he didn't know better, he'd think she'd just died a thousand deaths asking him that favor. Belligerent and proud, with an underlying vulnerability that knocked a sane man senseless. Like mother, like daughter. Daisy's words flooded back, 'I *need* this job.'

She *needs* my money, Marcus thought. However, he had a difficult time associating Daisy Malone with the typical gold diggers he'd encountered in his life. She lacked the charm and schmoozing abilities of your average kiss-up. Hostile, that's what she was. Rude and disrespectful. He should've fired her yesterday. She'd given him plenty of reasons. Insolence. Wrongful accusations.

"Daisy'll get the job done," Angie insisted, holding tight. "Please, Mr. Van Buren, don't dismiss my daughter because her mother stuck her nose where it didn't belong. I couldn't help myself. It's the Malone in me. I thought she was in danger of..."

Marcus stared down at her. "Of what? What is Daisy in danger of?" Again with the questions. He backed away from Angie's touch. Distance. He needed distance.

"Never mind," she said, untying the strings to her apron.

Good. She didn't want to tell him. Fine. Perfect.

"Just promise me—"

"No promises."

She flinched at his harsh tone.

Marcus raised his palms. "Sorry. I'm sorry. It's just...I don't make promises." Promises were too easily broken. Intentional or not. He tried to remember the last time he'd made a promise but was distracted by the encroaching migraine.

Angie pressed her lips together. Again tears filled her eyes.

Marcus cursed and looked away. "I hired Daisy to conduct a four-day investigation." He jammed his hands into his pockets. If they needed the ten grand so desperately, so be it. It was a drop in the ocean to him. "She's got four days."

"Thank you," she said, face brightening with relief. She grabbed her purse from the counter and headed for the back door. "You won't regret this, Mr. Van Buren."

"I'm sure I won't, Mrs. Malone." Marcus waited until she left then let out a pent-up breath. "Because I've got a contingency plan."

Seven

His scent. It tangled with her senses like a vine stretching toward the sun. She let it wrap around her, entwine her, hold her captive in its sweet, delectable embrace. A heady mix of old-world charm and a masculinity no gentlemanly cloak could disguise. She felt his daring as he thundered through the mist on his hard-muscled thoroughbred. Felt his passion as he made love on the plush velvet seat of his vintage Rolls Royce.

And here he was tempting her. Daring her to act impulsively, shamelessly. Without thought. His body pressed against hers, muscles tense, burning with restraint. Her own skin burned from his heat. She wanted to tear at her clothes, rid herself of the barrier between them, but she was trapped beneath his weight, with no desire to escape.

Why should she escape? Daisy thought. This was her dream, and it'd been so long since...

She was only human. And Jonas Van Buren was more real to her than any man she'd ever encountered. More genuine, more compassionate, a complex soul capable of loving greatly and hurting even greater. And he did so hurt. As she pressed her palms to the hard wall of his chest, she felt the pain pulsating in his heart. The guilt. She wanted to kiss away that hurt.

Where she was a willing captive of his invisible bonds, he held himself a prisoner of his own remorse. He could forgive anyone but himself. Control. He should have had better control, he believed.

"Oh, Jonas," she whispered, touching her fingers to his cheek.

He stiffened, his breath suddenly gushing warm currents

upon her face like an angry bull.

She smoothed his skin. "You've suffered so much, my sweet."

The warm fanning of breath ceased.

She whimpered, not wanting him to flee again. *Let me heal you.*

In the next instant, his hands raked into her hair, pulling her mouth to his. She immediately opened to him. And immediately regretted it. His desire for her spiked down to her very soul, exploding into a white-hot geyser of sparks that singed and scarred her forever. More powerful than she could have imagined, he stole her breath, her will, her heart. Could one die of such exquisite torment?

It's only a dream.

It's only Jonas.

A dead man.

You're having a wet dream about a dead man.

Her eyes flew open. She sat up so fast, she banged her head against his. "Ow!"

Fully awake now, she gaped at him sitting on the edge of her bed rubbing his forehead. Her heart pounded in her throat. "Oh, my God," she croaked. "Jonas?"

He glared at her. "You've got to be kidding."

She shrank back against the headboard, dragging the sheets up to her chin. Maybe she would die after all. "Oh, my God. Marcus?"

"In the flesh," he said with a growl. "Unlike your beloved Jonas. My grandfather. My *dead* grandfather."

She touched her fingers to her trembling lips. "But your scent...you smelled just like—"

"Let me guess. Jonas." He rose from the bed. "Are you saying I smell like my grandfather? Do I even want to know how my dead ancestor smells?"

"Like cigars," she mumbled, confused. How could she have made such a mistake? The kiss in the library had been gentle, compassionate, full of comfort. This kiss...this kiss....She continued to trace her lips. This kiss had jolted her like a thousand watts, warmed her like a sunny meadow, and awakened something inside her she'd thought long dead. Marcus had been right. When he kissed her, she damn well knew she'd been kissed!

How could she have believed she'd been dreaming? It was both exhilarating and terrifying.

She dropped her fingers as she realized Marcus' turbulent eyes studied her every move. Their murky depths darkened by the second. He shoved a hand through his hair, the same hand that had plowed into hers and drove her right out of her mind. A fallen angel. That's what he reminded her of. His beautifully etched face, all sharp angles and shadowed hollows, enticed as it intimidated. She should've been wary of his brewing menace, of the tension that clenched his jaw like a trap, but her mind still reeled from whatever alternate universe she'd just been dumped.

"Your pain," she continued. "I felt it. Buried deep...so like Jonas'."

He narrowed his eyes. "What pain? What are you talking about?"

"I don't know. You tell me."

He stepped back from her. "I don't have any pain, Ms. Malone, except for you. If you want to play amateur psychologist, open a booth on the Boardwalk."

Despite what he said, the wound did exist. She felt it, hidden beneath a labyrinth of barriers and shields. Whatever caused the underlying torment, it had been too long denied.

Like she should talk. She'd been running from her fears so long she wondered if she'd ever be able to stop.

She shivered with a sudden chill. Wait a second...

She whipped off the sheets and jumped to her feet. "Listen, Van Buren. I understand you might be upset that I called you by another man's name, but, excuse me for asking...what the hell were you doing in bed with me in the first place?"

That seemed to take the wind out of his self-righteous sails. "Pardon?"

"You know damn well what I'm talking about. I was sleeping. You were on the bed with me. Why?"

His cheeks actually flushed. "I...I..."

She smiled to herself, knowing she was one of very few who'd ever witness Marcus Van Buren both blush *and* stutter.

He shoved his hands in his back pockets. "You'd fallen asleep in the hall. I carried you here instead of dumping you on that tattered rag you call a sleeping bag. Your mother came by and—"

"My mother?" she cried. "My mother was here! You were downstairs talking to my mother while I was up here in your bed?" Daisy smacked her forehead and sank to the mattress. If her mother had caught her in Marcus' bed—

"Relax. She came by to make peace with you. Hell of a cook."

"She cooked for you?" She shook her head and pouted. "Of course she did. That's Mom. But she knew I was here alone with...I can't believe she didn't demand to see me. Make sure I'm all right."

He grinned. "She said I remind her of her favorite choir boy."

"Our church doesn't have a choir," she snapped. "Answer the question. What were you doing in bed with me?"

He rolled his eyes. "Not to ravage you, I assure you. I came in to grab my watch off the nightstand, but then you started mumbling something. I leaned in closer to hear you, and you grabbed me and pulled me down. *You* grabbed me."

Her cheeks burned. She wanted to blame him. She wanted to rant and rave. But she'd sensed the truth from the moment she'd awoken. His unblinking stare confirmed it.

She'd kissed *him.*

She'd thought of kissing him earlier, hoping to untangle her twisting thoughts of Marcus and Jonas, but now she was more confused than ever. She'd thought it was Marcus kissing her in the library. He'd denied it. She'd thought it was Jonas kissing her in her dream. It turned out to be Marcus in reality.

As he continued to stare at her, her mortification mounting with the silence, she wished he really had been trying to cop a feel.

This was getting way out of hand.

She stood again. "Where's the document?"

"What document?"

"The legal paper stating Laguna Vista ghost-free. Give it to me. A pen, too." Her hands shook. She had to get out of here. Mistakes were for learning. Not repeating.

"I thought you said you needed four days."

"Um, not necessary. There's nothing on the machines. Not a blip. Everything's clear. Where's the paper?"

He seemed suddenly alert. "One night is not enough proof for me, Ms. Malone. I want a thorough investigation."

"According to Rufus, you just want the paper signed. What do you care when or how? As long as I sign, right?"

"Despite what Rufus may have implied, I told you that I require a full investigation. You said it would take *at least* four days. You committed to do this job, Ms. Malone."

"I did the job. There's nothing. Let's move on."

He continued to stand, not moving on. "If you leave now, I'll be forced to stop payment on your deposit check and charge you an early-termination fee."

Early-termination fee? He was bluffing. Wasn't he? "How much is that?"

He studied his shoe. "I prefer not to delve into all this unpleasantness, Ms. Malone. I need the investigation completed this week. I don't have time to interview anyone else. You're obviously a woman of reason."

She waited for him to choke on that last word but he held steady. What was the rush with the investigation? What was he planning with the house, she wondered not for the first time.

"What if I offered you an additional five thousand a day?"

"Five thousand? As in dollars?" She quickly calculated the bonus money and swallowed. *Oh, my God.* Under any other circumstance, she'd be jumping up and down like a lunatic. Right now she felt backed into a corner. He knew she wouldn't say no. *She* knew she couldn't say no. Her family was more important than her raging hormones. She would just have to practice better self-control, like Jonas—no like Marcus— thought he should.

"Fine. You have a deal. I'd like it in writing by the end of the day."

"Fine." He stripped off his shirt as though it was suddenly offensive. He flung it to the floor and glared at it a second before reaching into the closet to grab a clean one.

"Fine," she muttered, getting in the last word as she stormed from the room. The image of his naked, muscled torso burned in her mind. What kind of woman needed five-thousand dollars a day to keep her hands off a man?

***

Marcus wondered if there were any reputable analysts in Atlantic City. Surely he needed his head examined. A multi-million dollar deal hinged on proving Laguna Vista ghost-free. Yet instead of allowing his so-called parapsychologist to sign on the dotted line, he'd insisted on a more in-depth investigation, another seventy-two hours at least, and he'd promised her five-thousand dollars a day for her time and trouble! Though trouble seemed to be something she dispensed freely.

Marcus walked down the hall, buttoning his clean oxford shirt and questioning his sanity. Easy answer. He was mad. But not as mad as she. She had the hots for his grandfather, who, by his calculations, would've turned one-hundred-and-six last April.

Suddenly, Kimberly dumping him for another man didn't seem so earth-shattering. At least his competition on that end was alive and under a century old.

Jonas. Daisy whispered the infamous Van Buren's name as though he were a saint. Marcus knew better. Jonas Van Buren had been a narcissistic, adulterous bastard. Work, women, and booze. That's all he'd cared about. He'd show up for the Sunday family dinner, spend a couple of hours with his wife and son and then be off again to who knew where. His son, Regis Van Buren, Marcus' father. Another self-obsessed bastard. Regis had followed his father's footsteps right into the grave.

Jonas. How in the hell could she mistake him for Jonas? *Pain buried deep, so like Jonas.* He doubted his amoral kin had ever suffered one ounce of remorse. As for himself...Marcus stuffed his shirttails into his navy trousers with an irregular amount of zeal...as for himself, he had regrets. Sure. What thirty-six-year-old didn't? But he'd learned from his mistakes and moved on. That's what being a mature, learned adult was about.

Jonas. She'd pulled him onto the bed, into her arms, thinking he was Jonas. Another man. Great. Another ding in his dented ego. So he'd kissed her. Any man with a shred of pride would've done the same. To prove a point. To make an impression.

He frowned, pacing the last quarter of the east corridor. He'd made an impression all right. When Daisy realized she was kissing him and not Jonas, she'd freaked. She'd wanted to leave. Well, he'd put a stop to that. Idiot. What had possessed him? She was ready to walk out on her own accord, leaving him to owe her nothing and free to contract a *reputable* parapsychologist and be done with this whole ghost business.

But no. He was *intrigued.*

Just like he couldn't leave *The New York Times* crossword puzzle unfinished, it would drive him crazy if Daisy left before his fascination with her faded. Obviously it was going to take more than a damned kiss.

That kiss. He'd nearly lost it just kissing her. He could only imagine making love to her. Despite the fact that she seemed to have personality issues, he wanted the chance to find out...so he'd bribed her. Bribed her to keep her from running fast and far away.

Jesus. Rufus' matchmaking plot had barreled toward him like a Mack truck. He'd seen it coming from a mile away, and still he'd stepped right in front of it. In the aftermath, he could call the bribe anything he wanted. Stupidity. Compassion. Curiosity. But the mangled wreck couldn't disguise the truth.

He wanted Daisy Malone.

Rufus snickered in the back of his mind.

Shut up.

Jonas. This was all his fault. Marcus pitied his grandfather should he ever come face-to-face with the womanizing bastard. He'd rip him a new...Marcus froze, hands jammed in his pockets, brow furrowed, heart pounding. He was thinking about Jonas as though he were alive, or at least an entity to be reckoned with. A ghost. Could it be? It would make Daisy psychic rather than psycho. A somewhat appealing prospect. What had her mother called her? A sensitive? *If a ghost is on the premises, she'll feel it.* Great. Just great. And what if, just what if Laguna Vista was haunted? What then? Marcus saw his dream sale disintegrate before his eyes, saw himself chained to Laguna Vista forever.

His head began to throb again.

Ghosts. There are no such things as ghosts, he assured himself. But what if Daisy did see a blip on her machine? Or picked up something with that supposed spirit radar? What if she changed her mind and refused to sign the document?

What was he thinking? Even if she signed it, it wouldn't matter. She hadn't the credentials to back up the signature.

Unbelievable. He'd risked a multi-million dollar deal to get Daisy Malone in the sack. Well, he was getting screwed all right, just not in the way he'd hoped.

Get a grip, Van Buren. You've got a backup plan.

Maintaining J.B.'s empire taught him early to cover all of his bases. Some called him ruthless. He preferred practical.

He rolled his shoulders back, feeling better now that he'd regained control of the situation. He trotted down the first few stairs, mind racing over the past two days' events, formulating how much to tell Thaddeus, and wondering for the umpteenth time what exactly he'd stepped into. Midway down the spiral staircase, the muck got deeper.

"*O Romeo, Romeo! Wherefore art thou Romeo?*" A young girl on bended knee raised her hands to him in appeal. "Actually," she said, springing to her feet. "It would work better if we switched places. Do you mind?"

Wearing red high-tops with the laces undone, baggy jeans, and an oversized Leonardo DiCaprio t-shirt, he guessed her about fourteen. Cute. Petite. The budding image of her mother, though her chestnut hair fell in waves to her waist. She easily resembled a modern-day Juliet. "Danielle, I presume?" He came down two steps to greet her.

"Mr. Van Buren?" she asked, bounding up three.

"Guilty as charged. How'd you get in?"

She fished a key from her pocket and dangled it before her freckled nose. "Daisy made it for me. In case of an emergency. So where is she?"

"Upstairs." He eyed the key, wondering how many emergencies Daisy expected.

Her face lit up. "Is Jonas up there?"

"What? No. Of course not." He cringed at his own gruffness.

"Bummer." She heaved a dramatic sigh, stuffing the key back into her pocket.

"Jonas Van Buren died over seventy years ago," he pointed out in a softer tone.

"Duuuh," Danielle said, rolling her big brown eyes. "Everyone knows that."

"So why would you think he was upstairs with Daisy?"

She shrugged. "I was hoping, that's all. I've never seen a ghost."

"There are no such things as ghosts."

"Not according to Daisy." She squeezed by him to race up the steps. "So, which room is she in? This place is huge. Did you ever see *The Shining*? *Redrum*," she drawled in a creepy voice, "*Redrum*."

Marcus shook his head, but smiled despite himself. "She's in the shower."

"Oh, more like *Psycho* then." She scrunched her face as she checked her watch. "At ten a.m.? Don't tell me she just woke up. Daisy never sleeps late."

"She was up all night, prowling the house for ghosts. She didn't find any, of course."

Danielle smiled as though he were amusing. "She will. Jonas is probably just playing hard to get."

"Hardly," he mumbled to himself, then stiffened. Again he was reacting like a jealous suitor. Jealous of his dead grandfather, for crying out loud! "What makes you so sure she'll find him?"

"Duh, because she's already found him once before. Didn't

she tell you?"

Everything inside Marcus stilled. "Uh, she mentioned something about it," he lied, not wanting to tip off that she might've betrayed her sister's confidence. "But we never got to finish the conversation."

"Well, I wasn't even born yet and Daisy was like ten when she and Mickey came out here one Halloween night. They were messing around outside the house, Daisy looked up, and there was Jonas staring out the window."

"Which window? How did she know it was him?" He could barely breathe as something squeezed his throat shut. This was just a ghost story the Malones had made up to scare their siblings. That's all. Nothing more.

"I don't know," she answered, her attention beginning to wander as she fiddled with the edge of her tee shirt, "but Daisy kept sneaking back here at night to see him again. At least until the cops brought her home for trespassing. Then the doody hit the fan. I wish I could've seen Pop's face!"

Marcus finished walking down the steps. It was worse than he'd thought. Not only did Daisy have the hots for his dead grandfather, but she'd been obsessed with him for nearly twenty years! How could he ever hope to compete with that? Even more shocking was the fact that he wanted to. What in God's name was going on in Daisy Malone's head? And, more importantly, what was going on in his?

He ran a hand over his face. He'd been at Laguna Vista for less than twenty-four hours and already his life had turned upside down. He should've scrapped this place a long time ago. To hell with profit.

Mental note—kill Rufus.

As he walked to the coffee table, thinking this was the perfect time to start smoking, he spotted the single red, unblinking eye. Daisy's video camera. She'd strategically placed a number of them throughout the house, though how one applied logic to something that didn't exist he'd never know. He hit the stop button. She may be doing her job, but while he was in the room, he preferred not to be taped. The Malones were loose cannons, and he didn't trust this little candid camera bit not to end up on television.

"*O Romeo, Romeo! Wherefore art thou Romeo?*"

Marcus turned to find Danielle one floor up, leaning over the wrought-iron banister, her arm extended as though reaching down to him.

His heart slammed against his chest.

"Yes," she exclaimed. "This is how it should be. Me up here. You down there." She leaned farther over, pointing to something behind him. "Would you grab my script out of my backpack and run the balcony scene with me, Mr. Van Buren? I have nightmares about forgetting my lines. And since Daisy's in the shower and opening night is tonight— "

"Come down from there, Danielle." His heart hammered and blood rushed through his ears, drowning out a distant voice. "*Did you see that, Marcus?*" A voice he knew but couldn't place. The harder he tried, the sicker he felt.

"It's not like you have to act the part. Just feed me my lines. I—"

"Come down here," he roared, hoping to stifle the phantom voice in his head as well as to startle Danielle. He had no children of his own, but by the way she screwed up her face and dragged her feet down the stairs, he imagined he'd pretty much sounded like an angry father.

She sulked past him, arms folded over DiCaprio's teen-idol face. "You're too old to play Romeo anyway."

Marcus wiped the sweat from his brow. He waited for his heart to settle back into place before turning to face the girl. She was sitting safely on the couch, backpack on her lap, braiding a front section of her long hair. "I'm sorry, Danielle." He sat down across from her. "I didn't mean to yell."

"Pop yells," she said, still focused on her braid. "You were just rude."

Feeling awkward, he leaned forward to rest his forearms on his knees. "I'm sorry. I didn't mean to be rude. But it's dangerous leaning over like that. You could fall." The distant voice in his head cried out, echoing as though down a long, deserted corridor. Another voice told him to quit listening.

Danielle snorted. "I wasn't going to fall."

"Things happen. Lean too far forward, lose your balance..."

Again she snorted. "Are you afraid of heights or something?"

He wished for an aspirin the size of Texas. "I'm not fond of them."

She flipped the half-finished braid over her shoulder and offered a forgiving grin. "I've got a thing about spiders."

He grinned back, charmed by her compassion and maturity. He'd never felt comfortable around kids. Yet something about this one...."Spiders, huh?"

"Hate 'em. Mickey dangled a rubber spider over my face once before waking me up. I screamed and swung at it, whacking Mickey in the nose instead. It bled like crazy." She giggled. "He never did *that* again."

Marcus laughed, too. They bonded that instant, he and freckle-faced Danielle Malone. It was a foreign and frightening feeling, though not as frightening as that recurring distant voice, now silent. "How old are you? Fourteen?"

She sat taller, thrusting her small but proud breasts forward in the process. "Fifteen."

He pointed to the baggy shirt that, until this moment, had concealed her developing shape. "And head over heels for Leo."

"Claire Danes played Juliet to his Romeo in a modern version of the story. It's on video. Have you seen it?"

"Afraid not."

"I would have given anything to be in her shoes. Anything." She looked down at DiCaprio's image and sighed. "He's to die for." She looked up and smirked. "And who do I get?"

Marcus shrugged.

"Jason Murdock."

"Who isn't, I take it, to die for?"

"Well, he's cute, I guess. But he sucks as an actor."

Marcus bit back a chuckle. "Is that so?"

"He keeps screwing up the balcony scene. I've saved his butt like a million times."

"A million, you say."

"Maybe more. But what if he throws me off tonight? What if I space?"

"That explains your nightmare." Marcus pointed to her backpack. "Want to dig out that script?"

Her eyes widened. "You mean it?"

"I know I'm a little old for the part—"

She blushed. "Sorry about that."

"Don't worry," he said with a grin. "Compared to Leo and Jason, I am old."

Twenty minutes later, Danielle glanced at her watch. "Holy moly, I've gotta run!" She nabbed the script from Marcus' hands and stuffed the book into her bag. Hauling the straps over her shoulders, she jumped up and headed for the front door. "Thanks for running my lines with me, Mr. Van Buren."

"My pleasure, Danielle." And he meant it. He couldn't remember the last time he'd read Shakespeare, or for that matter, the last time he'd read anything that wasn't a contract or a report. He stood and glanced at his watch as well. Saturday. Ten-thirty. Laptop lifeless. Morning paper untouched. Cell phone silent. Not an ordinary day in his life.

And where the hell was Rufus?

He followed Danielle into the hall.

She spun around, causing him to pull up short. "Uh, Mr. Van Buren?"

"Marcus. Call me Marcus. Mr. Van Buren makes me feel," he winked, "old."

She laughed. "Gotcha. So Marcus. You're coming tonight, right? To the theater? For opening night?"

He jammed his hands into his pockets. An evening out with the Malones? He suddenly felt the poor, pitiful orphan being included in The Osmond Family Christmas celebration. The feeling was awkward to say the least. "I don't think— "

She nabbed his forearms and squeezed. "Pleeeeease."

"Well, I—"

"Good!" She released him and tugged on the antique glass knob of the front door. "Curtain goes up at six-thirty. Daisy'll give you directions."

"Speaking of Daisy," Marcus said, holding the door open for her, "wasn't there some sort of emergency?"

"Nah," Danielle said as she walked out. "Just tell her I'll see her tonight."

Marcus shut the door and leaned against it. The pipes groaned as Daisy turned off the shower. He imagined her stepping out, soft skin slick, hands running through her dripping hair, steam curling about her curves. Then he recalled the message scrawled across his fogged mirror.

He stiffened.

What if Jonas and not Rufus...could Jonas watch her...

Marcus slammed his fist against the door. She was making him think crazy!

He'd had enough of Jonas Van Buren, real or imagined.

Pushing off the door, he glared up at the ceiling despite himself. "This is war, Grampa."

Eight

"*War! He has no idea who he's dealing with!*" James punctuated the air with an outraged finger.

Lined up in a row on the mantle of the grand fireplace like the see-no-evil, hear-no-evil, speak-no-evil monkeys, the Van Buren ghosts gaped at Marcus in shock. Though Jonas still disapproved of his siblings' matchmaking antics, he found it difficult to completely disassociate himself from the two. They'd been inseparable for too long.

"*War,*" Isadora shrieked, leaning so far over she nearly toppled off the marble ledge. "*Why that little snot-nosed...*" She looked to Jonas, who sat stone-faced in between her and James. "*Your grandson just declared war on you. What do you have to say to that, somber puss?*"

Jonas quirked a sad smile. "*I'm not surprised.*"

"*Come again?*" Isadora and James gaped at Jonas as though he'd praised the Prohibition Act of 1919.

He merely stymied them further by mumbling, "*Apparently, the apple didn't fall far from the tree.*"

Ignoring their perplexed expressions, Jonas crossed his arms and leaned back against the stuccoed wall. In life, he'd dotted all of his I's, crossed all of his T's. When it came to getting his way, he'd been merciless, leaving no stone unturned, no possibility unexplored. He'd been one hell of a corporate raider. A bastard at times, not caring how many dead bodies he had to climb over, caring only that he arose the victor. Just now he'd glimpsed a shadow of that same ruthlessness in his grandson. In life, he would've been damn proud, proclaiming Marcus a chip off the old block. Just now...just now he felt a little bit ashamed.

Daisy Malone was an innocent. Well-meaning and too good for her own good.

She didn't stand a chance against two ruthless bastards with only one thing on their minds. Especially when those things really had nothing to do with her at all.

He allowed himself a moment to wallow in the shallowest pool of remorse. Daisy Malone deserved better than to end up a casualty of his grandson's family feud. Another casualty of the Van Burens. *"Reminds me of someone else I once knew."*

Isadora snapped her fingers in front of Jonas' face. *"Helloooo. Anybody home? What are you babbling about?"*

"Daisy," he said, thinking aloud now. *"There's something about her."*

James wiggled his tawny brows. *"I'll say. Thinking back on the way she kissed Marcus, I'm beginning to see the appeal."*

Jonas frowned. *"Is that all you think about? Sex?"*

James shrugged. *"It's not all I think about. I think about the Yankees now and then."*

"Since when did you become so pure?" Isadora asked Jonas. *"You used to boff every skirt who wiggled her fanny in your direction."*

In life, he'd been proud of his countless conquests—

Jonas stopped. Why, after seventy years, did that suddenly sound pathetic? If he were honest with himself, he'd admit it was more like 'easy dame gets it on with rich sugar daddy.' Jonas frowned and looked away.

"What's this?" Isadora said. *"Don't tell me you've suddenly developed morals on top of everything else?"*

James looked as though his hero had suddenly fallen from grace. *"Say it ain't so."*

Jonas ignored him. *"I've been thinking."*

Isadora snorted. *"Well, there's your problem."*

"We didn't lead the best of lives."

"We led the very best of lives!" Isadora countered.

"And how!" James exclaimed.

Isadora flung her arms wide. *"Who had it better than we did?"*

James ticked off their perks on his fingers. "*We wore the best clothes, drank the best hooch, drove the best cars, scored the best broads—*"

"*Don't you have any regrets?*"

Isadora and James gaped at their older brother. "*Regrets?*"

Jonas shook his head. What the hell was happening to him?

"*Are you sick?*" Isadora asked, eyes narrowed. "*Can ghosts get sick?*"

Jonas looked at his sister, not really seeing her. What in God's name were these sentiments charging through his head and out his mouth? *Pathetic? Regrets?* He'd shocked himself as much as his siblings. He'd lived as fast and hard as they had, maybe harder. He'd never looked back. Never apologized. Never regretted.

Until now.

It was as though an emotional power line had snapped, thrashing wildly, sparking and zapping everything it touched. Jonas stared down at his hands and uttered a sudden revelation. "*I'm thinking I wish I'd spent more time with Sara and Regis.*"

James pushed his fedora onto the back of his head. "*Your son I can understand. But your wife? You said it plenty of times yourself, Jonas. Sara was a cold fish.*"

"*She was introverted, that's true. She had an aversion to wining and dining my business associates—*"

"*She had an aversion to socializing at all,*" Isadora butted in. "*She was stuck up.*"

Jonas glared at his sister. "*She was shy.*"

Isadora gave a dismissive wave. "*She was a stick in the mud. Why you married her, aside from her being a filthy rich heiress, I'll never understand.*"

Jonas reflected on Sara's wholesome face and quiet strength. She was a doting mother, practically raising their son on her own, and though she probably guessed that Jonas was less than faithful, she never wavered in her devotion to him. "*There was something about her.*"

James snapped his fingers. "*That's it! Daisy reminds you of Sara!*"

Isadora cocked her head. "*And Marcus reminds you of yourself.*"

Jonas started pacing. "*He's practically walking in my wing tips. Buries himself in piles of work, and when he finally comes up to breathe, it's with some dame he chooses from his stable. And Daisy. I don't think I've ever encountered a lonelier soul. This is by her own choice. More than ever, I'm convinced. They're absolutely wrong for each other.*"

Isadora spread her fingers, inspecting her manicure. "*How droll, Jonas. You're jealous.*"

"*For the last time, Izzy. It's not like that. There's something between us. A connection. I can't help thinking there's some bigger purpose in her being here.*"

"*As in helping you cross over,*" James said.

"*As in helping us cross over.*" Despite his earlier declaration, Jonas couldn't imagine leaving them behind.

Isadora folded her arms over her chest. "*Cross over. To what? Where? What did Father always say? If your friends jump off a cliff does that mean you have to? I'm not jumping over this cliff until I know what's at the bottom. You can just count me out of your little paranormal prison break, buster.*"

Jonas stopped pacing and looked his sister in the eye. "*I prefer crossing over to the alternative.*"

Isadora furrowed her precision-lined brows. "*What alternative?*"

"*I'm beginning to think all that hooch you drank addled your brain long before Jimmy drove the Pierce-Arrow into the bay.*"

James grunted. "*Leave me out of this, will you?*"

"*Marcus intends to sell Laguna Vista,*" Jonas continued. "*The buyer, if he has any business sense, will tear down this place and build one of those malls we've heard about, or one of those casinos. We're chained to Laguna Vista, Izzy. If Laguna Vista is no more, what does that mean for us?*"

Isadora twisted the diamond ring on her forefinger and regarded Jonas with a nervous smile. "*But in order to sell Laguna Vista, Marcus needs a document stating the property ghost-free. Isn't that what he said? So I'll step up my matchmaking efforts. Marcus and Daisy will fall madly in love, get married, move into Laguna Vista, and we'll all live—well exist—happily ever after."*

Both Jonas and James looked at her as though she'd just cheered for the Cardinals.

Isadora skimmed her fingers over her pearls while mulling over the situation. *"All right. Maybe I should switch my game plan altogether. Maybe we should spook blondie. Put on a show for all that wire-and-button nonsense she's got set up. Prove our existence. No document. No sale."*

James nodded. *"Works for me."*

A lonesome ache twisted in Jonas's gut. *"But I don't want to be here anymore."*

Isadora threw her lanky arms wide. *"At least we know what we're dealing with here. What if we succeed in crossing over, only to cross over into Hell? Or what if we fail? What if we can't break free of Laguna Vista? What if they tear down these walls? What if we're pulled to separate corners of the Earth? I don't want to haunt this world alone, Jonas. I'm scared!"*

Jonas caught his sister's hand and entwined his fingers with hers. *"You'll never be alone, angel,"* he said. *"No matter what happens, no matter where you end up, Jimmy and I will be right there with you. But we've got to start working together on this."*

Isadora sniffed. *"But..."*

Jonas shushed her. *"Together."*

Isadora remained silent, her frightened eyes staring through the room's giant window to the highway beyond.

James chewed his lip. Izzy hated to be afraid. She'd do anything to avoid it. Jonas was a fool to mistake her silence for acceptance.

The turbulent fault line widened between brother and sister, even if James was the only one who felt it. Longing for their past unification, he said, *"All for one and one for all."*

Just then the kitchen door swung open. Rufus strode into the living room, a bacon sandwich in one hand, a mug of coffee in the other. He plopped down on the leather couch and shivered. "It's freezing in here."

"I just started a fire." Marcus turned to face him, hands on hips. "Where have you been?"

Rufus propped his feet on the coffee table while biting into his breakfast sandwich. Mouth full, he said, "I told you I'd be out all night, *Dad*."

Marcus eyed his assistant's rumpled appearance, mentally arranging the order of his growing complaint list and wondering where to start. "You're wearing mismatched socks." Not even on his list. But the safest segue, considering Marcus' foul mood. Rufus may have been the master of seduction, but when it came to controlling his emotions, Marcus was the guru.

Rufus pointed to his left foot. "Barbie's. The only one she had without ruffles or bows."

"Where's *your* sock?"

"Good question. I've narrowed it down between the beach and the boardwalk Skyride. We had our clothes off twice before we stumbled into Barbie's hotel room. And it wasn't in her hotel room. Trust me. We looked."

Marcus stared at him. "You did it on a carnival ride?"

"Hasn't everyone?" Rufus took another bite of his sandwich then a sip of coffee. "So," he said wiggling his brows, "did Gidget make breakfast for you or the other way around?"

Marcus knocked Rufus' feet from the table before dropping into the chair across from him. "Her mother made breakfast."

Rufus' brows stilled then raised a half inch. "Her mother?"

"Don't ask."

He didn't. He merely shrugged and bit off another corner of his sandwich. "Something eating you?"

Rather than slugging his traitorous friend, Marcus leaned back in the chair and crossed his arms over his chest. "Why do you ask?"

Rufus cocked his head thoughtfully. "Oh, I don't know. The flame-thrower lodged in your throat. The steam blowing out of your ears." He took another sip of coffee. "Oh, wait, I forgot. You're always like that."

Marcus glared at him.

"Daggers shooting from your eyes." He set his mug on the table, no coaster. "Now I know something's wrong. What's up, Chief?"

"That's what I'd like to know."

Rufus furrowed his brows. "You're not mad because I got a little last night and you didn't?"

Rufus never knew when to quit. "It's more like what you didn't get."

His assistant mulled over the accusation while finishing off his sandwich. Brushing the toast crumbs from his hands and onto the floor, he confessed, "It could be the remnants of cognac and two bottles of champagne fogging my memory, but I don't recall any outstanding projects."

Marcus leaned forward, keeping a tight rein on his temper. "What about hiring me a reputable parapsychologist?"

"What are you talking about? I did that. Daisy Malone. She's your reputable parapsychologist."

"Is she?"

Rufus leaned forward, replicating Marcus' combative stance. "It's not like you to beat around the bush, Marc. Spit it out. I'm not a mind reader."

"According to Daisy's mother, Daisy's schooling consists of one semester of parapsychology at a community college *and* she flunked the technical exam."

"Oh."

"*Oh*? Did you examine her professional credentials at all, Rufus?" Marcus could no longer keep a lid on his anger. "Or was it like the chopper pilot? Since when is a pretty face the sole requirement for employment at VB Enterprises? Where are your principles? Where's your integrity?"

"Wait a minute—"

"Where's your loyalty? A multi-million dollar deal is at stake. I'm shocked. What's more, I'm disappointed." There. He'd said it. He'd chastised his assistant for royally screwing up. So why didn't he feel better? Why didn't Rufus seem contrite? On the contrary, he appeared every bit as angry as Marcus.

"Have I ever, in the two years we've been together, given

you reason to doubt my abilities? My loyalty?" He rose to his feet and tugged at the cuffs of his mis-buttoned shirt. "I thought we were beyond that, Marc. I thought we'd established a certain amount of trust. I thought we were friends." He looked offended, hurt, and ready to roll up his sleeves and duke it out. "I've obviously overstepped my bounds."

Marcus' own temper suddenly cooled. He stood as well, reminding himself Rufus' intentions had been good-hearted, if not misguided. Rufus, his many faults aside, was unequivocally the best friend he'd ever had. He was allowed an occasional screw up. Though he'd probably beg to differ, he wasn't perfect. "Damn, you're sensitive, Sinclair. Shake it off. I was pissed. I'm over it. Let's move on. Luckily for you, I've got a backup plan."

Instead of showing interest in Marcus' plan, Rufus dug in his heels and started to tick off his defense on his fingers. "(A) I conducted a thorough background search on Daisy. She may not be a technical whiz, but she has other applicable talents. In addition, she's owner of one of the most reputable ghost-investigation societies in the tri-state area. Her signature will carry a lot of weight with Zigfreid."

"How can you be so sure?"

"Because (B) Zigfreid's lawyers provided our lawyers with a list of six U.S. parapsychological teams, any of whose word would be acceptable to Zigfreid. I interviewed all six. The S.P.S. was number four on that list."

"Why is this the first I'm hearing about this list?"

"You told the lawyers to pass all information concerning this case on to me. You said you didn't want to be bothered with the details. You told me to take care of it. I did. So Daisy Malone didn't earn a formal degree in Parapsychology. Cliff Newsome and Randall Creed did. They're the founders of the S.P.S., and that'll be enough for Zigfreid."

"Again, how can you be so sure?"

"Because I have a signed document from Newsome and Creed testifying to Daisy Malone's talents and credibility should Zigfreid question it. Apparently they're quite fond of her."

Marcus ran his hand over his face. Jesus. When had this gotten so complicated? "Wouldn't it have been simpler to hire one of the other five teams?"

"You're the one who asked me to keep this low profile. Daisy isn't interested in a write-up in some journal. She isn't interested in being interviewed on a talk show. She's interested in the monetary payoff. End of story. Besides, it made sense. Laguna Vista is in Atlantic City. The S.P.S. is based in a small town not thirty minutes away." Rufus plunged his hands into his pockets and shrugged. "Then there were the extenuating circumstances."

Marcus snorted. "As in Daisy Malone is a dead ringer for my dream girl and you saw a chance to play Cupid for your jilted friend?"

Again, Rufus shrugged. "That was part of it. She's also—"

"Let me guess. She's also in a financial jam and you felt sorry for her."

Rufus slumped back on the couch and let out a weary sigh. He looked up at Marcus, sincerity in his eyes. "I know how much this sale means to you, Marc. If you want to dump this old place and score a few mil, then that's what I mean to see done. I know she's the new kid on the paranormal block. But considering there are no such things as ghosts and the fact that the S.P.S. was on Zigfreid's list, I figured it was a mere technicality. I covered all the bases, Marc."

"So I see." Marcus crossed to the fireplace, tossed in another log, then reclaimed his seat opposite Rufus. How could he condemn Rufus for hiring Daisy Malone when he himself, knowing full well she wasn't the real deal, had offered her a raise to stay not forty minutes ago? His ire instantly gave over to curiosity and concern. "Did you take into account the possibility she might not sign?"

Rufus shook his head. "Not a concern. She'll sign."

"So you've said. But it's become apparent to me that she truly believes in ghosts."

"Show me a ghostbuster who doesn't."

"What if she finds evidence—"

"She won't. Ghosts don't exist. You've said it yourself dozens of times."

"But—"

Rufus cut him off with raised palms. "No buts. She'll sign. No signature. No money."

Marcus nodded. "Ah. The financial dilemma."

"Exactly."

Marcus thought back on Angie Malone's visit. "This involves her family, doesn't it?"

Rufus crossed his arms over his chest. "I see you've been doing some investigating of your own."

"Not by choice."

"I'm sorry, Marc. I kept you in the dark because I thought it's where you wanted to be."

Marcus plowed his hands through his hair. "It was."

Impersonal. That's how he preferred his relationships. Intimacy on any level led to the possibility of broken promises, hearts, and lives. Some chances weren't worth taking. His friendship with Rufus Sinclair had been a miracle in itself. Unfortunately, Kimberly hadn't fared as well. He realized now that he'd deserted her long before she'd run out on him.

"Are we square on this?" Rufus asked, rising from the couch for the second time.

"Sure. Just do me a favor and stop trying to meddle in my love life."

Rufus quirked a worried grin. "Who said anything about love?"

Marcus waved him off. "It was only an expression. Speaking of *flings*, when did you leave Barbie's?"

Rufus glanced at his watch. "About a half hour ago. Why?"

"You didn't drop by here earlier this morning, say around eight-thirty?"

"Hell, no. I was sound asleep. Or, wait, we might have been going at it at that time. The way she woke me up..."

Marcus rolled his eyes. "Who's Louise Brooks?"

"Who?"

"You didn't send me an email using the name Louise Brooks?"

"No. Who's Louise Brooks?"

"I don't know. Find out. While you're at it, I want to know what a parapsychologist means by the term *sensitive*."

"I can tell you that," Rufus said. "Newsome and Creed used that word to describe Daisy. They said it's like being an antenna to the spirit world. She can tune into ghosts and emotions and things like that." Rufus looked over his shoulder as though worried they weren't alone anymore. "Is there a problem?"

Marcus shook off another chill and a dull throbbing at his temple. He could still smell that cigar even though he'd changed his shirt. "Did you borrow my blue oxford shirt?"

"Yeah right," Rufus said with a snort. "I don't even like that shirt."

Marcus groaned and pushed off the chair.

"What?"

"Just get that information on Louise Brooks," he said, plucking his cellular off the desk and heading for the kitchen

"Where are you going?"

"To set my backup plan in motion."

Nine

A panic attack.

Daisy recognized it for what it was. She'd had one before. Shortness of breath. Erratic heartbeat.

She sank down onto the edge of her bed and dropped her head between her knees.

Hyperventilating. She was definitely hyperventilating.

It all started when she'd found a positive reading on the EMF detector. She couldn't believe it. It had to be a mistake, she'd thought. She wasn't ready for it not to be. She went over the reading ten times, even checked the unreliable equipment for malfunction. When she'd found none, she considered alternative explanations. Logical explanations. Just when she'd convinced herself it was definitely a power surge, the music started.

Piano, bass, drums. Simple instrumentation that faded to a muted backdrop when a woman's sultry voice began to croon, "*I'm heart over head, head over heels, out of my mind, c-c-c-crazy for you...*"

It played over and over like a broken record, echoing throughout Laguna Vista as effectively as phantom laughter. By the fourth time through, Daisy had been ready to scream.

Rufus, she'd thought. It had to be Rufus. Marcus had gone into town hours before. Business, Rufus had told her when she'd finally ventured down for breakfast around noon. Which was fine with Daisy, since the less she saw of Van Buren the clearer she could think.

Of course, the husky-voiced songstress had other ideas. Unable to concentrate as the song started once again, she'd abandoned her research books and marched off to pull the plug on Rufus' musical love-fest. Funny, she'd guessed him more the Melissa Ethridge/Sheryl Crowe type. Jazz seemed more like Marcus' style...if he listened to music at all. She'd wondered if Marcus Van Buren could dance. She imagined herself in his arms swaying to a Duke Ellington classic, "Mood Indigo" or maybe "Sophisticated Lady." Then "*I'm heart over head, head over heart, out of my head, c-c-crazy for you*," chimed out for the umpteenth time, shattering her Ginger Rogers/Fred Astaire fantasy.

Cursing, she'd searched the second floor for the offending CD, tape, or record player and found zilch. She was on her way to the first floor when she'd bumped into Rufus on the circular stairs. "Doesn't that CD of yours have another track?"

"I was coming up you to ask you the same thing," he said. "Although I doubt it's a CD. Sounds too old and scratchy. Still, that broad has one hell of a sexy voice. Who is it?"

"How should I know?" Daisy brushed by him and surveyed the living room with a frown. "It's as loud down here as it is upstairs."

Rufus eyed the ceiling. "Maybe it's being pumped in by some sort of central-speaker system. This place used to be a disco, you know."

Daisy shot him a derisive look. "I know. It was also a bed and breakfast and three, no, four different restaurants. Before that it was actually a home." She snorted. "Imagine that."

Rufus ignored her sarcasm. "Let's just find the source. I'm dying to know who that singer is."

So they searched. And searched. For twenty minutes until at last the music abruptly ended mid-chorus. Rufus stuck to his central-speaker-system theory and something about a short in the wires. Obsessed with finding the source and even more obsessed with identifying the sexy singer, Rufus extended his hunt to what used to be the garage, leaving Daisy alone and with a very bad feeling.

Dragging herself back up the stairs and into her room, she'd assured herself that "C-C-Crazy For You" was a classic, covered by hundreds of different artists over the decades. She assured herself that, just because the song had been written in the 1920s, well, that was no cause for alarm.

Then she'd walked over to her bed to find her notebook, the one filled with vintage newspaper clippings, sitting wide open. On top, like the cherry on a sundae, an article featuring a round-eyed, cupie-lipped socialite cheek to cheek with a Valentino look-a-like. *Isadora Van Buren-Valentine-Mueller-Tadmucker, daughter of department store mogul Jonathan Bernard Van Buren, widow of taffy tycoon Roy Tadmucker, marries Hollywood producer in secret ceremony.*

The impetus of Daisy's panic attack had lurked the next line down.

She sucked in a long, calming breath. She should check it again. Maybe she'd misread.

Sitting up, she scanned the article a second time.

Isadora Van Buren, a touted lover of the arts and infamous ne'er-do-well, re-recorded the popular song 'C-C-Crazy For You' along with five original compositions and presented them to her fourth husband, Hollywood producer, Monty Carr, as a wedding present.

She hadn't misread. Oh, my God.

She also hadn't unpacked this particular notebook from her backpack. She'd been busy flipping through her textbooks on paranormal activity and old files given to her by Cliff and Randall. The backpack still rested in the corner by her sleeping bag, but the three-ring binder was here, on her bed, open to a page she'd never really looked at before. A skinny column from a gossip page that had nothing at all to do with Jonas.

Who'd been rooting through her bag? Marcus? Doubtful. He hadn't been around all day. Rufus? Impossible. He'd been with her for the last twenty minutes, scouring the mansion for a defunct disco's turntable. After that, she'd watched him stalk off for the garage.

So if not her...if not Marcus or Rufus...then...

Daisy dropped the notebook like a hot potato. She paced her room, wringing her clammy hands, chanting, "Oh, God, oh God, oh my God."

They were here.

And they were letting her know it. It hadn't been her

imagination all those years ago. She'd really seen Jonas in that window. In the tower.

The west tower.

Daisy flew out of her bedroom and plowed into Rufus, who yelped like a goosed schoolboy. Wide-eyed, he caught her shoulders and steadied her. "You scared the shit out of me, Malone! Where's the fire?"

Smoke. She'd smelled smoke in the west corridor. The same heady scent she'd smelled on Marcus' shirt this morning. Cigars. "Does Marcus smoke?"

Rufus frowned at the urgency in her voice. "No. Why?"

It was all she could do to breathe now. She felt like one of Sean's yo-yo's. Her emotions up, down, round and round. Giddy. Terrified. Thrilled. Morose. What if it was true? What if it wasn't? "But you do. I've seen you."

"So what?"

"And you probably borrow Marcus' clothes once in a while. You're roughly the same size."

He looked at her as though she'd lost her mind.

"You know, when you feel like wearing something different but can't afford to go shopping. Jill and I swap skirts and shoes all the time."

"I've been able to shop whenever I feel like it for a while now. What's more, I don't even like that shirt."

Daisy's breath stopped altogether. "Which shirt?"

"Marc's blue oxford."

Oh, my God. It was true.

Rufus narrowed his eyes. "First Marc accuses me of borrowing that stuffy oxford and now you. What's going on?"

Daisy stared at him, excitement churning in her stomach and threatening to bubble up and out. She was dying to share the news. But she couldn't share it with him. Not Rufus Sinclair. He'd been the one to officially hire her...and he'd hired her to disprove the existence of ghosts, not the other way around. If she wasn't careful, she could kiss the mortgage to her family's home and business good-bye. *Although*, Marcus had specifically told her to direct all of her complaints, concerns, and findings to his Number One Man.

And here he stood, waiting, clearly uncomfortable with the notion that she knew something he didn't. "What's the deal with Marc's shirt?"

After a moment's thought, she pushed him back against the wall. "Okay. But, you have to promise—swear to me— that you won't say a word to Marcus."

"I'm not comfortable with that."

She backed off, palms raised. "Fine. Forget it."

Curiosity flashed in his golden brown eyes. "Allow me a consideration."

"Being?"

"I won't offer the information. But if he corners me about that damn shirt again, if he asks me specifics and I know them...then that's that. I won't lie to Marc."

"Fair enough." She sucked in a bracing breath. "It was Jill."

He cocked his head. "Excuse me?"

She couldn't believe how easily the lie had slipped past her lips. Then again, it wasn't a lie in the mean-spirited, dishonest sense. It was a tiny, harmless fabrication. Besides, Rufus and Marcus were hell-bent on remaining oblivious to the truth. Who would blame her? All she wanted was a little more time, a chance to salvage her family's home. Jill would understand. Hell, Jill would gleefully play along. Not that Daisy would let it come to that. "Last night, somewhere around one a.m., Jill snuck back into the house. She must've lifted that shirt from his closet. I was making my rounds, checking the video cams, when I found her sitting on the leather couch downstairs, puffing away at one of *your* Cubans, wearing little more than *Van Buren's* shirt."

He paused, digested the information, formed a visual, then grinned.

Men.

He shook his head. "Why would she do that?"

"She has a crush on him."

The grin widened. "Kinky."

Daisy frowned. "My sister isn't kinky, she's just a little...wild."

"You don't say?"

"Impetuous." This had gone far enough. "The point is. No harm done. I slipped the shirt back into Van Buren's closet and warned Jill against pulling another stunt like that. Believe me, her stalking days are over." She waited for him to say something, waited for him to wipe that silly grin from his face. A disarmingly handsome face, she had to admit. One that probably turned nine out of ten articulate, sane women into babbling, moony-eyed airheads. Luckily, she was in the one/ tenth minority. "So what's it going to be, Sinclair? Is my secret safe with you or what?"

He slipped his hands into the pockets of his dress pants. "For future reference, Marc's fastidiously organized. This includes his bureaus and closets. Pants with pants. Shirt with shirts. You get the idea."

Daisy rolled her eyes. "Don't tell me he folds his underwear."

"No." His eyes sparked with amusement. "He lets his valet do that." He glanced at his watch then set off for his room. "See you later, Malone. I've got just enough time to shower and shave."

"You're going out?"

"I've got a hot date with a showgirl." Cockily, he added, "See you tomorrow."

If she wasn't so ecstatic about being left alone in the house, she would've blasted him for his moronic insinuation. As if a *showgirl* was a sure thing. Sinclair was either a chauvinist pig or overly conceited. "Probably both," she muttered, taking off in the opposite direction. Point was, he'd be out of her hair for the rest of the night.

Bursting with excitement, Daisy hurried around the corner to the far wall of the west corridor. To the same wall she'd run to this morning. She was certain now that Jonas had tried to contact her. She'd *felt* him. Then as he'd fled, she'd followed his emotional trail to this very wall.

She pressed her palms against the peeling wallpaper. Nothing. No sadness. No regret. No feelings at all.

She sniffed the air. No smoke. "Damn."

It occurred to her that she'd left her infrared thermal scanner and micro-cassette recorder back in her room. She also didn't have a journal to document her findings. "Forget it." If there was a significant drop in temperature, she'd feel it. If there was any sudden audio activity, she'd hear it. As for catching paranormal sights and sounds on failing equipment that had given her more trouble than a rowdy drunk at the pub...

Daisy stalked midway down the hall and punched the stop button on the camcorder stationed there. She walked two more steps and plucked the cassette from another audio recorder and stuffed it into the back pocket of her jeans.

The Van Buren ghosts were ready to come out of the closet, so to speak. The last thing Daisy wanted was to catch their antics on tape.

No evidence.

So long as there was no hard evidence of their existence, Marcus couldn't take issue with her. He couldn't boot her out only to employ an exorcist or something equally desperate. He couldn't deny her the payoff she so badly needed.

Daisy paced the hall, willing her mind to think as fast as her heartbeat. A plan. She needed a plan. A plan to appease Marcus and to collect that money while simultaneously helping Jonas. He needed her. She wasn't sure why or how she knew that, but she knew it. She'd always known it. Jonas Van Buren needed her help.

"What is it?" Daisy asked the air. "What do you want from me? What can I do?" Her questions floated unanswered with the dust. What had she expected, a booming disembodied voice? A transparent image of Jonas bogged down in chains, like the miserly accountant Jacob Marly in Dickens' *A Christmas Carol*?

"*Where are you?*" She sounded desperate even to her own ears.

It was then that she heard it. The agitated clicking of...heels? Daisy cocked her head and listened to the faint but repetitive sound. She retraced her steps, following the sound to its loudest point. The end of the west corridor. Again she placed her palms, then her cheek, to the wall.

Anger. Dissention. She held her breath as the turbulent emotions stormed through her. The clicking stopped, then just as suddenly resumed. *Clickety-clickety-click.* Faster. Louder. Spiked heels on cement or marble. Running, no, pacing. Isadora? They were above her. The west tower. If she could just speak to them...to Jonas. Daisy glanced left then right. No doors. No obvious panels.

She zipped around the corner into Marcus' room. Nothing. The library. Zilch.

Her room. Zero.

Where was the entrance to the west tower?

The clicking stopped.

She was still determined. Perplexed, but determined. She was standing in the hallway, staring at the walls, when Rufus strolled out of his room, looking spruced-up and ready for anything. Tall, dark, and graced with the good looks and charisma of a young Elvis. He flashed her a one-dimpled smile that wiped the west tower from her mind for at least a second. Begrudgingly, she realized that Rufus' conceit had merit. That poor showgirl, no matter how virtuous, didn't stand a chance against his bad-boy charm.

"Nice suit," was all she gave him. He needed to fit his head out the door so she could be left alone.

"Thanks." His smile faltered. "Say, did you hear all that clicking?"

"The wind," Daisy said. "Tapping branches against the windows."

"Branches. Wind. Right." He smiled as though relieved, then tugged up his sleeve to glance at his watch.

Daisy rolled her eyes. Chauvinist pig, conceited, *and* gullible. What a mix.

"Seven-thirty. Right on time. See ya, kid. Happy hunting."

"Yeah. You, too."

Waltzing off, he called over his shoulder, "If you find that recording, hang onto it for me. I can't get that chick's voice out of my head."

Daisy blinked after him. "Seven-thirty?" She heard him

bound down the stairs and out the front door. "Danielle's play! Crap!"

She bolted to her room, tugged a red wool sweater over her head then grabbed her backpack. Midway down the stairs, she froze in her tracks.

Clickety-clickety-click.

She looked up and groaned. "Ah, hell."

Torn between the present Malones and the past Van Burens, Daisy raced back up and down the stairs three times before blowing out the front door.

Her sister came first. Somehow, she knew Jonas would understand.

Ten

"*You're all wet, Jonas! It's better this way.*" Isadora paced the upper floor of the west tower, trying to blow off some steam. It was either that or sock her stubborn, opinionated, know-it-all brother in the snout. He'd always been bossy, but this preoccupation with crossing over had stretched her nerves to the breaking point. "*We make our presence known, and the sale won't go through. We scare them off. Then things will go back to normal. We'll be safe. Bored, but safe. No one wants a haunted house.*"

"*We agreed to work on this together,*" Jonas bellowed, fists on hips.

"*I didn't agree to anything. It was Jimmy who jumped ship and sided with you.*"

"*Now just a minute,*" James said from the sheet-covered sofa.

"*I asked you not to interfere,*" Jonas said, plowing right over him. "*To let me handle this. But no! You couldn't listen to me. You couldn't show a little restraint. Though why I'm surprised, I have no idea. Restraint was never one of your glowing attributes.*"

Bull's-eye. An arrow to her heart. Isadora marched up to him and narrowed her eyes. "*Don't mince words, Jonas. Spit it out. Say it. Say what you've been thinking for the last seventy years!*"

Jonas stared at her.

"*Cat got your tongue? All right, then. I'll say it for you. It's all my fault!*"

"*Izzy,*" James cautioned.

"*Shut up, Jimmy!*" Isadora never looked away from Jonas.

Like two sworn enemies squaring off in the street, the showdown had come at last, the blazing orange sun in the distance sinking lower by the minute. "*I talked you into going with Jimmy and me to the speakeasy. It was the night before the eve of my thirtieth birthday, and I was horribly, wretchedly depressed. I begged, cajoled, and sulked until you finally agreed to forego your silly dinner party with your wife for a night of debauchery with your sister.*"

"*Izzy. For God's sake,*" James said.

"*You didn't seem to mind so much, Jonas. Not after a few shots of tarantula juice and a lusty toss in the backroom with Sally Langhorne.*" She cocked a brow. "*You always were a sucker for a vamp with long gams and big tits.*"

"*Izzy,*" James pleaded. "*She's just scared, Jonas. She's—*"

"*Shut up!*" Jonas and Isadora ordered as one.

"*But then it was three a.m. The band was packing it in, and we were lit up like the store window. You suggested we call a cab. 'What for?' I asked. 'Jimmy's only half-screwed. Besides he could drive us home blind-folded.' Being the egotistical sap that he was, Jimmy agreed.*"

James rose to his feet. "*Now just a minute.*"

"*So off we went in your Pierce-Arrow, stinko and zipping along in the fog as if guided by friggin' Rudolph-the-Red-Nose Reindeer himself.*" Isadora was screaming now. Tears scalded her eyes. She hadn't cried in seventy years. She wasn't even aware ghosts *could* cry. "*The World Series. I don't remember how we got on the subject, only that I wanted to talk about anything other than my birthday, anything other than turning another year older. Thirty. God, it sounded so...final. So I picked a fight with you. I said the Dodgers would take the Yanks in '29. I so loved to tease you, Jonas. I knew it would gripe your cookies. And did it ever. Cheering for someone other than the Yankees? You were outraged. I laughed and egged you on.*

"*Jimmy was shouting at us to clam up, fending off a couple of playful slaps I sent his way, then...then...*" She swiped away her tears, refusing to let them fall. God, she was angry with Jonas. Or was it with herself? "*Then we were free floating over the bay, a pathetic ghostly trio.*" She waved a limp hand through the tension-filled air. "*The rest is history. So go on, Jonas. Go on and say it. Get it out of your system. You'll feel better for it. We're dead because of me. We're stuck here because of me. This is all my fault!*"

A pickaxe couldn't chip the ice in his eyes. When he spoke, his voice could've frozen the sun. "*I don't know what you're whining about, Izzy. You should be happy. You got what you wanted. You're twenty-nine...forever.*"

Isadora shivered from her brother's cold cruelty. She felt like a beaten dog left to freeze in the night. It was more painful than dying. She backed away from him as though he were the devil.

Jonas said nothing to stop her, nothing to soothe her.

"*Izzy?*" James ventured. "*Jonas?*" He threw off his fedora and jammed his hands through his hair. Desperate to mend frayed bridges, he said, "*Come on, guys. All for one and one for all. Our childhood oath, remember?*"

"*Sorry, Jimmy,*" Isadora whispered as she drifted down through the marble floor. "*I think we've finally grown up.*"

Eleven

Daisy maneuvered the S.P.S. van through oncoming traffic. Like a salmon, she struggled upstream through honking cars and steady curses.

"Can't you people read the sign!"

The van's high beams lit up the red-and-white Entrance Only sign like a Fourth of July finale. God forbid anybody had to wait in line for two seconds. No, they had to block the entrance and screw up her life. What was their rush anyway? *They* hadn't missed their sister's play. If any of them had taken the time to read tonight's TV schedule, they'd know that everything was a repeat!

Or maybe, just maybe, these students-turned-parents hated this place as much as she did.

She flexed her shoulders. *Calm.*

She swiped her sweating palms on her jeans. *Calm.*

Guilt clogged her throat as decent and considerate family members swerved to avoid her. Danielle's opening night had been a box-office success. And she'd missed it. The entire thing.

She'd driven like a bat out of hell and on a near-empty gas tank. She'd hoped to catch the final scene at least. Sneak in, get a synopsis from Jill during the standing ovation, then congratulate Danielle on a stunning performance. Bluff Danielle. That had been her plan.

Desperate, Daisy jerked the wheel left, drove up and over a curb, a grassy median, and then another curb. She screeched the van to a stop beside the Malone station wagon. One of five vehicles left in the school parking lot.

She jumped out and raced up the steps to the side entrance.

Maybe, just maybe—

The Malone family breezed through the double glass doors, laughing and fawning over Danielle as though she were Meryl Streep.

Oh no.

Sean saw her first. "Daisy!"

The laughing stopped.

Too late to run.

Mickey and Candie both arched inquisitive brows. Her mother pressed her lips together as though unsure what to do. Danielle's eyes glittered with hurt before she stalked toward Daisy, small breasts thrust forward, chin raised. "I was brilliant," she announced, whisking by. "If you care to know."

Daisy winced, then cringed as the car door slammed. She turned to find Danielle sitting in the backseat of the Malone station wagon, spine rigid, arms crossed, looking angry enough to take on the Fighting Badgers football team.

"I'm sorry." Daisy started toward the car, her heart in her throat. More than angry, she knew Danielle was hurt. It was the first time ever she'd let her sister down. "Danielle, I—"

"Let it be."

Daisy paused mid-step, prompted by her mother's voice and gentle touch. "I let her down, Mom."

Angie squeezed Daisy's slumped shoulder. "She'll get over it. Just give her a little time to sulk. Marcus explained how he pressured you to speed up the investigation. How you had to work late. It couldn't be helped. Danielle will understand...in a couple of hours or so."

Daisy shook her head. "Marcus *explained?*"

"He's still inside. Poor thing. Missy Polanski cornered him."

"Missy?" she croaked.

"Nice guy," Mickey said.

"With the patience of a saint," Candie added. "Missy's drooling all over him."

"Dear, why don't you go inside and rescue him?" Her mother ushered the rest of the gang to the wagon. "Poor thing," she repeated as she climbed into the car.

Stunned, Daisy watched as Mickey steered the wagon toward the dwindling mass. Poor thing? Marcus Van Buren? The man who commanded every situation like an overconfident pirate king with too much gold bullion? Then again, this *was* Missy Polanski.

Daisy felt ill.

She could only imagine the little treasures Missy was feeding the overconfident pirate king. Daisy vaulted up the steps two at a time.

The door slammed behind her and echoed off the lockers. The hallway dissolved, and the scene unfolded as it always did. A troupe of *Rocky Horror* transvestites prancing out of the classrooms, singing about the time warp, and dragging her back to that day long ago when she'd walked down this deserted hall with her mother for the last time, never to return...as a student anyway.

She'd never experienced a more lonely day in her life. The image of her father sitting in the car at the entrance of the school, waiting, haunted her still.

Every time she came here, she remembered with acute clarity why she was still alone.

She trembled, shame washing over her in fresh waves. She hated this place.

"I can't believe I'm having a conversation with America's Most Eligible Bachelor!"

Daisy's stomach turned. She knew that voice. High-pitched, whiny, dripping with superiority...and coming from the mouth of a vulture who thrived on picking carcasses clean.

She spied them huddled near the trophy case. Or rather Missy was huddled. Marcus looked trapped. Daisy couldn't even enjoy the moment as she moved toward them.

Missy's lips curled as she spotted Daisy. "Well, if it isn't Easy Malone."

Daisy balled her fists at her side. "Millicent."

Missy fluffed her over-processed blonde hair and looped her arm through Marcus'. Though Daisy stood two inches taller, the witch still somehow managed to look down her nose at Daisy. "I'd like you to meet a friend of mine," she boasted,

"Marcus Van Buren. Maybe you've heard of him? Wall Street tycoon? America's Most Eligible Bachelor?"

"Ms. Malone and I are acquainted," Marcus said.

"Reeeeally?" Missy drawled, circling in. "I'm surprised. I mean, knowing how conservative you are, Marcus. I can't imagine you associating with Easy here."

Daisy clenched her fists tighter. "Leave it be, Missy."

But Missy was hell-bent on revenge. Her eyes fairly glittered for the kill. The years had obviously not been kind to her. Bitter lines fanned around her mouth, as though she hadn't smiled in a decade. Come to think of it, Daisy could never remember Missy smiling so much as sneering. Some things never changed. "I'd be careful I if were you," she told Marcus, leaning in as though she had a juicy secret, which she did. "She's got a thing for rich boys. You wouldn't know it to look at her, but she's a schemer this one."

A small crowd of teenagers began to form behind them. Daisy's cheeks flamed. Her throat burned. She may as well have been seventeen again.

Say something, you idiot. Anything. Defend yourself.

Marcus untangled himself from Missy's snare as Daisy's face turned crimson. Five tension-filled seconds stretched to ten, then twenty. Was this the same woman who'd accused him of having elephant-sized balls? Silent and humiliated, she looked ready to crumble. Worse, she looked defenseless.

Ignoring Missy's insinuations, he moved next to Daisy and placed a comforting hand at the small of her back. "I'm sure I don't know what you mean, Ms. Polanski. I know Daisy to be a genuinely warm person. I'm quite fond of her."

A strangled choke sounded from Daisy's throat.

"A wolf in sheep's clothing," Missy insisted. "But she got hers, didn't you, Daisy? Could've been Valedictorian, if not for—"

"Hey, Missy! Is that your husband cruising the parking lot every day after school?" Jill shoved into the small crowd, planted a hand on her haughty hip, and tossed her glorious red hair over her shoulder. "I mean, how many times do I have to refuse to get in the car with him? Buy a leash, woman."

The surrounding crowd snorted and heckled. Missy's face burned with the fires of hell as her mouth opened and shut. Shooting a murderous glare at Daisy, she spun on her heel and stormed off.

Jill glowered at the crowd. "Show's over."

The teenagers dispersed, still snickering.

"Does he really ask you to get into his car?" Marcus asked, horrified.

"Yeah, but right now I'm glad," she said with a cheeky smile. Then she clasped Daisy's arm. "Just ignore her, Daze. She's a bitch, and everyone knows it."

Daisy managed a shaky smile. "Thanks, Jill. Don't worry about me. I'm fine. Go on with your friends."

Jill looked unsure.

"I'll see her home," Marcus said.

Jill eyed him up for a second then nodded. "All right, but no funny stuff." She kissed her sister's cheek then left them alone.

"Old high school rival," Daisy muttered, tugging at the bottom of her wool sweater. "Sorry."

Marcus marveled at the quivering lamb before him. He'd never seen anyone cut down so quickly as Daisy Malone. *Easy Malone.* The empathy continued to flood through him, making him wish for the prick of a catty barb. His palm still pressed against her back, he felt her pain as though it were his own. Disconcerted, he raised his hand and tucked several stray hairs behind her ear. "What do you say we get out of here?"

Twelve

Daisy glared at her shot glass as though accepting some silent challenge. She raised her brows and glass to Marcus in a cynical toast, licked the salt off her hand then tossed back the tequila, exposing her long throat in temptation. He shifted in his seat when she slammed the empty glass to the table and sucked the wedge of lime as though it were the most succulent fruit of the earth.

He didn't know how many more times he could watch her wage battle with her demons before he yanked her out of her chair and kissed that luscious mouth until she tasted nothing but him.

He already knew she was a little off. How could anyone in her profession not be? But he'd never pegged her as cruel. Was she purposely torturing him with her decadent little drinking game? Was she enjoying watching him squirm in the hot seat?

He shrugged out of his suit jacket and turned his attention to the bar, unable to watch her with a sane mind. There was no way for him to know what she was thinking. The only words she'd spoken since they'd left her out-of-gas van in the school parking lot had been to give his chauffeur directions to this cramped, rotting dive along some forgotten highway. This wasn't exactly what he'd had in mind when he'd suggested an out-of-the-way place for a drink.

Whoever Mack was, he should be ashamed to have his name on the sign. The place was a wreck. Splintering wood walls. Mismatched linoleum floor. Stuttering neon beer signs and a flickering TV chained to the wall. A jukebox in the corner, struggling to play its songs through one tinny speaker.

"Listen, if you're embarrassed to be seen with me..."

Marcus brought his head around. Here it comes...salvation...the old Daisy...

But her words drifted off to mingle with the clots of dust dangling from the ceiling fan. She'd been poised and ready to nail him to the wall. Instead her voice cracked like the fragile shell of an egg. "You think I don't see you constantly looking over your shoulder? Waiting to see who comes in to find you here. With me."

Daisy's razor-sharp barbs usually pricked and scraped his temper. But as the fragments of her broken pride fell from her lips, she cut him to the bone.

She stared down into her empty glass.

Was this the same wise-ass Malone with the belly jewel and the bad attitude? The same quick-witted, smart-mouthed girl who'd maligned him, kissed him, and somehow finagled several grand out of him all in the space of two very short days?

The tarnished coin had been flipped. And he wasn't sure what to make of the other side. The side that caused Jill to fight through a crowd and send Missy off with her tail between her legs. The side that caused her mother to show up at a stranger's house and debate his intentions about her daughter. The side that caused Rufus to refer to her as the sweet and naïve Gidget.

The side that caused Marcus to experience a cold rush of fear as her vulnerability tugged at something within him.

She raised her head. Her troubled eyes pierced his soul and waited for him to run for his life. They also demanded an answer before he left.

He'd been thoughtless. She'd just been publicly humiliated, and here he sat twisting the knife, checking over his shoulder every time the front door creaked open. "I'm not embarrassed to be seen with you, Daisy," he said. "I swear. But there's this reporter..."

"And?"

"Never mind."

Daisy traced her finger around the rim of her glass. "And

you're afraid he might be lurking in the shadows, camera poised, waiting to catch you in a compromising moment?"

Fixated on the butterfly ring on her third finger, Marcus smirked. "Something like that."

"Kind of like the front page of the latest *Tattletale*?"

His smirk died. "Kind of. "

"Sorry about the crack I made about your ex yesterday. I didn't mean to make light of your breakup."

He glanced up. "Then why did you?"

"I'm not sure. It's just that guys like you—"

"Guys like me?"

It was her turn to say, "Never mind." She signaled the waitress. "Shirl. Another round for me and my guest." She eyed Marcus' Bloody Mary. "Something a little stronger for you, maybe?"

"What's wrong with what I'm drinking?"

Daisy rolled her eyes at Shirl, who'd sidled over, smacking her gum and sharing a gap-toothed smile. "Sugar," she drawled, leaning her flabby elbow on the table and giving him the once-over, "I ain't never seen no one who looks as good as you, dresses as good as you, and drinks a pansy-ass drink like you and ain't light in the loafers."

Marcus eyed the wilted celery stick poking from his glass then the roughnecks whooping and hollering around the smoky bar. "Martini. Straight up."

Shirl crossed her arms. "Nice shot of you with the bimbo twins, but not everyone believes what they read."

His temper heated to a slow burn. "Jack Daniels then."

"Good choice." Shirl patted his hand then turned to Daisy. "You know it's gonna get back to your pop that you were here, Daisy-girl. You know Mack's his biggest competitor. Them two fought like mongrels over a t-bone last year trying to attract the Super Bowl crowd."

Daisy fiddled with her empty glass. "I know what I'm doing."

Shirl shrugged as though she'd heard it all and ambled away.

Mack's was Malone's biggest competitor? Marcus forgot

his own troubles as he noted the faded and curling flyers stapled to the wall. The ones advertising year-old band appearances and a rusty El Camino for sale—Cheap! No wonder the Malones were in financial straits. How could a rundown roadside bar support a family of seven?

Shirl set the drinks on the table and left without a word.

As Daisy settled back into her sulk, Marcus almost wished the obnoxious waitress had stuck around. He hated making small talk, and Daisy's brooding silence seemed to demand it. When they'd first arrived, he'd expected her to cry in her beer, to work her way to his shoulder as she bemoaned her problems in the deserted corner of the bar. He'd dreaded every minute of it. Hindsight told him that would've been much easier. Drink, cry, be done with it.

He should have known better. One thing for sure about Daisy Malone, she was unpredictable.

Instead of seeking solace, she'd kept to herself. With the exception of her tag-team challenge over his drink preference and the mock toast before each shot, she barely seemed to notice him. The only signs of her inner struggle until now were the shredded cocktail napkins and mangled stirrers littering the scarred table between them.

She was driving him crazy. So many unanswered questions hung in the smoke-fogged air. So much had happened. Missing the play. Her baffling confrontation with Missy Polanski. The fact that she sat drinking in this anti-Malone establishment. And mostly, how the hell was he supposed to feel when she kissed him into a meltdown and then woke up horrified to find that he wasn't his dead grandfather!

After three shots of tequila, most people's tongues would have loosened. But not Daisy's. She'd shut up tighter than a clam.

She saluted him with her glass again. He groaned. At this rate, she'd drink him right under the table.

This time she performed her seductive cantina routine even slower...or was his mind slowing? Her tongue seemed to drag forever over her skin, and he thought for sure he was going to die. As she sucked on the lime, he tossed back his own shot, welcoming the distracting burn down his gullet. She dropped the lime and licked her lips.

Sweat popped out on his forehead.

He was damn close to making love to her right here, right now, on top of the sticky, wobbly-legged table between them. Jesus. He had to do something. Anything to keep his attention from the fire raging in his pants...

So it had come to this. Small talk. Jesus. "So how did you get into the ghosthunting business?"

The corner of her mouth kicked up like a sheet in the breeze. "Officially or unofficially?"

As he watched the whimsical smile flirt with her lips, he suddenly wanted to know everything about her. What memories lit her eyes as she thought about his question? Who had taught her about ghosts? Why did she believe in them? Warning sirens blared in his head. *No, no, no*— "Both," he heard himself say.

"It's a long story."

He signaled Shirl for another round, glad when he looked over his shoulder not to spy a certain short reporter with beatnik hair lurking behind the cigarette machine, or somewhere equally as clichéd. Marcus was convinced the cheesy, turtleneck-wearing Joe Rush had been transplanted from an old *Scooby-Do* cartoon. A bizarre incantation by rag reporters to summon their Rag King...right along with Daisy's hipster ghosthunting van, The Mystery Machine.

Deciding his quasi-privacy was safe, at least for now, he relaxed in his chair. "I've got all night."

Her smile faded, as though she hadn't really expected to relay her ghost story at all. "A long, *boring* story."

"If it involves you, Malone, it can't possibly be boring."

"Hmm." She shifted around in her seat. "Let's just say my interest in ghosts goes way back."

She paused, crossed and uncrossed her legs, then drummed her fingers on the table. Obviously weighing how much or how little to tell him. *Or* waiting for him to redirect the conversation. He let her wait. She shifted around again. "It wasn't until about six months ago that my interest moved from unofficial to official. I was schlepping beers at the Pub, doing my waitress thing..."

Again she paused, her eyes on him sharp as a hawk. Waiting for him to make some sort of cutting remark, perhaps? He didn't bite. Nor did he miss her careful omission that, as a kid, she believed she'd sighted Jonas. His mother's bitter words echoed in his head. *"Don't shit where you eat, Marcus. Don't be a Van Buren."*

Daisy cleared her throat. "...doing my waitress thing when I overheard one of Pop's regulars complaining how his wife had signed up for the new 'parrot psychology' course at the community college." She rolled her eyes and smiled. "I remember him shaking his head between long sips of his Budweiser, wondering when the town council would vote on giving the Lucky Charms leprechaun his own holiday."

Marcus laughed.

"I ignored his drunk ramblings until he dove into this long-winded tirade about how his wife was trying to contact her dead grandmother from Hungary—oh, and of course, Elvis. I stopped pushing my towel across the bar on that one. He'd meant *parapsychology*. The study of those things beyond the accepted laws of the universe. Werewolves, vampires, zombies...ghosts. I had no idea the college offered such a course. I took it as a sign. I'd been wanting to pursue other interests, to broaden my horizons. But ghosthunting as a reputable career choice?

"I enrolled in the class the very next day. After one semester and two field trips, Cliff and Randall, teachers and partners in the agency known as The Society of Parapsychological Sleuths, declared me their number one student." Embarrassed, she shrugged and grinned. "Seems I'm gifted."

He waited for her to explain that by gifted she meant "sensitive." Waited for her to tell him that she'd flunked the technical exam. That she didn't know a paranormal gadget from a spiritual-reading gizmo, as her mother had pointed out. Not that he hadn't witnessed that on his own. The woman was constantly jiggling cords and whacking monitors trying to get them to work properly. A practice he'd graciously not remarked upon.

She confessed nothing. "Not that I have anything against being a waitress. I mean, I love Malone's Pub. But I thought I'd finally tripped upon my true calling, and when Cliff and Randall announced they were moving to California on a fully-funded grant, I didn't think twice. I offered to buy them out lock, stock, and barrel."

Marcus cocked his head. "Right down to that rusted old van. Must have cost you a pretty penny." He knew it had cost her life savings. Rufus had managed to slip that one in before Marcus had cut him off.

She curled her fingers around her fourth shot of tequila. "It was worth it. It's just that my timing...Well, I've never been one for good timing."

There it was again. The kicked puppy look. The same one she'd worn not an hour before at the school, after that Polanski woman had attacked her. What had Missy said? *She's got a thing for rich boys.* What the hell did that mean? And why hadn't Daisy impaled the frizzy-haired bimbo with the same sharp tongue she used on him? Instead, Jill had been the one to skewer her like a shish kebob.

It should've been Daisy. All he could think was it should've been Daisy to snatch back her pride from Missy's bloodied hands, then maybe she wouldn't be sitting here trying to reconcile her place in a world gone mad. But obviously this particular game didn't follow the normal rules and regulations.

She closed her eyes, licked her hand then tossed back the shot. As she lost herself in the ritual of the lime, he felt his muscles tense, his skin heat. He wanted to know what this vulnerable vixen had done with the real Daisy Malone. Where's your evil twin, he wanted to demand, or are you the wolf in sheep's clothing? She slammed down the glass, opened her eyes, and smiled. A small but genuine smile. A slightly drunk smile. "No use crying over spilled tequila, right, Marc?" Her eyes sparkled like the Austrian crystals of Laguna Vista's chandeliers. She looked sexy as hell. His blood burned. His temples throbbed.

Daisy Malone screamed of scandal.

And he wanted her. Bad.

"Unless you want to put on a show for everyone in this bar," he said in a raw voice, "I suggest we take out our frustrations on that dartboard over there. Agreed?"

Her lips parted in surprise. She obviously had no clue what she was doing to him.

Could she possibly be that innocent? That naïve? That ... *Gidget?*

"Agreed?" he demanded through clenched teeth.

She nodded but seemed hesitant. He stood and turned, expecting her to follow of her own accord. She did, but not without teetering a bit and not before shouting to Shirl behind the bar, "Another round!"

He walked over to the dartboard. No darts. He looked around to find Daisy smirking at him, hands on hips. "You have to pay for them at the bar. This isn't exactly your private uptown men's club."

Ah, the Daisy he knew and...well, the one he knew. Compliments of four tequila shots? Thank God. "I see that. And for your information," he said as he walked over to the bar, "I don't belong to a private club."

"Have you ever played darts?"

"No, but how hard can it be? Throw the dart at the board."

She waltzed over and tapped a dingy strip of masking tape on the floor with her toe. "You have to throw from here."

He mentally measured the distance. "That's not so far. Piece of cake."

Shirl set their drinks on the window ledge to the side of the dartboard. Daisy lifted her glass. "Care to make a friendly wager?"

Marcus prided himself on his athletic ability. The way Daisy was drinking, she'd barely be able to throw the dart in a straight line. It almost didn't seem fair to take her money, but when he thought about how much he was paying her to walk around his house in circles..."You're on. How much?"

"Winner gets to sleep on that dream of a mattress they delivered for you today. Loser sleeps on the couch downstairs."

Salt. Drink. Lime.

He broke out in a sweat, preferring both the loser and the winner to sleep in that dream of a bed. He simply nodded. Her mood seemed to be lifting. Finally. Maybe he could find out what Missy Polanski held over Daisy like a brick about to be smashed into her skull.

He sighed. For a man who didn't want to know anything about her, he was sure doing his damnedest to find out *everything*.

He handed Daisy the red darts as he set down the blue next to his brimming glass. Loosening his tie, he wondered if it was wise to have another drink. He may not have to drive, but he did need every ounce of control to keep his hands off her. The last thing he needed was to wake up in a relationship tomorrow morning, especially with his sometimes-proud-sometimes-vulnerable little ghostbuster. She wasn't 'big-O-faking' material. She'd get attached, cling to him, not understand that when the week was up so was their fling. As much as he wanted her—and God did he want her—he couldn't do that.

She set down the lime and licked her lips.

The Jack Daniels burned all the way to his toes.

"Damn, it's hot in here." She fanned her flushed face. It was about time the liquor started to affect her. *He* didn't seem to be, and as his own buzz started to kick in, he didn't want her to have every edge over him.

Without warning, she lifted her sweater. For a second her head was lost in the material, giving him a chance to stare at the tight tank top that left nothing to the imagination. What was she doing to him? As the sweater cleared her head, it pulled that infernal ponytail band with it.

His breath caught as her hair spilled out of its confines and floated free around her face and over her shoulders. The glow from the TV behind her lit her like an angel, the static lifting blond strands as though blowing with the clouds.

He was a dead man.

A wolf whistle sounded from the bar behind him.

Don't get uptight. They do that kind of thing here. Besides it was plain that she was with him. No cause to get riled.

He gave her his cockiest smile. "Are you ready to play?"

She smoldered at him through thick, soot-colored lashes. "I'm always ready."

Definitely drunk, he thought, as he bowed and waved her to the line. "Ladies first."

She stepped up to the masking tape and smirked. "You asked for it, Van Buren. Get ready for the ass-whipping of your life." With that, she sent the dart whizzing straight into the bull's-eye.

He closed his eyes. Sucker bet. Idiot. She had grown up in a pub. Of course she'd be an expert. She probably had her own set of darts in her glove compartment, ready to lure unsuspecting suckers into a challenge at any given moment.

Maybe she wasn't drunk.

All right. Shake it off, man. Shake it off. It can't be that hard. He stepped up to the masking tape. It was so close. He felt as though he could lean over and tap the board.

She strutted up to him and planted a hard one right on his lips. "For good luck." She winked and sat down on the window ledge.

She's just trying to rattle you. Concentrate on the board. He tossed the dart. It bounced off the wall and clattered across the floor. He turned on her. "You did that on purpose."

"Don't be a sore sport, Marc. It's not becoming." She accepted the new round of shots from Shirl. "How 'bout if I give you a do-over?"

"Don't bother," he muttered. He stalked over and picked up his glass. "This is the last drink, Daisy. I think we've both had enough."

Fear and pain flashed in her eyes. It was gone in an instant, but he'd read it as easily as a billboard. Her excessive drinking, this outrageous act. She was numbing her emotions, distracting her thoughts. Daisy was the kind of girl who wore her heart on her sleeve. Unlike him, she couldn't harden herself against vulnerability and despair with sheer will. She felt too deeply. Loved too deeply. It was all too much for her right now—

How did he know that?

Shaking his head, he let it go, leaving his preaching and interrogation for another time, another place, if at all.

When he dropped the subject and picked up his dart, gratitude showed in her eyes. Sometimes it was better to leave things alone. Maybe it was a blessing in disguise. He was weak tonight. Tomorrow he'd appreciate the wall of unknown still solid between them.

As his dart landed in the thick black border outside the scoring area, he turned to find her licking her arm and pouring salt on it.

This was just too goddamned much.

He was only a man. A Van Buren man at that.

He stalked over and nabbed her wrist. Staring into her eyes, he ran his tongue over her salt-encrusted skin. With his other hand, he threw back her tequila. It scalded his throat, but he ignored it as he kissed her palm, lifted the fingers clutching the lime to his mouth and sucked.

Her eyes burned a deeper shade of blue. Her arm went limp. Satisfied that he'd finally gotten to her, he let her hand drop to her lap. "Your turn."

She stared at him, looking confused.

"Darts. We're playing darts, remember?" He felt like strutting.

She looked down at the dart he handed her as though it was some foreign object. "Oh," was all she said. She shuffled on wobbly legs over to the masking tape. This time it was her dart that clattered across the floor. She turned and glared at him.

"All's fair in love and darts, sweetheart." He kissed her hand as he passed, and this time he nearly hit the center circle.

His victory was short-lived. The hard glint of challenge was back in her eyes. He should be happy to see more of the old Daisy, but somehow he'd liked having her dazed by his kiss.

Not good.

Bull's-eye.

She jumped up, arms raised, and stuck her tongue out at him. "I'm the master! Who wants to take me on?"

Marcus lowered her arms, but she kept jumping all the same. Her perfect breasts bounced in invitation to every randy hothead in the bar. "Cut it out," he said, telling himself this was a matter of safety and not jealousy.

But it was too late. Two men, both dressed in jeans and flannel and unshaven chins, strolled over to accept Daisy's over-ambitious invitation. Marcus blocked her flushed body from their view. "She was just teasing, gentlemen. We're about to leave."

One flicked his unfiltered cigarette to the floor, just missing Marcus' brand new Italian loafers. The other simply grinned as though it was all he knew how to do. The rude one spoke. "Mack's got rules. Winner plays whoever's got his money up next." He poked his sizable chest with his equally sizable thumb. "That would me."

Daisy pushed past Marcus. "Out of the way, Van Buren. I need a bigger challenge than you."

Stewing and not having a valid excuse to punch the man's lights out—not yet anyway—he hunkered down on the window ledge and watched them like a prison guard. Shirl delivered another round. Just what this volatile situation needed. More alcohol.

Before he could stop her, Daisy licked her arm, downed the tequila, then sucked the lime. With those two big goons looking on, her routine suddenly seemed obscene. He gripped the window ledge to keep from dragging her out of the bar.

His sudden possessiveness scared him. He'd never felt protective of anyone in his life. It was insane. He barely even knew her, yet...yet he felt like a junkyard dog guarding his property, ready to snarl and shred anyone who dared to trespass.

It must be the liquor, he decided. How many times had he seen strangers get drunk at parties and become best friends or even lovers before the morning light? And in that harsh morning light, nine out of ten of those people groaned, threw up, then asked God what they'd done. He and Daisy were in danger of crossing that line. Complicating matters, her infatuation with Jonas rankled him beyond reason. He could imagine his letter to *Dear Abby*. "Dear Abby, I'm attracted to a woman but she's in love with my dead grandfather. What to do? Signed, Glutton for Punishment."

Mr. Personality eased in behind Daisy as she prepared to throw. "The name's Don. Let me show you my special technique, baby." He splayed his hand across her stomach and pulled her back to his chest. The other burly hand curled over her fingers on the dart.

Daisy's smile faltered as she tried to shrug him off. "I'm doing fine on my own, thank you."

Don ground his hips against her backside. "It's always sweeter to play together, honey."

Marcus stood. "Let her go. I won't ask you twice."

Daisy continued to struggle, but Don held her tight. "Mind your own business, fancy pants. You might break a nail."

"I warned you. *Don.*"

Marcus whipped the man around and socked him square in the jaw. Don went crashing back into a pair of empty stools. Grabbing onto the bar, Don shook his head, then lowered it to charge Marcus like a bull.

Marcus sidestepped him at the last second. Unable to stop, the arrogant son of a bitch rammed his head straight into the wall. He crumpled to the floor.

Marcus turned to Don's buddy, whose silly smile had disappeared. "You want to take me on, too?"

Thirteen

RAGING REBOUND!
MAD MARCUS IN BARROOM BRAWL OVER NEW
GAL PAL!

Daisy could see the headlines now. Well, maybe through a blurry haze she could read the newsprint. Willing herself sober, she squinted and scanned the bar for that meddlesome reporter Marcus had mentioned. If this wasn't front-page material....

What was Marcus thinking? Taking a good look at him, she realized he wasn't thinking. Not rationally, anyway. She'd never been to the wilderness, but his cold, deadly eyes reminded her of an animal too long without food.

She had to get him out of here. That reporter might not be around, but Mack had debts and couldn't be trusted not to have a handy Polaroid stashed behind the bar.

Daisy slid next to Marcus and rested her hand on his arm. His corded muscles tightened and flexed as he clenched and unclenched his fist. She swallowed at her mind's image of peeling off his stuffy shirt. Now was not the time. No time was the time.

"You won, Marcus," she said. "Let's go."

He slowly straightened and relaxed his hands. Without a word, he stalked to their table to retrieve his jacket. He glared at her with those animal eyes as he tossed some bills onto the bar then thrust her sweater, very un-Marcus-like, at her.

She swayed as she tried to push her arms through the sleeves. Muttering an oath, he helped her with her pullover then prodded her out the door. He grabbed her elbow and steadied her as she tripped over an empty beer can in the parking lot.

"I guess I drank a little too much," she said with a sheepish smile. So much for willing herself sober.

"You don't say?"

He was mad. Really mad.

He tried to help her into the limo, but she stumbled and fell in anyway. As she lay sprawled facedown across the carpeted floor, she realized Marcus had been right. She shouldn't have had that last drink. It had been the straw that broke the dam, or whatever.

Scrambling into the seat across from him, she pondered his scowl. When they'd first arrived at the bar, she'd been so caught up in her own private hell that she'd barely noticed him. But after a couple of shots, she'd become aware of how he'd stared at her, all hot-eyed and intense when she'd do the salt and the lime. After that, she couldn't help herself. She'd liked the way he'd looked at her. So she kept ordering round after round to see it again and again.

Somehow, in the midst of it all, he'd charmed her into talking about herself. About Cliff and Randall. Had she said too much? Was he wishing he'd hired a more experienced ghosthunter? Did he even care?

As he sat across from her in the dimly lit parking lot, he'd never looked more handsome. His perfect hair ruffled. His starched shirt loose and unbuttoned at the throat. His eyes gleaming in the darkness like the animal now fresh from the kill but hungry for more.

Hungry for her.

He moved in for the attack. "You played a dangerous game back there, Daisy. It could have ended a lot worse."

She refused to point out that she felt a lot worse now alone with him in the dark limo than at any time in the bar. Instead she said, "Who'd have guessed you weren't the Wall Street wimp after all? Where'd you learn to fight like that?"

"Prison."

Oh, his mood was foul.

The driver, O'Brien, called over his shoulder. "Where to, Mr. Van Buren?"

"Home," Marcus barked. "I mean, Laguna Vista."

Daisy frowned. "I have a better idea." She leaned forward and tapped the chauffeur's shoulder. "Take a left out of the parking lot and head for the White Horse Pike."

"What are you up to now, Malone? I'm not in the mood for any more games."

Her temper flared. "If you think this morning was a ploy to squeeze you for more money, you're wrong."

"If I'd believed that, I would have shown you the door myself."

"Then what are you talking about?"

"Confusing me with Jonas. Pretending I'm my dead grandfather. I don't understand this obsession you have with him, but I wish you'd stop calling me by his name. Especially after I kiss you."

So that's what was bothering him. Jonas.

Too bad she couldn't tell him what she'd discovered that afternoon. It might be fun to watch him shoot through the moon roof. However, the liquor insisted on talking, because she couldn't believe her own ears when she said, "I liked when you licked the salt off my arm."

His brown gaze eased over her like hot maple syrup. "So did I."

The shadows mingling with the soft glow of the floor lights no longer felt like a safe barrier. Instead they beckoned hot images from her mind into reality.

"Daisy..." he said softly, leaning toward her.

She turned to O'Brien. "Take a left at the light and head toward the marina. Park in the back lot, past the piers."

When she turned back, Marcus had retreated to his corner. "Do you always pull away so quickly?" *Dammit!* She'd done it again! The liquor must've opened a direct line from her brain to her mouth.

"Daisy, before this goes any further, you should know that I don't like emotional entanglements."

As the limo rolled to a stop, she snorted. "Tell me something I don't know."

He peered out the tinted windows, scanning the remote

section of the bustling marina. "Why are we stopping here?"

She drew a shaky breath, focusing on the bridge that spanned the choppy waters of the bay. It'd been so long since she'd come here. "You don't know where you are, do you?"

He crossed his arms. "I presume you're going to tell me."

Instead of answering, she opened the door and stepped out. The autumn wind blew in off the bay and through her wool sweater. She breathed in the tangy salt air as she crossed over to the rail to look up at the bridge. "Of course, it wasn't as tall then."

Marcus came up behind her. "What are you talking about? What's all the mystery, Malone?"

"Jonas died here."

"Daisy," he warned, "if this is your idea of some kind of warped family reunion—"

"I thought if they became more real to you, then maybe you'd change your mind."

Marcus swore. "My big-mouth assistant told you about the sale, didn't he?"

She turned and blinked at him. "What sale?"

He narrowed his eyes. "Are we on the same page here? Change my mind about what?"

"About your family. It's important to honor your heritage, Marcus. Without family, you don't have anything."

No one had ever looked at him with pity. Except sometimes his mother, who always denied she'd "done such a thing." He didn't like it. He didn't like it at all. "If by *family* you're referring to Jonas, Isadora, and James, then I'll thank you to mind your own business. Don't tell me what to feel. They were a bunch of drunks who didn't give a damn about anybody but themselves. If that's the kind of heritage I'm supposed to honor, I'd rather be an orphan."

He spun away from her and got back into the car.

She bit her lip and followed. She hadn't planned to bring him here. When the idea struck her in Mack's parking lot, she never believed for a moment he'd melt into a quivering mass of emotion. She also never expected him to renounce his own family in the very place they'd died.

He was peeved. Even more peeved than when they'd left the bar. So peeved that he forgot his usually impeccable manners and got into the limo ahead of her. She tried to maneuver her way around him, but he wasn't helping. As hard as she tried to avoid it, it happened. She touched him.

Anger. Hurt. Betrayal.

They all twisted like vipers inside him. She felt terrible. What had she stirred up?

"You could use the other door."

"You *could* move." Rather than walking to the other side, she crawled across his lap then fell into the seat beside him.

Without looking at her, he shut the door and ordered O'Brien to Laguna Vista.

As the car floated down the road on luxury shocks, she felt her own heart bump and skip in uneven beats. "I'm sorry, Marcus. I had no idea you disliked them so much."

His face remained stony. "Now you know."

Despite the dark emotions warring inside him, she touched his cheek and turned his face to hers. "You really have no idea how sorry I am."

She touched her lips to his, softly, tenderly. Her own heart filled with sadness. Family had been the only wonderful and true thing in her life. For some reason, his only represented misery and pain.

She didn't expect him to respond. The gentle kiss was meant only to convey that he was not alone in the world. That someone cared. She drew away after a moment.

For countless seconds, he stared at her with an intensity that created sweat between her breasts. She began to move to the opposite seat, but he grabbed her arm and pulled her back. Before she could think, he crushed his mouth to hers.

She wanted to cry in that kiss. She felt the desperation. The loneliness.

He needed her.

More than physically. He needed someone to hold on to, someone who could spend his emotions. She'd like to think not just any warm body would do. She'd like to think it was only her warm body he needed.

As he plunged his fingers through her hair, she felt a white-hot passion raging along with his turmoil, and it went straight to her head. And other places. Shifting her knee across his legs, she straddled his lap and deepened the kiss.

It was a match to dry tinder.

Their tongues silently communicated what they refused to utter in words. She raked her hands through his hair.

It was hot, so hot.

At some point, Marcus closed the tinted glass between them and O'Brien and opened the moon roof.

He smelled so good. Like expensive cologne and Italian leather. She traced his full lips with her tongue. God, how many times had she dreamed of that in the last twenty-four hours? It was better than she'd imagined.

Out of her mind, her urgent fingers fumbled with the buttons of his shirt. She had to see that perfect chest once more, touch it, taste it. He leaned his head back and groaned as she sampled the sweet hollows of his neck and unfastened the last of his buttons. When she sat back and spread his shirt wide, her breath caught. Oh my, he was beautiful. So damned beautiful she almost didn't know what to do. She tentatively touched him with her fingertips, afraid something so magnificent might disappear before her eyes.

His breathing grew ragged. "My turn."

With hands much more adept than hers, he relieved her of her sweater and tank top in one fluid motion. His fingertips grazed the lacy edges of her white push-up bra. "Incredible."

His gaze caressed and scorched at the same time. The cool evening breeze brushing against her damp skin had nothing to do with the shiver coursing down her body.

He trailed his fingers down to the snap of her jeans. She sucked in her breath as he popped it open. Concerned, he looked up into her face. She leaned in and kissed him again, nowhere near having her fill of that mouth. His palms skimmed over her rib cage and down to her hips, grinding them against his. Before she could think, his head dropped to suckle her nipple through its lacy confines. Her brain exploded into full tilt.

She groaned. "Marcus..."

His hands returned to her waistband. "I have to see that belly jewel, Daisy. Before I die, I have to kiss that red gem."

In pure ecstasy, Daisy leaned back to let him unzip her jeans. Her breast was left cold, bereft as his mouth plunged past the soft hollows of her ribs to the treasure he sought. His tongue caressed, circled, and darted around the red ornament, bathing it in such lavish attention that she wanted to cry with pleasure.

She couldn't take anymore. She wanted him. Sitting up, she reached for his belt. He moaned. "Daisy..."

She'd just cleared the buckle when the limo hit a crater in the road, crashing the top of her head into the roof. She was too swept away to care, either that or so drunk she couldn't feel anything. But she did feel. Oh, how she felt...

As she reached for his belt again, he clasped her hands between his. "Believe me, Daisy, I don't want to stop. But we should, before we both do something we'll regret."

Somewhere in the recesses of her mind, she knew he was right, but she couldn't help feeling hurt. Would he regret making love to her?

She must have visibly pouted because he planted a reassuring kiss on her lips. "We've both had too much to drink. It wouldn't be right."

But it *felt* so right, she thought, trying to wade out of the haze fogging her brain.

"We only met yesterday."

The heat in her blood chilled. A familiar humiliation settled over her as she eased off him and pulled on her sweater.

"Daisy, I want you so bad it hurts. You felt it. Please don't look at me like that."

His eyes were so sincere. Not at all like Brad's.

She burst into tears.

"What is it?" he asked.

"Thank you for making"—sob— "excuses to my family for me tonight. It's the nicest thing anyone's"—sniff—"ever done for me."

He pulled her into his arms and stroked her hair.

She cried for all the mistakes that had led her to this moment. She cried for her family, which seemed to be falling apart day by day. She cried for Marcus' family, which seemed to be nothing more than a dusty pile of rubble. She cried for...

Something he'd said earlier suddenly poked through her misery.

She pulled away from him. She was never a pretty crier, and she cringed as she imagined her blotched face and blood-shot eyes. "You mentioned something about a sale."

He stopped a tear with his fingertip. "I guess it won't hurt for you to know, though I get the distinct feeling you won't like it. I'm selling Laguna Vista."

She gaped at him in horror. "You...How..." She sputtered, unable to believe her ears. *Oh, my God.* About to dive into a long-winded tirade, she felt those twisted viper emotions writhe up inside him again.

She shut her mouth.

Throwing herself back into his arms, she cried all the way back to Laguna Vista.

Fourteen

She was going to kill Sean. What the *hell* was he doing practicing his drums at...what time was it anyway? Daisy tried to open her eyes, but her lids, heavy as cinder blocks, refused to budge. The banging and clanging continued. Her head pounded like the underside of the Steel Pier on a Friday night. Daisy opened her mouth to yell, why the *hell* hadn't he taken up the harp? The soft soothing strains...but all that came out was a garbled croak. Her tongue lay impotent in her mouth like a rolled-up bath towel. And that taste in her mouth...What the *hell* had she eaten? An entire bag of nacho chips? Tacos? Something Mexican.

Lime. Salt.

Tequila.

She groaned as last night came back to her with all the clarity of a drizzle-laden fog.

Trashed. She'd gotten trashed with Marcus Van Buren.

What else? What else? Come on. Come on.

The banging and clanging grew louder. Daisy punched the mattress as visions of locking Sean in the bathroom scattered the memory clouds she'd been gently luring.

Dammit.

Forcing her eyes open, she squinted against the sunlight pouring into her room. No, Van Buren's room. No, her room, but certainly not her room in her tiny condo. Not her old bedroom at her *home* home. Which ruled out Sean.

Laguna Vista.

What the *hell*?

She tried to sit up, but her head throbbed double-time in protest, so she rolled out of bed. And fell face first on the cold hardwood floor. She was either numb, dead, or still drunk. She didn't feel a thing. She pushed herself to her hands and knees, head spinning like a planet off its axis. Wait. Scratch that. She felt plenty. Nausea. Dry mouth. A piercing pain in her temples like a pile driver trying to open a line to her brain.

How much had she drunk? Three, four shots? She normally held her liquor better than this.

What had she said exactly? More importantly, what had she done? A fleeting image of crawling across Van Buren's lap and kissing the living daylights out of him skidded across her mind. *Great.* What else had happened in the back of that cozy, no-tell motel on wheels? Glancing down, she figured she couldn't have done anything too horrible. She was still dressed. Wearing the same jeans and tank shirt she'd worn when she'd stumbled out of the bar, albeit rumpled and with a very curious stain. "Thank God for small favors."

Music then flowed in to join the percussive assault, interrupting Daisy's sketchy reflections. Music she'd heard before. Last night. "*I'm heart over head, head over heart, out of my mind, c-c-crazy for you.*"

Isadora Van Buren. For someone who'd been a dedicated party animal, she seemed to have lost her respect for the holy hours of hangover hell. Her voice crooned louder with each passing phrase. At this rate, she'd wake the entire city.

Oh, God.

Daisy forced herself to her feet and lumbered toward the door. How was she going to explain this one away? Don't panic, she told herself. A panic attack on top of a hangover might very well lead to cardiac arrest. Maybe she'd slept into the afternoon. Maybe Marcus had gone into town again on business. Maybe Rufus hadn't gotten home from his date yet. No need to panic.

She stumbled into the hall, knocking into both men. Squinting and prying open her eyes at the same time, a difficult task to say the least, she found neither man looking any happier or healthier than she. Perversely, that made her feel somewhat better.

"It's friggin' seven a.m. in the morning," Rufus

complained, bracing one hand on the wall to hold himself erect.

Marcus glared at Rufus. "That's redundant." Then he glared at Daisy. "If this is another one of your long-lost family member's surprise visits," he growled over the racket while trying to button his silk pajama top, "I'm tossing you over my knee and spanking you for each and every one of those damned *emergency* keys you've seen fit to hand out."

Daisy stared at the two grumpy men through bleary eyes. Always impeccably combed hair stuck up and out every which way. Five o'clock shadows. Bloodshot eyes. A haggard sagging of the jaw commonly sported by those who'd gone to bed three sheets to the wind. Marcus was the only one who'd managed the transition to pajamas. Like she, Rufus had slept in the clothes he'd started out in last night. She grinned, clinging to her last shred of amusement like a life preserver. "What happened to your *sure thing* with the showgirl?"

Rufus glared. "Her mother waits up for her."

Daisy snickered. "You look like something the cat dragged in."

"Yeah, well you're no beauty queen yourself right now."

Daisy's smile slipped as she swiped her tangled hair out of her eyes. She could only imagine how awful she looked. Her lids felt puffy and sore. From crying, she suddenly remembered. Oh, yeah. She'd had herself a big 'ol crying jag right there in Marcus' arms. Great. Just great.

Mortified, she swiped at the dried mascara no doubt staining her cheeks and winced.

Marcus gently nabbed her chin and inspected her face. "What happened to your cheek?"

Her skin flushed, from his touch, from embarrassment. "It's nothing. I fell out of bed." She fluttered a careless hand. "Happens all the time."

"You slept in that deathtrap? I told you to sleep in my bed. You won it fair and square." He eyed her wound more closely. "Dammit, I should've tucked you in there myself. You had to be bullheaded..." He turned to Rufus, who stared at him, mouth agape. "Order her a new bed today. Preferably something with guard rails."

Rufus held up his hand. "It's friggin' seven-o-two in the morning, Marc," he repeated as the music grew louder.

Marcus skimmed his thumb over her cheekbone. "That's going to be some shiner."

The song built toward a deafening crescendo.

"Seven-o-three," Rufus shouted with his hands pressed to his ears.

"I'll take care of it," Daisy said, but she didn't move. She was too transfixed by the way Marcus studied her lips, as though they held the answers to the universe. The maple-syrupy heat in those brown eyes melted her all over again. Maybe they hadn't made love last night, but something had definitely passed between them. Her wobbly knees proved it. Uncomfortable with his lingering inspection, she stammered, "I...I know. I look awful."

He quirked the side of his mouth. "I was thinking you look kind of cute."

"Excuse me," Rufus grumbled, pushing off the wall and dragging himself toward the mounting cacophony, "but I have to murder somebody."

"Wait!" Daisy tore herself from Marcus and grabbed Rufus by his shirttail. "Wait. I'll go." Her mind raced—well, it tried to race but instead inched along like a geriatric turtle. "Marcus was right. That crazy family of mine. You never know what they're gonna do next." She grappled for a reasonable excuse.

"*C-c-crazy for you-oo. Gotta have you-oo!*"

"Jill," Daisy blurted. "It's probably Jill." She lowered her voice, cajoling Rufus with narrowed eyes. "You know. Trying to draw attention to herself."

His face remained blank, if not pained.

She rolled her eyes and whispered, "The crush."

"Aaaah." Rufus nodded slowly then stopped. "The love song I get. But what's with the tin-pan alley marching band?"

The music blared louder, as though someone had spitefully turned the volume knob to ten.

Marcus groaned and pushed past Rufus. "Maybe you've reconsidered murder, but I haven't."

Daisy sprang into action. "I'll do it!"

"Before you kill her," Rufus shouted, "find out who that chick singer is."

She raced ahead and down the spiral steps, fighting a fresh wave of nausea as she smelled frying bacon. Sick as a dog, she'd absolutely retch if Marcus discovered the ghosts just now. She wasn't ready. She needed more time. Time to reason with them. Time to help them cross over. "Cut it out, Izzy," she pleaded through clenched teeth as she stumbled toward the source of the mayhem.

Pushing through the kitchen door, Daisy's heart stopped. Her jaw dropped like a busted elevator, and her eyes sprang fully open. It was like something out of *Ghostbusters*.

Spoons, knives, and ladles drummed autonomously against various pots and pans. Apples, oranges, and bananas danced midair while dishtowels twirled and shimmied around them in bizarre Buzby Berkley fashion.

She gasped. It echoed in both ears as Marcus and Rufus joined her. Together they gaped at the most eerie player in this 3-D spectral circus.

At the stove, brandishing a spatula as though she'd never handled one in her life, wearing Daisy's plaid flannel shirt and little else outside of a long pearl necklace, glittering studs, and diamond rings, hovered a fuzzy image of a sleek-haired, doe-eyed flapper.

The apparition turned to smolder at Rufus. "*C-c-crazy for you-oo. Gotta have you-oo,*" she crooned, then winked at him, "*Cu-cutie you. Ooh!*" Then, like a magical zipper, she faded away from the ankles up.

Daisy nearly choked. "Isadora."

The flannel shirt crumpled to the floor, utensils clattered to the counter, fruit dropped and rolled across the floor. The music stopped.

Deafening silence.

Until two slices of bread popped out of the toaster with a chipper ding.

Because it was all she could do, Daisy muttered, "Houston, we have a problem."

After a brief moment, Marcus stepped over the impromptu

fruit salad, crossed to the stove, moved the sizzling bacon to the back burner, then poured himself a cup of conveniently brewed coffee.

Taking a deep breath, Daisy crisscrossed to the refrigerator, nabbed a carton of orange juice, traversed the fruit-littered floor to the pan-ridden counter, calmly poured the juice into a glass, drank, gargled, then spit it into the sink. She then turned on the faucet and proceeded to down two glasses of water. Wiping the back of her hand across her mouth, she said, "I never realized how much Isadora looks like Louise Brooks."

Rufus shot Marcus a look, as though the name meant something but he didn't want to believe it. He proved the point when he glanced back to Daisy, croaking, "Louise Brooks? The 1920s film star?"

Daisy nodded. "She and Isadora Van Buren were great friends."

Rufus pinched himself. "I'm dreaming. I must be dreaming."

"You're not dreaming," she said.

Owl-eyed, Rufus slapped his hands to his face. "Did you..." he pointed to the discarded shirt, "she was..." He plowed his fingers through his disheveled hair. "How can you two be so calm? We just saw a...a..." He threw his hands in the air. "It winked at me!"

Marcus swallowed a mouthful of coffee, welcoming the caffeine and the chance to jolt his stunned brain. "I think she likes you."

"Is that all you have to say!" Rufus shouted, then pressed his palms to his temples and groaned. He sank into a kitchen chair. "I'm hallucinating. It's the vodka. I'll never drink vodka again."

Daisy's stomach churned. "I feel the same way about tequila."

Rufus dropped his forehead to the table. "I feel like shit."

Marcus grabbed a plate, plucked the toast from the toaster, five strips of burnt bacon from the pan, and handed Rufus the makings of a sandwich. "Maybe this will help." Coffee mug in hand, Marcus dropped into a chair himself and nudged the plate toward his friend's lowered head. "You definitely have a fan, Ruf. She made your favorite."

Rufus raised his head and glared at Marcus through squinted, bloodshot eyes. "How can you joke about this, Marc?"

"I don't know." Truly, he didn't. Maybe it was because he'd already suspected as much. That ghosts, at least in this house, did indeed exist. The email, the message on the mirror, the incident with his shirt, the uncanny feeling of being watched. Then there was Daisy. Accusing him of kissing her when he hadn't. Mistaking him for his grandfather time and again.

Although he'd probably sprout white hairs from what he'd just witnessed, he welcomed proof that Daisy wasn't a whacked-out space-case. After all, it was highly disturbing to be attracted to someone who suffered from hallucinations.

Unfortunately, the revelation shed some unflattering light as well. If Daisy had known beyond a doubt that Laguna Vista was haunted, then it meant she'd planned to lie all along. To accept his money under false pretenses.

"*Whatever it takes. So long as she signs,*" he'd said at one point to Rufus. His words came back to haunt him, so to speak. He knew it was hypocritical, but it bothered him all the same. She'd withheld the fact that as a child she'd seen Jonas. Withheld the fact that Laguna Vista was indeed *haunted.* What else was Tight-lipped Malone keeping from him?

He swiveled in his seat and gave his rented ghostbuster a skeptical once-over. She was staring at her crumpled flannel shirt, lost in thought and looking nearly as panicked as Rufus. Amazingly, he wanted to give her the benefit of the doubt. Clearing his throat, he motioned her over and into an opposing chair. "Have something you want to tell me?"

She sagged into the chair as though the weight of the world suddenly weighed too much. "Laguna Vista is haunted."

"Aw, crap." Rufus drooped over and buried his head into his folded arms. "I think I'm gonna be sick."

Marcus set his mug on the table. "How long have you known?"

He braced himself for a lie but hoped for the truth. Somewhere between last night and this morning she'd come to mean more to him than a walking-talking ego-repair kit. He'd never forget the way she'd blindsided him with her wise cracks and tequila routine. The way she'd settled herself on his lap as if it were her private property. How could he ever forget that? And the way she'd cried like a war widow in his arms...

Yesterday he'd awakened to the same structured world he'd always known. This morning...well, hell, he'd seen his dead great aunt frying bacon and coming on to his best friend, and he'd merely sipped his coffee.

He wouldn't go so far as to call himself a new man, or even a changed one for that matter. More like...more like a man who'd just discovered another side of himself. He'd always done fine without it, but once exposed, well, he needed to explore, find out where it could take him.

Daisy squared her shoulders. "I've known since I was ten."

Marcus released his breath, unaware he'd been holding it.

"It was Halloween. I came here on a dare. I was standing outside, staring up at the west tower. That was the first time I saw him."

"Jonas," Marcus clarified, feeling ridiculously buoyant.

"Uh-huh. That tower's up pretty high, yet somehow we...connected. I don't know how else to explain it. It's not as if I could read his expression or hear a ghostly voice bemoaning his woes and sorrows, but I still knew he was sad. Sad and lonely."

Playing the neutral investigative reporter, Marcus asked, "How'd you know it was Jonas?"

"Spooky stories about the Van Buren deaths have been circulating this area for decades. I knew it was a ghost, and I knew it was a man, which narrowed it down to Jonas and James. My gut told me it was Jonas. A vintage newspaper photo confirmed it. However, after countless stakeouts with no repeat sightings, not to mention years of Pop's persuasive reasoning, I finally wrote it off to an overactive imagination.

"When I took this job," Daisy continued, as though reading Marcus' thoughts, "I still thought it was my imagination. I had no proof that Laguna Vista was actually haunted. I fully intended to prove it was *not*. But if by some quirk it was, well, I had a backup plan."

"A lot of those lately," Rufus said in a muffled voice.

Marcus kicked him under the table, eyes locked on Daisy. "Which was?"

Daisy offered a weak smile. "I was going to help the ghosts to leave."

Rufus raised his head a half inch. "You can do that?"

She nodded, her fingers plucking at the shirt in her hands.

Marcus raised a brow at her, giving her one last chance to come clean. "You can do that?"

"Yes."

Daisy shifted as Marcus leaned back in his seat. He looked as though she'd fed him some foreign food and he wasn't sure whether he liked the taste.

Two days ago she wouldn't have given two figs whether or not he believed in her. Two days ago he'd treated her with the disdain of a boardwalk charlatan. But two days ago turned into last night, and she'd learned more about Marcus Van Buren than any bush-prowling, self-respecting tabloid reporter ever had. The fact that he'd covered for her with her family carried a lot of weight. Not to mention the way he'd punched out *Don's* lights in her defense. Or the way he'd slammed on the brakes and avoided certain disaster in the back seat of his limo. Oh, yes. Last night was flooding back to her now, and with each memory she felt herself sinking deeper into a sea of regret.

She'd likened him to Brad. Why? Because he was good-looking and rich. She'd treated him rudely from the get-go, assuming him to be another self-obsessed bastard. Another charm-her-pants-off-and-leave-her-to-deal-with-the-circumstances prick. She'd been so blind with the memories of the past, warped and twisted in her mind, that she'd failed to listen to her gut. Failed to see the wondrous possibilities of the present.

But today she was feeling brave. Incredibly, deliciously brave. Carried on a wave of something she didn't want to inspect too closely, but holding on for the ride just the same. "Yes," she repeated more confidently. "I can help them to leave."

Rufus popped his head back up. "How soon?"

Daisy searched Marcus' eyes. Unable to read him, she reached forward and clasped his folded hands. "Will you let me try?"

Marcus leaned across the table and raised her hand to his lips. "I just want you to know," he said with an engaging smile, "that when we first met, I doubted your mental stability. After all, you believed in ghosts."

He kissed her palm then her forearm, reminding Daisy of the sensual way he'd licked the salt from her skin the night before, of the way he'd tongued her belly jewel and driven her to the edge of insanity. Her cheeks blazed as an unexpected sigh escaped her lips. "And now?"

"Your wish is my command."

"Good Lord," Rufus complained, his gaze darting back and forth between Marcus and Daisy. "As if that fat-grizzled bacon wasn't enough to make me sick. What have I done?"

Fifteen

"Tell me again why we're not moving into a hotel?" Rufus looked miserable as he nursed his bowl of bland oatmeal.

"Because I refuse to be railroaded out of my own home by relatives who are too stupid to know they're dead." The last half-hour played over in Marcus' head like a foreign movie with fuzzy subtitles. Daisy's list of possible reasons for why his grandfather, great aunt, and great uncle were haunting Laguna Vista had been lengthy, and murky at best. Ticking them off to better understand them, he recited, "Either they don't know they're dead, know they're dead but are confused as to where they are and why they don't feel like they used to, know they're dead but are unwilling to leave the physical plane, are in shock and reliving over and over again the events leading up to their untimely deaths, or are bound to the physical plane because they're too emotionally attached to feelings of guilt or revenge to 'let go.' "

"It's as confusing coming from you as it was from Daisy. I wish she'd hurry down with those research books so we can hurry the hell up and de-ghost this place." He held up his spoon with one hand, his head with the other. "One day, Marc. I'll give it one day. Then I'm moving into a hotel with or without you."

"I probably left out a couple of possibilities," Marcus rambled on, "but my brain is in no condition to recall. That's what I get for mixing Bloody Marys, Jack Daniels, and tequila."

Rufus turned a whiter shade of pale. "Marc, please."

"Whichever reason, they all strike me as selfish." Marcus refilled his coffee mug to the brim then bit off a corner of dry toast. "Which is in perfect keeping with my grandfather."

Oatmeal dripped off Rufus' spoon before he could get it to his mouth. Frowning, he said, "You sound as though you hate him. You never even knew him."

"I know of him. That's enough."

"Let's get back to something you said a few seconds ago. You said, *my* home."

"What?"

"*I refuse to be railroaded out of my own home*, that's what you said. Since when did you start thinking of Laguna Vista as your home?"

Marcus set down his toast. "What are you talking about? It's always been my home. I inherited it. I own it. Thus it is mine. My house."

"There's a big difference between a house and a home. A piece of property and a place where you hang your hat."

"I don't own any hats."

Rufus leveled him with a derisive look. "You know what I mean. Something's happening to you, Marc. I'm used to seeing you poring over charts and reports."

"I'm working at night, before I go to bed."

"Back-to-back appointments..."

"Yesterday I met with a tax assessor, the county clerk, an electrician, and a plumber."

"You're usually on the cell phone twice an hour fleshing out one deal or another. If Kelly has called here three times—"

"I asked *Ms. Bishop* to hold my calls until Monday."

"You're kidding."

"It's the weekend."

"That never mattered before."

"I'm on vacation."

"You don't take vacations."

Marcus regarded his friend with a curious grin. "Why are you being so contrary? Wasn't it you who suggested I go on a free-for-all weekend? Loosen up, you said. Dead, you called me."

Rufus eyed the fruit that had been dancing mid-air thirty

minutes before. "I'm beginning to appreciate the mundane."

"Do you know what I did last night?"

"I'm afraid to ask."

"I played darts."

"Darts?"

"In a bar. A redneck bar."

"Oh, God."

"Rufus."

"Yeah?"

"I punched a man."

"What? Why?"

"He put his hands on Daisy."

Rufus jumped to his feet and converged on Marcus, fists on hips. "All right." He sucked in a deep breath, studied his bare toes, then released the breath and started to pace. "All right. We can fix this. No need to panic."

"What are you talking about?"

"We've got to put some distance between you. That's the first thing."

"Between who? What are you babbling about, Sinclair?"

"Do I have to spell it out?"

"I guess you do."

He stopped before Marcus, regarding him with something akin to pity. "I'm going to give it to you straight, Marc."

"Please do."

"No use in sugar-coating it."

"Spit it out, dammit."

"You're in love."

Marcus laughed. "I'm not in love."

"Denial. Predictable. Well, that's something, I guess."

"I'm not in love," Marcus repeated. "I'm..."

"Yes?"

"Intrigued."

"Intrigued?"

"Yes. Intrigued. And attracted. Definitely attracted."

"So intrigued that you're ready to chuck a multi-million-dollar sale?"

"If you're referring to Laguna Vista, and I assume you

are, nothing has changed."

"You're still hoping to sell to Zigfreid?"

"I'm planning on it."

"But the place is haunted!"

"Unfortunate. But fixable."

"According to who? Daisy? As parapsychologists go, she's as green as the White House lawn."

Marcus cocked a brow. "You knew that when you hired her."

"But that was different. The circumstances were different. We weren't dealing with...with," he jammed his hands through his spiked-out hair and whispered, "*you know.*"

"Ghosts." Marcus grinned. "You can say the word, Rufus. It's not like they're going to appear on call."

"How do you know? How do you know anything about what they're going to do? Based on what we just saw, they're capable of about anything. Cooking. Juggling fruit. Spinning invisible records."

"Flirting," Marcus added.

"Poke fun, go ahead. When that dame whisks me off into some third-dimensional wormhole to make me her love slave, then you'll be sorry. I'm the best damn assistant you ever had."

"And the horniest."

Rufus shrugged his shoulders, as if there was nothing left to say.

"Listen, I'm not any happier about this little spiritual surprise than you are. But panicking won't help. Sticking our heads in the sand won't help. The best course is a calm, logical course. Accept that Laguna Vista is haunted and do what we can to rectify it. We're not in any danger. The ghosts aren't hostile."

Rufus snorted. "Again. According to Daisy. You're placing your trust in a woman whose credentials are as shaky as a politician's word. Tell me again you're not in love."

"I'm not in love. And I'm not stupid. Help is on the way."

Rufus snapped his fingers. "Your backup plan."

"Thaddeus Bookman."

"I recognize that name. He was on Zigfreid's list. An expert in the field. Respected by his peers." Rufus shook his head. "Out of the country. Scotland. Special assignment. Wild horses couldn't drag him away."

Marcus sipped from his cup. "He'll be here by week's end."

"How..."

"He owes me."

"You know him?"

"We go way back. Feel better?"

"If one of the most renowned parapsychologists in the country is on his way to deal with the...*you know*...then why is Gidget the Ghostbuster still here?"

"I intend to honor our contract. She deserves a chance. Besides, she has a history with Jonas. I have a feeling it could help."

Rufus cocked a brow. "Yeah, you have a feeling all right. Now who's thinking with his one-eyed trouser snake?"

***

Daisy sighed in relief as she spread a fat glob of toothpaste across her brush. She thanked Isadora Van Buren for setting her free. The war with her conscience had begun to take its toll. It had been bad enough when she'd first arrived, knowing she might have to lie about the ghosts' existence in order to collect the money her family needed. But after last night, after Marcus' explicit kindness, how could she have in all good conscience continued to lie to him? Lying had never come easily to her, but it had certainly helped when Marcus Van Buren was simply, in her mind, a Brad Worthington clone.

She still needed the money, however. Nothing had changed there. She hoped Pop had heard about her escapade in Mack's Pub. Served him right to know his eldest daughter preferred to consort with the enemy rather than with him. Maybe then he'd get the message, because she'd sure as hell been too much of a coward to tell him to his face. She loved her father with every minute of her existence, and it crushed her that he'd been the one to uncover the vindictive bone she never knew she had. Not even Brad Worthington had pushed her so far.

She rinsed and spit.

At least her relationship with Marcus had improved. Considerably. Not that she'd call it a relationship exactly. More like "a thing." It was too new to know what it was for sure, and they'd had no time alone since he kissed her cheek goodnight at her bedroom door.

She wiped her face on the pink towel she'd packed.

She had another reason to thank Isadora for her surprise coming-out party. Marcus now believed in her. Before, she could have been the world's foremost parapsychologist, and he'd still have thought she was a flake avoiding the real world. Given time, he would have figured out she was the average girl next door with nothing up her sleeve, but now she didn't have to wait. He'd seen Isadora Van Buren for himself, and there was no going back.

As she walked out of the bathroom, she tripped over Danielle's Cookie Monster slippers. Guilt twisted inside her. It seemed her father wasn't the only selfish Malone these days. How could she have forgotten the most important night of her little sister's life?

Obsession. She was obsessed with the ghosts. She wouldn't deny it, and she'd tell Danielle the truth, despite the excuse Marcus had generously provided. Danielle was nearly as excited as Daisy was about the ghosts, and once she told her sister that not only Jonas was here, but Isadora and maybe James as well, surely she'd find it in her heart to cut her big sister some slack. Hopefully.

Still, the world seemed brighter now that she could no longer taste the vile remnants of tequila in her mouth. She just had to grab her books off the bed and—

Jonas.

She could tell the difference now. He stood at the foot of her bed dressed in one of Marcus' well-cut suits. Loneliness, guilt, sadness. The same as Marcus, but something more. An edge of desperation. Impatience, too. And a cutting regret that almost made her double over. His dark eyes, so like Marcus', burned with silent entreaty.

She stepped forward. "Jonas..."

She wanted to reach out, touch him, hold him. He appeared

solid, but she left her hand at her side, afraid he'd flee. "What can I do?" she whispered.

He set the book he'd been holding onto the bed. His eyes bore into hers. *Help me*, he mouthed.

"Anything."

He glanced down at the open book.

She moved slowly to the bed, as though in dream. *Chapter Fifteen. Crossing Over: Do You Have What it Takes?*

Her gaze flew back to Jonas.

He was gone.

***

Daisy flew into the kitchen, book clutched in her sweating hand.

Marcus looked up and smiled. "Your mother just called. She invited us for dinner tonight. Well, she didn't invite Rufus, but he refuses to stay here alone, so he made me call her back and invite him, too. She said she's handcuffing Danielle to the banister so you two can make up."

Daisy gave him a shaky smile. "That's great. OK. I, um, well, your grandfather just showed up, and he invited us to help him cross over."

Rufus dropped the spoon into his oatmeal and groaned.

Marcus frowned. "How did he do that?"

She plunked the book down on the table and pointed. "He had it open to this page. I read his lips. He said 'help me.' Marcus, he's desperate. I can feel it. Maybe he knows about the sale. Maybe he can't take being cooped up here anymore. I don't know. But he wants it bad, and for some reason he can't do it alone."

Marcus narrowed his eyes.

"Cross over, I mean."

An orange flew across the room and bounced off the refrigerator.

Rufus looked ready to scramble under the table. "I better get one hell of a bonus this year, Marc."

Marcus watched Daisy twist her tank top in her hands, and he pushed out the adjacent chair with his foot. "Sit down, Daisy. Take a deep breath."

She did. Her racing thoughts began to slow.

"Now, what's in this chapter? Why does Jonas think we can help?"

"It's like I said before, they're chained here for some reason or another. Though we can rule out the theory that they don't know they're dead. That's another chapter. This one is about those who die but get stuck between worlds because of something they did or didn't do. A regret. A guilt. They died suddenly, so who knows what could've been left undone or unsaid. They might not even know themselves."

Marcus leaned back in his chair. "If they don't know, how are we supposed to know? Those two were dedicated hell-raisers. They probably have a red-carpet rap sheet a mile long."

"You seem to know a little about them. Anything immediately spring to mind?"

His eyes hardened. "I told you about Jonas. He ignored his family. And Isadora. She was married so many times there should be a law against it."

A banana whizzed past Marcus' ear.

"I thought you said they weren't hostile," Rufus grumbled, keeping a wary eye out for more torpedoed fruit.

Daisy scanned the room, rubbing the chill from her arms. "Can you feel the tension in here? I felt it Friday, too."

Marcus nodded. "I thought it was just me."

Rufus gaped back and forth between them as though watching a psychotic tennis match. "Of course there's tension. Your dead aunt is chucking fruit at our heads."

"No, it's deeper than that," Daisy said. "It's like there's a black cloud hovering over us."

Rufus picked up his oatmeal and his tomato juice. "That's it. If anyone wants me, I'll be outside." With a sharp eye toward the ceiling, he stormed out the back door.

"You can feel it?" Daisy asked quietly, afraid he'd deny it if she expressed too much enthusiasm.

His forehead creased. "Don't make a big deal out of it. Everyone can pick up on vibes here and there."

"Rufus didn't feel it."

"Rufus is scared out of his wits. He's not feeling much of

anything right now."

"His reaction is pretty standard. Yours, on the other hand..."

He scooted his chair next to hers then rubbed his hands up and down her goose-pimpled arms. "Let me guess. You're thinking, for someone who so vehemently denounced the existence of ghosts, I converted rather easily. Maybe too easily."

Easy. Daisy blew non-existent hairs out of her eyes. Nothing about Marcus Van Buren was easy. Not the smile that stole her breath. Not the eyes that burned her skin. And his touch. Oh, God. His touch, innocent though it was, left her clawing the dirt somewhere between annihilation and resurrection. She could think of nothing but pinning him to the kitchen table to finish what they'd started in the back of his limo.

She shook her head clear and answered, "Something like that. I understand that it's hard to argue with your own eyes." She glanced at the stove. "Isadora was standing right there, cooking. Then there was the dancing fruit. The floating utensils. I checked for strings, for hidden cameras, for trickery on any level. Nothing. We saw what we saw, and it was real. What I don't understand is your lack of anxiety. Most people fear what they don't understand."

Marcus quirked a playful grin. "I ain't 'fraid of no ghosts."

"No. You're not afraid of them." Daisy shivered as a realization hit home. "You're angry with them."

His grin faded, then a moment later he took her hands and stroked his thumbs over her knuckles. "It's ridiculous, I suppose. Being ticked at a trio who have been dead for seventy years. A trio I never even knew. But they hurt a lot of people, Daisy. Jonas, he...well, I don't remember my father ever speaking his name. His own father's name. Although that might have been J.B.'s influence at work."

"What do you mean?"

"After the accident, J.B. packed up the family, what remained of it, and moved them into the Manhattan residence permanently. His wife. His daughter-in-law and his two grandsons."

"Two?"

"Jonas' son, my father, Regis Van Buren; and Isadora's son, Richard."

Daisy blinked at him. She thought she knew all there was to know about the famous Van Buren siblings. "I wasn't aware Isadora had a son."

"I'm not surprised. She kept it low profile, from what I understand. Shielded the boy from the media with the ferocity of a lioness protecting her cub."

"Isadora? A mother?" Daisy couldn't imagine. "Was she a good one?"

"J.B. thought so. In fact, it was the one and only thing he gave her any credit for being good at. She certainly wasn't good at being a wife. She went through four husbands, for chrissake. And God knows how many lovers."

"Richard's father was..."

"Husband Number Three. Roy Tadmucker."

"Of Tadmucker Taffy?"

"That's right. The founder. Suffered a mortal heart attack the night of their third wedding anniversary."

"She can hardly be blamed for that."

Marcus raised a brow. "She was twenty-one. Roy was fifty-one. He died underneath her with a smile on his face."

Daisy blushed. "Oh."

"At any rate, as much as J.B. disapproved of his children's decadent lifestyles, he was devastated by their deaths. His suffering was such that he threatened to disown any family member who dared utter the names Jonas, Isadora, or James in his presence. He was a stubborn old man. He never forgave them. For the way they lived. For the way they died." Marcus shrugged. "After several years, the famous Van Buren siblings were little more than a bad memory, for those who even cared to give them a second thought."

At once an aching sadness consumed Daisy, a rush of darkness as though the sun had fallen from the sky. It seeped through her skin and into her bones, making her want to curl up into a pathetic, self-pitying ball. "Stop it! Don't say anymore. I...I..." She jumped from her chair and ran from the kitchen, tears burning her eyes.

Marcus was right behind her. He nabbed her in the living room and spun her around, holding her by the shoulders to keep her from crumpling to the floor. "What is it? What's wrong?"

"She may be dead, but she still has feelings!"

"Who?"

"Isadora! She heard you. Everything you said. And she felt, I felt...what you said hurt her."

"I'm sorry," Marcus said, then frowned. "Wait a minute. What am I sorry for? She made her bed."

"I don't care if she did or didn't, just don't say anymore. Not now. Not here." She shrugged out of his hold, wiped her eyes, and knotted her hair into a loose bun at the base of her neck.

"Maybe Rufus was right. Maybe we should move into a hotel."

"No. I'll...no. Just give me a minute." She took a deep breath, rolled back her shoulders, flexed her tensed fingers, then exhaled, shaking off Isadora's sadness like a bad mood.

Marcus folded his arms and waited for her to complete her ritual, concern still marring his expression. "Better?"

She nodded. "It just happens sometimes."

He guessed that's what Newsome and Creed had meant when they'd called her a *sensitive*, though he refrained from mentioning it. Then she might ask him how much he knew about her background and when he'd learned it. He wasn't ready to open that can of worms.

"How'd you know all that?"

"What?" Startled out of his thoughts, Marcus busied himself with the drawstring of his pajama bottoms, realizing with a frown that he'd been traipsing about Laguna Vista as casually as he lingered about his own penthouse.

"All that stuff about J.B. and his feelings. How could you possibly know all that?"

"He kept journals."

It was as though a light suddenly glowed from within. Her face beamed. "Your great-grandfather kept journals?"

"One for every year of his adult life. I came across them about ten years ago when my office was being redecorated. It was his office first, then my father's, then mine. I found the books hidden behind a secret panel, along with some old family documents and keepsakes. I skimmed a few, out of curiosity. But I felt like I was eavesdropping, reading his personal thoughts, so I stopped."

"Where are they now?"

"Where I found them. I figured if J.B. wanted them read, he'd have left them out where anyone could have browsed them."

She moved forward then, wrapped her arms about his waist and pressed her cheek against his chest. She sighed and snuggled closer. "I didn't think you possessed any."

He held her tight and smiled down into her rumpled hair. He had no idea what she was talking about, nor did he care. At the moment his heart was racing like a teenager's on his first date. Amazing. He'd never felt giddy in his life. Men like him didn't get giddy. But he couldn't think of another word to describe how he felt every time she moved willingly into his arms. "Any what?"

She looked up at him. "Sentimentality. Family loyalty."

He kissed her forehead. Then the bridge of her nose. Then the crevice of her upper lip. When he got to her mouth, he surrendered to the lust that had been growing since he'd first set eyes on her this morning. Unlike giddiness, lust he understood completely.

But instead of losing himself, a chill shot down his spine as her small hands tenderly framed the sides of his face. She'd thrown herself into the kiss with every bit as much passion as he, but something more than lust fueled her enthusiasm. Either the ghosts were interfering, or Daisy was falling just a little bit in love with him. Either way, the realization made him pull back.

He needed a breath. A moment to think. "Don't go putting me on a white charger yet, sweetheart. My motivation was somewhat self-centered. J.B. recorded more than a few scandals in those journals. If they fell into the wrong hands..."

His words stuck in his throat.

They stared at one another for a moment—breath ragged, hearts pounding, hormones fogging their brains—then pushed themselves to arms' length. "The journals!"

Daisy's eyes sparked with hope. "Whatever Jonas did or didn't do. Whatever's holding him back. Surely we'll find a clue in your great-grandfather's journals."

Marcus was already on the move.

Daisy hurried after him back into the kitchen.

He opened the back door. "Rufus!"

Rufus, already on his way in, jumped two feet. His glass and bowl went flying. Tomato juice soaked the front of Daisy's white tank. The last of the oatmeal landed on Marcus. "Jesus! Don't sneak up on me like that!"

Marcus ignored the globs of cereal clinging to his pajama top. "I need you to go to New York."

Rufus sagged with relief. "Thank God."

Jill burst through the kitchen door, startling them all. "Hey, guys!"

Rufus clutched his chest and sucked in a choked breath. "I can't take it."

Jill surveyed the strewn fruit, spilled juice, and splattered oatmeal. "Damn," she complained with a sullen pout, "a food fight, and I missed it."

Sixteen

Two things struck Daisy as she pulled the S.P.S. van into her parents' driveway.

First, "America's Most Eligible Bachelor" was attempting to fix her broken glove-box door.

Second, Rudolph and his plastic reindeer gang frolicked in thousand-watt suspended animation across the front lawn.

"What month is it?" she asked.

The glove-box door clicked closed. And stayed closed.

"You fixed it!"

Marcus wiped his hands in the air and smiled. "Despite public opinion, not all millionaires are useless."

She smiled. "So I've noticed."

His eyes warmed as he perused her pink faux-cashmere sweater and form-fitting denims. "I've been noticing a lot of things myself lately."

Her cheeks burned. She was flirting with the man every woman in America dreamed about, and it was disconcerting to say the least. How many before her had dropped like pulsating blobs at his feet, helpless against his powers? His charisma had nothing to do with wealth. He was all man—hard muscle and sinew. Though his movements were gentle, restrained, she'd seen the power that lay beneath his courtly façade. And she'd felt how much of a man he was pressed against her in the back of the limo, where he'd proven how much of a gentleman he was as well.

He was simply perfect, and as the lights from the decorations provided that same soft glow as the limo, she wished she'd agreed to come here in the luxurious, black, *private* car. And wouldn't that be the icing on the cake of her life. Making love in her parents' driveway with a man she'd only known for two days. She turned away from his hot brown eyes before she completely lost her mind. Her voice croaked as she fumbled with her seatbelt. "We'd better go in. The windows are already fogging up on the van. I'll never hear the end of it."

He caught her hand as she grabbed her wallet from between the seats. Those damn syrup eyes melted all over her. "Might as well make it worth the abuse."

He pulled her over and met her in the middle. His kiss was gentle at first, a tentative tasting that gave her a moment to consider her acceptance. Like she had a choice. She buried her fingers in the back of his hair, pressing him closer, crushing her breasts against his suit-jacketed chest. His tongue glided and darted around hers, ensnaring her in a tango hot enough to melt the plastic off the seats. She hadn't been the praying sort for some time now, but as his fingers slipped up the back of her sweater to caress her back, she begged God for this heaven to last forever.

Unfortunately, He wasn't listening because Marcus broke away and playfully kissed her nose. "I think that should do it."

"Do what?" she asked, her head spinning.

He smiled. "You have this very cute habit of forgetting things when I kiss you. I like it."

With that, he hopped from the van. Since when did Marcus hop, she wondered, still in her trance. She stepped out unsteadily and met him at the sidewalk.

Rudolph's nose flickered as its hidden bulb clung to life.

"Wow. Your family is really into Christmas."

She suddenly felt self-conscious. When Marcus got a good look at where she was from and what she was about, would he still be this starry-eyed about her? She immediately killed the thought. Daisy Malone was who she was. She wouldn't pretend to be any different. She'd tried once to be something she wasn't. Never again.

So her family ate processed cheese and frozen waffles. So they had oil spots on their driveway and oil spots on the kitchen paneling where Pop rested his head back at meals. So they went a little wacky and hung the Christmas lights on the house in October. At least they didn't leave them up all year round.

If Marcus Van Buren couldn't handle that, better to find out now and be done with it.

Though she had to give him some credit. He hadn't put up much fuss when she refused to arrive at her parents' house in the chauffeured limousine. After a couple of "Are you sure's?", he simply shrugged his shoulders and climbed into the van. No pained look, no scrunched nose, no sideways glance. It was a good start.

"Daisy, where the hell have you been?" Jill stood in the front doorway, shouting. "Dinner's almost ready and Mom's having a fit."

Marcus took Daisy's hand and smiled. "I think I'm going to enjoy this."

She furrowed her brow. "I don't think you've ever had a dinner like this before."

"That's why I'm going to like it." His kissed her hand then her lips. Right in front of Jill.

She wondered if their "thing" was progressing into something more. Surely a man who was only interested in a weekend fling wouldn't kiss her in front of her family. For a man ready to bolt out of her life, he seemed awfully comfortable spending an evening with the Malones. But, as usual, Daisy preferred to play it safe. She wouldn't get her hopes up. She'd take it slow. One day at a time...

Jill stepped outside, and they met her on the steps.

She glared at Marcus, her white tee shirt and baggy khakis seeming to flare with her huff. "I thought you said hell would freeze ten times over before you slept with Daisy."

"Jill!"

"Daisy!" she parroted, then squinted in the dim light of early Christmas. "What's with the shiner? Don't tell me you fell out of bed again."

"All right, I won't. Now apologize to Marcus."

Jill crossed her arms. "I'm only looking out for your best

interests. A man like him is used to getting what he wants, sometimes without asking."

Daisy poked a finger at Jill's chest, pressing her into the front door. "You're insulting our guest. Apologize. Now."

Jill rolled her emerald green eyes. "Fine. Sorry, Marc, but family's gotta look out for family, you know?"

Mortified, Daisy turned to apologize to Marcus. He was grinning again. What was he finding so amusing? And just what had he meant by "hell freezing over?"

"Don't worry, Daisy," he said. "I think it's great you have someone who cares about you so much. Can't fault her for that, even if her tactics are a bit barbaric."

Jill blinked. "That's a new one. I don't think I've ever been called barbaric." She twisted her locally famous lips as she contemplated his fate. "I can live with that."

Daisy sagged with relief. Marcus had been accepted into the fold. "Whose bright idea was it to put out the Christmas decorations before Halloween?" she asked.

"Mom's. She said the place needed some cheering up." Jill's look turned serious. "I think she's cracking, Daisy. Pop only comes home to sleep for a couple of hours on the couch, and then he's back to the bar again. He doesn't even eat here."

Daisy frowned. The only reason she'd agreed to come tonight, besides hoping to make amends with Danielle, was because she'd known Pop wouldn't be here. It was Mickey's night off, and with football season in full swing, it'd be hours before Pop closed the bar. But no one had told her he'd been hiding out. He was ashamed. They all knew it. He was a good man who'd screwed up, and no one seemed to know what to say to make things right. Secretly, she was hiding out from him as well. He was still her perfect Pop. What if she said something she couldn't take back? What if she said something that changed their relationship forever, even if that was already too late to worry about?

She should be able to forgive him, but whenever she imagined little Sean's frightened face or Mickey's tired eyes or Jill's college fund about to go down the drain, she couldn't help it. She loved the rest of her family just as much as she loved him, and she'd protect them just the same.

"Hang up Marcus' jacket, Jill. It's the least you can do."

"Yeah, sure."

They followed her inside the closed-in porch. Marcus shrugged out of his suit jacket and handed it to Jill. "I guess being the oldest, Daisy's accustomed to bossing you around," he teased.

But Daisy didn't bite. For the first time in her life, she hesitated at the door of her family home. She touched her fingers to the rough wood. The door needed to be sanded and repainted. "Mom's not exactly herself, huh? I thought it was odd that she didn't make a big deal about my staying at Laguna Vista."

"Maybe she'll talk to you, Daze. You being the oldest, like Marcus said. She's vacuumed the house three times since yesterday. She even cleaned the windows. Inside *and* out. You know how much she hates to clean windows."

Daisy felt another point being chalked up against her father. Not only had he scared his kids, he'd scared their mother as well, and he didn't have the gumption to stick around and see her through it. Daisy knew he was busting his butt down at the pub trying to save his business, but it didn't excuse the fact that his wife needed him and he was nowhere around.

Daisy laced her fingers with Marcus'. It was strange. One minute his touch set her pulse racing, her skin burning. The next, it calmed her like a gentle river, flowing through her with a silent serenity she'd never known.

Something deep, something base cried out to her. In a blind rush, she heard his soul calling. She knew he didn't hear it, probably wasn't even aware of it. The curse of the sensitive. What would he do when he heard it? Drop to one knee? Run for his life? Maybe it wasn't even calling to her, but it was calling for something, loud and clear.

Sometimes she wished she couldn't feel these things, they only tended to complicate her own feelings...and right now they were telling her exactly what she didn't want to hear.

Marcus reveled in the feel of Daisy taking his hand as if it were her right. It surprised him that such a simple gesture could affect him so deeply. He'd been acting like a smitten idiot the entire day, but he couldn't seem to stop himself. Thank goodness he'd sent Rufus to New York. His assistant would be prying them apart like the Jaws of Life this very minute.

They stepped into the house, and all hell broke loose. A phone jangled off the hook. A television blared. Sean pounded on a nearby door. "Danielle, hurry up. I have to pee!"

Candie and Mickey Malone sat smushed together on a sagging loveseat that probably held more history than all of Marcus' furniture combined. They looked cozy and happy, and Marcus felt a twinge of envy. These two had dedicated themselves to one another, trusted their lives with one other. Would he ever be able to do that? Would he ever allow himself to play such an irrevocable role in someone's life?

Candie untangled her hand from Mickey's then waved. "Hey, Marcus. Hey, Daisy."

"Daisy fell out of bed again," Jill announced as she leaned a hip against a bookcase full of old encyclopedias.

There was a collective groan, a wince, and some "not agains" as they all exchanged easy greetings. It was so casual, Marcus felt as though he'd been here a dozen Sundays already. No one treated him like a visiting dignitary. No one rushed forward to claim his attention before someone else whisked him off. No one seemed to care about Marcus Van Buren, President and CEO of VB Enterprises. They only wanted to know about Marc and how he was doing.

Photos of children at various ages, all with the same blue backdrop, covered the paneled wall above a faded plaid couch. He found Daisy immediately. All the way from the little girl with missing teeth and braids to the beautiful young lady whose eyes still glittered with the promise of the future. A young lady, he'd wager, who'd yet to make an enemy of Missy Polanski.

"Daisy, Danielle won't get out of the bathroom!"

Daisy dropped her wallet on top of the TV. "Did you give her five minutes, Sean?"

Sean hopped from one leg to the other. "No, but—"

"You know the rule," she said, ruffling his tawny hair.

"Whoever's in the bathroom gets five minutes. After that, you can make a fuss."

"But, Daisy, I really have to *go-o-o*. No fooling this time."

"Seven people and only one bathroom?" Marcus asked in pure wonderment.

Mickey grinned. "Let's just say I'm glad I moved out before Jill hit her teens."

Jill grabbed a pillow from the couch and threw it at Mickey's head. "At least I don't forget to flush the toilet."

This is what a real family is like, Marcus thought to himself. In your face, in your business, in your life. His mother had groomed him from birth like a child inheriting a throne. In a sense, of course, he was—following his father's and his grandfather's steps into the controlling seat of VB Enterprises. But she'd never let him be a kid, and he remembered her shrieks when he'd pedaled his bike down the main hall, whooping like a banshee at the top of his lungs so their house didn't seem so empty.

"Wish me luck," Daisy said before she left him to knock on the narrow bathroom door. "Danielle, open up. Sean really has to go."

"I'm not talking to you," came the muffled reply.

"Don't make me get a hanger and jimmy this door open. You know I can do it. Besides Marcus is here and—"

The door flew open. "Marcus!" She sailed past Daisy. "Thank you for running my lines with me yesterday. I was so relaxed. Even Jason managed not to be an embarrassment."

Sean ran into the bathroom and slammed the door.

Daisy winced but remained strong as she moved next to her sister. "Danielle, I want to explain about yesterday."

Danielle sniffed. "I know Marcus didn't keep you late to work, Daisy. No matter what he says to stick up for you. He wouldn't do that."

Marcus' eyes widened.

"No, he didn't," Daisy said, "and it might not make up for it, but I'm going to tell you the truth. I hope you'll understand."

The teenager waited, arms crossed.

"Jonas. The ghosts. They're at Laguna Vista. They're real,

and I found them right before your play. I was so stunned that I forgot everything else."

Jill and Danielle squealed at the same time. "We knew it!"

Mickey shook his head and reached for his wallet. "I should've known Daisy's instincts would be dead on." He raised his hand to Marcus. "Pardon the expression." He doled out a five-dollar bill to each girl. "Swindlers," he muttered.

Danielle wrapped her arms around Daisy. "If you miss next Saturday's performance, I'll kill you."

Daisy's face radiated pure happiness. Marcus smiled. He'd bet the yacht she had no idea how beautiful she was.

Then it hit him. No one was the least bit phased by Daisy's announcement. Mickey continued to watch the game. Candie was scanning a fashion magazine. The two teenagers performed a victory dance, waving their newly won booty around the living room.

His mother would've had a heart attack. Or at least claim to be having one.

A fire alarm suddenly shrilled through the house, followed by a plume of smoke from the kitchen.

Daisy bolted toward the smoke.

Marcus was hot on her heels.

Grim-faced and with tears in her eyes, Angie Malone stared down at the blackened, smoking steaks on the counter.

"Are you all right?" Daisy yelled over the piercing wail of the alarm. "What happened?"

Marcus opened the kitchen door to let out the smoke.

Jill scrambled onto a chair and plucked the battery from the alarm.

Angie wiped her hands on her apron. "I guess I forgot the time. I left the steaks in too long. I don't know..."

The panic on Daisy's face settled into concern. "You never overcook anything, Mom. What's wrong?"

"Nothing...I...I'm just tired." She surveyed the charcoal briquettes through bleary eyes. "Look at this mess," she said, voice quivering, hands wringing.

Was this the same feisty woman Marcus had met only

yesterday? Though he was concerned, he now understood where Daisy had inherited her unpredictable nature. Mr. Malone couldn't be too bad a guy, he thought. He'd survived a house full of Malone women all these years.

Daisy wrapped her arm around her mother's shoulder. "Mom, don't worry about the steaks. We'll order pizza. No big deal."

"Everything is such a mess," she whispered, looking about the kitchen as if it were all suddenly overwhelming. Then her gaze landed on Daisy. She gasped and cupped her eldest daughter's chin. With a gentle thumb, she skimmed the now infamous shiner. "You really have to stop falling out of bed, Daisy."

"I know," Daisy said, shrugging off her concern. "Now stop fussing over me, and let me fuss over you for once. I want you to lie down for awhile. It's been a tough week." Daisy, her face etched with worry, led her mother from the kitchen.

Angie didn't fight it. Something Marcus knew to be uncharacteristic. Like mother, like daughter. Two women ready to take on the world, yet, since yesterday, both had experienced some sort of emotional breakdown. What was going on? And why did he feel the insane urge to wrap Daisy in his arms and steal her away from everything?

Marcus walked back into the dining room and sat down. Sean lay sprawled out on the living room floor watching some sort of superhero cartoon, oblivious as he now controlled the abandoned TV.

Jill strutted into the dining room and flopped into the chair next to his.

"Just because you have money doesn't mean you're not a pervert." Her voice carried little vehemence this time. Her statement seemed more like the disgusted snort of a lion that'd been forced to give up the hunt.

"So, when do you graduate?" he asked, paving the way to civility.

"June. Thank God."

"Going to college?"

She picked at one of the fake yellow flowers decorating the fully set table. "I was accepted to Princeton."

She must've seen the surprise on his face because she narrowed her catlike eyes at him. "What? Just because I'm beautiful I can't have a brain? You men are all the same," she muttered. "Pigs."

"That wasn't why . . ." but then he stopped because the real reason for his surprise would be just as insulting, and embarrassingly priggish. From what Rufus had told him of the Malone's financial state, he was surprised they could afford such an expensive education. But they were a tight-knit clan who seemed to do anything for each other. With a twinge of envy and at the same time warmth, he realized that, somehow, the Malones would manage to send their smart-as-a-whip, lethal-as-a-two-ton-mega-bomb daughter to Princeton. "My old roommate is a history professor at Princeton. I bet he'd be delighted to give you a personal tour. I think he knows every dusty corner and mildewed book on campus."

She lowered her eyes. "That's really nice of you, Marcus, but I'll have to take a rain check on that. I'm going to work for a few years first. You know, get a taste of reality."

Candie Malone strolled in and dropped herself into a chair with a sigh. "It's all my fault."

"What's all your fault, Doll Face?" Mickey followed her and planted a kiss on the top of her head.

Candie blanched. "I'd promised to watch my sister's kids today, but something came up and I couldn't. So I asked your mom if she'd babysit. I should've known it would be too much with all that's going on."

Mickey cocked his head. "Nonsense. Mom loves those kids." He snatched a celery stick and some dip from a platter. "Where'd ya go?"

Candie ducked her head, and Marcus knew she was struggling. "I had some things to do. You know, the usual."

Sean rolled over. "She got a job."

"Sean, you sneaky little eavesdropper!" Jill leaped from her chair. "You're gonna get it!"

He jumped up and ran behind a recliner. "Mom!"

"She can't save you now." Jill chased him around the living room and out the front door.

"A job?" Mickey asked.

Candie lifted her chin. "We need the money. I'm able, and since you wouldn't listen to me..."

Mickey rose from his chair. "You lied to me."

"I thought it was best for the family. Mickey, I'd never hurt you, honey."

"If you went back to stripping, I swear to God—"

She jumped up, knocking into Marcus in the process. He reached out to steady her, amazed to find her shaking. Her face flushed with anger as she pinned Mickey with narrowed eyes. "You're still ashamed of me. I knew it!"

"Do you think I want the guys from the bar to see my wife naked? Are you insane?"

"Fine. I don't want to be around anyone who's ashamed of me. I'm going home." She turned on her heel and stalked out of the house.

Mickey scratched his forehead. "What the hell just happened?"

"Is her last name Malone?" Marcus said, still digesting the fact that Candie—sweet, mild-mannered Candie—had once been a stripper.

"Only by marriage, but I guess it's contagious. We're an ornery bunch." Daisy's brother sighed. "Dammit, I gotta go get her."

"Good luck."

Mickey raced out the door.

The phone rang, and Danielle blew through to the kitchen to answer it.

Marcus sat alone in the Malone dining room. He checked his watch. Fifteen minutes. They'd been here a total of fifteen minutes. He closed his eyes and leaned his head back on the chair. He heard Sean yelp from outside. He heard Danielle's voice rambling on the phone.

He wished Daisy would come back. He missed her.

Then Candie's words sailed through his mind. *We need the money. I thought it was best for the family.*

Green, gullible, and broke, Rufus had said on the chopper ride from Manhattan to Atlantic City. *Daisy Malone needs your money.* But Marcus hadn't wanted to know the specifics. He hadn't wanted to get involved in someone else's life. He hadn't wanted to feel.

He cracked open his eyes. Daisy walked toward him, brows furrowed, sweater twisted in her hand.

He felt.

He suddenly wanted to know everything. What had *she* been like as a child? What did *she* do for fun? Why was her pop hiding from his family? Just how far in debt were they? The questions shot through his mind in rapid fire.

How could *he* help?

That one ground things to a screeching halt. He waited for terror to come chase away the idea, but it planted itself right there in his mind, like a heavy piece of furniture no one could move.

Daisy's troubled gaze took in the field of empty plates. Her lip trembled, but she breathed deep, settling herself.

She was a fighter.

She'd never ask for his help. Pride ran through her as thick as her ancestors' brogue. It was the first thing he'd noticed about her. Well, the first thing right after her cute body. One call, and he could fix her problems forever, monetarily at least. She'd hate that. She'd accuse him of charity. But he hated watching that crease in her forehead deepening by the second.

She fiddled with a paper napkin. "I'm sorry, Marcus. This wasn't quite what I meant when I said you'd never had a dinner like this."

He rubbed her arm and grinned. "We didn't exactly make it to dinner."

She searched his eyes. A grin touched her own lips. "No. We didn't, did we?"

"Tell you what," he said, recalling her cocky sportsmanship at the bar. "I'll give you a do-over."

Her eyes brightened. "Oh, really."

He shrugged. "It's only fair. I mean, after the way you led me into that dart game like a lamb to slaughter..."

She jumped up from the chair. "Danielle, get off the phone!"

"What are you—" Before he could finish, she pulled him up by his tie and proceeded to kiss every thought but one right out of his head.

She pulled back, her blue eyes hot as a tropical sky. "I'm ordering the family a pizza, then we're getting the hell out of here."

Seventeen

Daisy shoved the transmission into park. "*Now* can you tell me why we're here?"

Marcus leaned over, cut the engine, and slanted his mouth over hers, sending a fresh blast of heat down her already overheated body. She clutched his strong shoulders, more than ready to continue where they'd left off the night before. Parking lot or not.

He broke the kiss. "It's a date," he said, voice thick.

Her head spun with a curious fog. "What is?"

He gave her a lopsided grin. She swore she saw affection in his eyes. "Here. Now. Though I admit, we are kind of working backwards."

The breath of his words hit her like a heat-heavy wind blowing off an inferno. Blowing away the fog. Just plain blowing her away. Images of the previous night kicked up in her mind. His tongue sliding oh-so-slowly down her arm. His capable hands on her backside, grinding his hips against hers. His lingering heat a red-orange sun dipping into the horizon, a promise of another scorcher to come. She wrapped her arms around his neck, her voice scorched earth. "You don't have to do this."

"You took me home to meet your parents," he said, kissing the tip of her nose. "Sort of. You can't expect me, in all good conscience, to take you home and make love to you when we've never even been on a date."

Yes. Yes, I can. "Doesn't last night count?" she said, knowing she sounded desperate and not caring. "You know, drinks? Darts?"

Limo.

His eyes darkened. Dare she hope he felt the same flames threatening to burn him as well?

He traced his finger over her lips, cool, calm. "Nope."

She pulled away in frustration and gripped the steering wheel. God, what was happening to her? She felt like a horny teenager trying to coerce a prom date into the backseat. "I'm not drunk tonight."

He smiled. "I know."

She clung to the last shred of her self-composure. "How the hell do you do it?" she demanded.

He casually peered out the windshield to the colorful, whirling amusement rides cramming the Steel Pier. "Do what?"

"Stay so cool and calm when I've got a death grip on my steering wheel, fighting not to rip your clothes off."

He turned and flashed his lady-killer smile. Ooof. Right in the gut. Fate was cruel. Cruel. Cruel. Cruel.

"Sweetheart, I'm so hard for you right now I'm afraid I'm going to hurt myself."

Sparks cooked and snapped in his eyes. She searched for her voice. "So why are we here?"

"Because neither of us can think straight. When we make love, we're both going to know exactly what we're getting into."

"And what is that?"

His dark eyes melted into hers. "I have no idea."

She swallowed hard. "You don't have to do this, Marcus. I know you don't like emotional entanglements. You told me so yourself last night. I know you'll leave when Laguna Vista is settled, but I want you anyway, even if just for tonight."

He grabbed her hand, held her eyes captive. "I'm not playing games, Daisy, I swear. This has been the best and worst weekend of my life. You're beautiful, wonderful, and keep me on my toes. I can't honestly say what's going to happen tomorrow or the next day because I don't know. But I like you, I really do, and I'm going to treat you like anybody I like. With respect."

Her jaw worked, but nothing came out.

He kissed her on the nose again then opened his door. "Now get out. The sooner we start this date, the sooner we," he winked at her, "you know."

He slammed the door. His scent lingered in the dark, stuffy air. Right along with the distinct remnants of charred passion. She watched him walk around the front of the van and wondered how this man, in three short days, had turned her world upside down. She hadn't lied. She wanted to spend the night with him, and she'd never guilt him to make him stay. But, as always, the curse of the sensitive reared its ugly head. She'd felt more than just loneliness, guilt, and sadness in his heart. She'd felt his goodness, his compassion, his warmth. She'd felt it, and somehow it had slipped into her own heart when she wasn't looking. But no matter how foolish she knew it to be, she couldn't stop it anymore than she'd be able to stop the devastating loneliness when he left her for good.

He opened her door and took her hand, purposely standing close so she'd have to slide down his hard body. Her cheeks burned. "Tease."

He smiled innocently as he locked her door. Taking her hand, he led her toward the Atlantic City boardwalk. The clear night sky stretched into forever, the far-flung stars battling the halo of casino lights for top billing. As they climbed the steps, the ocean breeze lifted her hair and cooled her skin. Thank God for small favors.

"I'm sorry about dinner—"

He held up his hand. "Tonight it's just you and me. Getting to know each other. No one else exists for the rest of the night."

"All right," she agreed, not having much more to lose.

Marcus caused quite the stir as they strolled down the planked avenue. Some women did quick double takes. Others stared him down hoping, to get his attention. Some dropped their jaws then looked away, faces red. She could relate to that one. Every time she looked at him she remembered him without his shirt. She smiled as she watched the phenomenon unfold around her, Marcus completely oblivious, or pretending to be, as he was good at. She pressed herself closer to him. He was hers, for tonight at least, and she wanted everyone to know it.

The best thing of all, however, was watching him soak in the Atlantic City nightlife. The flashing rides, the noisy games, the seedy people. Something in her stomach fluttered as the wealthy, sophisticated Marcus Van Buren stared at corn dogs and stuffed pandas in pure delight.

Right in front of the public eye for all to see.

"You've never been here before, have you?" she said.

"No. My mother rarely let me out of New York when I was a kid, unless it was out of the country. Now I'm lucky if I can snatch a few days a year to relax on my yacht." He stopped short and rolled his eyes. "That sounded terrible, didn't it? Poor, little rich boy. I'll understand if you want to throw up."

She swiped a lock of midnight hair from his forehead. "Did you always want to be a suit? I mean, didn't you have any other dreams besides shuffling paper and working deals?"

He stared up into the night sky. "I wanted to be a fireman."

How apropos, she thought, still willing the night air to cool her skin. "Every boy wants to be a fireman. I'm talking about something you craved. Something that excited you, haunted you deep in your sleep."

He cocked his head. "How do you know I didn't want to be a fireman?"

"It's just that..." She waved her hand. "Never mind. It's stupid. You'll think me even more weird."

"Impossible," he said, pulling her into his arms, eyes glittering.

"Smart ass," she muttered.

"I'm learning from the best." He kissed her thoroughly, right smack in the middle of the boardwalk. "Now tell me."

"What?" she asked breathlessly, the stars beyond him spinning.

Looking satisfied, he stepped back, allowing the breeze to wash over them. "You were going to tell me something stupid."

"Oh, right. Well, yesterday morning in your bed, while I was kissing you, I saw some things."

He cocked a jaunty brow.

She rolled her eyes. "A racehorse and an antique car?"

He stiffened. He said nothing as he suddenly pulled her over to a concession stand, bought a caramel apple, and stuck it between her fingers.

"Marcus?"

He walked away with his hands in his pockets.

She trotted to catch up to him. "What? What is it?"

"You're incredible," he said, his gaze peering out into the black ocean.

The hair on her arms stood. She'd never been able to read anyone's thoughts before. She'd only been able to channel emotions, never dreams or memories or thoughts. Her connection with Marcus was stronger than any she'd ever experienced, even with Jonas. "I take it I was close?"

He didn't look at her, just continued with that faraway look, his voice low and even. "For as long as I can remember, I've dreamed of settling down on a horse farm. Waking up to a misty dawn, putting my latest contender through her paces, one day watching her race at Churchill Downs."

A horse trainer. Marcus Van Buren wanted to be a horse trainer. Nervous, she took a bite of her apple and instantly regretted it as the sticky coating stuck in her teeth. "And the car?" she ventured, wondering what this startling connection meant.

They stopped at a water-gun booth, and Marcus laid a bill on the counter. The suspense was killing her, but maybe this new second sight was too much for him. It was disconcerting enough for her. She probably shouldn't have mentioned it. Now she'd probably ruined the entire night.

The gruff game runner snatched up the money. "Whenever you're ready," he barked. Daisy tossed the apple into the garbage, happy to be rid of the messy treat that should definitely be on the 'food-not-to-eat-on-a-date' list. She began to lick her fingers, but when she looked up, Marcus' intense gaze nearly turned her to dust. He eased toward her, took her fingers and, one by one, suckled the sweet remains. She grew lightheaded, her knees nearly buckling.

The game runner cleared his throat. "Any time you people

are ready."

"My other dream," Marcus murmured, "my late-at-night, never-told-a-soul dream, has been to make love on the soft, velvet backseat of my vintage Rolls Royce. There's something about a plush interior and a naked woman." He let go of her fingers. "Ready?"

She swallowed. "Yes."

She didn't move.

He smiled. "The game."

She shook her head. "Right."

They each picked up a heavy pistol, some sort of muted metal painted black and attached to a hose.

"Spray the target," the game runner droned, his bored eyes staring off into the distance. "First one to pop their balloon wins."

Another game she'd grown up on. No way Marcus had ever played a game like this. She could beat him with her eyes closed. But she wouldn't. She wanted to be conquered.

The bell rang. They were off.

Marcus had one eye squinted, looking like the Dirty Harry of water balloons. She grinned, something she couldn't seem to stop doing, and concentrated on her target. She hit it dead on, then let her aim stray a little, go back, stray a little.

Pop!

Marcus set his gun on the counter and traced her ear with his tongue.

Pop!

"Thanks for letting me win, kid."

She swallowed. "My pleasure."

He claimed her hand again, and they walked along in silence. Normally she would've felt compelled to talk and fill the void. But there was no void. No chasm to bridge. Hand in hand, she felt everything she needed to know. Affection, happiness, anticipation. She raised her face to the ocean breeze. If nothing else, she'd always have this night.

Out of nowhere, a body swooped down over their heads, only to be yanked back as if trying to escape Heaven's clutches. Some sort of bungee ride.

"I would pee my pants if I had to do that," she said, watching the flying body with a dubious eye.

Marcus eyed the height of the drop tower. "I would do more than that."

She turned to him. "What's the most embarrassing thing that's ever happened to you?"

He quirked a grin. "You don't want to know."

She tugged his arm. "Yes, I do. Come on. We're supposed to be getting to know each other."

He looked down at her. "All right. We were driving to Nantucket once when I was twelve. I had to go to the bathroom, bad, and was making my mother crazy. She refused to stop at a fast-food restaurant or a gas station. God forbid. Finally I squirmed and whined and made her so miserable that she forced the driver to pull over at a gas-n-grocery place. I got the key from the attendant and ran into the bathroom. I'm finally relieving myself, ecstatic after drinking a gallon of soda. Suddenly the door swings wide open. Somehow I forgot to lock it."

Daisy grinned up at him. "That's not so bad. Your back was probably turned to the guy."

"I was so stunned when the *woman* walked in that I turned all the way around with my you-know-what in my hand. She sized it up for a second and said, 'Don't worry kid, it'll grow.' I thought I was going to die. My mother was shocked when I didn't talk through the whole state of Connecticut."

Daisy pressed her mouth against his. Something about him made her completely wanton. "So did it?"

"Did it what?"

"Grow?"

He chuckled deep in his throat. "You'll just have to wait and see," he said. "What about you?"

She recalled her last day of high school, but shook it off. "I was in seventh grade. I had a crush on Mitchell Pierce. Only my close friends knew that whenever I saw him I walked into things."

He kissed the bruised skin around her eye. "I couldn't hope that this shiner has anything to do with me, could I?"

"Maybe. If you hadn't looked like you were going to eat me up while I did the salt and the lime, I wouldn't have been forced to drink so many."

He smiled, self-satisfied. "Good answer. Go on."

"I was walking down the middle of the cafeteria, lunch tray loaded with Wednesday lasagna, when he walked past and said 'Hi.' I was so befuddled, I walked right into the principal. Lasagna all over his favorite suit."

He threw his head back and laughed. "Doesn't something like that usually make you a star for a day?"

"Not when everyone saw me staring at Mitchell like a lovesick puppy." *Exactly how I'm looking at you.* "It was hell for months."

He cupped her chin and kissed her. When he pulled away, he asked, "So what did he do?"

"Who?"

Marcus smiled big and pulled her on. He insisted on buying her cotton candy so he could lick her fingers some more. Both of their lips turned pink. "Good thing you advised me against the blue," he said.

He dragged her on ride after ride. The Tilt-A-Whirl. The Himalayan. He couldn't seem to get enough. As they claimed their car for the Scrambler, she said, "I think you're only doing this as an excuse to squish me."

His eyes danced. "You're right." But he must have been getting the hang of the rides, because this time he sat in the squish seat and clutched her tight in his arms. She enjoyed it so much, she insisted they go around again.

As they made their rounds from ride to ride, game to game, food cart to food cart, Marcus seemed to lose years. He looked like a kid who'd been locked away all of his life and then suddenly set free in an amusement park, literally. His excitement was infectious, and he seemed to be savoring every minute, eating it alive.

As they waited in line for the Octopus, the guy operating the ride had his music pumping so loudly she thought it might beat a hole through her chest. She didn't recognize the song nor did she care. She leaned back against Marcus and watched the people pass by. Again they didn't speak. Their bodies said it all. Restraint wearing thin. Desire boiling beneath the surface. And always that little missing part of him, the lost piece of the jigsaw puzzle, like the hole in the blue sky of a landscape or a crater in the middle of a flower-draped meadow. That missing piece that kept him from getting too close to anybody. That missing piece that undoubtedly broke his engagement and would eventually take him from her as well.

As she contemplated how a man like Marcus ended up engaged in the first place, the latest song by Heart Valve came blaring through the speakers. She knew this song, and without warning, Marcus grabbed her hand and sent her twisting away from him like an unfurled sail. "What..." He brought her back to his chest, and then she was sailing again.

He was dancing with her. In the middle of a ride. On line for the Octopus. Was this the same man who'd been so concerned about drawing unwanted attention to himself, specifically the unwanted attention of an overzealous reporter? He hadn't looked over his shoulder once tonight. Now this.

When she was reeled back into his hard chest, he sang to her. "You make me breathe a little heavy....," then he growled along with the lead singer and planted a wet one on her lips.

Before she knew it she was giggling and following his lead. He was an excellent dancer, and the crowd had moved back to give them room. Howls and whistles flew from all directions.

He coiled her back into his arms. "You know I want you," he crooned. After five more spins, her hair slipped from its ponytail. He plucked the band from her hair and tossed it far into the crowd.

When the song ended, he dipped her low and kissed her as if posing for an old-time post card. Everyone cheered. She tried to catch her breath. Her senses reeled. She'd never danced like that in her life.

She placed her hand on his arm. "I'm too dizzy for the ride," she breathed. "I need to sit or walk or something."

He maneuvered her through the crowd at a sedate pace. The spinning in her head began to slow. "Scratch what I said before. I now have a new most embarrassing moment." She looked up at him. "When did you learn to dance like that?"

"About fourteen. My mother was grooming me for the deb parties. She's very ambitious where I'm concerned. She figured her one son should expect only the wealthiest daughter on his arm. A strategic alliance. Groomed and prepped for stud service."

"Yikes," she said, "and I thought my dad was harsh because he wouldn't let me stay home from Girl Scouts to watch *Dukes of Hazzard*."

He cocked his head.

"Never mind. Sounds like your mother kept a pretty tight leash on you."

"You could say she was overprotective. Still is."

She stopped and looked at him earnestly. "What would she say if she knew you were here with me tonight?"

"She'd fake a heart attack."

Her jaw dropped. "You're not serious."

He grinned. "Serious as a heart attack."

"I can't believe we just danced in front of all those people. You're wild, Marcus Van Buren." She kissed him, unable to get enough, their hands moving more easily and free as the night progressed.

It struck her then that he was trying very hard to impress her. But why? Why did it seem like he was trying to cram their relationship into one night? To make himself feel better when he had to leave? Feel less guilty? She'd told him he didn't need to worry about that. As the night wore on, however, she knew the truth. She would be crushed when he left, but she'd never let him know it.

"So I guess you'd say I'm sort of unpredictable? A fun date, even?"

"Definitely," she said. "Nothing like the stuffy creep they make you out to be in the rags."

She cringed at the reference as soon as she said it. Marcus didn't flinch. In fact, he seemed pleased with her answer. So much so, he pressed her into the side of a ticket booth to show her just how much. He pulled away, his breathing hard, his face close. "I don't know what it is, Daisy. You bring out the Van Buren side of me."

Her interest piqued. "What Van Buren side? Tell me something you've done."

"I got a tattoo when I was sixteen. The deb parties were in full swing, and my mother was making me put those dance lessons to use. It drove me crazy, so I went to the seediest joint I could find, popped a cigarette in my mouth, yanked down my pants, got a tattoo right above my ass and showed my mother the pictures to prove it. She went into her usual state of cardiac arrest."

She laughed. "Maybe it's a good thing you've got a Van Buren side. No offense."

"My mother's been through a lot," he said, the crease in his forehead threatening to make an appearance. "Her husband was just like his father. Regis was the spitting image of Jonas in every way. He pulled the same tired tricks, and she turned bitter, determined for me not to end up that way. The urge to be wild was always in me, but I've fought it for as long as I can remember. I don't want people to suffer because of me, Daisy."

She touched his face. "You would never purposely hurt anyone."

He looked into her eyes. "No. Not on purpose."

She knew exactly what he meant. He didn't know where this relationship was going any more than she did, but they were going to make love. They both knew that.

"It's okay, Marcus. I know."

His eyes darkened. "You're too good to be true," he whispered, then kissed her.

"No, I'm not," she rasped, but the words were lost as their hands buried themselves in each other's hair, pockets, anywhere within reach. It wasn't until the ticket taker tried to get out of her door that they finally broke apart.

"Come on," he said, eyes swirling with desire. Ten steps later, he stopped in front of the Skyride. He looked wistfully up at the dark, cozy cars cruising twenty-feet above the beach. His shoulders sagged, and he turned to her, disappointed.

"Dammit."

"What's the matter?"

"I've got a thing about heights."

She rubbed his arm. "It's okay. I think I've had all the rides I can take for tonight." She glanced down and cleared her throat. "We could go back to my condo."

"I thought you lived with your parents."

"Not for a few years now. Though I have to admit, I do spend most of my time there."

"Daisy, we don't have to—"

She touched her fingers to his lips. "I want to see your tattoo."

***

Daisy slid Marcus' tie from around his neck and let it drop to her kitchen floor.

He pressed her back against the wall, his hands possessive at her hips, his thumbs strumming the exposed skin at her waist. Pale white squares splashed across his face from the streetlight outside the window. "Any emergency keys you want to warn me about?" he asked, his warm breath fanning her cheeks.

She freed the tiny white button at his throat. Ducking her lips inside his collar, she tasted his skin. "Everyone has a key to my condo," she murmured, losing herself in his scent. His pulse raced beneath her lips, the blood rushing hot with desire for her. Its intensity stole her breath. "Marcus..."

He raked his hands through her hair. "I know, Daisy," he breathed, "I know." He lifted her face and traced his tongue along her lips as though memorizing every curve, his fingers clasping her head as though something might tear them apart at any moment.

She felt like the moon poised on the edge of night, waiting to rise, waiting to shine high in the heavens, waiting for Marcus to take her there. She clutched the smooth cotton of his shirt, a ridiculously flimsy dressing when compared to the heavily muscled chest beneath. She suddenly imagined him draped in chain mail, powerful thighs clenched against his war horse, his heart exploding with honor, his warrior body straining for the rigor ahead. It seemed almost criminal for a man like Marcus to be decorated in a common suit and tie. She spread her fingers over the material, saturated with heat. He was too magnificent for mere cotton and thread.

The longer she touched him, the more she felt it. The painful echoes of some lost misery, buried like an ancient tomb. The dark fear that lurked, guarding some secret part of him, even as every molecule in his body hurtled in her direction. That missing piece that would forever trip up his life, no matter his confidence that nothing was wrong.

A rush of tenderness spread through her. She touched his cheek, delectably rough from probably the first shave he'd skipped in years.

He clasped her fingertips and raised them to his lips. "So sweet," he whispered then leaned down to kiss her slowly, thoroughly. "You taste good, too." He trailed his lips to her throat.

She let her head fall back, feeling wanton and wonderful and never wanting it to end. Groaning, she ran her hands over his shoulders and pushed his jacket down his arms. "I want to see you."

He shuddered beneath her touch. "Daisy..." He slipped his hands beneath her sweater, his long fingers nearly spanning her rib cage as he caressed the skin just below her breasts. "You're so beautiful," he whispered in her ear, his breath hot, the hairs on her neck tingling.

Her knees began to give. She started to sink down the wall. Good, she thought through her crimson haze, another inch and those glorious hands would be on her breasts. Closer, closer...

He pulled back.

She moaned.

He titled up her chin. "Open your eyes, sweetheart."

No. No. She didn't want to talk anymore. Enough talking. She wanted him to touch her. On her breasts. Her thighs. Everywhere.

"Daisy."

She moaned again but opened her eyes.

His eyes burned into hers. "You know who I am, don't you?" he asked, his voice broken with breath and desire.

Her mind moved like an ant through hot tar. "What?"

"You know I'm not Jonas?"

She splayed her fingers through his hair, delighting in the contrast of her pale skin buried in those raven tufts. God, he was beautiful. His lips moist from her mouth. His dark eyes burning with intensity. He took her breath away.

As she felt the quiet beseeching within him, any lingering doubt about Marcus Van Buren's integrity disintegrated. Something fluttered in her heart. "That's why I brought us here. I don't want any confusion. I want to be sure that what I'm feeling is..." She cut herself off. *What was she saying?*

"And just what are you feeling?" he murmured as he leaned back into her, nibbling on her ear and lifting her sweater higher.

She gasped as his hand slipped under her satin bra to gently cup her breast. "More than I should," she admitted, her voice a croak.

His mouth claimed hers once again, shooting her senses into the stratosphere to whirl among the stars. She wanted his mouth all over her. Hot. Possessive. She wanted to know what it felt like to be loved by Marcus Van Buren.

Letting her hand glide down to the front of his slacks, she touched the hard and heavy evidence of his desire. He stiffened, something low and guttural rumbling in his throat.

"Daisy..."

"You have too many clothes on," she breathed, the air between them stifling. She fumbled with the tiny buttons of his shirt, her fingers clumsy and eager. She couldn't see clearly, her head spinning, spinning...unable to stand it any longer, she tore apart the sides of his shirt, scattering buttons like b-b's across the floor. "Sorry."

His labored breath fluttered her hair. "No problem."

Easing the shirt over his biceps and down his forearms, she sighed, her knees weakening. She leaned forward and pressed her lips to one hard pectoral, her tongue tasting the place she'd only dreamed of. "You're the most beautiful man I've ever seen," she whispered against his burning skin. "Inside and out."

His grip on her waist tightened. "That mouth of yours is nothing but trouble," he said, his voice sounding as though it had been raked over hot coals. He yanked her flush against him, kissed her nearly breathless, then pulled her sweater over her head and tossed it into the darkness. Eyes burrowing into hers, his fingers caught the straps of her bra and guided them down her arms. "Now you're going to pay," he vowed softly.

Shivering under his potent gaze, she felt his fingers flick open the front clasp of her bra and the cups fall away, catching on the tips of her nipples. She had to concentrate on breathing as his thumbs caressed the soft edges of her breasts, working their way under the material to stroke the most sensitive flesh. She cried out as pleasure pierced through her, so exquisite to be almost painful, but not quite.

She reached for his belt, needing to feel his torment as much as her own. He sucked in his breath. "Sweetheart, if you touch me there again, this'll be over before it starts."

His deep, dark eyes, so earnest, so honest, so hot. She felt herself drawn deeper and deeper into some kind of out-of-control vortex, spinning and spinning. Her mind and body tumbling through space.

He dropped to his knees. *Oh, God.* She clutched fistfuls of his hair as his tongue flicked over her hard nipple, sending her back arching over the counter. "Marcus...Marcus..." She cried his name over and over as he tasted, suckled, dangled her over the edge of endurance. Gripping the countertop, she pleaded, "I can't take much more of this."

He unbuckled her belt and whipped it from the loops of her jeans. It clattered somewhere across the floor.

"That's not fair," she said, somehow managing to speak. She wanted to enjoy his writhing and squirming as much as he did hers. With a finger under his chin, she guided him to stand. Her heart thumped against her chest as she tugged the leather belt from around his waist and tossed it into the dark. Something untamed flickered in his eyes, something that warned her his chivalrous breeding was about to be tossed off like an old coat. Quickly undoing the button of his slacks, she rose to the challenge, her hand lingering over his zipper, caressing it, tugging it down a bit, then back up, and down again. A thrilling sense of danger hovered about him as he watched her with predatory eyes.

Her breath came fast and hard. She wanted him to lose control. She wanted to experience Marcus Van Buren in unleashed glory...but not on the cold linoleum of her kitchen floor. Not for the first time anyway. Despite her earlier convictions, this meant more to her than she'd ever imagined.

Sensing her hesitation, he touched her cheek. "Are you sure about this, sweetheart?"

A giant lump formed in her throat. Somehow, this man—this masculine, beautiful, too-good-to-be-true man—always thought of her needs first. His voice, so gentle, so concerned, as though soothing a frightened animal. Admittedly, she was frightened for her heart, her tender heart with the scars of a punching bag. And she did feel like an animal, wild and crazed with a passion she'd never known. But she wasn't fragile in that delicate, china doll sort of way, and she knew her mind. She knew what she wanted. She wanted Marcus. No matter the circumstances. Right now, in her mind, in her life, he was the most wonderful man in the world.

She smiled through her lover's haze before kissing him softly. "Take me to bed."

He hesitated, and she pointed. "That way."

He swept her off her feet and carried her to the bedroom, kissing her, nibbling her lips, and in those moments, Marcus Van Buren did something no other man had. He made her feel like a woman. Treasured and handled with care. Dangerous and seductive.

He set her down on the bed, her double mattress sagging under his weight as he followed.

"I just want you to know," she managed, as Marcus nipped a playful trail to the hollow of her throat, "that I don't do this every day."

"I know."

The warm skin of his chest brushing against her bare breasts almost stalled her thoughts. "I mean, I'm not accustomed to inviting near strangers into my condo, let alone my bed."

"I know."

She nearly shot off that bed when his mouth moved lower to claim her nipple. The delicious torture landed her somewhere between heaven and hell. His tongue circled, hot and moist...she was losing herself, her body no longer belonging to her...

Headlights splashed across her ceiling as someone pulled into the parking lot. Her stomach dropped, and just as she was about to jump up and cover herself, she stopped. Her heart pounded against her ribs. She wasn't a teenager anymore. This wasn't the backseat of a car.

This wasn't a mistake.

Lust and shame twisted into a single ugly vine. She felt it wrapping around her vulnerable heart. Felt it squeezing. Strangling. "I'm not a slut."

Her croaked words stopped him cold. She closed her eyes and groaned. What had she done? She hadn't meant to say that aloud. Hadn't meant to spoil the moment with a past long dead. Dammit! She hadn't seen hide nor hair of Brad Worthington in ten years, and yet she was still letting him ruin her life. She was pathetic.

Marcus rolled off her and onto his side.

This is it, she thought. He'll either accuse me of being a tease, or worse, frigid. She braced herself. It was even worse. He said, "I know."

She opened her eyes.

Propped up on one elbow, Marcus was studying her with an expression that obliterated years of shame and regret. He looked at her as though she were an innocent. A lamb. A virginal goodie-two-shoes armed with more enthusiasm than experience. She felt like Doris Day in *Pillow Talk*. Flattered and saddened at the same time, tears welled in her eyes. If he only knew.

He smoothed his hand over her cheek and wiped away a tear with his thumb. "You're not a one-night-stand kind of girl, Daisy. I know. I've always known. Considering I'm here, in your condo, in your bed, I should be scared as hell right about now." He smiled down at her. "Apparently I'm not in my right mind."

Apparently. An hour ago he wasn't sure where this relationship was headed. Now he was ready to commit? Poor Marcus. He was getting so wrapped up in his weekend adventure that he was starting to mistake fiction for reality. And poor Daisy, once again, when he came to his senses and took off for New York like a bat out of hell. She had to nip this "thing" in the bud before it nipped her. "Don't confuse lust with...well, just don't confuse it. I don't want any promises."

Relief and tension mixed when he didn't pull away as expected. Instead he stroked the stray hairs from her face, his eyes sympathetic and making her feel like a babbling idiot. "What are you so scared of, Daisy?" he whispered, as though afraid if he spoke too loudly, she might bolt.

She swallowed. "It's just happening so fast."

His fingers smoothed her furrowed brow. "We can slow down. Say the word and it's done."

She looked past his face, not really seeing, but unable to stand the tenderness softening his features. She didn't want to slow down. She wanted him. She wanted...she wanted...her mind stuck. Just what did she want?

"It's not as complicated as you think," he said.

"Isn't it, though?" Marcus Van Buren, America's Most Eligible Bachelor and one of the richest men in America. Daisy Malone, cocktail waitress and amateur ghost hunter. Used goods. In her mind, she couldn't make the two jibe. She had no plans of crashing into the same wall twice.

"If you're not willing to risk it—"

She brushed her fingers over his lips, quelling his words. Such a beautiful mouth. A mouth made for kissing. She wanted that mouth. Wanted this man. For as long as this insane attraction burned between them. And that's what it was. Insane. Impossible. The fact that she admitted as much, even if only to herself, somehow eased her apprehension. She rolled on top of Marcus, wanting to crawl inside of him and never come out. Splaying her fingers through his ebony hair, she looked into his impossibly dark eyes. "I'll risk it."

As he pulled her into a mind-numbing kiss, she assured herself that her heart was safe. This time she was walking into a doomed affair with her eyes wide open.

Marcus closed his eyes. He thought he'd almost lost her there. She was so passionate about him reconciling his hurts, his fears—ones that he was positive did not exist—yet she dwelled in her own dark past. He knew it had to do with what happened outside the high school on Saturday night, but he wouldn't push her. He wanted her to trust him, to tell him her deepest, darkest secrets because she wanted him to know. Because she knew he would continue to feel the same and nothing would change.

But she wouldn't know that until she put her faith in him. He wouldn't beg for it. He shouldn't have to.

When had this sassy-mouthed girl worked her way under his skin? Into his blood? His very breath? He'd never before understood what it meant to ache for someone. What it felt to become a part of them. He'd always been able to gauge people's emotions, but never to this extent. He'd known the moment Daisy had surrendered herself to him. Not because of the words she'd spoken, but because something undefined had passed between them. Not only were their bodies meshing, but something more...if only she would see it.

Why couldn't she tune in her sensitivity to him? How could she feel Jonas' emotions? A dead man, when Marcus was right there beside her, a living, breathing, hot-blooded male with more emotions than he could handle?

He rolled her onto her back, kissing her, trying to make her feel him. She framed his face with her hands, holding him tenderly but firmly, as though afraid he might go away. Hope flickered inside him. Maybe all wasn't lost. She suckled on his lower lip, her legs holding him hostage, her hips nestled against his. God, she made him so hot...he couldn't think...

As he moved down her body, her fingers buried themselves in his hair, messing it up and turning him on beyond belief. He sampled the valley between her ribs, delighted at the goose bumps cropping up as he slipped down farther, destination imminent. Unbuttoning her jeans, he parted the material and savored that most exotic place that had ambushed his dreams. The red belly jewel.

Her skin glowed smooth and fair in the moonlight, and the devilish jewel winked at him, as though knowing the havoc it wreaked. Well, he wreaked it right back, and soon Daisy writhed beneath him like the deeply sexual woman he knew her to be. It angered him that somewhere along the line a man had made her feel ashamed of her sensuality.

He slipped from the bed and pulled her jeans lower, expelling a long, appreciative sigh. Without a doubt, he stood at the edge of heaven. She was incredible. So beautiful. So sweet. He tugged the jeans over her feet then peeled off her socks. As he looked down on her, naked on the bed, hot and wanting him, he nearly lost it. His hands flew to his zipper, but she scrambled to her knees, her eyes glazed and glimmering with heat. "Allow me."

He groaned.

She slowly lowered his zipper, no teasing this time. He stood still, afraid to move and embarrass himself like an inexperienced kid. Her mouth trailed along his chest, savoring every dip and curve, her moist heat making him want to cry out as she pushed his slacks over his hips to drop and puddle around his feet. He stepped out of them. She leaned back, her eyes roving over him, touching, caressing.

She whispered, "Thank you, Marcus."

"For what?"

She looked straight into his eyes. "Sharing yourself with me."

He sucked in his breath, feeling like he'd been kicked in the gut. "Daisy..." He leaned forward to kiss her, but she held him away, smiling, relaxed, hot, and looking more gorgeous than he could stand.

"Tattoo," was all she said.

Groaning, wishing he could take back that day twenty years ago, he turned.

He heard a snort from behind. Before she could do so again, he turned back around.

She cocked her head. "'Mother?' In a heart no less?"

He almost laughed at the absurdity now. "If you knew her, you'd understand. I wasn't always able to please her, but I sure knew how to torment her."

Daisy's hands glided over his abdomen to caress his lower back. "How come you never had it removed?"

He grinned and pinned her down to the bed. "Van Buren wild streak."

She grinned back just before kissing him breathless. He nearly lost his mind feeling her naked against him, clutching, moving, silently calling him to the inevitable. He didn't know how much longer he could last, but he wanted to be sure she was ready. The last thing he wanted to do was hurt her in his own blind rush.

Her soft thatch of curls shimmered blond in the moonlight, warm, inviting...a prelude to the paradise beyond. He drew her nipple into his mouth at the same time he slipped his finger inside her. Gasping and arching her back, she clutched his hair for dear life.

He shivered with heat. She was ready.

He straightened himself over her, hovering a hair's breadth away, touching his lips to hers. Wrapping her legs around his hips, her hands clawed at his back, urging, begging, demanding. He entered her slowly. His body sagged with pleasure as he found her exquisitely tight. She moaned and opened her eyes. He stared into them, held them captive, wanting her to know what this meant to him.

Feel me, Daisy. Feel me.

A moan escaped from somewhere deep inside her. She urged him deeper, lifting her hips, wanting more.

He lost it. Holding her to him, heart to pounding heart, he thrust harder, faster. "Say my name," he whispered in her ear, not wanting any confusion this time.

"Marcus," she rasped, fingers grasping, riding him with an abandon that he'd never forget until the day he died.

"Louder," he urged, growing wilder by the second.

"Marcus!" Her cry echoed off the walls as she climaxed beneath him, shuddering, gasping.

He followed her straight into the oblivion, crying out, shattering into a million pieces he could never put back together.

Eighteen

The next three days passed quickly if not quietly.

Monday, bodysurfing on a wave of exhausted euphoria, Daisy wasn't prepared for what greeted them at Laguna Vista. Neither was Marcus.

They found their bags packed and waiting inside the foyer. Like a scene from a bad gangster movie, the message GET OUT was scrawled in red lipstick across the wall. Regardless, they'd moved inside, dread churning in Daisy's gut.

Heat blasted like angry breath from the living room. It must've been ninety-five degrees, though the thermostat was set at sixty-two. To make matters worse, a fire stubbornly raged in the grand fireplace no matter how many times they extinguished it. The kitchen, on the other hand, was freezing. Frost had formed on the inside of the windowpanes, the pipes had frozen so that the faucet was useless, and the brand new, high-tech stove and refrigerator were mysteriously on the blink.

Apparently they weren't wanted upstairs anymore than down. Their bedrooms had been ransacked. Mattresses overturned. Belongings scattered. The pages of Daisy's research books ripped from their bindings. The chapter Jonas had pointed out, the chapter referring to crossing over, was missing completely. She knew in that instant that this wasn't Jonas' dirty work, but Isadora's.

Though she couldn't explain it, she felt as though Jonas and his sister had engaged in an all-out war. And she was standing in the middle of it.

Hostility and fear pelted her from every direction.

Stay. Go. Stay. Go. Help me. Mind your own business.

As the battle waged on, she'd wondered where James stood in all of this. She hadn't felt a peep out of him yet.

Then there was Marcus. Whereas she had grown increasingly anxious and distraught as the day wore on, he grew angrier. When they weren't snapping at each other, she was crying and he was suffering inexplicable anxiety attacks and popping aspirin like candy.

An unhappy Rufus had returned from New York in the middle of the cleanup, but for every wrong they righted, Isadora committed two more. The vase she winged through the air, barely missing Rufus' head and smashing into the wall behind him, proved his last straw. He stomped out of the mansion not more than ten minutes after entering it. Refusing to spend another second under its 'possessed' roof, he plucked his cellular from his pocket and checked himself into a suite at Atlantic City's most extravagant casino. "If you want me or your great-grandfather's journals," he yelled to Marcus from the driveway, "you know where to find us."

An hour later, Marcus had found Daisy on the second floor, curled up against the west wall, bawling her eyes out and lamenting Jonas' and Isadora's sorrows as though they were her own.

"That's it." Ignoring her protests, he'd hauled her up and dragged her from the house, grabbing the luggage waiting at the front door, compliments of Isadora. He kicked the door shut behind him. Loading their possessions into the S.P.S. van, he said, "I'll check into the hotel with Rufus after I take you home."

That only made her cry harder. *Home* to her was 318 Newberry Street, the Cape Cod with the peeling all-weather paint, the seven-room house she'd grown up in, the place she went back to when she'd had an extremely bad day, or week. The place she went to feel better. Who could feel bad in a house filled with the home-cooked smells of Mom's Cooking Channel dessert of the week? Filled with the sound of Pop, Mickey, and Sean cheering and shouting at the television during Monday Night Football? Filled with the sight of Danielle and Jill giving each other fashion makeovers? Who could feel bad in a house filled with laughter and love?

Only now the house was filled with tension. Home wasn't *home* at the moment. If she went there, she'd feel worse.

As though knowing her mind, Marcus had taken a left off Route 40 onto English Creek Road. Daisy dried her eyes with the sleeve of her flannel shirt, breathing easier once she realized he considered her home her condo. Her thoughts drifted away from her family and to the man sitting in the cracked vinyl seat beside her. Jaw clenched, eyes narrowed, posture rigid. If not for the tiny vein throbbing at his right temple, she'd think he was some sort of wax-museum escapee. What was he thinking about? The ghosts? Her? Work? His penthouse?

His ex-fiancée?

What was her name? Kimberly. Kimberly something-or-other. She'd read it in a tabloid somewhere. Seen a picture of her, too. Tall. Skinny. Beautiful. Of course. Weren't all women born into money tall, skinny, and beautiful? Wasn't it like a rule or something?

Marcus' ex. Jealousy moved through Daisy in a sickening wave. Did he still love her? Had he ever loved her? He'd never spoken her name. Was it too painful? Too embarrassing? Their breakup had been splashed across the front page of *The Tattletale*. Not that she ever bought that printed trash. But who could help skimming the pages while waiting in line at the grocery store? And who could miss it? Front page. A grainy paparazzi shot of Mr. & Ms. Wealthy, Beautiful, and Engaged in happier days, holding hands and weaving through a crowd to the entrance of some exclusive premiere. *DUMPED*. The word had been stamped across Marcus' chest like a rejected side of beef.

At the time she'd laughed. Cheered for the skinny woman with bony elbows. Told the grainy image of the CEO that it "served him right." But that had been before she knew Marcus Van Buren. Before she'd learned he wasn't a self-centered, manipulative, cruel-hearted bastard, snake-in-the-grass. Before she'd realized he wasn't a Brad Worthington.

Brad had never asked her if it was all right to make love to her. He just assumed she would. After all, he always got what he wanted, and a girl like Daisy should be honored that he paid attention to her at all. Of course, he'd never said any of this, and it hadn't occurred to her to say no.

Brad had never taken her to the boardwalk or danced with her or played darts with her to cheer her up. Brad had only taken her to his parked car or to the pool cabana behind his house. Always at night, sneaking by the big house to impress her but never actually inviting her inside.

When she thought about it now, she wished she could reach back in time, grab that girl by her shoulders, and shake some sense into her. So what if he'd sat with her family a couple of times? God, what he must've been thinking as he'd sat all proper and polite on the plaid family couch. *Open up, Daisy, while I spoon-feed you and your family a load of crap the size of an elephant's. Mr. Malone, I'm sorry, but we can't listen to anymore of your boring prattle about microbreweries. I have to go screw your daughter before my next date.*

What a fool! A sap! She'd mistaken his lust for love.

She didn't want to make the same mistake again.

How easy that would be with Marcus. Despite his unrepentant obsession to sell Laguna Vista, he was turning out to be everything she wanted in a man. Loyal, considerate, passionate. When they made love...when they made love, she knew his soul. They connected in a way that defied words. She'd never felt anything like it before. Not even with Jonas.

Watching Marcus pop another aspirin, Daisy wondered, not for the first time, if Marcus was—at least a little bit—a sensitive. It would explain his emotional reaction to the tension and anger plaguing Laguna Vista, especially when Rufus seemed oblivious to anything beyond the physical. It would explain his anxiety this afternoon as Isadora's pranks escalated. Maybe it would even explain his headaches. The thought consumed her. She was barely aware that Marcus had parked the van and escorted her up the steps to her condo. She was barely aware that he'd fished her key out of her backpack.

He unlocked her door. "I don't want you going back there, Daisy."

The sound of his voice startled her. "What?"

He placed his hand on the small of her back and ushered her inside. "I don't want you going back to Laguna Vista."

"I have to go back." She dumped her backpack on the hallway floor and flicked on the lights one by one as they moved into the kitchen. She needed brightness. Anything to help dissipate the gloom that had traveled with them from Laguna Vista. "I have a job to do, remember?"

"I'm not sure it's safe for you to be there." He filled her tea kettle with water—the one she'd picked up at a garage sale two weeks before when life had been so much simpler—and set it on the front burner. Adjusting the flame, he said, "Something's changed. You felt it. I felt it."

The curse of a sensitive. "They're not dangerous," she said, trying to ease his mind. If he did possess *the curse*, he certainly wasn't tuned into it. "They're angry."

He turned to her, half-grinning. "That doesn't make me feel better."

Her heart skipped. That smile. That face. For a few foolish moments last night she'd thought that once they'd made love, he'd be out of her system. The curiosity satisfied. The three-year drought brought to a quenching end. But no. All he had to do was flash that killer grin and...*pow!* Right in the gut. The hormones kicked up like dust in a stampede.

With their lovemaking still humming through her body, she resisted the urge to pin him against the cabinet and have her way with him. *Don't get attached, Daisy. Don't get used to him being around.*

She waved him aside and chose two mismatched china cups from her cabinet. "How about this?" She set the cups on the counter, dropped an herbal tea bag into each, then turned to him, hands on hips. "How about if I tell you they're angry with *each other*, not with me. How about if I tell you with one-hundred-percent certainty that I'm in no physical danger. Does that make you feel better?"

Marcus moved in and took her into his arms. "This makes me feel better." He kissed her neck. "This makes me feel better. This...," he stole her breath with a kiss that melted her heart like a cherry cordial, "...makes me feel better."

So much for distance. Sighing, she sagged against him. Maybe she hadn't learned her lesson after all. Maybe she was doomed to live for one incredible moment and suffer for years afterward. It certainly seemed to be a pattern, especially when her mouth opened and said, "Then maybe you should stay here instead of with Rufus."

He lowered his smiling mouth toward hers. "I thought you'd never ask."

Laguna Vista suddenly flashed in her mind. It was dying. Not the quick, pull-the-trigger kind of dying. But a slow, grueling, behind-the-scenes rot. A rot that would never see its natural demise if Marcus made his sale. Not only would the rot be destroyed and carried away, what about the souls inside?

Before he kissed her again and stole her wits completely, she said, "I have to go back."

He pulled away, looked as though he was going to argue, then surprised her by saying, "All right. But not for more than a couple of hours at a time, and never alone. If I can't go with you, then make sure you drag along Rufus, Jill, or Mickey." He traced her lower lip with his thumb. "Promise me."

His touch. Strength. Goodness. *Heat.* A sensual fire burned low in her belly. She'd promise him anything right about now. "I promise."

They never had their tea.

Somewhere after midnight they pulled themselves out of bed and feasted on tuna sandwiches and apricot margaritas, two things Marcus had never had. Regardless of the apricot, she honored his request and gladly treated him to her salt-and-lime routine. As a reward, he gave her something *she'd* never had. An orgasm on her kitchen table.

Tuesday came and went in a blur. Marcus couldn't accompany her to Laguna Vista. Calls started jamming his cell around eight a.m. Between his secretary and the ten or twelve other associates who seemed unable to function without him, he told her he'd be tied up most of the day.

Her phone call to Rufus produced an expected reaction. Something along the lines of "fat chance, honey." So she'd joined him at his plush suite to study two of the twelve journals he'd transported from New York. By two o'clock they'd annihilated a pot of coffee, a plate of Danish, four caffeine-loaded sodas, two Rueben sandwiches, and a giant order of cheese fries.

At three, feeling pumped up and slightly queasy, Daisy drove to Laguna Vista. Jill met her out front. They entered the mansion together. Jill lasted a half-hour. She freaked out when, wanting to reapply her lip gloss, she looked into the bathroom mirror to find a seventy-something version of herself staring back.

Daisy drove her distraught sister home, then drove back to her condo where Marcus had dinner waiting. Spaghetti with jarred sauce. Something he'd never had. That night they drank blue martinis, something *she'd* never had. Followed by more great sex, this time on her Victorian settee.

Wednesday proved much the same. Except this time Marcus had meetings to attend, and she and Rufus made it through only one journal, though they finished an entire six pack of soda. Mickey was her appointed escort of the day. Being a male Malone and made of more egotistical stuff, he lasted forty-five minutes.

While searching for the entrance to the west tower, he'd peeled away a strip of wallpaper hoping to find a hidden panel. The wall instantly bled.

Marcus had given her a cell phone for "on-the-job emergencies," so she'd called Danielle. Mickey refused to wait inside, so they'd sat on the front step until Danielle's friend dropped her off. Mickey's tires spit gravel as he tore away from the house. Ignoring his warning, Danielle eagerly entered the mansion with Daisy. "This is *sooo* cool. I can't wait to meet Jonas."

"I have a feeling he's hiding out in the west tower," Daisy told her. "If we could just find the entrance."

After an hour of futile searching, Danielle declared herself "over it." Isadora's antics didn't faze her in the least. In fact, she ranted to the air that Isadora was an amateur compared to the ghosts in *Poltergeist.* The carpet literally pulled out from under her. Danielle landed on her butt. She smirked to the air.

"Kid stuff." Bounding to her feet, she rolled bored eyes and asked Daisy, "Can we go now? I've got a ton of homework."

Since she wasn't making any progress, Daisy drove her home. She watched her little sister skip past Rudolph and his gang and into the festively decorated Malone home. As she slammed the door behind her, a stuffed bunny wreath bounced against the weathered red paint. Once. Twice. A bunny wreath. Good Grief. Mom was up to Easter. At this rate, she might make it to Halloween—the real Halloween—by this Saturday.

She sighed and backed the S.P.S. van out of the drive. She should've gone in. Should've checked on Mom. But it was Wednesday. Pop's usual night off. Chances were he was camped out in front of the TV watching '*Wheel*' with Sean. He'd watched that show with all of his kids, challenged them to come up with the phrases before he did. Daisy had been fifteen before she'd figured out it was his bizarre way of making sure his kids were learning something in school.

Pop. She couldn't bear to see him right now.

Seven days. She'd avoided him for seven agonizing days. An eternity. What would she say when she finally did see him? *Hey, Pop, sorry Jill can't go to college?*

Seven days. Jesus. How much longer before the bank slapped a padlock on the front door of Malone's Pub? How much longer before they got evicted from the house?

Seven days.

Six days into the investigation. Two days longer than she'd told Rufus it would take her to prove Laguna Vista ghost-free. One day longer than she'd told Marcus it would take her to help Jonas and his siblings cross over. She was no closer to helping Jonas cross over than she was to being crowned Miss America.

Marcus was right. J.B.'s journals were packed with scandals and schemes instigated by his children. Jonas could be feeling guilty for any one of a dozen she'd discovered so far. As for tuning into Jonas' thoughts, Isadora was doing her damnedest to jam that frequency. Her own emotions were so fired up that Daisy couldn't tell where Isadora left off and Jonas began.

Seven days.

How long before Marcus demanded that signed declaration? What if he wanted it regardless of whether the ghosts were there or not? Then she'd be back to lying. For what? So she could collect a fat paycheck she hadn't earned?

No. So that she could save her family from financial ruin, she reminded herself.

Daisy pulled the S.P.S. van into her assigned parking space, the space she'd paid for with her hard-earned money. For years she'd scrimped and saved, played it safe, never really going anywhere or doing anything. Saving her pennies for a rainy day. Keeping a low profile. Preserving the tattered remains of her reputation.

Well, it seemed no matter how cautious she was, life still jumped up and bit her in the butt.

She switched off the ignition then rested her forehead on the steering wheel. Why was it, despite all his tender words and thoughtful gestures, did she suddenly feel like Marcus Van Buren's high-priced whore?

A knock on her window startled her. Finding his handsome face on the other side of the pane wasn't exactly the medicine for what ailed her.

Seven days.

Four days into her and Marcus' thing, fling, affair. Whatever the hell it was. Her troubles with the ghosts not withstanding, four of the happiest days of her life. How long before it ended? How long before he returned to Manhattan? To his real life? She'd told herself that, when the time came, she'd handle their parting like a sophisticated woman. No pleading, no crying, no regrets. She'd been that route. She was older now. Wiser. Worldlier.

Yeah, right. He hadn't even hinted that he was leaving, and she was already imagining several finales to their short-but-sweet union. One involved him staring at her retreating form while massaging the shoulder she'd socked in lieu of a good-bye kiss.

Yeah, real sophisticated. Frowning, she rolled down the window.

Marcus regarded her slumped shoulders and drooping ponytail with furrowed brows. He tucked several loose locks behind her ears. "You look like you could use a drink, Malone."

The last time he had made that observation they'd ended up at Mack's. Tequila. Darts. A barroom brawl. Making out on the back seat of the limo. The stuff Springsteen songs were made of. "I don't like that look in your eye, Van Buren. What do have in mind? Grasshoppers? Blow-jobs? Sex on the Beach and a pineapple pizza?"

Marcus braced his palms on the van's roof and leaned forward, giving her a naughty once over. "I could do without the Grasshoppers."

Sexy *and* charming. She couldn't accuse the media of wrongful advertising. Although there was much more to Marcus Van Buren than any of the magazines had revealed. It was the 'much more' that captivated Daisy. For all his fame, she knew something the world didn't. Marcus Van Buren was one of the "good guys."

The vice around her heart tightened. She snorted a disgusted breath. Was it possible, regardless of her silent vow not to fall in love with this man, that she'd done just that? Daisy glanced at her reflection in the rearview mirror. The term *loser* immediately came to mind. Her mood slipped from bad to downright foul.

Groaning, she motioned him away from the van then hopped out. Hands on hips, she regarded him with a frown. "Listen, Aladdin. This adventure has got to end at some point or another."

"Aladdin?"

It was then she noticed he was wearing jeans. Expensive jeans, but jeans nonetheless. And no tie. No buttoned-up, stiff-collared oxford. Just a black crew neck and a houndstooth sport jacket. He looked like Rufus, only better. "You know what I mean. Darts. Tuna sandwiches. Sex on the kitchen table." She flicked her gaze to his faded blues, trying very hard not to notice the way they accentuated his muscular thighs. "Jeans. It's *A Whole New World*. I get it. I understand. You're on vacation. Experiencing things you've never experienced before. A collection of 'firsts.' I'm sure your society buddies will get a big kick out of hearing how you attended a high school performance of *Romeo and Juliet*, especially as you're tooling down Park Avenue in your limo on the way to some exclusive Broadway premiere."

Brow raised, Marcus stepped forward. "I rarely take Park Avenue to get to Times Square."

"You know what I mean."

"Yes. I think I do." He backed her against the van. No escape. Framing her face in his hands, he said earnestly, "I won't hurt you, Daisy." Then he kissed her.

It was like being swept up inside a tornado. A turbulent whirlwind of emotions spun around her, disorienting her. Guilt. Exhilaration. Hate. Affection. Sadness. They twisted together, strangling her with their intensity. Panicking, she pushed Marcus away with a force that had him stumbling to catch his balance.

"Daisy?" His dark eyes rounded with confusion, concern.

She held up her palms as he took a step toward her. "Don't touch me. Not now. I'm too...I feel...the anger, the tension...it's unsettling."

He stiffened. "It's Laguna Vista. I knew it was a mistake to let you go there."

"No, Marcus," she said, swiping windblown hair from her eyes with shaky hands. "It's you."

He stared at her. Not uttering a word, he simply stared. Not appearing stunned or angry, not looking like anything. He was, at this moment, unreadable.

A phone chirped. His cellular. He let it ring.

Daisy grew increasingly uncomfortable. Although his mangled emotions were no longer crushing hers, the impression lingered, and his silent stare and annoying phone didn't help. On the seventh ring, she snapped. "They're not hanging up. It must be important."

Nine rings.

"For God's sake, Marcus, answer the damn thing."

He yanked the cell from his jacket pocket and turned his back on her. "It's six o'clock, Ms. Bishop. Go home. I'm

ordering you to get a life." He paused. "Oh." His voice gentled
considerably. "Hello, Angie. Yes, she's right here." He turned,
brow raised, and handed the compact receiver to Daisy. "It's
for you."

She scrunched her face. "Hello? Mom? Why are
you...What? Come where? Why? What's wrong? Don't tell
me nothing. I can hear it in your voice. Tell me...who's crying?
Is that Jill? Why is Candie crying? What's all that racket?
Mom...calm down. What about Pop? What? Mom...hello?
Hello?"

Dead air. Daisy blinked at Marcus, her heart lodged
somewhere between her chest and her throat. "We got cut off.
We..." she threw the phone at him. "I have to go."

Marcus caught the phone one-handed then nabbed the
sleeve of her denim jacket. He tugged her across the lot toward
a steel-gray foreign job. "I'll drive."

She didn't argue. Nor did she ask where the limo was or
what he was doing with a Rolls Royce. She knew the exact
purpose behind the luxury car. "*My other dream has been to
make love on the soft, velvet back seat of my vintage Rolls
Royce.*"

Yesterday she would've thrilled at fulfilling one of Marcus'
fantasies. Today it merely struck her as "another first."

She tucked away the hurt as Marcus revved the engine
and instead focused on her Pop. Her feelings be damned. The
mint-condition Rolls sounded a lot faster than her beat-up van.
And the sooner they got to Malone's Pub the better.

Nineteen

An ambulance outside Malone's Pub, engine running, lights flashing. A crowd of concerned patrons hovering nearby, whispering, wondering. Two paramedics rolling out a gurney, another one holding an oxygen mask over Pop's pallid face. Her mother eerily calm in contrast to her hysterical sisters. Mickey trying to wrench the keys out of the driver's hands shouting that he'd drive faster.

The scenario played over and over in Daisy's mind. *Pop.* The last time she'd seen him he'd been confessing his gambling sins, hanging his head in shame. She'd done nothing to comfort him. Not then. Not in the week that followed.

Guilt gnawed her gut. Grief. Trying to fight her rising panic, she fixed her teary gaze on the familiar landscape. It was dark now, but she knew the area like the back of her hand. Pine trees. Ridgemoor townhouse development. Pine trees. Country Claire's Corner Market. One mile to go.

"Don't imagine the worst, Daisy," Marcus said as he whizzed through a flashing caution light.

Too late. She'd imagined a heart attack. A stroke. What could be worse?

"You don't know for certain that anything is wrong."

"Candie was crying, Mom was..." her words trailed off as Marcus took a hard right into the pub's parking lot. No ambulance. No gurney. No gawking patrons. Her previous scenario shot to hell, her imagination took wild, horrific flight.

Daisy shoved open the car door and jumped out before Marcus could park. She raced for the entrance of Malone's Pub. Wrenched open the front door—

"*Got to celebrate!*"

Heart pounding, brow sweating, Daisy froze on the threshold. In the hundred-and-one scenarios she'd imagined, she'd never envisioned her mother leading a conga line through the crowded bar, singing a song about celebration with the twenty or so patrons following her. Peering through the din, she saw Danielle and Sean popping quarters into the jukebox, seemingly anxious to bring the musical entertainment somewhere closer to cool. Jill was playing pool with three men twice her age, and Mickey and Candie were making out in the corner by the pay phone like two horny teenagers.

Faces, faces, and more faces. Familiar faces. Friends, neighbors, regulars. Drinking, laughing and, from the looks of things, having the times of their lives.

What the hell?

"Hi, Daisy."

"Hi, Chuck." Another regular. A watered-down-domestic beer drinker. A pig in denim. Daisy shrugged off his arm when he draped it over her shoulder. She'd lost count of the times he'd asked her out and she'd said no.

Chuck smiled in spite of her rejection and swilled three-quarters of his long-neck. "Danny sure knows how to throw a party."

"Everything all right?" Marcus stepped up behind her and slid his arm around her shoulder, much in the way Chuck had.

When she didn't shrug him off, Chuck frowned and retreated to the bar.

Daisy scanned the chaotic scene for her father. "It seems Pop's throwing a party."

"What's he celebrating?"

"That's what I'd like to know."

"Daisy! Marcus!" Daisy's mother raced across the room, leaving Danielle in charge of the conga line. "Oh, Daisy!" She threw her arms around her daughter, hugging the breath out of her. "I'm so glad you made it."

Daisy wriggled from her mother's grasp. "What's going on, Mom? We ran red lights to get here. I thought something was wrong with Pop."

Her mother crinkled her nose. "Why would you think

that?" Then the light went on. "Ooooh. The phone call. I tried to explain, but we got cut off."

"Candie was crying."

"Happy tears. Everyone else was either whooping it up or trying to catch their breath like me. The relief. I can't tell you..." The strains of "Copa Cabana" stole Angie's attention. She laughed and pointed to the far side of the room. "Like mother like daughter."

Daisy turned and found Danielle, yellow feather in hair, swiveling as though born to lead a conga line.

Angie broke into an impromptu cha-cha.

"Mom."

"Mmm?"

"*Mom.*" Daisy gave her a gentle shake.

Her mother turned, cheeks flushed, eyes twinkling. Her smile was unusually goofy. "What is it, dear?"

Daisy blinked as an absurd thought popped into her head. "Have you been drinking?"

She gave an indelicate snort. "Nooo. Well, maybe just a little. Okay. Yes. If a few flutes of champagne count."

"Of course they count. Especially when you don't drink to begin with."

"It's a party!" Angie patted her daughter's cheek. "Lighten up, Sunshine. Our problems are solved. You should be dancing on air. Speaking of dancing...Marcus!" She struck a challenging pose in his direction then cocked a saucy brow. "Ever cha-cha with an ex-showgirl, mother of five?"

"No. I..." He looked from Angie to Daisy to Angie, then shrugged. "No."

"Then this is your lucky night. Come on, City Boy."

"But, Mom..." Too late. Daisy swallowed a frustrated scream as her mother pulled Marcus deeper into the dancing crowd. He went willingly. Now that all was apparently well with the Malones, he seemed happy to distance himself from her. She'd hurt his feelings in the condo parking lot. She didn't need to be a sensitive to know that.

Daisy massaged her temples. The day had gone from bad to worse.

She started out as a moving target for Isadora's antics, then moved on to pick a fight with Marcus, and finally—the icing on the cake—spent the last twenty minutes digging Pop an early grave.

Not one of her better days.

Or was it? What had Mom meant? Our problems are over.

"Copa Cabana" faded, making way for "Happy Days are Here Again." The conga line turned into a Mummer's Parade, with Sean leading the pack. Jill's hoot echoed across the room as she tossed her pool cue on the table and joined in the goofy, strut-your-stuff parade. Mickey and Candie fell in behind her. Danielle brought up the rear. Her mother tried her best to get Marcus to join in. To his credit, he endured and moved to the bar.

Danny Malone emerged from the storeroom, arms loaded with bags of chips and cans of salted peanuts. He dumped the snacks on a nearby table to join in the celebration. Smiling like an idiot, he grabbed Angie, kissed her, then lured her into the strutting parade.

Daisy swallowed an emotional lump as tears pricked her eyes. This was the Pop she knew. Full of life. Full of love for her family. A week ago he'd told them he was in danger of losing this place, not to mention their home. After which, he'd holed up here in the pub, working himself to death, trying to sort through the financial mess he'd created. Trying to find a solution. Apparently he'd found it.

Questions swirled in her mind, demanding answers, but she found it impossible to rain on her father's makeshift parade. Instead she sagged against the wall, her emotions tangled in a suffocating knot.

"Your family sure knows how to have a good time."

"That they do." Daisy took the beer Marcus handed her, only to pick at the bottle's metallic label.

"The bartender...Phil? He said this was your usual."

"It is. I'm just not in the mood, I guess."

He took the bottle from her and placed it in line with the empties on the windowsill behind him. After a moment's silence, he said, "So this is where you work."

Daisy scanned the crowded pub. So like Mack's, she realized, no wonder they'd always been in head-to-head competition. But unlike Mac's long, drab, boring bar, Danny's square mahogany bar was finished in a thick, clear gloss, its deep, varnished wood soaking up the warm lighting. Danny's pride and joy. Of course, the black vinyl padding edging the bar had seen better days. Duct tape colored with permanent marker sealed the holes made by jewelry, cigarettes, and fights. The felt on the two pool tables had begun to fade, as had the old tile floor with its red-and-white-bowling-ball-swirl pattern.

The back of Daisy's neck prickled with self-consciousness. What was Marcus thinking as he looked at this place? Was he disgusted by the eclectic décor and spirited clientele? He'd survived a visit to the wacky Malone home without complaint. He'd endeared himself to her family in six short days and seemed genuinely fond of them in return. Then again, Brad had played the same game until the stakes had risen. Then he'd shown his true colors. Pub owner's daughter, Daisy Malone, was an interesting diversion for fun, but for life?

She couldn't keep the bitterness from her voice. "Granted it's not Tavern on the Green, but it's my second home."

"I didn't expect Tavern on the Green."

Daisy cast him a sideways glance. "Oh, that's right. You're broadening your horizons these days. Well, there's a foosball game in the back room, along with an ancient Pac Man arcade, in case you missed out on that the first time around."

He moved in front of her, blocking her view of the partying patronage. "You've been in a foul mood all night, Malone. Stop dancing around it. Spit it out."

She stiffened her spine, spoiling for a fight, welcoming one. "All right. You're filthy rich." She uttered the words with the same disdain as "mass murderer" or "child molester." She knew she was being unreasonable, ridiculous, but she needed distance. He was becoming too important for a man who would soon phase out of her life.

"Comfortably well off."

"You say tomato, I say *to-ma-toe*."

Marcus leaned forward and braced his hands on the

paneled wall, pinning her as he had that first day in the library. The same anger sparked in his eyes, the same hard edge roughened his tone. "You knew who I was when you went into this, Daisy. I'm the same man I was a week ago. What's the problem? The fact that I was born into money? Or the fact that I work hard to maintain that legacy? I'm rich. So what? I work hard. So shoot me. I'm also a classic car fanatic and diehard Yankees fan. I'm uncomfortable around kids, and I'm afraid of heights. I've got quirks and strengths and flaws like everyone else.

"You've got a chip on your shoulder, Malone. It was never clearer than on the day I met you. Now here it is again. Since I have never, to my knowledge, done anything to hurt you, I can only assume you're comparing me to someone who did. Another *rich boy*. Is that it, Daisy? Give me a clue here, because I'm damn close to losing my temper."

Like a crumbling statue, a chunk of her heart broke off and lay forever ruined. He'd opened himself to her, ready to accept anything she needed to tell him. An amnesty of the soul. A clearing of the conscious by sharing the one thing about her life he didn't know. He wanted her to confide in him. A request so simple, yet so complicated...and so impossible.

He thought he was ready. She wasn't so sure he was. And, more importantly, if she was. Telling him meant risking his respect, his affection. Maybe withstanding his disdain or worse his disappointment. Telling him meant making herself vulnerable.

She wouldn't do it. Couldn't do it. She'd foolishly fallen in love with him. And he would be leaving.

She looked into those maple-syrup brown eyes and felt her own color drain from her face.

Shit. Yup. There it was. The Big L. The real thing. True love.

Against her better judgment, she'd fallen head over heels, heart over head in love with Marcus Van Buren. Instead of fortifying her, thereby allowing her to leap the inches between them and put her life in his hands, the realization created a coward with a yellow streak a mile wide. The thought of his reaction to her tawdry secret terrified her. Actually terrified her. So much so, it would remain just that, she decided. *Her* secret. What did it matter? He'd be leaving her soon anyway. Back to Manhattan. Back to his *real* life. Would it be so bad if he forever carried the illusion that she was as sweet and pure as he'd imagined? Couldn't their fairytale fling remain just that, a fairytale?

She darted her gaze around the crowded pub. The thudding of her heart rivaled the pumping music as she contemplated lying to him.

She couldn't do it. It wasn't in her. So instead she did what she always did. She avoided the subject. *Danced* around it. "I'm sorry, Marcus. You didn't deserve that. Any of that. Being rich doesn't make you bad, just luckier than ninety-percent of the population," she added, hoping to lure him into playful banter.

He didn't bite.

"Anyway, I apologize. I've been under a lot of stress, and I took it out on you." She crooked a genuine smile and nodded toward the bar. "Buy you a shot of tequila?"

Unsmiling, he said, "No, thank you."

"Challenge you to a game of darts?"

He stepped back and crossed his arms, regarding her like a child who'd been caught red-handed but continued to deny it. "Daisy..."

Pop's voice rang loud and clear, penetrating her thick, emotional smokescreen. "Sunshine!"

He must've just spotted her. She watched him hurry across the crowded dance floor. Her pop. Danny Malone. The good-hearted Irishman with more generosity than good sense. The light of her life.

Winded from his Mummer's antics, he stood before her now, half bent over, hands braced on hips, wheezing for air. He signaled her to give him a moment to catch his breath.

Her heart twisted. She hadn't realized just how much she'd missed him. Old memories—ones that should be faded and yellowed by now—snapped to mind in full color. She wasn't the only one who'd suffered from her scarlet past. Her entire family had suffered. Pop especially. He'd taken it hard. Real hard. But he hadn't yelled. He hadn't preached. He hadn't blamed her in any way. Instead he'd taken her in his arms and promised her it would be all right. She was sure she'd disappointed him, but he'd never once betrayed that emotion. He'd just tried his damnedest to make it "all right."

Daisy lowered her gaze, embarrassed by her less-than-tolerant reaction to his one and only screw up. Instead of offering her understanding and support, she'd avoided him. Left him alone to stew in his remorse and shame. Instead of helping him to figure a way out, she'd taken it upon herself to repair the damage. Why? Because she couldn't face him. Because she was disappointed in him. Because she was angry with him. Angry that he'd shattered her illusion. After all these years, she'd still thought he was perfect.

He smiled. No hurt. No anger. "It's good to see you, Sunshine." Unconditional love.

Her heart soared to the moon and back. "Hi, Pop." His green eyes moved to Marcus. "Pop, this is Marcus Van Buren. Marcus, this is my father, Danny Malone."

The men shook hands.

"Mr. Van Buren."

"Mr. Malone. Marcus, please."

"Call me Danny."

"Danny." Marcus nodded, seemingly pleased at the invitation to address her father by his first name. "Nice to meet you."

"Likewise, Marcus."

Her father shifted as an awkward silence fell between them.

The reality of the situation hit Daisy like a head-on collision. She'd just introduced her father to the man she was sleeping with. A rash prickled at the base of her throat, burning its way up to her cheeks. She twisted her butterfly ring in an endless reel. "Mr. Van Buren—that is, Marcus—owns Laguna Vista, Pop. He hired me to investigate whether it's haunted or not. The ghosts—his ancestors, Jonas, Isadora, and James—died tragically in 1928 and, well, they didn't lead the purest of lives and—"

Danny rested his hand on Daisy's to still her nervous gesture. "I know about the ghosts, Sunshine. I also know about Mr. Van Buren."

Daisy's voice cracked. "You do?"

Danny cocked his head toward the passing parade. "Sean."

She rolled her eyes. "Who else?"

"Your mother. Mickey. Jill. Danielle." He winked at Marcus. "You've made quite an impression on my brood." He hooked his arm about Daisy's waist." Mind if I steal my daughter away for a few minutes? We have something to discuss."

"Please." Marcus looked to Daisy, his brown eyes hot with warning. He hadn't forgotten their conversation. "I'll be at the bar."

She would be alone now. With Pop. No more cowardly buffers.

As he steered her through the supply room and beyond into his office, she felt her composure—what was left of it—slipping away with each step.

He closed the door, shutting out the sounds of the celebration, then pointed to his chair. "Sit down, Sunshine. We need to talk."

Rounding the old desk, she slipped into the worn leather chair, nearly sighing as she settled into the molded pocket of Pop's shape. She rested her forearms on the closed account ledger, hands clasped, lips pursed.

"You've been avoiding me, Daisy girl."

It was all she could do not to drop forward and bury her face. She was that ashamed.

"I understand."

That only made it worse. "Pop, I—"

He cut her off with a wave of his hand. "It's all right, Daisy. I made a mistake. A terrible mistake. I gambled money that I didn't have." He paused, looked down at the toes of his shoes, then sniffed and glanced back to her. "I don't know how it happened exactly. I gambled a few bucks here and there, Thursday afternoons mostly. Me and a couple of the regulars, we'd drive over to one of the casinos, have lunch, toss a few bucks on the craps table, roulette, blackjack. For fun. I don't know when it got out of hand, but it did. Lost more than I could afford. Then I'd borrow, win some back, and instead of quitting while I was ahead, well...it's a cycle. A sickness. I thought I could handle it, but in the end it handled me."

Daisy's eyes filled with tears. "Pop—"

"Let me finish. I put this family at risk. Our business. Our home. I don't blame you for being disappointed in me, Daisy. I was disappointed in myself. So much so, it was hard to come home at night and face your mother. So you see, I understand the avoiding part." He moved forward now, slid a chair next to hers and sat down. "You expected better from me." He smiled sadly. "I expected better of myself. That's the real hell of it."

Knowing the feeling, she touched his arm. "You can't go on beating yourself up like this, Pop. It was a mistake. It could happen to anyone." If she could only take her own advice.

Danny smiled and placed his warm hand over hers. "I know what you were up to, Sunshine. I know you took that cockamamie ghostbusting job to try to bail me out. I heard Van Buren waved a mighty large paycheck under your nose to prove Laguna Vista ghost-free."

Daisy bristled. "Who told you? Jill?"

"It doesn't matter who told me. What matters is that you put yourself in a dangerous situation with no other thought than to collect that paycheck, thinking it was our salvation."

Daisy pulled her hand from his and balled her fists in her lap. "It's not a dangerous situation. The ghosts aren't hostile, not to me anyway. Mickey told you about the bleeding wall, didn't he?"

"Bleeding wall? No." He narrowed his eyes. "What the—"

"Danielle. What did she come crying to you? If she hadn't taunted Isadora, then Isadora wouldn't have pulled the rug out from under her. But that was it, the furthest it's gone. Other than Danielle's bruised butt there have been no other physical injuries."

His lips thinned. "Well, that's good to know."

"As for the torpedoed fruit—"

He placed a finger to her lips. "Shush. When I said dangerous, I meant the emotional ramifications."

She blinked. "The emotional ramifications?"

"Laguna Vista upsets you. It always has. Why do you think I ordered it off limits for all those years?"

"Vagrants? Rats?"

"Even when you were a little girl, you sensed things other people didn't. I don't care if I was dancing a jig, if deep down I felt miserable, you knew it. When you came home at ten years old swearing you'd seen a ghost at Laguna Vista, carrying on about how sad he was and how you had to help him, well...you cried yourself to sleep for weeks, for chrissake. I couldn't take it. I did my best to convince you it was your imagination. I thought it was for the best. Something about that place, it always felt dangerous where you were concerned, Daisy. You don't know how happy it made me when you lost interest in it.

"When I heard you'd gone to work there, I pulled myself out of my self-pitying funk pronto. I racked my brain. Racked your mother's brain. Money. A hundred-fifty grand. How in the hell could I generate a hundred-fifty grand?" Danny recaptured her hands and smiled. "Yesterday we found a solution. Today we sealed the deal. So you see, our problems are solved. You don't have to go back to Laguna Vista. You don't need that paycheck. Let someone else sort out that para-whatcha-ma-call-it mess."

Daisy tensed. "What deal, Pop? What have you done?"

"I signed a contract with a silent partner. An investor. We're going to turn Malone's Pub into a high-tech sports bar. Renovations start in two weeks!"

***

When Marcus saw Daisy emerge from the back room, his dart sailed astray and into the pockmarked paneling. Her father was on her heels, smiling and talking and pointing to various parts of the pub. She smiled, too, though hers was forced. A real Daisy Malone smile flowed across her face like a meandering river, catching the sunshine as it eased on by. This smile cracked like pond ice, stiff and cold.

He knew her every expression, her every nuance. For instance, he knew a rash broke out at the base of her throat when she so much as skirted the truth or faced an uncomfortable situation. The rash had crept up her neck when she'd neatly avoided his inquiries into her past, and again when she'd introduced him to her father. He'd known that having him stay at her condo these past few days had been a major step for her. However, standing in her father's pub, watching them together, he realized just how big of a leap she'd taken.

For all of her sass and wild ghost chases, Daisy Malone was an old-fashioned girl. With old-fashioned values. Mixing that with her "sensitive" gift, he came up with a girl who probably took things harder than most people. A girl who felt deeper than most people. A girl who took things to heart and held it there for a very, very long time. A girl who held grudges. Hence the chip on her shoulder.

He couldn't hide his disappointment when she'd sidestepped her past like dog crap in the street. He'd asked her a direct question. Had hoped for a direct answer. Not that he hadn't already figured it out on his own. Missy Polanski had eagerly supplied at least two pieces to the puzzle. "*Daisy has a thing for rich boys*," she'd said. "*Easy Malone*" she'd called her. Add in Daisy's explanation that Missy was an "old high school rival" and, that, Marcus thought, cast a pretty clear picture. "Rich boy" had dumped Missy for Daisy, who probably fell into heart-wrenching puppy love with the man only to be dumped by him later on down the line...more than likely for a rich girl.

It made sense, yet it didn't. Why was Daisy being so evasive over something that had happened ten years ago? So she'd fallen in love. So he'd dumped her. Had she loved him that much? So much that she still pined for him after all these years? So much that she couldn't speak his name?

Frowning, Marcus pulled his dart from the wall then leaned against the cigarette machine, waiting for Mickey to take his turn. Wasn't it enough that he'd taken on Jonas? Now there was another ghost in the mix? Speaking of Jonas, he wondered what his dear dead relatives were up to tonight. They'd been hell on wheels these past few days, trashing Laguna Vista, terrorizing anyone who stepped foot in the place.

Each day Marcus prayed Vladimir Zigfreid wouldn't pop in for a surprise visit. The ghosts would no doubt scare the old man to death. *Literally.* Then bye-bye sale. Although these days, Marcus found himself thinking less and less about the sale and more and more about Daisy.

Daisy. His sweet, stubborn Daisy. She'd spent the last three days trying to reason with the ghosts, trying to calm their antics, trying to reach Jonas. But they weren't speaking to her, she'd advised in frustration, nor apparently to one another. While she struggled at Laguna Vista, Marcus had spent his time wheeling and dealing with various number-crunchers, lawyers, and loan officers. However, at night they were always together, floating on that new-lover cloud that Daisy seemed convinced would fall to the ground and fog up their lives at any moment.

She was right about one thing. This was all a first for him. Every day with her he experienced a first. It was amazing, refreshing. She brought out a side of him he barely knew existed. The side Rufus treated like an endangered species. His wild side. The side he'd always been afraid to turn loose because it reminded him of his father, and even worse, Jonas. After years of playing the buttoned-up, by-the-book executive, after years of strategically avoiding any kind of passion or play that might detract from his cool, controlled reputation, he'd finally let loose.

He'd never been happier.

Like thumb separated man from beast, he realized there was one irrevocable difference between himself and his male predecessors.

Fidelity.

He knew this because he could draw blood today and swear that he'd never want another woman the way he wanted Daisy. She was the gentle pink sky at daybreak. The fierce red at sunset. He may not be a poet, but she sure as hell made him feel like trying to be.

He'd thought, perhaps foolishly, that no matter their social differences, no matter their backgrounds, they'd somehow work it out. But apparently Daisy had her doubts. It hurt, and he wanted to shake her. They were in a new millennium, for crying out loud, hanging out in seedy bars and chucking needles with wings at the walls. He was beside her no matter where they went, what they did. Why couldn't she give him enough credit? Why couldn't she see that no spring-loaded trap waited for her to take what she deserved?

He knew why. It didn't matter how nice he was. How understanding. He could send her roses every day for the next six months and it wouldn't change a thing. *He* was paying for whatever that prick rich kid did to her all those years ago. For that nameless man's sake, Marcus hoped he never crossed his path. The best plastic surgeon he knew had just retired.

Daisy. Again Marcus thought of her telling rash while she'd introduced him to her father. A father she so obviously adored. Who'd have guessed "elephant-sized-balls" Malone was a daddy's girl.

And Marcus had been sleeping with her.

Not that Danny Malone knew that for sure, but he must know they'd been living together in Daisy's tiny condo these past three days. Jill knew, which probably meant Danielle knew, and if they'd been gabbing about it, no doubt "little pitcher, big handles" Sean knew. In which case, everyone in Atlantic County probably knew.

Looking back, Marcus considered himself lucky Danny hadn't pulled a shotgun the first time they'd met.

"You're up," Mickey called, pulling his fancy metallic darts from various sectors on the board.

Distracted, Marcus stepped up to the tape and threw. His plain-blue dart bounced off the board's metal rim and clattered to the floor. The second did the same.

"If you focused more on the bull's-eye and less on my sister, Van Buren, you might hit your mark." Mickey paused. "Unless my sister *is* your mark."

Marcus reached for his scotch, took a sip, then set it aside. He picked up the third dart. "Has she always been so proud?"

The dart sunk two inches left of center.

"Always," Mickey said, handing Marcus his darts then sailing his home. "Bull's-eye!" He repeated his skill twice more until the center of the dartboard looked like a silver bouquet. Smiling, he plucked the darts and made his way back to Marcus. "It's a Malone trait. She's also generous, fiercely loyal, quick to temper, and can hold her liquor like a true Irishman."

Marcus nodded. "I've noticed."

"Which part?"

"Pick one." Marcus resumed his watch against the cigarette machine, drink in hand. She was wearing those jeans again. The ones she'd been wearing the first time he'd set eyes on her. Tight and worn in the knees, not to mention the seat, which was where his eyes were trained at the moment. She turned and looked up, observing the lighting fixture her pop pointed to. Marcus' gaze consumed her from head to toe. Ponytail. White ribbed tank and flannel shirt, unbuttoned and tied at the waist. Faded jeans. Hiking boots. The look that was wholly Daisy. Down to earth, unassuming. A girl who kept a few bucks stashed away in a peanut butter jar. His most unlikely, illogical match, and he was crazy about her.

He was certain she felt the same about him. In fact, he was almost certain she'd fallen in love with him, though she'd probably rather die than admit it.

All right. So maybe she had cause to be concerned.

He'd pulled on her lifestyle like a comfy old pair of jeans and a Downy-fresh sweater. But how would she wear his? He imagined her at one of his mother's social functions, looking angelic in a gown he'd surprised her with, flanked by overly tanned women with tummy tucks and capped teeth. She'd radiate a natural beauty, an inherent goodness. She'd shine as she talked about how proud she was of her pop, his renovated pub, and her beloved brothers and sisters.

They'd hate her.

Missy Polanski was an amateur compared to these women who'd cut their teeth on hauteur. He knew Daisy would manage a tough act for a while, her chin in the air, muttering something about "sticks and stones." But it would get to her. It would get to anybody. He wanted to protect her from that. Wanted to protect her from anything that upset her. That's why he'd decided to take matters into his own hands.

You can't always save those you love from getting hurt, an inner voice told him. *Sometimes circumstances are beyond our control.*

A familiar ache throbbed behind his left temple. Marcus sipped his scotch, hoping to fend off the invading migraine. "But sometimes you can change the circumstances, thereby changing the outcome."

"You talking to me?" Mickey asked, grabbing his beer from the table.

Marcus shook his head, his gaze locked on Daisy. "Myself."

"You're not going to break her heart or anything, are you, Van Buren?" Mickey pointed the neck of his beer bottle at Marcus. "I kind of like you. I'd hate to have to kick your ass."

"Blinding devotion to family," Marcus said with admiration. "Another Malone trait." One surprisingly shared by his own ancestors. Jonas, Isadora, and James. All for one and one for all. For the first time ever, he actually envied the hell-raising trio. At least they had a sense of family devotion, if only to each other. Marcus' family consisted of only himself and his mother, who wasn't exactly the June Cleaver of Park Avenue.

He did have cousins down the shore in Cape May, but he'd had no contact with them. A feud between his father and Isadora's son, Richard Tadmucker, had severed those family ties long ago. Once, when Marcus was eighteen, he'd considered reaching out to his uncle, but his mother instantly suffered one of her "episodes," calling Marcus a traitor to his father between gasps and the Tadmuckers a disgrace to the Van Buren legacy. Rather than arguing with her, he'd relented, figuring if the Tadmuckers wanted to reunite the two families they could always contact him. They never did.

Sean and Danielle raced over then to plant themselves in front of Marcus and Mickey. Gyrating their hips and shoulders in some sort of hip-hop maneuver, they sang the latest hit at top of their lungs. *"Fam-i-ly is everything! Mess with my sisters and brothers, you mess with me!"*

Danielle told Marcus, "We added the brother part," while Sean pulled Mickey onto the dance floor. Candie joined them as Jill, too, made her way toward the sibling circle. Danielle tugged on Marcus' hand. "Come on," she yelled over the pumping music. "They're playin' our song!"

Across the room, he saw Daisy being prodded by her pop toward the center of the floor. *"Fam-i-ly is everything!"* he sang off key. *"Without it you don't got a thing!"*

As Danielle dragged him onto the dance floor, Marcus marveled at the way life spun on a dime. Last week he'd been on his yacht, miserable, wanting to be alone. Now here he was, bustin' a move with the Malone family.

"We're together and we live in love, that ain't no lie," they all sang.

Jill and Danielle flanked him in a slick bump and grind. *"Come and join our fam-i-ly and let love get you by!"*

Surrounded by the Malones, the irony of the moment was not lost on Marcus. A pop song's lyrics had never been more poignant. And Marcus had never felt more at home. When Mickey gave him a conspiratorial wink and twirled Daisy into his arms, he enjoyed a split second of brotherly camaraderie. A split second of the light in Daisy's eyes before it flickered out.

She tried to back away, but Marcus slid his palm down her back and pulled her closer. Her heart pounded against his chest. A heart betraying its master. A heart that had tricked her into thinking she ever ruled it at all.

He knew exactly how she felt.

He skimmed his other hand down her arm and locked their fingers. He knew without a doubt that he'd made the right decision. He knew their destiny, even if Daisy didn't.

Grooving to the beat of the bass and drums, Marcus kissed her furrowed brow, willing away her tension. She leaned against him and sighed, giving in to the moment as though she hadn't the will nor the inclination to resist. He smiled into her hair as she pressed against him. Home was more than just a place, he suddenly realized. It was a state of mind.

The beat continued to pulse. His hips began to sway. He closed his eyes as Daisy rocked with him as though on the tide of an approaching storm. Together they descended into a dance all their own. Her breasts brushed his shirt. Her threadbare-clad thighs clenched against his. He was about to lose his mind. Choreographed lust. Passionate as the Lambada. Sexy as the Tango. They as good as made love on the dance floor. Right there in the middle of Malone's Pub. Right there in front of Daisy's family and friends.

When the song ended, the crowd burst into applause. Their dark, tender world shattered. Daisy backed away from him, palms pressed to her flushed cheeks, tears glistening in her eyes. Over her shoulder, Danny and Angie Malone winked at him. Mickey and Candie gave him the thumbs up. Jill and Danielle gave each other the high five, and Sean made mushy kissy faces at him. One by one the Malones drifted toward the bar while the rest of the patrons resumed their former partying.

Marcus and Daisy stood breathless, staring at each other. Daisy spoke first. "We need to talk."

Hoping she was as overcome as he, Marcus grabbed her hand. "How unusual," he said with a grin. "You read my mind." He guided her through the masses, heart thudding in anticipation. He'd planned on doing this tomorrow night, but why delay their happiness any longer? If she understood how he felt, then maybe she'd see that they belonged together.

Shutting the door and the Bee Gees' falsetto strains of "How Deep Is Your Love" behind him, Marcus scanned the parking lot for an appropriate place to talk. His gaze flicked to his Rolls. He'd had it brought down from New York for this express purpose. He'd envisioned the entire romantic scenario. Suddenly it didn't seem romantic enough. What he wouldn't give to be in Central Park. A hansom cab. A single, long-stemmed rose. Champagne.

"How'd you know how to get here, Marcus?"

It was as if someone had ripped the parking lot out from beneath him. Unflinching, however, he guided her along the side of the building to the rear of the pub, toward privacy, as his mind fumbled to shift gears.

"We've never been here before," she said. "And I didn't give you directions as you were driving. I was too upset to notice at the time, but you knew exactly where you were going. You've been here before." She pulled her hand from his grasp and slumped against the bar's back wall. She wrapped her arms about her to ward off the fall chill. "You're the silent partner Pop told me about."

A dull yellow light shone down on the dumpster behind them. The soft glow did nothing to gentle her pained expression. Accusation. Distrust. Betrayal. All crashed out from her in angry waves. The approaching storm. He held her troubled gaze, wondered if she saw his own.

Life spun back on that dime.

He'd screwed up. Driving her to the pub as though he'd been here a dozen times.

She'd been so distraught. How could he have known Danny would throw a party? After that phone call, he'd been genuinely worried. For her. For her family. "Let me explain."

"Oh, God." She buried her face in her hands and shook her head. "I knew it. I just knew it."

He nearly dropped to his knees at the hitch in her voice. *What had he done?* Aching to reach out to her, he shoved his hands into his pockets instead. He couldn't bear watching her pull away in disgust. He'd meant to tell her. In his own way. He'd specifically asked Danny to let him tell her in his own way. At an appropriate time. Although now that he witnessed the wreckage, there probably was no such thing as an appropriate time. A bomb was a bomb. The damage was done. No matter the extent of his good intentions, she'd construe the partnership as a pity offering.

Pride. The one Malone trait he could sure do without right now. Gauging how best to clean up his mess, he decided to proceed as the calculated businessman she believed him to be. "I'm going to make a hell of a lot of money off this place, Daisy. It's a smart investment."

"Oh, pleeease." She threw her arms wide, her teary eyes

suddenly sharp as she gestured at the rundown pub. "It's a blue-collar hang-out thirty miles from the lights of Atlantic City."

"Which is precisely why we'll appeal to the residents of this county and the next by renovating Malone's Pub into a high-tech sports bar. Add on an adjacent theme restaurant, and you'll double your profits by drawing entire families."

Daisy glared at him. "What do you know about running a bar? Or a restaurant for that matter? What do you know about families?"

The last one stung. She'd meant it to, but he plowed on. "I have several investments outside of VB Enterprises. My interests are diverse. As for this particular venture, running the bar and the restaurant will be your father's role in the partnership. I provide the backing. He provides the expertise. All I have to do is sit back and rake in profits. Trust me, Daisy. I was bred to make money. I know a good investment when I see one."

"Bullshit."

Why was she making this so difficult? Didn't she see he just wanted to help? Just wanted to make her happy? Since when was that a goddamn crime! He advanced on her, head cocked. "Run that by me again?"

She swiped away her tears before confronting him, fists on hips. "Everything you said. All that 'it's a wise investment' crap. It's bull. You don't need this place. You don't need the headache. My family wormed their way into your heart and, knowing the financial mess we were in, you went and did what you always do. Threw your money around. So easy to do when you've got so much of it! But it wasn't for you to bail out *my* family. They're my kin, not yours. My responsibility, not yours. When I rid Laguna Vista of *your* family and collect that honest paycheck, I'm going to buy you out."

He raised his brows. "You're going to buy me out with my own money?"

"Yes. And don't look at me as if I'm crazy. It makes perfect sense to me. It's a matter of principle."

"Are you saying I don't have any principles?"

"I'm saying you entered into a partnership with my father for the wrong reason."

Marcus clenched his jaw as his temper simmered toward a slow boil. "What would that reason be?"

She was crying openly now. A moment ago his arms would've been around her, comforting her, but her spiteful words had done their job. He kept his distance.

"You did it because you feel sorry for me. For my family. Oh, those poor, wacky Malones," she mimicked, her throat thick with sobs. "They're this close to being evicted from house and home, and their only hope is a daughter who thinks she can save the day by helping some guilt-ridden ghosts get to Heaven. I'm sure your intentions were good. How could they not be? You're a good man, Marcus Van Buren. But we're not one of your tax-deductible charities."

He clenched his fists at his side. "I'm going to skate right over that one, Daisy, because you're upset and you tend to make asinine comments when you're upset. And for your information, there's a vast difference between a donation and an investment."

She sniffed and dragged her flannel sleeve beneath her nose. "It's not just the money. It's my family. They like you. A lot."

"So?"

"So? They're already envisioning the wedding ceremony. You and me, walking down Holy Redeemers red-carpeted aisle."

"So?"

She stared and sniffed, speechless for a second. "So...so...that's not going to happen."

Before he could think, he dragged her into the woods behind the pub, into the dark. Caging her against a thick oak, he said, "Don't be so sure."

"Don't," she pleaded. "Don't tease me with promises of happily-ever-afters." Her voice cracked. "I'm not Cinderella."

Marcus framed her face in his hands, thankful for the stream of moonlight so he could stroke away her tears. "I'm not the man who did you wrong in the past. So stop comparing us. Stop thinking about what was and focus on what could be."

Daisy let out a sob. "It's not that easy."

"Yes, it is." He kissed her then, hard and intense, a transfusion of his desperation and sincerity. "Can't you feel it?" he whispered on her lips, his breath like a hot, desert wind.

She shuddered and clutched his shirt. He tried to read her eyes, but the moon was playing tricks. Could she feel him? Could she feel his heart clutched in her hand?

With a sharp tug, she brought his mouth down to hers. She kissed him just as hard, just as fiercely, but hers was the kiss of a woman about to be torn from her lover's arms. He tasted her tears, her fear. Her resolution.

As she pulled him down into the grass, Marcus declared his own resolution.

They belonged together. He was the best thing that had ever happened to her. He just had to convince her.

As for the partnership, she'd been dead wrong. He hadn't done it because he felt sorry for her. He'd done it because he loved her.

Twenty

"Scaredy cat."

"I'm not scared."

"Are too."

"Am not."

The taller boy nudged the smaller boy in the shoulder. "Are too."

The smaller boy puffed out his little chest. "Am not."

The taller boy, though only taller by an inch, crossed his arms over his chest. "All right then, squirt, prove it."

"All right, I will!" Turning on his heel, he marched toward a steep stairwell. "But I'm tellin' you, Marcus, there's nothin' up there."

"Betcha' my Joe DiMaggio special edition card there is."

The smaller boy paused on the fourth step and looked down over his shoulder. "Dust doesn't count."

"Course not, bean brain," Marcus said. "But anything that has to do with Jonas, Isadora, or James does."

The smaller boy frowned. "You're not supposed to say their names out loud, Marcus. It's bad luck."

Marcus braced his fists on his hips. "Are we gonna do this or not? We don't have all day. If our moms find us here..."

The younger boy pursed his lips in thought. "DiMaggio, huh?"

"Yup."

"Honest Injun?"

"Yup."

The smaller boy shrugged then resumed his awkward ascent up the rickety stairs. "All right. But I'm tellin' ya, Marcus. There's nothin' up there. Ma said so."

"And I'm tellin' you there is," Marcus argued as they reached the top landing.

The smaller boy pushed open a rusted door and stepped out onto the roof. "How can you be so sure?"

Marcus stepped up beside him, shielding his eyes from the setting sun. He squinted at the tower, its arched window only a few feet from where they stood. "I don't know, squirt," he said softly. "It's just a feeling."

Someone touched his shoulder.

Marcus shot up like a catapult. Heart hammering. Brow sweating.

The shadow blocked the moonlight, looming large and close. It smelled of expensive cologne, cigars, and cognac.

Jonas.

The man bent forward, a silencing finger pressed to his lips.

Rufus.

Marcus sagged with relief as he fought to adjust his eyes to the dark. For a second there he'd thought...remnants of the nightmare flickered through his mind then faded like an old TV shut down for the night. Shaking his head, he swung his legs out of bed and squinted at the bedside clock. The digital numbers glowed 4:25 AM. "What the—"

Daisy stirred beside him. "Marcus?"

Rufus stepped back into the shadows. Marcus turned and smoothed his hand over her hair. "Go back to sleep, baby. I'm just getting a drink of water."

She murmured something then turned her face back into the pillow. Marcus rose from the bed and prodded Rufus toward the living room, quietly shutting the bedroom door behind him.

"The kitchen," he said, coming up behind Rufus. "Now."

Rufus followed Marcus into the tiny room and waited for him to flick on the bulb above the stove. "I'm sorry, Marc, but—"

"Lower your voice, will you? How the hell did you get in here?"

"An emergency key. Daisy gave it to me the day before yesterday."

Marcus pressed his fingers to his throbbing temples. "I

should've known."

"I'm sorry," Rufus repeated. "I tried calling, but you didn't answer."

Marcus filled a glass with tap water, nabbed his aspirin off the spice rack, and downed two extra-strength tablets. "I turned off the ringer so Daisy could get some sleep. She had a rough night."

"And your cell..." Rufus eyed the tap water as if it were poison.

"I shut that off, too."

"That explains why they called *me*." Hiking up his slacks and bracing both hands on his hips, Rufus looked wide awake and ready to take on Mike Tyson. "They knew *I'd* get to you."

"Who?"

Rufus stepped back. "Do you want the good news first or the bad news?"

Marcus was ready to pummel his assistant. "Spit it out already!"

"Looks like you could use the good news first. Your mother's in town."

"That's the good news?"

"She got in last night, demanding to know why you're at Laguna Vista. She said she almost had a heart attack when her PI told her where you were. You really should return her calls, Marc. She sounded frantic, more so than usual. I almost didn't recognize her voice." Rufus took in the small space of Daisy's kitchen. "Don't worry, I told her I didn't know where you were."

Marcus ran a hand over his face, not wanting to ask but knowing he had no choice. "What's the bad news?"

"Joe Rush."

Marcus stilled. "What did he want?"

"To make your life a living hell, I believe. He told me to tell you *thanks*."

"For what?"

"He said that this morning's edition not only paid off his bogus trip to Paris but also bought him a brand-new BMW. That slippery son of a bitch."

Marcus closed his eyes, the hum of the refrigerator like a jackhammer in his brain.

"I scoured the town for a copy," Rufus went on, "but deliveries don't start rolling in 'til around four-thirty a.m."

Marcus opened his eyes and glanced at the microwave's clock. 4:29. With a guttural curse, he pushed off the counter and strode for the front door.

Rufus was right behind him. "Uh, Marc?"

Marcus spun on him. "What, dammit. What?"

Grinning, Rufus lowered his gaze. "You might want to put on some clothes."

***

The headline was bad.

"*DUMPED CEO SLUMMING IT,*" Rufus read aloud. "That son of a bitch."

The photos were worse.

"What in the hell kind of zoom did he use to get *this* shot?" Rufus squinted at the grainy montage. "Jesus, Marc. You did it with Gidget on the kitchen table?"

Marcus stared at the image, unable to find his voice. Seeing himself half-naked on the front page of *The Tattletale* was the lowest moment of his life. That was until he flipped to the inside story.

"Jesus Christ," Rufus erupted, having already turned to the feature article. "And Daisy thought *you* had elephant-sized balls?"

The store clerk cleared his throat and pointed to his female associate, busy making four pots of flavored coffee.

Rufus steered Marcus toward the dairy section. "Where does Rush get this stuff?" he asked, lowering his voice to an outraged whisper. "We'll sue his pants off."

"For what?" Marcus snapped, still reading.

Rufus snorted. "Oh, I don't know," he said, each word a sarcastic growl. "Defamation of character. Invasion of privacy. *Slander.*"

Marcus reached the bottom of the first column and skimmed the second, his mouth growing drier with each passing sentence. "Unfortunately, Rush is pretty on the mark this time."

Rufus blinked at him. "Daisy's mother was a topless showgirl?"

"I don't know about the topless part."

"And her sister-in-law," Rufus glanced back over the article, "Candie. She was a stripper?"

"I believe she refers to it as exotic dancer."

"What about this part about Daisy? This can't be true." Rufus lowered the paper but Marcus ignored him, choosing to stare at the yogurt display instead. "Marc? The part about Daisy..."

"I don't know."

Rufus scrunched his brows. "What do you mean, you don't know?" He pointed to the article. "It says here—"

"I know what it says." Marcus folded the tabloid in two.

"But that would mean she's a gold digger."

She's got a thing for rich boys, Missy Polanski had taunted.

Rufus shook his head. "That would mean she's—"

"A liar."

"I don't believe it," Rufus said.

Marcus rubbed his hand over his face. "I don't want to believe it." He didn't. But if it was true, then that meant Daisy was one hell of a goddamned actress.

"And all this stuff about Jonas, Isadora, and James?"

"You've been studying J.B.'s journals. What do you think?"

Rufus sighed. "Probably true. I'm sorry, Marc. Dead for seventy years, and they're still making headlines. Although I have to say, Daisy and her family are giving your relatives a run for their money." Rufus shook his head. "Scandal. Everything you didn't want."

"And more." Striding for the store's front door, Marcus felt everything around him fade. The pile of day-old subs, the rack of pink cupcakes, everything became a muted backdrop to the riot in his heart. Even his movements blurred, like the slow motion of a man reaching for an attacker's gun a moment too late.

"Where are you going?" Rufus asked, snatching up the

entire bundle of the day's *Tattletale*.

"To get to the bottom of this."

Rufus slapped a fifty on the counter. "We'll take all of these." He reached over and snatched the copy from the smirking clerk's hands. "Including this one."

***

Daisy Malone stared up at the yawning window of Laguna Vista's west tower, its bleary pane appearing tired and vacant in the soft glow of dawn.

But like a lazy, sun-flecked river hid phantom creatures and surging currents beneath, so did Laguna Vista's west tower window hide the forgotten lives and capricious currents behind its blank face.

How impossible it all seemed.

Yet as she stood rooted next to her van, the cool morning breeze weaving through her hair like gentle fingers, here she was again. Not the jaded cynic who'd rolled into Laguna Vista nearly a week ago to collect a fat bribe from a boss she scorned. But the little girl who'd shown up on the front lawn of the infamous mansion one Halloween night, found a ghost, and believed without a doubt that she could help him. That same little girl who knew without a doubt that if she just believed enough she could accomplish the impossible.

Instead of feeling overwhelmed, she couldn't wipe the stupid grin off her face.

So this was what being in love felt like.

She peered into the van's dirt-and-bug-smattered side mirror. If you took away the goofy grin and dreamy doe eyes, she looked exactly the same. Funny, since she felt like a whole new person.

Marcus. Jonas's grandson.

The connection.

God, when she thought about the cosmic implications her stomach did a funny little dance.

Kismet.

Destiny.

Whatever it was, she loved Marcus Van Buren.

Her heart swelled as giddy joy bubbled in her throat. She

loved him. Madly. Senselessly. Seamlessly. She could find no edges to her love for him, nor a hole nor a snag nor a fray.

She imagined herself, a freckle-faced, no-name girl from a no-name town, splashed across the tabloid covers holding hands and smiling with Marcus as their love was made public to the world. Yesterday that very notion would have seemed ludicrous. A joke. A far-fetched fantasy. But when she woke up alone this morning for the first time in nearly a week, all the sad, pitiful endings she'd imagined for them spun like a well-oiled weather vane to point in a completely new direction. Feeling the cold, empty sheets beside her had struck a terror in her like she'd never known. Then she'd remembered hearing Rufus' voice and she'd calmed down...for a split second. That's when the second wave of terror, this one more frightening and violent, crashed over her. The fear of never again waking up with Marcus. Never having his warm, solid body wrapped around hers, protective, possessive, their hearts beating strong and steady as one.

Hence why she'd raced over here at the crack of dawn, foregoing a much-needed coffee stop.

She had to help the ghosts cross over.

Now. Today.

She didn't know how. She didn't know why. She just knew that her life with Marcus could not begin until she helped Jonas. It hadn't hit her right away, but she suddenly had the sneaking suspicion that the raw, empty ache inside of Marcus had something to do with his grandfather. Somehow, somewhere along the line, even though they'd never met, their lives had tangled together like a mass of string, kind of like the unruly bonds of family, the beginning and the end lost somewhere in the genes and mayhem. She knew that neither of them could move on until someone helped unravel the jumbled mess. And, somehow, just like she had that moonlit night seventeen years ago, she knew she was the only one who could do it.

A soft pink and yellow haze crept over the part of Laguna Vista's roof facing the bay, like a baby's blanket being pulled across the sky to ward off the night chill. She snuggled into her jacket, warmed more by the wonder of Marcus' love than by the material. Yes, his love. He loved her, too. She felt it in his every touch, his every glance. Though she longed to hear the words, he didn't need to say them. He didn't need to say anything at all. She'd felt him. Everything about him. Which only made her blush with shame that she'd taken so long to believe in him. But who could blame her? It'd been a whirlwind seven days. Seven days! If a friend came to her talking of marriage and forever after only seven days, Daisy would lock her in the closet until she came to her senses. But there was no one to lock her in a closet. Her family loved him, as did she.

Of course, because this was Daisy Malone's topsy-turvy week on *This is Your Life*, things couldn't go *too* smoothly. She had, after all, accused Marcus of buying her family's affection. She cringed to even think about it. However, after a night of fitful sleep, she'd realized why she'd acted so irrationally. He'd turned her world upside down. He'd stolen the only chance she'd had in redeeming herself to family. She'd wanted to be the one to save them. It had taken her years to figure out how, and she owed her family so much. That's the only reason she'd come back to Laguna Vista in the first place—well, the main reason anyway—and the only reason she'd managed not to run from the house those first couple of days when she and Marcus didn't get along...or especially when they did.

She deserved a ruler across the knuckles from old Sister Josephine. How could she have accused him of such a thing? He'd done so much more than offer money to her family. He'd offered them a chance to restore their lives, their dignity, because he'd cared about her, about them. He wanted his new friends to be happy, and he'd been able to give them the tools to do it. He was right. His funding was no guarantee. The Malones would still have to work hard to make their new business a success, and she knew they wouldn't want it any other way. Did it really matter who made it possible, just as long as her family was safe? Couldn't the fact that she'd tried be good enough for her?

Yes. It finally could. After she'd seen the light of

unconditional love and forgiveness in her father's eyes, she knew he expected nothing but the same in return. That's all he'd ever wanted. That, and for her to get on with her life. To stop living in the past. To stop blaming herself. Unlike her, he wasn't watching her every move, waiting for her to step in the next pile of crap and make her mother cry. He only wanted her to be happy...just like Marcus did.

With the past week behind her, she understood now that measured time had nothing to do with the rhythm of the heart. Seven days. Seven months. Seventy years. What difference did it make? No matter how you packaged it, there were still three dueling ghosts bound to their childhood home for a reason they didn't understand. There was still a handsome millionaire love struck by a high school dropout he barely even knew. The heaven above had its own rules, its own game to play, and didn't ask its pawns whether they liked it or not.

And, at first, she hadn't liked it. Not one bit. Marcus Van Buren had terrified her. He'd terrified her the way he'd scrutinized her, holding a mirror in front of her face and demanding she take a long, hard look at her life. She hadn't wanted to look. She'd been doing just fine with her past buried in some dark corner behind her heart. He'd made her feel things, want things. Things she'd always been too afraid to think about because she wanted them so badly she'd ache. But she'd never settled her past, not really. Its grave may have been deep, but it was still inside her, festering, and the idea of sharing it with Marcus, flinging all of her demons into the sun and watching them burn, made her feel lighter than she had in years.

An unburdening of the soul.

He'd given her the perfect opportunity last night. Hell, he'd practically proposed, and she'd fumbled that like the perfect butterfingers. But when he'd confronted her so blatantly, demanding the truth, dangling it in her face, she couldn't rise to the bait. She'd already been of the mind that day that she would be telling him goodbye. That last sweet lovemaking in the woods behind the pub had been her way of saying it without words. She hadn't known if she *could* say the words. She knew now that she couldn't. Ever.

A rush of tenderness swelled through her as she thought about Marcus, so sweet and devoted and so ready to understand whatever she had to tell him. As soon as the ghosts were safe in the "beyond the beyond," telling him the truth about Brad was third on her agenda. If they were going to start their future off on the right foot, they needed to get everything out in the open. She wanted to hear from his own mouth that his ex-fiancée, Kimberly Langford, no longer meant anything to him. She knew that already, of course, because Daisy knew that somehow she and Marcus Van Buren had been custom-made for one another. But he'd also refused to talk about his past relationship, and that wasn't fair. If she had to be honest, so did he. No secrets. No hurts. No fears.

Second on her agenda, however, was to tell Marcus that she loved him. In the past days, he'd given her nothing but warmth and affection and trust. He'd already put his heart in her hands, even if she'd been too scared to see it. Unfortunately, the only reward she'd offered him was attitude, suspicion, and disbelief. Thank God for his patience and persistence. She planned to pay her debt in full. And what better way to prove her sincerity than to be the first to jump off the cliff and say, 'I love you'? No bungee cords. No parachute. No net.

But first she had to set things right.

She wanted a happily ever after for everyone.

Yup, just like a fairy tale. Just like Cinderella.

***

Drawing a steadying breath, Daisy opened the door to Laguna Vista and stepped inside. The weak morning light had yet to penetrate the dark interior, forcing her to feel along the wall until she found the light switch.

It was freezing. She could see her breath. It was colder inside the house than out. That was until she stepped into the living room.

A fire blazed in the grand fireplace.

If she hadn't known it was Isadora's doing, the shadows writhing on the walls like frenzied voodoo dancers might have creeped her out. All the same, she flicked on the chandelier, the floor lamp, and a desk lamp, flooding the room in artificial light.

Her enthusiasm flagged as the reality of the situation hit her. There were still so many things she didn't understand about the spirit world. She sank down on the arm of the leather couch. What made her think she could do this? What expertise did she really have? A community college course and a stack of dusty books she'd read before bed. What made her so sure that only she—a novice, a beginner, a greenhorn—could pull off such a thing as helping ghosts cross over into another world?

Jonas.

That's who made her so sure. He sensed something in her. He'd sensed it seventeen years ago, and he sensed it now. The connection. She knew it, too. Had always known it. But it was so intangible, so inexplicable, how would she know?

She'd know.

She jumped up and whipped off her jacket. She just had to pay attention and listen and feel. She'd just know. There was simply no more explanation than that.

"I can do this," she assured herself for good measure, rounding her shoulders and giving herself a full-body shake.

Infused by the image of Marcus waiting for her at the end of Holy Redeemer's aisle, she swept through the entire downstairs, unplugging her video cams and monitors. She collapsed her tripods and leaned them in the foyer corner, gathered her audio recorders, assorted cameras and wires and piled them haphazardly in various crates. "Look, guys," she called between rushes of breath, hurrying back to the warmth of the living room. "No gadgets. No gizmos. Just you and me. That's it. Jonas? Isadora? James? Please. I know you're here. I know you're hurting. I want to help. Please." She heard the hint of desperation in her voice, but she couldn't help it. She *was* desperate. Desperate to help them cross over. Desperate for their pasts to be healed and their fresh, new lives to begin.

"*How wretchedly pathetic,*" a disembodied voice taunted.

"*Lay off, Izzy,*" a male voice countered.

"*Well, well, well, if it isn't the knight in the shawl-collared suit come to save his damsel in distress from his naughty little sister. Ain't that the gnat's eyebrows?"* Suddenly a transparent image of Isadora Van Buren appeared. Lounging on the couch in one of Daisy's flannels, a cigarette holder poised between her fingers, the sleek-haired flapper leveled her dark gaze on Daisy. She cocked one thinly tweezed brow. "He's in love with you, you know."

Jonas materialized not four inches from where Daisy stood. "Don't listen to her, Daisy. It's not like that."

"I know." Daisy smiled at him, days of angst and confusion melting away. Something was different. Something that allowed her to see Jonas more clearly. To hear him. Although Isadora was no more than a transparent image, Jonas appeared deceptively tangible. Real. *Whole.* And he wore not a stitch of mortal clothing. Only the old-fashioned, tailored suit she assumed he'd been wearing the night he'd died.

Something had shifted.

A semester of parapsychology told her to assess the situation in a calm and rational manner. Cliff and Randall's explicit lectures on how to deal with an apparition played in her ears like a broken record. But despite their insistent instruction, Daisy couldn't summon the scientist in her. She couldn't analyze. This moment, all she could do was *feel.* In this strange and wondrous moment, she knew Jonas Van Buren's every dream. And more poignantly, his every regret. "I remind you of her."

Jonas stashed his unlit Cuban into the inner pocket of his suit coat and nodded. "Sara was a gentle soul with a pure heart...just like you. Her wants and needs were simple, despite her affluent upbringing. And like you, she was fiercely loyal to family, to me, to our son. All she wanted was my love, my devotion, my...attention. She had one of the three at least. I loved her. Very much."

"Then why did—"

Jonas raised his palm. "I'd never been able to resist temptation, Daisy. God knows I'd tried, but once the baby was born, I put my wife on a pedestal, treated her like the Virgin Mother. I could no longer bring myself to touch my perfect Sara with dirty hands."

"So you stayed away."

Again he nodded. "Work. Women. General debauchery. It all came easily. You see, I have a natural wild streak." He gestured toward Isadora and presumably James who'd yet to appear. "All of us do."

"Like that's a crime," Isadora cracked, flicking her ashes onto the carpet where they disappeared.

"I don't know why I'm telling you this. I've never told a soul my true feelings for Sara, not even Sara." He closed his eyes, his hands clenching into fists. "After a while, the hurt and disappointment in her eyes became so unbearable that I couldn't stand to go home anymore. It all seems such a waste now. I should've let her go. I should've given her a chance to find someone else to love. Someone who deserved her." He let out a long, ragged sigh and opened his eyes. "But I didn't. I was too selfish to give her up. As for my son, well, I barely knew the tyke. At the time, I'd never considered the devastation my absence would cause. Unfortunately, he turned out just like me. And Marcus..." he paused and stared down at the toes of his wing tips.

"Is nothing like you."

Jonas glanced up, a sad smile crooking his lips.

Daisy shook her head. "What I mean is, he's the best parts of you. There is good in you, Jonas. I know it. Sara knew it. It just took a while to surface."

He slid his hands into the pockets of his creased trousers and chuckled. "Thirty-four years on Earth plus seventy in spiritual limbo. More than awhile. More like a lifetime and beyond."

"And if God granted you a do-over?"

"On my life?" His smile turned wry. "I'd do it quite differently."

"Not me!" Isadora shouted, rocketing off the couch. "I'd live my life exactly the same. Exactly!"

Jonas ignored her. "Thank you, Daisy."

"For what?"

"For being you. For bringing out the best in my grandson.

For introducing the Malones into this selfish household. For showing me the true meaning of family."

Isadora shook her fist behind her brother's back. "I'm this far from poppin' you in the snoot, Jonas! We're your family. Me and Jimmy. All for one and one for all, you moronic traitor!"

Daisy tried to deflect Isadora's frenetic vibes. "I'm sorry I haven't figured out how to help you cross over, Jonas. But please know, I haven't given up."

He reached out and cupped her chin. "It doesn't matter. You've already given me so much."

Daisy shivered as he brushed his lips across hers. Just like that day in the library, only different. The guilt, the sadness that had linked her to Jonas Van Buren for so long were no longer overwhelming, but oddly bearable. "That felt like goodbye."

"It's time for you to move on, Daisy. You've wasted enough of your life worrying about a trio of unworthy ghosts."

"But—"

"I know. You want to help me cross over. Forget it, kid. I'm a lost cause. Even if I wasn't, well," he jerked his thumb over his shoulder, "I'm not going anywhere without them. You heard Izzy. For better or worse. Not even death did us apart."

Daisy leveled serious eyes at him. "Not so fast, Jonas. You were right to liken me to Sara. I don't care how stormy the sea gets, I'm hanging in. I'll figure it out. I'll help you," she looked to Isadora, "all of you, cross over."

"Leave me out of this, Blondie!" Isadora folded her arms over her small bosom.

Jonas ignored his sister. "No, Daisy. This connection goes both ways, and it's time I'm the one who tried to help. I've been feeling sorry for myself all of these years when it's my grandson who's been suffering the brunt of my mistakes. And now you."

"What do you mean?"

"I guess there was a rhyme to the reason I told you about Sara. I can't stand to see anymore waste. I may not be able to change the past, but I can sure as hell try to fix my grandson's future."

"I know the feeling," she said, reaching for his hands before realizing the futile gesture. Then his words sank in. "Jonas, something happened to Marcus, didn't it? Something in the past that's still eating him alive today."

Jonas nodded, his features taut. "Yes. I'm sure it's the reason he never came back to the house again."

Daisy furrowed her brows. "But Marcus was never here before..."

"He was. A long time ago. God, when he first stepped into the house last week, his guilt and resentment cut right through me."

"It's more than a grudge over your bad parenting, isn't it?" Daisy's nerves tensed. "What happened, Jonas? You have to tell me. We have to help him."

"I have an idea, but we'd have to act fast, before the house is sold." He reached for Daisy's hands, and somehow, some way, she felt his urgent touch. "I swear, Daisy, I'd spend eternity in this godforsaken house before I let my mistakes hurt my family for one more minute."

"Good," Isadora snapped. "Then let's just stay here. It's about time you remembered where your home is."

Jonas glanced over his shoulder. "Izzy's scared to cross over."

"I know," Daisy said, her heart thundering with her own fear of the unknown. "What about Marcus, Jonas? Tell me!"

Isadora swooped in on her. "You *know*?" She circled Daisy in a blur of energized anger. "How could you possibly know what I'm feeling? How does anyone know what I'm feeling? When has anybody ever known? Truly known? I'll show you what I'm feeling."

Jonas reached for his sister. "Izzy!"

"I'll show you what I'm feeling!"

"Izzy, don't!" came another man's voice. Daisy made out the fuzzy image of a young man in a snap-brimmed fedora. James?

Suddenly her senses intensified. The room shifted. The

colors too bright. Daisy swooned as Isadora's rage and confusion overpowered her.

Jonas reached out to her. "Daisy!" But with a blinding flash and a loud whoosh, Jonas was sucked up the spiral staircase in a chaotic cyclone.

Then all went still.

Twenty-one

"For a smart man, Jonas Van Buren, you're one thick-headed sap."

The whirlwind of bold, blinding hues faded, and Jonas found himself standing in the west tower, dizzy and confused. He focused on the stranger before him. "Who are you?"

"They call me Newborne."

Jonas gave the soft-spoken man a once over. White sneakers. White slacks. White crew neck sweater. Even his hair was white. Pure as freshly fallen snow, except for the ornery twinkle in his dark brown eyes. It was then Jonas noticed the colorful aura hovering about the fifty-something man. "*What* are you?"

Newborne perched himself on the arm of the sheet-draped sofa and smiled. "A heavenly escort."

James materialized at Jonus' side. "Holy..." Eyes wide, he swiped off his fedora and slapped it to his thigh. "He's an angel or something, Jonas. Come to help us cross over. After all this time." He whistled. "Ain't that the eel's hips! I'll zip down and fetch Izzy!"

Newborne pointed to Jonas. "Sorry. Just him."

James' face fell.

Jonas squared his shoulders. He willed his voice steady. A difficult task, considering he'd never been more nervous in life or death. He'd been praying for this moment for seventy years. But not like this. "I'm not going anywhere without my brother and sister."

Newborne sighed, flicking non-existent lint from his sleeve. "If it took you this long to figure it out, think how long it'll take Isadora and James. They're not going anywhere."

James charged forward. "What is it? What do we have to do?"

Newborne held up his hand. "Start by paying attention."

"Now just a minute—" Jonas began to protest, but James touched his shoulder, resolute. "Don't say it, Jonas. This is your chance. Don't worry about Izzy and me. We'll catch up with you later."

Jonas knew James was putting on a brave front. Without his big brother around... Then there was Izzy. Daisy. "Marcus—"

"Is responsible for his own happiness," Newborne said, rising and stretching.

"The incident—"

"Not your fault." Newborne glanced at his watch. "I've got a schedule, Jonas."

"I—"

"Sara's waiting."

"That's low, Newborne."

The man shrugged. "Just stating the facts."

Jonas felt as if he were being ripped in two. He thought of his sweet wife, his heart soaring in anticipation of their reunion...then he glanced at James.

"Wait for them," Newborne warned, "and you could be waiting an eternity." He moved forward, his colorful aura glowing brighter with every step. Coming sneaker to oxford with Jonas, he cocked a white brow. "So, what's it going to be, old boy?"

***

"Marcus?" A man's voice echoed from down the hall, as did his footsteps as he approached the living room. His size twelve Hush Puppies sank deep into the carpet. "Marc, I—" He stopped upon seeing Daisy, her hair wild and tumbling down her back. Her eyes bright with mischief. "Oh, hello. I'm sorry. I thought...that is...I didn't mean to burst in, but I knocked and no one...the door was ajar, so I..." he thrust out his hand and moved forward. "Let me start again. Hi. I'm Thaddeus Bookman. A friend of Marcus Van Buren's. And you are?"

"Extremely pleased to meet you." She curled up her lips into a coquettish grin. "Hiya, Doll Face."

Thaddeus cleared his throat and straightened his crooked bow tie. "Hi."

She thrust out her newly rounded breasts and arched a curious brow. "A friend of Marcus', you say? Tall, rugged, adorably disheveled. My kind of man. Although it's been so long at this point, any man is my kind of man." She smiled seductively and swept her hand toward the couch. "Won't you sit down?"

Dumbfounded, he did.

She promptly sat in his lap.

Again Thaddeus adjusted his tie. "Would you by any chance be," he cleared his throat as she skimmed her fingertips along his stubbly jaw. "Are you Daisy Malone?"

She winked. "You can call me Sugar Lips." She reached up and removed his wire-rimmed glasses. "You have beautiful blinkers."

"Blinkers?"

"Eyes. And a swell kisser." She mooned over his lips.

"Thanks." His voice cracked as she scooted higher on his lap, "Uh, Daisy?"

Her mouth hovered close to his. "Sugar Lips," she insisted.

Thaddeus fumbled with his tie. "Is it hot in here?"

Flashing a naughty grin, she whipped the tie from his neck, tossed it aside, and loosened the top three buttons of his rumpled white shirt. "It's about to get a lot hotter."

"Bookman?"

Thaddeus jumped up, bringing Daisy with him. "Marcus."

"Oh. Hi, Marcus." Daisy yawned, barely sparing him a glance.

Marcus clenched his fists at his side. Stuck to the Princeton professor like a dryer sheet to a towel, Daisy stared dreamily through lowered lashes at his old college roommate. He would've slugged his tweed-suited friend if not for the fact that Thaddeus looked so miserable and out of sorts, not to mention half blind. He kept squinting between Daisy and Marcus, trying to nab the glasses she playfully dangled just out of his reach.

"We were just...I was just..." Tiring of her shenanigans, Thaddeus hauled Daisy closer and grabbed his specs. "She was about to clean my glasses," he explained lamely.

"Actually," Daisy drawled, trailing her finger down Thaddeus' bronzed neck, "I was about to clean his pipes." She narrowed her eyes at Marcus. "Then *you* walked in."

The front door slammed. "Marc? You in here?" Rufus strode into the living room toting four bundles of twined newspapers. "Good. I could use your help. I've got more in the car, but—"

"Rufus!" Daisy pushed Thaddeus away with such fervor that he fell back against the couch. She sailed across the room, threw her arms around an owl-eyed Rufus and planted a kiss full on his lips.

The bundles thudded to the floor. Rufus, in obvious shock, endured rather than participated, his arms frozen at his sides. Ten seconds later, nine seconds longer than Marcus thought it should've taken him, Rufus managed to push Daisy to arms' length.

She smiled a lazy, sexy smile. "You taste better than I imagined. And I've got a hell of an imagination, Sweet Cheeks." She fluttered her fingers over her shoulder at Thaddeus. "Marcus, you sure know how to pick your friends." She took another brazen step toward Rufus.

Stunned speechless, Rufus held up ink-stained palms to ward off another advance.

Marcus nabbed her by the elbow before she tackled his best friend with another lip lock. He shook with fierce, gut-wrenching jealousy. Joe Rush's commentary, planted in his mind like an evil seed and watered by Daisy's illicit behavior, sprang full to life. "So you've seen the morning paper," he said, grasping for an explanation. "You figured you've blown your chances with me, so now you're working your wiles on Bookman and Sinclair. How desperate can you be, Daisy?"

She wrenched her elbow out of his grasp and smirked. "Desperate enough to tangle with the Van Burens," she said, backing away toward the fireplace. "The *infamous* Van Burens.

The ones who have a history here. Memories. The ones who stick together, all for one and one for all."

She looked to Rufus, winked and crooned, "C-c-crazy for you, gotta have youuuuu." Looked to Thaddeus and blew him a kiss, "See ya 'round, Doll Face." Then fainted.

Marcus rushed forward and caught Daisy before she hit the floor.

The lights flickered twice. The fire blew out as an icy wind whipped past them and up the stairs.

Thaddeus leaped off the couch without missing a beat. "Put her here, Marcus."

Rufus went for the scotch.

Marcus's hands shook as he rested Daisy on the couch. She looked so fragile, so vulnerable lying there limp in her baby pink sweater and faded denim overalls. Her hair fell loosely about her face, taunting him that *his* Daisy was sweet. She wasn't the kind of girl to play games.

A wolf in sheep's clothing? His heart ached. He'd never known a heart could physically ache. If what he'd read was true, then this little pink fluff had had him dancing to her tune like a circus pig in a tutu. He didn't know what he'd do if that were the case. He just goddamned didn't know.

But if the article wasn't true...Marcus stopped. He knew some of it had to be based in fact. It was how Rush operated. Maybe he'd embellished to hurt Marcus. If so, it worked. And that was almost worse because it meant that Daisy hadn't trusted him enough to confide in him. What more could he have done? He'd asked her for the truth, given her every reassurance that, no matter what it was, it wouldn't matter. But she hadn't been able to do it. She just didn't trust that he'd be around for her when things got real. Why, he thought with pent-up frustration, could she feel everything else but his love for her?

Angry and confused, he didn't know whether to throttle her or comfort her. Instead he gently tapped her cheeks. "Daisy. Wake up, Daisy."

Thaddeus took off his jacket, rolled it into a ball and tucked it under her head. Buttoning all but his top button, he adjusted his suspenders and crouched next to Marcus. "Nothing happened, Marcus. I swear."

Marcus shook his head. "It doesn't matter. It wasn't Daisy."

Thaddeus pushed his glasses up on his nose and squinted at the girl whose eyes were fluttering open. The same blue eyes that had devoured him now stared at him with confusion. "But..."

"It was Isadora." Rufus downed his scotch and poured another. He stumbled toward the couch. "Jesus, Marc. I've been kissed by a ghost." He touched his forehead and cheeks, leaving inky fingerprints on his clammy skin. "Do I look different?"

"Give me that." Marcus took the scotch from Rufus and placed it in Daisy's trembling hands. "Drink this."

"What happened?" she asked.

"Somehow," he explained, trying to calm his turbulent emotions, "Isadora entered your body."

Thaddeus stroked his chin between his thumb and forefinger. "Who's Isadora?"

"My great-aunt."

"His *dead* great-aunt," Rufus clarified, heading back toward the liquor cabinet. "A horny dame with the hots for none other than *moi*."

"A ghost," Thaddeus said, a smile softening his weathered face. "Interesting."

Daisy blinked at him. "Who are you?"

"Thaddeus Bookman." He thrust a big hand at her. "Pleased to meet you, Ms. Malone."

Instead of shaking his offered palm, she shoved her untouched drink into it. "Professor Thaddeus Bookman? Author of *The Paranormal Enthusiast's Guide to the World Beyond*?"

Thaddeus beamed. "You know my work?"

Daisy leaped off the couch, pushing past both men. "You bet I do. It's practically required reading for anyone in the industry. It's brilliant."

Thaddeus rose, a proud smile on his face. "Thank you, I—"

"How could you?" she railed at Marcus.

"We need help," Marcus said, digging in for the fight.

"You mean *I* need help." Her eyes shadowed with hurt even as she planted stubborn fists on her hips. "How long have you been planning this? I thought you believed in me."

Those soft eyes, the soft voice...he wouldn't be swayed. Couldn't. Not now. Not yet. Not before he at least had it out with her.

She waved her hands in front of her, as though erasing an invisible chalkboard. "No. No, you're right. I haven't given you any reason to believe I can do this. I haven't done a thing to prove to you that I can." Her features culminated in a longing so intense, he had to hold himself steady. "You just have to understand that it's something *I* have to do. It has to be me. The connection—" Her gaze jolted toward the stairs. "Oh, my God. Jonas!"

She bolted for the staircase.

"Where are you going?"

"To find Jonas. He needs me." She devoured the steps two at a time.

Thaddeus tapped Marcus on his tensed shoulder. "Who's Jonas?"

"My grandfather."

"Dead," Rufus confirmed before Thaddeus could ask. "And if you think that's creepy, get this. Jonas and Daisy have a *thing*."

"Shut up, Rufus," Marcus snapped, heading for the stairs.

Thaddeus rubbed his palms together. "Interesting," he said as he followed Marcus. "Coming, Mr. Sinclair?"

"And risk another mauling from Izzy the lusty ghost? I think not."

"How do you know she's upstairs and not—"

Rufus slammed down his glass. "I'm right behind you."

"Daisy, slow down," Marcus called down the hall. "I want to talk to you."

"No, he needs me now!" She disappeared around the corner.

"*Very* interesting," Thaddeus said with a chuckle.

"Shut up, Bookman." Where was she going? Marcus wondered. There was nothing at that end of the hall, except..."Daisy!"

He moved forward to run but Thaddeus tripped and plowed right into him. Both men landed with a heavy thud. He heard an *oomph* and a door slam.

Then pounding. "Let me out!"

"Rufus." Marcus pushed Thaddeus off him.

The pounding grew louder as did Rufus' voice. "Marc! Professor? Somebody! Get me the hell out of here!"

Marcus backtracked down the hall until he found the door behind which Rufus was trapped. He jiggled the brass knob. "Locked."

Thaddeus came up behind him. "What is it?"

"A linen closet."

"Marc?"

"Right here, Ruf. Hang on."

"Someone pushed me into this goddamned closet, and now I can't get out!"

"Don't panic. Bookman will get you out." Marcus turned to Thaddeus. "Get him out."

"Where are you going?" Thaddeus and Rufus asked as one.

Sweat trickled down Marcus' back as a fuzzy image of a young boy came to mind. "*I'm tellin' ya, there's nothin' up there.*" Marcus struggled to breathe. "I've got to get to Daisy."

Rufus pounded his fist against the oak door. "Marc?"

"He's gone." Thaddeus jiggled and twisted the knob.

"Professor?" Rufus whispered, his voice suddenly an octave higher.

"What?"

"I'm not alone in here."

                                    ***

Marcus raced around the corner and skidded to a stop at the end of the corridor. He did a three-sixty. Daisy was nowhere to be seen. He stared at the wall. A door. There should be a door. He didn't question how he knew that. There hadn't been a door in the blueprints he'd studied last year. But he knew, as sure as the fear in his heart, there should be a door.

Marcus flattened his hands against chipped paneled wood and layers of peeling wallpaper, palming his way down the wall, the wall where a door should be. Then he felt it. Excitement. Foreboding. Daisy. Jonas. And someone else. Someone dear.

"*Scaredy cat!*"

A small boy.

"*I'm not scared!*"

Two small boys.

Overwhelmed, Marcus leaned his forehead against the wall and gasped for a steadying breath. Then he saw it. Near his shoe. A small hole in the wooden baseboard. A mouse hole? No. He knew better. Crouching down, he reached in and flipped a trick lever. The secret panel swung open. Steep, spiraling steps ascended before him, years of cobwebs freshly disturbed. Daisy's footsteps tracked in the dust and now echoing above him.

"*But I'm tellin' you, Marcus, there's nothin' up there.*"

Dry mouthed, Marcus gripped a decrepit banister and forced himself to climb the stairs, one terror-filled step at a time. Daisy's voice rang in his ears. "Pain buried deep. So like Jonas." Like a tidal surge, repressed memories flooded back to him in vivid clarity.

"*Betcha' my Joe DiMaggio special edition card there is.*"

"*Dust doesn't count.*"

"*Course not, bean brain. But anything that has to do with Jonas, Isadora, or James does.*"

"*You're not supposed to say their names out loud, Marcus. It's bad luck.*"

"*Are we gonna do this or not? We don't have all day. If our moms find us here...*"

"*DiMaggio, huh?*"

"*Yup.*"

"*Honest Injun?*"

"*Yup.*"

"*All right. But I'm tellin' ya, Marcus. There's nothin' up there. Ma said so.*"

"And I'm tellin' you there is."

"How can you be so sure?"

Marcus pushed open a rusted door and stepped out onto the roof of Laguna Vista. A breeze ruffled his damp hair as the rising sun warmed the back of his neck. The west tower loomed a few meager feet ahead. Fighting a wave of nausea, he whispered his boyhood explanation, "It's a feeling."

He saw her then. Carefully picking her way to the edge of the roof.

"Daisy, stop! Stop right where you are." His words were little more than a strangled whisper.

"He's in there, Marcus," she said, kicking aside broken red shingles. "Jonas is in the west tower. I know it. I feel it. He's waiting for me. If I can just get to him, I can help him. I know it. All this time, I couldn't find a way in. Then it occurred to me, the window. I can climb in through the window." She inched her way nearer to the edge and onto a raised ledge. "All I have to do—"

"Climb down, Daisy. *Now.*"

His harsh words stopped her. On precarious footing, she grabbed onto a decorative wrought-iron railing for stability then looked at him. "What is it? What's wrong?"

She sounded scared. Not for herself but for him. He must look like shit. He certainly felt like shit. He was barely breathing—that is, if he was breathing at all. His heart had most definitely stopped. He felt sluggish and disoriented, and he was sweating. Buckets of sweat, as though he was facing his death. Or someone else's.

"Acrophobia," she said. "I forgot! You're afraid of heights. My God, Marcus. You shouldn't be up here at all. Just stay calm. Breathe deep and step back against the door. Better yet, sit down. Sit down, breathe deep, and stay calm. I'll come back for you. This won't take long. I'm almost there."

Though his feet felt like cinderblocks, he somehow managed to inch forward. "Come away from the edge, Daisy. Please."

She navigated the ledge like a circus tightrope performer. "I climbed a zillion trees as a kid." A chunk of cement fell away. Her left foot slipped. "I'm okay. It's okay. Did I mention I was a crackerjack gymnast in grade school?" She kept moving. "Almost there."

Marcus felt as though knives twisted in his temples.

The railing groaned.

"*Almost there, Petey. We're almost there. Hold on to the railing. That's right.*"

"*Did you see that, Marcus?*"

"*What? Pay attention, Petey. Watch where you step. Almost there.*"

"*In the window. I thought I saw—*"

Petey's scream echoed through Marcus' head.

"*Marcus!*"

"*Hold on, Petey!*"

"*Help me!*"

"*Hold on! I've got you!*"

"Marcus!" Daisy's scream pierced his heart and soul, calling him to the here and now. Paralyzed, Marcus watched as the railing gave way.

"*Help her,*" an older man's voice pleaded. "*You can do it, boy.*"

Marcus felt a sudden and foreign rush of love flow through him. Intense fatherly love. A connection. It shook him to his core as time stood still, then briefly ceased to exist at all.

"*I'll help you.*"

Marcus glanced up. In the window, palms splayed against the filthy pane. Jonas.

God, it was like looking into a mirror.

Jonas reached out. "*All for one and one for all.*"

Marcus lunged forward, meeting him halfway. They caught Daisy by her wrists. She dangled three stories above the paved circular drive. "Hold on, baby!"

Another woman screamed. A frantic woman somewhere down below.

Marcus paid no heed. He locked gazes with Daisy, her eyes filled with tears. He felt her fear. He'd felt this sort of fear before. Sheer terror. Only then he hadn't been quick enough, strong enough. "It's all right, Daisy. We've got you."

This time it was different.

"We?"

A chill raced down his spine. He tightened his hold on Daisy and glanced over his shoulder. In the window. Jonas. Smiling.

"Marcus?"

He tore his stunned gaze from his grandfather.

Her voice trembled as a single tear slipped down her cheek. "Can you help me up, please?"

Sobered and shaking, he hauled her up over the crumbling ledge and into the safety of his arms. When he glanced back to the window, Jonas was gone.

Twenty-two

He'd killed his cousin.

Gambled Petey's life, offering a goddamned baseball card as stakes, and he'd lost.

He'd known the roof was in disrepair. Creeping along the crumbling edge to climb into a third-story window, he'd known it was dangerous. Yet he'd as good as dragged Petey onto the roof. He'd as good as pushed him over the edge.

It was his fault.

And Jonas'.

"Marcus?"

How the *hell* could he do something like that and not remember it?

"Marcus, you're hurting me."

Daisy's plea reached him from some far-off distance. He dropped her hand, the air cool against his sweating palm. His temples throbbed, as though the twisting knives had been yanked out to leave deep, gaping wounds.

"*I thought I saw...*" Petey's last words echoed in his ears.

He remembered it now. Vividly. That last second...he'd glanced in the window, the second before Petey fell, catching a glimpse of a retreating figure.

Jonas.

Marcus glared at the vacant window. His deep-seated grudge with his grandfather. *Pain buried deep*...It all made sense now. And yet it didn't.

All these years, such hot animosity toward a man he'd never met. Oh yes, he'd been angry at Jonas his whole life. Angry for turning a once loving family into a dysfunctional mess. Angry for caring more about his one-night flings than his own son's future. Angry for the tears Marcus' own mother had cried whenever her husband called to say he wouldn't be home, or especially when he didn't call at all. Oh, yes. He'd nurtured his anger from an early age, and he'd never questioned it. Why would he? It was only natural for a child to resent someone who'd sabotaged his family's happiness. Jonas had always been like the Grinch who stole Christmas, except he'd died before he could have a change of heart. Before another little boy could be born to make him see the error of his ways.

However, what was unnatural was the corrosive loathing that had been boiling on the back burner of his memory for over twenty-five years. An anger and a hatred that had bordered on self-torture. A grown man should've been able to leave behind the disillusionment of childhood dreams and get on with his life.

But how did a man know which way to run when he didn't know what he was running from?

Now he knew.

As though struck by lightning, he walked in a daze down the attic steps.

"Marcus, tell me what's wrong."

He heard fear in her voice. How could he explain? How could he explain that for years he'd been terrified to let a passenger ride in his car? That he'd handpicked the people around him, knowing they wouldn't get too close? That he'd spent years constructing a life that never went beyond his control? A life that wouldn't be responsible for someone else's. A life that had been reduced to rubble in a matter of minutes.

How could he explain that all he wanted to do was curl up in a corner and weep like a little boy, for a little boy who'd remain so forever?

He felt her hand on his arm. Comfort.

He shrugged it off. He wasn't ready for comfort. Not yet.

He pushed open the secret panel.

Thaddeus waited on the other side, brows creased with worry. "I heard a scream. Two screams. Then the door flew open, and Sinclair fell out. He followed one scream. I followed the other...here." He motioned to the wall. "But I couldn't...there wasn't...a hidden door. No wonder." He stopped, his gaze computing the menace on Marcus' face. "Christ, what happened up there, Marcus?"

Marcus ignored him, choosing instead to investigate the second scream. A familiar scream. The same scream he'd heard when he'd grabbed for Petey.

Jesus.

Petey's terror-stricken face filled his mind as he pushed past Thaddeus. He could still see the wide, brown eyes filled with tears, begging Marcus not to let go. The sheen of sweat on his freckled cheeks. The desperate little fingers that clutched at his...

Marcus swallowed an anguished sob, preferring instead to slam his fist into the railing as he descended the circular stairs. *How the hell had he forgotten!*

"Marcus!"

His mother, looking deceptively prim in her lavender silk pantsuit, rushed toward the steps, hand pressed over her heart. Her eyes were wild, frantic, tears spilling out of their artfully lined corners. "Are you all right?"

Rufus stood behind her, his tense face asking the same question. Marcus held his friend's gaze a full two seconds, not really seeing him, willing himself a modicum of control before making eye contact with the faithfully overdramatic Mary Van Buren.

Her hands fluttered over him to be sure he was in one piece. "What in God's name were you doing on that roof? How did you get up there? That wall's been sealed for years."

His stomach heaved.

She knew. Of course, she knew.

His glare must've been hot and deadly because she turned panicked eyes toward Daisy. "How dare you risk my son's life," she accused shakily. "What were you thinking?"

Daisy opened her mouth, shut it.

"What are you doing here, Mother?" His voice was calm, controlled as he picked up Rufus' forgotten scotch and tossed it back. The liquid fire did little to warm him.

She sucked in a practiced breath of offense. "I don't hear

from my son in days. I find out he's actually *sleeping* in this," she looked about the house with disgust, "firetrap...with this..." she gestured a harried hand toward Daisy..."what was I supposed to do? You weren't here last night. You weren't checked into any of the hotels. I was worried."

"I've gone away before without telling you. What's the big concern now?" He eyed her jeweled fingers sardonically. "Since I don't see a fire extinguisher, I can assume it's not the house burning down around me."

His mother sniffed and eyed Daisy as though she were a used dress on a discount rack. "Well, if you really want to know..."

Marcus snapped. "What I really want to know, Mother, is how the hell I forgot about Petey! You remember him, don't you? Your nephew? My cousin, Peter Tadmucker?"

Daisy touched his arm again, tentatively this time. "Marcus, please."

He shook her off, eyes blazing. "No, goddammit. Tell me! Why, until five minutes ago, couldn't I remember killing my own cousin?"

He heard Daisy's breath sputter. His mother's catch.

She clutched her heart and sank to the edge of the leather couch. "I don't know what you're talking about."

"Don't you dare fake a heart attack! And don't you dare lie to me!"

She dropped her hand, but her tensed fingers remained curled. "But you didn't, sweetheart."

He hurled the glass into the fireplace.

His mother jumped up. "No, I mean it!" She reached out her hand, then pulled it back as though afraid he'd bite. "It was an accident. You grabbed for him. You tried. But you were so young, so small," she said, her tan face now pale and looking ten years older than when she'd first walked in.

His voice was low, like a panther's warning growl. "Why didn't I remember?"

"I thought it was for the best. You were so upset. You couldn't sleep. You wouldn't eat. I found a doctor, a hypnotherapist, who helped you forget. What was I supposed to do?" She reached out her hands again. "My poor boy. Hurting so. I couldn't let you get bogged down by this."

Marcus sniffed, stepping away. "That's right. Because I had such a promising future as the head of VB Enterprises. You always had high ambitions for me. I guess something like that would've put quite the nasty mark on my reputation. A reputation you've guarded like a pit bull."

Her lips trembled. "You don't understand—"

"Oh, I understand. I guess I can't blame you, seeing as how you had to live in the soiled shadow of my father's reputation, but, tell me, Mother, how much did it cost you to keep this out of the papers? Or, for that matter, how much did you pay the Tadmuckers to stay away from me and keep their mouths shut? Hmmm? How much does something like that cost?"

She looked ready to break down into hysterics, but as he moved in for the kill, Daisy grabbed his arm and pulled him to face her. "Stop it, Marcus! You've said enough."

His laugh sounded strange to his own ears. "I've only just begun, sweetheart."

"But she looks ill."

He eyed his mother's chalky pallor. "Looks like she's seen a ghost," he accused, unable to summon an ounce of mercy for the woman who'd given birth to him. "Don't let her fool you. She always plays this game, Daisy...but then I guess you should understand all about playing games."

She blinked at him, stunned. "What are you talking about?"

"So easy to play innocent when you've had the practice."

Her eyes narrowed.

So she wasn't going to take this lying down. Good. He welcomed the fight. Welcomed her impassioned explanation. But then, didn't the guilty always deny the loudest?

"Spit it out, Marcus. What exactly are you accusing me of?"

The air crackled between them. He could barely look at her without his heart seizing. He'd dreamed a thousand dreams on that beautiful face. A thousand dreams now dead in their tracks. He couldn't breathe. The pain, the long-buried pain he'd never understood, had been tapped. It was gushing out faster than he could handle. He didn't know how he could feel anything else, but he did. A new agony, like freshly tilled earth, raw and exposed. His mother. Daisy. The only two people he'd ever loved. And both had betrayed him.

He went for the bundle of tabloids.

Rufus stepped in. "Marc, no. Not like this."

Marcus waved his assistant aside, gritted his teeth, and snatched a newspaper from the pile. "Let's cut to the chase, shall we?" He thrust it into Daisy's hands. "I assume it needs no explanation."

She scanned the front page. Her hands trembled, but he felt no satisfaction. "DUMPED CEO SLUMMING IT?" Worse, instead of the fear he expected in her eyes, he found ire. "You think *I* had something to do with this?"

"Keep reading."

He could see the bold type of the story's lead-in from where he stood. HARVARD GRADUATE ROMANCES HIGH SCHOOL DROPOUT. DETAILS INSIDE. And those details were emblazoned in his mind. *Young girl drops out of high school after getting pregnant. Young girl blackmails prominent lawyer to keep college son's name out of paper. Ten years later, same girl scams Wall Street tycoon, Marcus Van Buren, claiming she can exorcise dead relatives from his ancestral home.* Though Rush had omitted her name, he'd supplied plenty of damning photos.

Daisy Malone: high school dropout, unwed mother, scam artist.

Marcus Van Buren: Fool.

The paper fluttered to the floor as blood drained from her face. "My God, not again. My family..."

Marcus felt the knives that had been yanked from his temples plunge into his heart. His voice scraped with shattered emotion. "So it's true?"

Tears filled her haunted eyes. "I was going to tell you. Today. I was going to tell you so many things today. I shouldn't have waited."

Something inside him died as he stared down at her with

stone-cold eyes. "It wouldn't have mattered if you were honest, Daisy. If I'd known the truth, I wouldn't have touched you with a ten-foot pole."

Twenty-three

Her hand stung from the slap.

It was nothing compared to her heart as she watched Marcus Van Buren walk out of Laguna Vista...and her life.

Short, angry breaths stabbed her lungs.

Her eyes burned, but no tears would come.

She must be in shock.

That would explain why her heart kept beating, like a tire spinning eerily after a wreck.

As the deafening silence pressed down on her, threatening to snap her chilled bones, she realized Marcus Van Buren had done exactly what she'd predicted. Exactly what he'd vowed he never would.

He'd hurt her. Then he'd left her.

If I'd known the truth, I wouldn't have touched you with a ten-foot pole.

Her stomach clenched. It felt as though he'd run that pole straight through her gut.

She pressed a trembling hand to her waist, recalling another time she'd felt such raw despair that she'd wished her body would shut down and give her a moment's peace. A time when she was a seventeen-year-old girl who'd miscarried her departed lover's baby two days into her second trimester.

Her knees weakened as her bones seemed to finally crumble.

It hadn't mattered that Brad had deserted her, that he'd wanted nothing to do with the baby, that his father had offered her father twenty-five thousand dollars to sever any ties between the two families. An offer Pop had thrown back in the pompous lawyer's face. No need for the Worthingtons to reject the Malones. The Malones rejected the Worthingtons.

None of that had mattered.

What mattered was that Daisy had wanted the baby, even though she was seventeen and scared to death. So much so that she'd dropped out of her senior year at the first signs of a troubled pregnancy.

Through it all not once had her family judged her. She'd disappointed them, shamed them, and yet they'd stood beside her. Ready to battle anyone who breathed an unkind word about Daisy or her untimely situation.

Unlike Marcus. *I wouldn't have touched you with a ten-foot pole.*

He'd not only judged her, he'd condemned her.

Not twelve hours after he'd said marriage wasn't a ludicrous idea.

Her fists clenched. The invisible pole twisted inside her.

How dare he? How *dare* he?

He'd cursed his mother for being obsessed with avoiding scandal. Then in the next breath, he'd shown himself to be no better. Even worse, the man who'd damned his father for breaking promises and bailing out when things got tough had just walked out on her without looking back.

Damn him. *Damn* him.

A strangled sob caught her ears, drawing her attention away from the front door. In her tumult, she'd forgotten she wasn't alone.

"What have I done?" Mary Van Buren, ashen faced and trembling, fainted into Thaddeus Bookman's arms.

Daisy took that as her cue.

She was out the door and halfway to her van before she realized someone was chasing her. "Daisy, wait!"

"Go away, Rufus." She wrenched open the driver's door and climbed inside, reaching immediately for the glove compartment, which opened on the first try. Of course it did. Marcus had fixed it. Another twist of the pole. *Look, Daisy, I'm just a regular guy.* Yeah, right.

"He didn't mean it."

Daisy snorted. "Seems chronic." She rifled through the

glove compartment, pulling out the crumpled pack of cigarettes. Thankfully, Jill, the wanna-be-smoker, had spared her one cigarette, bent and stale though it was. Finding a match was another story. The van's lighter had disappeared sometime during the Reagan administration.

She looked up at Rufus who'd opened the passenger door and climbed in without an invitation. "Got a light?"

"You don't smoke."

"I used to—and I want to *now*. So either make yourself useful or get the hell out of my van."

Frowning, he produced a flashy ultra-slim lighter, steadying her hand as he lit what had once been an enjoyable crutch. She inhaled and sighed, expecting a sudden and familiar calm to descend over her. However, the heady smoke had no effect other than to leave a bad taste in her mouth. Much like Marcus' nasty remarks.

"Learn something new about you every day," Rufus said, eyeing the mangled cigarette perched between stiff fingers.

Daisy fumbled through her backpack, searching for her keys. "Well, you can rest easy, Rufus. The cat's out of the bag. After today, you know all there is to know about Daisy Malone. No more secrets, no more skeletons lurking in my closet. Your Mr. Rush has certainly seen to that."

"Why didn't you tell him, Daisy?"

She jerked up her head at his soft words. The levity of his gaze broke the dam of tears. "What? That I'm an ex-smoker? Or that I fell in love at seventeen, got pregnant, and miscarried three months later? Or wait, maybe it was finding out that I'm a high school dropout that blew his self-righteous mind. I guess studying my ass off to get my GED doesn't count for much in a Harvard man's book."

"You miscarried?"

"Yes," she snapped, resuming the search for her keys so Rufus couldn't witness her tears. "Didn't you read the article?"

"Yes."

"Weren't the sordid details spelled out in black and white?"

"Yes. I mean, there were sordid details. But nothing about a miscarriage."

Daisy's hand froze in her backpack. The smoke from the cigarette streamed unchecked into her eyes as she homed in on Rufus. "What *exactly* did that article say?"

Rufus jammed his hand through his disheveled hair. "That you seduced a rich kid, got pregnant, then tried to blackmail his family into buying your silence. Among other things."

Daisy opened her mouth, but words failed her. Fury roared through her like a freight train, her heart pounding deafeningly in her ears. Mumbling obscenities under her breath, she ditched the cigarette out the window.

"I take it the facts are wrong?" He shook his head. "Of course the facts are wrong, or twisted at the very least. Rush wrote the story. That son of a bitch." He slammed his fist on the dashboard. The glove compartment popped open. He slammed it shut. "When Marc questioned you on the article," he asked irritably, "what did you think you were confessing to?"

"The truth."

"Joe Rush wouldn't know the honest-to-God truth if it walked up and punched him in the face." His hand fisted, and his eyes took on a dreamy cast before he rushed on. "But he's not so stupid as to write a total work of fiction. He got his mangled data from somewhere. Someone who knew Marc was here and not in Paris. Who would sink so low as to call that bastard?"

"I have a good idea." She jammed her key into the ignition and revved the engine. "Get out, Rufus."

"What?" Noting her murderous expression, he fumbled the door open. "Why? Where are you going?"

Daisy ground the gears into reverse. "To take control of my life."

***

"You snake!"

Missy Polanski's eyes popped open. Two cucumber slices fell into her plastic-draped lap. "Jesus, Daisy. You scared the daylights out of me. What do you want?"

Daisy ripped *The Tattletale* out of Missy's blood-red claws and waved the tabloid in front of her clay-masqued face. "An explanation."

"I'd say that reporter needs a stronger telephoto." Missy
snickered. "Nice picture," she said, pointing to the front page.
"Though I'd preferred a less grainy view of Van Buren's cute
behind." She squinted. "Is that a tattoo?"

"That *reporter* was under the impression Marcus was in
France. How did he find out Marcus was here in Jersey? How
did he know about my condo?"

"That's what reporters do, Daisy. They sniff out news."

"This isn't news," Daisy spat, turning the foiled heads of
four other salon clients. "It's gossip."

Missy snatched back the paper and perused the inside
story. "Juicy gossip at that." She passed the tabloid to the
woman in the next chair. She winked at the other clients. "Great
stuff. Make sure you all pick up a copy."

"You contacted that reporter," Daisy accused, disregarding
the stares of the other women. "That Joe Rush. You told him
Marcus was here. You told him about my past, or your warped
version of it at least."

Missy closed her eyes and leaned her head back. "Do you
mind, Malone? In case you haven't noticed, I'm getting a facial
here."

"Why?" Daisy plowed on. "Why drag my family into your
grudge against me? Why embarrass Marcus like that? Because
he paid more attention to me than to you? That's it, isn't it?
You hated it that Marcus favored me over you the other night
in the hallway. Just like Brad favored me over you more than
ten years ago. For the last time, Missy, I didn't steal Brad
Worthington away from you. He was tired of you. Just like he
got tired of me. He used us. Why can't you see that? He's the
bad guy, not me."

Missy sat straight up. The clay masque cracked as her
face contorted with fury. "Brad loved me. You lured him away
with your sickening goodie-two-shoes innocence. It fascinated
him. But fascination only lasts so long. I was working on
getting him back and was damn close to succeeding until you
went and got yourself pregnant, you stupid twit. You scared
Brad away. He never came back after that summer. Because

of you, I missed out on being who I could've—*should've*—been. Mrs. Brad Worthington. You ruined my life, Malone. And at long last, I've finally ruined yours."

Daisy blinked at her high school rival. The woman who spent more money on plastic surgery than groceries. The woman who'd married a suspected pedophile. The woman who, without an ounce of remorse, had dragged Daisy as well as her family's reputations through the nation's mud. For a moment, Daisy considered dumping a nearby bowl of dye, the hue a bright hooker red, over Missy's bleached locks. The moment was fleeting. "You're wrong, Missy. You haven't ruined my life at all. My life and my happiness are in my own hands." On her way out the door, she added, "If I were you, I'd stop worrying about the past and start worrying about your future."

"What's that suppose to mean?" Missy shrieked, running after Daisy, plastic cape flying.

But Daisy was already climbing into her van. She had her own future to address.

***

Daisy couldn't begin to sort her warring emotions about Marcus until she made sure her family was all right. By now, they'd more than likely received a phone call from a concerned neighbor or an extended relative, alerting them to the surprise in this week's *Tattletale*. Or perhaps Missy had left a rolled-up copy on the front stoop early this morning. It would've been the crowning touch.

She knew her family would be more outraged than embarrassed. Pop would be pissed at Rush for making Mom's stint as a showgirl sound as though it were something to be ashamed of. In truth, Danny was proud of his wife's Vegas career.

And Mickey. Yikes, his head had probably exploded because Rush had referred to his love as a "Candie stripper." Candie had worked as an exotic dancer to pay her way through college. But then she'd met Mickey and fallen in love. She'd given up dancing and school, neither of which she'd cared for, and focused her energy on their relationship. Now she was his wife, and Rush had publicly humiliated her. Daisy suddenly worried that Mickey, wild with wrath, might track down Joe Rush and beat him to a bloody pulp, landing himself in jail.

And they would all, the entire Malone family, be furious that Rush had twisted Daisy's sad past so horrifically as to be unrecognizable. She shuddered to think what they as a combined unit could do to that New York City upstart.

A huge, chrome bumper pulled into the road. With a cry, Daisy screeched her van to a halt, just missing the family station wagon as it backed out of the Malone driveway.

The station wagon's brakes chirped. Her mother climbed out. "I was on my way to find you."

Daisy jumped out of the van and met her mother halfway. "You've seen it?"

Angie, eyes bright and fierce, nodded. "Oh, yes."

"Pop?"

Again she nodded. "He took off after Mickey. Candie called here in hysterics. Said Mickey was on his way to Manhattan to murder that reporter. I don't know if your father's going to head your brother off or help him." Tears filled her eyes as she stepped forward and took Daisy into her arms. "My poor, dear, Sunshine. Secretly, I hope your father and brother pound that dickhead Rush into the ground."

Daisy smiled against her mother's shoulder. "I'm okay, Mom."

Angie pulled back and touched a comforting palm to her daughter's cheek. "Are you sure?"

"No." Her lower lip trembled, making her feel like a five-year-old clinging to her mother's apron. She didn't care. Right now she needed comfort. An anchor in a sea of confusion. A voice of reason. More than anything else as a child, Daisy remembered her mother's soothing voice, soft and understanding, eager to lift the weight of the world from her daughter's shoulders. Daisy, running on adrenaline and in danger of a nosedive at any moment, needed her Mommy.

"How did Marcus take it?"

Daisy lowered her eyes and focused on her hiking boots.

"Not well."

"He must be angry as hell at that reporter."

"He's angry as hell at me."

"You? Why on Earth would he be mad at you?" She placed a finger under Daisy's chin and forced Daisy to look her in the eyes. "Tell me you already told him about Brad."

Daisy said nothing.

"All right then, tell me you set Marcus straight. That you told him the truth."

Daisy swallowed hard. "I told him the article *was* the truth.'

"What!"

"I hadn't read it. Only the front page. It all happened so fast. He was so angry. I confessed without even knowing what I was confessing to. He walked out on me, Mom."

Angie took her by the forearms and pulled her close. Looking Daisy dead in the eye, she asked, "Do you love him?"

Tears pooled in Daisy's eyes. It killed her to admit it, but there was nothing left at this point but the truth. "Yes. With all my heart."

"Then go after him, Sunshine. Make this thing right." Her mother smiled. "Love means working through the bad times as well as reveling in the good. You've been in this family long enough to know that."

Daisy didn't move. She didn't know what to do. "He's probably halfway to New York."

Angie inclined her head. "Then you better get going." Lifting Daisy's hand, she shoved her keys into it. "Here, take the station wagon. It may be old, but it looks faster than that van of yours." She prodded her daughter toward the family car and practically pushed her in. "Oh, and take this." She handed Daisy a state-of-the-art cell phone through the rolled-down window.

Daisy stared at the phone. "Where'd you get this?"

Angie smiled. "From Marcus. He wanted me to have it. In case of an emergency." She leaned in and kissed Daisy's cheek. "Fight for him, sweetheart. He's worth it. And you deserve the best."

Daisy allowed her mother to push her into the car and

send her after Marcus because she didn't know what else to do. Now, watching her mother wave to her in the rearview mirror, she knew she better figure out something. Quick.

She turned the corner, made sure she was out of sight, then pulled up to the curb and cut the engine.

Now what?

Something inside her wouldn't let her chase after Marcus. As much as she wanted to spend her life with him, she couldn't make it easy. Her mother said you had to take the good with the bad when it came to love. She knew that. Hell, she was living proof. But what about the fact that he'd scorned her and walked out? What about self-respect? What about making Marcus work for her forgiveness...if he even wanted to?

She certainly wouldn't go after him to change his mind. He either wanted her or he didn't, and there didn't seem to be any mystery there.

She absolutely would not go tearing up the Parkway to convince a man she was worth something. For ten years she'd believed she deserved the snide comments from Missy Polanski, the sidelong looks and behind-the-hand whispers of local gossips as she walked the aisles at the supermarket. Well, she'd put an end to that today. Telling off Missy had been a long time coming, and it felt good.

But what about Marcus? Could she just let it end like this?

Her gaze fell to the curled and faded family snapshot that Pop kept tucked into the dashboard. Tears burned her eyes as she stared at his proud, smiling face, his burly hand on her young, slim shoulder, and she realized more than ever just how lucky she was.

She'd never doubted her family's love, even in the worst of times. She'd always known they'd be there, just as they'd huddled around her in the picture. Always known there'd be someone there to catch her when she fell.

But what about Marcus?

Who would catch him?

Suddenly the entire morning played out before her, but through Marcus' eyes. The way he'd gripped her arm as though she were a lifeline. The way he'd punched the stair railing in anger and frustration...agonized over the death of a beloved cousin he'd never even remembered, a cousin he believed had died because of him.

Hot tears coursed down her face. God, that was enough to bring down any man, even one as strong as Marcus.

But it hadn't stopped there. Oh, no.

His mother, the only person he'd ever trusted, the one person who represented anything good in his life, had been lying to him for most of his life.

Daisy plucked a burger-joint napkin off the floor and wiped her nose.

Then, as if his mind hadn't already been blown to complete bits, his lover stupidly confirmed to be true horrendous lies about her past. Lies that made him believe he'd been betrayed yet again.

How could she blame him? How could she blame him when, if such a thing had happened to her, she would have reacted ten times worse?

She picked up the compact cell phone from the seat.

He'd given her mother a phone. In case of an emergency.

She looked around the old car, the one that had carried her family to the doctor, to twirling practice, to the library...just about everywhere they'd ever gone. Marcus had known the car had broken down the night of the play, and he'd given her mother a phone...because he wanted her family safe. Because he cared.

Fight for him. He's worth it.

Daisy knew all about second chances. She'd been blessed with her fair share this past week alone, and if she loved Marcus Van Buren anywhere near as much as she claimed, didn't he deserve one, too? The world had turned on him. He was alone. She needed to show him that he wasn't.

She plucked the picture from the dash, dropped it into her pocket, and started the car.

Isn't that what love and family were all about?

***

The dark green stalls of the tollbooth loomed before Marcus like the giant gates of Hell. He eased off the accelerator.

His foot cramped and he muttered an oath as he was forced to slow down. Panic prowled the edges of his fury. He didn't want to slow down. Slowing down meant he'd start to think again. He didn't want to think. He wanted to burn the blacktop until it dumped him off the edge of the planet. Until the snarling emotions were finally shaken loose and left in a dead heap somewhere on the Garden State Parkway.

It wasn't just the fact that he'd forgotten his wallet at Daisy's condo that made him swerve the Rolls to the side of the road amidst blaring horns. It was the finality of crossing yet another threshold out of Daisy's life. Somehow it jolted him from his headlong dash into oblivion. Somehow, the hulking green bays stood perched before him like an ominous warning. Once he crossed, there'd be no going back.

He checked his side mirror, ready to storm the gates. It was too late to worry about what lay on the other side. He already knew his life would be a living hell. He didn't need to come back here to torture himself. What would be the point? To jump back into the flames that had burned him once already? To watch the crumbling ashes of his hopes and dreams scatter with the autumn winds?

But then he heard those chill, careless winds in his head, whipping across the dead lawn of Laguna Vista, the dried, curled leaves scratching along the bare-patched earth, buffeting the front door of the abandoned mansion. Her defeated whisper gusted through its dark, empty halls. *Not again. My family.*

He threw the transmission into park and sagged into the plush seat. His limbs suddenly fell limp. The blood that had been pounding in his head ebbed back to the seeping wound he'd once called his heart.

Not again.

So this had happened before. Publicized scandal.

My family.

Marcus' mind raced, his forehead creasing in puzzlement. Rush's article had portrayed Daisy as a teenaged seductress, a schemer, a blackmailer, an unwed mother who apparently abandoned her child when it failed to afford her the posh life she'd plotted. In short, Rush had declared her a calculating, heartless slut, and yet her concern had not been for herself. It had been for her family.

His thoughts slowed.

The winds stilled inside him, leaving an eerie silence.

He no longer saw the red glare of brake lights through the windshield. Instead he watched the memory of Jill Malone threatening to have him maimed if he touched her sister. Watched Danielle Malone frantically searching the crowd at the play for her beloved Daisy. Watched Danny Malone's face radiate pure heaven whenever he set eyes on his Sunshine. And watched Angie Malone cook ten pounds of her daughter's favorite breakfast to help mend bridges.

Rush's story suddenly developed a thousand holes. This was not the family of a woman who'd given up her child for adoption when the rich kid who got her pregnant wouldn't pay.

These were the Malones. Fiercely proud and loyal to a fault. To them, family was everything. And Daisy was every inch a Malone. Giving up one of her own? Not in a million years. Not for a million dollars.

Dread hung heavy in the air, along with the scent of fear.

Blackmail. Rush had accused her of blackmail. Yet Daisy wasn't about money. She'd proven that last night, when she'd realized he was the silent partner in her pop's new venture. A venture that would save her beloved family from financial ruin. She'd thrown a fit. God, not even the threat of bankruptcy had put a dent in that godforsaken Malone pride.

With sudden and vivid clarity, he remembered their emotional scene behind the pub. He'd felt her. As much as he'd denied it, she wasn't the only one who could feel things. Which was one of the reasons he'd kept himself safely distanced behind his ocean-sized desk and buried under a mountain of paperwork. He hadn't wanted to feel. He hadn't wanted to be involved. But Daisy sure as hell made him feel, and she sure as hell made him involved. Involved in a life that had been passing him by.

Last night behind the pub she'd been ready to say goodbye to him. She'd been afraid. Afraid because she loved him. Afraid that he would leave.

Oh, God. How many times had he begged her, *Feel me, Daisy. Know the truth.*

Well, she must have known all along. Just when she'd needed him to feel her truth and live up to the promises he'd made, he'd plunged a knife into her heart and walked away.

He shook his head, his eyes burning.

All those years of blaming Jonas and Regis for deserting their wives, their families. For turning their backs on broken promises and ignoring the destruction they left behind. For all the years he'd vowed not to be a Van Buren...

He'd done just that.

He'd screwed up.

Royally.

How easy it had been. That was the most frightening part. To learn he was human. To learn that, no matter how vehemently he denied the blood in his veins, it still flowed red and ripe with Van Buren imperfection. The same blood as Jonas and Regis. Men with faults and failings. Not god-like patriarchs with cloven hooves whose legends certainly outweighed the reality.

He'd never once considered that there might be two sides to the stories his mother had told him. She'd been bitter and had grown to loathe the Van Buren name and all it represented. It was possible, even though his father and grandfather had committed inexcusable acts, that somehow they'd simply lost their way, and the longer they were gone, the harder it was to come back. Maybe that was the romanticized version he suddenly very much wanted to believe, but he couldn't dispute the love he'd felt radiating from Jonas on the roof. As sure as the numbing lock of Daisy's fingers, he'd felt his grandfather's apology.

They'd screwed up.

They'd all screwed up.

Daisy, who in one lifetime had given her heart to two undeserving sons of bitches.

Danny, who'd gambled away his family's security despite his bone-deep love for them.

His mother, whose own hurt had turned her son's vulnerability into an obsession.

Jonas, who'd somehow been lucky enough to find a second chance at redemption.

And Regis, who had not.

The Malones were no different than the Van Burens when it came to mistakes tangling up their lives. But the Malones had something the Van Burens did not. Forgiveness. They forgave each other with all the passion with which they loved.

Would Daisy have enough forgiveness in her heart for him?

And what about himself, he wondered, as he sat there parked on the side of the road, idling in one of those major intersections of life. What would he do?

He still had a chance to set things right. He still had a chance to create a new beginning for the Van Buren family. Wasn't that the reason he'd gone to the house in the first place? To settle old scores and renew his family name with a fresh, clean slate? Who said he had to forget his family, his heritage, his roots? Instead of denying their existence, maybe he should learn from their legacy.

He wondered for a wistful moment if his father could see him now, if he was proud that his son had learned from his mistakes. Proud that, despite his unconventional upbringing, his wife had raised a fine son.

Everything seemed brighter all of a sudden, almost blinding, as though he'd spent his entire life walking in shadows. An undiluted joy surged through him, so potent as to be painful. For the first time in his life, he felt whole, complete.

Well, almost.

Panic rushed his crumbled wall of defense. Leading it, like a battering ram to his heart, was the vision of horror and disbelief that had slacked Daisy's jaw a second before it tightened with fury and she struck him. God, he'd been so caught up in his own raging emotions that he'd forgotten who she was.

The woman he loved.

Daisy Malone.

But her admission of guilt still made no sense. Why would she agree to such libelous accusations...unless...unless she'd never read them. She'd just assumed it reported the truth. She hadn't known Rush's fiendish tendencies. Marcus had.

Still he'd condemned her.

He was a fool. A damned fool.

He gunned the accelerator and cut an illegal U-turn across four lanes of traffic.

Not only did he owe Daisy Malone the groveling of a lifetime, he owed Petey Tadmucker. He refused to allow the little boy's death to be in vain. He would bring the family back together. All three families. The Malones, the Van Burens, and the Tadmuckers.

As the dark green stalls diminished in his rearview mirror, he somehow knew his father was proud.

Twenty-four

Marcus steered the car with one hand and fumbled with the cell phone in the other. It wasn't easy punching the tiny numbers with shaky fingers and one eye on the road, and he nearly dropped it when Rufus started shouting into the phone the second he answered. "Are you out of your frigging mind?"

"I was," he admitted.

"Where are you?"

"On the Garden State Parkway."

"Well, hang a U-ie and meet me back at Laguna Vista, pronto." There was static, then a muffled whirring sound. "Dammit, Barbie, not now! Pay attention to the stick!" Pause. "Not mine! Ah, for God's sake!"

Marcus shook his head. "Rufus, what the hell are you doing?"

"Looking for you! Now turn around. Not you, Barbie. Marc!"

"Rufus, I don't have time for this. I need to find Daisy."

"That's what I'm trying to tell you. I found Daisy on her mother's cell phone and sent her back to the house. I told her you'd be there. I knew you'd come to your senses."

Everything inside him stilled. She'd gone to the house...thinking he'd be there. He didn't know how, because he surely didn't deserve it, but there was hope. "I owe you."

"Damn right you do."

"But I can't meet her at the house."

There was a pause, then Rufus' Brooklyn accent turned low and lethal. "You better—"

"Get her to meet me at the Steel Pier, Ruf. I need your powers of persuasion."

"Well, *I am* the one who got you two together in the first place. And Marc?"

"Yeah?"

"It's not what you think. She didn't know what she was admitting to."

"I know."

"She—"

"Just get her to the Steel Pier, Rufus. And...thank you."

***

"Where's Mrs. Van Buren?" Daisy asked.

Thaddeus Bookman emerged from the kitchen with a hoagie sandwich and a glass of iced tea. "Looking for Marcus."

"Where's Rufus?

"Looking for Marcus. Where were you?"

"Looking for Marcus." She felt a sickening flutter in her stomach as she stood in the exact spot where Marcus had left her. "Rufus said Marcus would be here. I guess he doesn't want to be found."

"Oh, Mr. Sinclair will find him. I'm certain of that. He's determined and seems on friendly terms with a helicopter pilot." He studied his watch. "Though I think he planned to be back by now."

Moving farther into the living room, Daisy barely noticed the comfortable temperature and odd sense of calm. Her own stomach gurgled with nerves and fear, not to mention the manic fidgeting of her fingers as they wound into the hem of her shirt. Just because she was willing to take a chance on Marcus didn't mean he wanted it. After all, the ever-resourceful Rufus hadn't been able to find him. There was no guarantee that Marcus would come back...ever.

She'd risked what was left of her heart by coming here, and she'd felt a painful kick when she'd pulled into the drive and not seen his car.

She'd wait, but how long she didn't know.

"Rufus planned to get you two back together so you can kiss and make up. He thinks you two are in love. So do I." Thaddeus looked down at the goodies in his hands as though he'd forgotten they were there. A place mat sat waiting on the coffee table, and he set his plate and glass on top of it.

Daisy ignored his observation and instead looked around for the bundles of *The Tattletale*. "What happened to the newspapers?"

Thaddeus sat. "I burned them."

Her gaze shot to the big man perched on the leather couch. She didn't know him, not really. Not enough to thank him for a gesture that couldn't possibly burn away her past or what had happened. Not enough to care what he thought about her. Only she did care. He was Marcus' friend. "It wasn't true."

"I didn't read it," he said, reaching for his glass. "Even if I had, I wouldn't have believed a word of it. Tabloids are only good for lining the litter box. Obviously you didn't read it, either, or you wouldn't have confessed to its content. Marcus should've seen that, but he was too blinded by his own ghosts, so to speak. He's angry. No matter her good intentions, his mother screwed up."

"She hates me."

"Mary Van Buren hates anyone who brings so-called scandal to the Van Buren name. She's not an easy woman. Then again, she hasn't had an easy life. Don't let it bother you, Daisy. She doesn't like me, either."

Daisy stuffed her hands into the pockets of her baseball jacket. "You brought scandal to the Van Buren name?"

"Uh, no, not really. I didn't instigate it anyway. It's a long story. Maybe another time." Thaddeus gestured toward his sandwich. "Can I make you something to eat?"

Her stomach gurgled. "No, thank you." Then she saw the melted cheese on his hoagie. "I thought the appliances were on the blink."

"They look in working order to me."

Daisy swept past Thaddeus and into the kitchen. Bright sunshine streamed through windows that this morning had been caked with frost. The refrigerator was humming. The water running. Normal. For the first time in four days, everything appeared to be normal. She returned to the living room.

"Everything all right?"

"Apparently." She gestured to the fireplace. "What happened to the fire?"

"After I burned those insidious tabloids, I doused it. It was sweltering in here."

"How long ago was that?

Thaddeus shrugged. "Twenty, thirty minutes."

"It hasn't flared up again on its own?"

"No, why?"

"Isadora spent the past three and a half days wreaking havoc on this house. Keeping the home fires burning was one of her tricks. Vandalizing the kitchen and plunging it into an Arctic freeze was another. I don't feel her anger anymore. Nor do I sense Jonas' despair. I don't feel...anything."

"Ahh." Thaddeus snapped his suspenders. "Well, Jonas is somewhat at peace. Isadora's energies are otherwise focused. She's pouting. And James is trying to cheer her up."

Daisy slumped into the oversized chair. "So they're still here."

"Mmm-hmm." Thaddeus bit into his hoagie then wiped a spot of mustard from his mouth. "Why so glum?"

"Since I didn't feel anything, I thought maybe Jonas had crossed over. I had this crazy idea that once he faced his past, that once he learned the lesson he needed to learn, he'd be allowed to move on. I guess I was wrong."

"No," Thaddeus said, taking sip of iced tea. "You weren't wrong. He learned his lesson. The importance of love, of family, as in his wife and son. He earned the chance to cross over. He didn't take it."

Daisy leaped out of her chair. "What! Why? When?"

Thaddeus motioned her to sit.

She did, but not before pacing a few steps. "I can't believe this. When did this happen? Why didn't he go?"

"Remember what Marcus said about Isadora entering your body?"

"Yes."

"Remember anything that happened during that time?"

"No. Why?" Daisy leaned forward, eyes wide. She'd swear the man was blushing. "Did I do something wrong?"

"No, just..." Thaddeus cleared his throat and adjusted his glasses. "No. You didn't do anything wrong. What about before that? You were talking to Jonas."

"That's right. He thanked me for showing him the importance of family. Said he regretted not being a better husband and father. Then he was sucked up the steps." She snapped her fingers. "Just like that."

Thaddeus grinned. "Dramatically summoned to the west tower by a Mr. Newborne."

"Mr. Newborne?"

"A heavenly escort. An angel, if you believe in that sort of thing, sent to bring Jonas to Heaven, if you believe in that sort of place. Apparently, Jonas tried to bargain with the man. Tried to get Isadora and James in on the deal. Your rooftop escapade interrupted the negotiation. Newborne warned Jonas he was on a tight schedule. Jonas ignored the warning in order to help Marcus, who in turn helped you. When it was over, Newborne was gone."

"No!" Her cry was muffled as she buried her face in her hands. "Poor Jonas. What have I done?"

"What you've done, Daisy," Thaddeus said, reaching over with his long arm and titling up her chin, "is quite remarkable. You've given a tortured soul peace. Yes, quite remarkable."

"What are you talking about?"

"You said it yourself. You said, 'I don't feel Jonas' despair.' He's at peace, Daisy. He's a changed man. A happier man. "

"But he wanted to cross over. I promised I would help him. Instead I prevented it."

"You prevented nothing. Jonas would've refused Newborne regardless. He still wants to cross over, to be with Sara and Regis, but he won't leave without Isadora and James. *All for one and one for all* I believe was the quote."

She studied Thaddeus as he cleaned the lens of his glasses. "How do you know this? I know you're a crack parapsychologist, but how could you possibly know all this?"

Thaddeus slid his glasses back on. "James told me."

"James Van Buren? He spoke to you?"

Thaddeus sipped his iced tea then nodded. "He has a

fondness for hanging out on the refrigerator. He explained the whole scenario while I made my lunch."

"You saw him?"

Again he nodded. "Almost as clearly as I see you. I've never conversed with an apparition. I found it most interesting."

Daisy swiped her hair from her face. "I'm confused. I thought my seeing Jonas had something to do with being a sensitive. I even thought Marcus might be a sensitive since he seemed affected by the ghosts and their moods. He saw Isadora, but then so did Rufus. There's also a possibility his cousin, Petey, saw one of the ghosts. Does that mean we're all sensitives?"

Thaddeus shook his head. "I saw James, and I'm by no means a sensitive. I'm a scientist. A historian. I don't feel things as you do, Daisy. I simply experience unexplained happenings, examine them, document them. Don't try to make sense out of this. We're dealing with the supernatural. The inexplicable. That's what makes it so," he wiggled his brows, "interesting."

Daisy leaned back in her chair and sighed. "Maybe it is useless to make sense of it, but I'm curious why each ghost latched on to a specific person. Jonas to me. Isadora to Rufus. Now James to you."

"Be interesting to find out." Thaddeus smiled and bit into his hoagie.

A familiar, heady scent settled around Daisy like a warm embrace. She scooted to the edge of her seat. "Do you smell that?'

Thaddeus wiped breadcrumbs from his mouth and sniffed the air. "Cigar smoke."

"Jonas." She smiled, feeling a strange sense of ease for the first time all day. "Do you see him?"

Thaddeus glanced around. "No. You?"

"No. But he's here. I feel him." She closed her eyes, wishing she could hold his essence to her. Then her eyes popped open and she sprang to her feet. "He just whispered in my ear."

Thaddeus rose from the couch, concern on his weathered

face. "What did he say?"

Not knowing why, Daisy wrapped her arms around Thaddeus and planted a smacking kiss on his lips. "Marcus needs me." She pushed away and darted for the door.

"But you don't know where he is."

Her mother's cell phone rang. She pulled it from her jacket pocket. "Rufus? I know. I know. Where? Got it." She smiled at Thaddeus. "Now I do. Wish me luck."

"Good luck."

The sentiment was voiced in tandem. One human. One ghost.

***

Marcus paced the edge of the Steel Pier. The screams from the whirring rides echoed his nerves. Would she come? Would Daisy give him another chance?

He was ready to tear out of his skin as he waited for her. Maybe he'd pushed his luck in asking her to come to him. It wasn't ego. It was the heavy pall of his betrayal hanging over Laguna Vista. The wounds too fresh, the air still singed with the heat of his words. He wanted to beg for her forgiveness with laughter in the background, with excitement and cheer infecting her every breath. He wanted the lighthearted atmosphere to swallow her and make her forget his cruelty. He wanted her to remember the good times they'd shared.

Yes, he was playing this from every angle.

He had everything to lose...and he was scared to death he just might.

The sun crested high in the sky, the tiny white ball beating down on his shame from between thin, gray clouds. He leaned over the rail to watch sea gulls bob for popcorn floating on the equally gray ocean. A child tossed the fat puffs then squealed in delight as the birds dove, snatched them up then screeched in demand for more. The little boy's blonde hair fluttered and shimmered in the breeze as he grinned up at his mother, clutching the red-and-white-striped popcorn bag.

A longing twisted inside Marcus.

He could envision his child, Daisy's child, as clear as the little boy with the sunshine hair and gap-toothed smile. Pride surged with shame. Deep down he knew that Daisy would be an incredible mother. No matter the circumstance, she'd cherish the chance to raise a child. Yet he'd believed Rush's lies.

He should've known better. He *did* know better. Still, there was something to Rush's story. Something that confirmed what he'd suspected all along. Daisy had suffered more than a broken heart from that rich kid. There was something deeper. Something that had eaten away at her for years. He wanted to understand. Most of all, he wanted to hear it from Daisy. No one else.

As it should've been all along.

This time, he'd give her every reason to trust him.

"I thought you were afraid of heights."

He spun around at her soft voice. She stood a good five feet away, obviously wanting to keep her distance. The Octopus's wily black arms writhed beyond her shoulder, as though struggling to make its way back to the water. He understood its need to try, if even in vain.

Her voice belied her look. A wild look. Thick strands of hair had slipped from her ponytail, waving in the breeze with the same rebellion as the mechanical tentacles behind her. Her eyes crackled and snapped with blue sparks, issuing a don't-mess-with-me warning he didn't quite know how to take. The unsnapped Phillies jacket billowed around her. He could see the shallow rise and fall of her chest. Had she been running? Dare he hope it had been to him?

He pressed himself against the rail, fighting the urge to snatch her up and steal her away before she ordered him out of her life. He didn't know what he'd do without her. He just didn't know.

As the wind snapped at the back of his shirt, the long drop behind him felt like mercy compared to Daisy Malone standing before him, maybe for the last time. "The height is nothing now. I must be cured."

She stared at him, seeming to weigh her words. She surprised him by addressing his feelings first. "Your acrophobia..."

"Spurred by Petey's fall."

"The headaches?"

"Repressed memories. Spurred by mention of Laguna Vista, or Jonas."

"It wasn't— "

"—my fault. I know. At least the logical, adult part of me knows. It's a hell of a lot easier to deal with guilt when you know what's causing it. It'll take some time, maybe a good therapist, but I'll make my peace with Petey...and with myself."

Daisy glanced at the ocean. "Seems you've got it all figured out."

His heart ached at the catch in her voice. "Most of it."

Her gaze drifted back to his. He expected tears. Instead Malone pride sparked at him from incredible blue eyes. He didn't know whether to feel relieved or worried.

She nudged at a melted blob of taffy with her boot, not giving him a clue either way. "Your mother—"

"Is she all right?"

Daisy shoved her hands into the back pockets of her jeans. "Shaken up. She fainted but Thaddeus caught her. He said she's back at her hotel." She paused and studied him, as though gauging the guilt that raged like rivers in the lines of his skin. "Marcus, you had every reason to be angry."

"Maybe. But it's no excuse for the way I treated her. And you."

"A bomb dropped on your head. Anyone would've been shell-shocked." She cocked her head. "But there is one thing I don't understand."

Marcus closed his eyes. Finally. He'd fast-forwarded his issues to get to hers, theirs. Now he wished for a pause button, dreading the possible end of what could've been, *should've* been the most incredible relationship of his life. Shit. *Shit.* He opened his eyes, memorizing her every curve, her every crook, her every lash. He drew a deep breath. "Go ahead."

"Don't you know me at all?" Her voice sounded small, fragile, out of place amidst the gasping hydraulic machinery and pumping techno music. She suddenly looked like a broken angel trapped among the faceless crowd.

He couldn't stand it any longer. Devouring the distance between them, he pulled her to him and pressed his cheek against the warm curve of her neck. "Yes, Daisy. God, yes. I know you. I do." He splayed his fingers into her hair, unwilling to let her go. "Forgive me. It wasn't you that I didn't know. It was myself." He felt her struggling to breathe in his desperate embrace. As much as it killed him to step away, he didn't want to scare her.

He captured her hands. They were cold, but she didn't snatch them away. His eyes, hot with beseeching, bored into the guarded blue gates of her soul. "The life I'd thought was mine suddenly wasn't anymore. The incident on the roof, the memories...there was a whole part of me I didn't know existed. I couldn't think. I couldn't breathe." He squeezed her hands, needing her to feel his truth. "I know I haven't been fair to you, but please, Daisy, feel my sincerity. Know that I've never before given anyone my heart. Know that I was scared, scared of letting anyone near me in the face of what I'd just discovered. I know you, Daisy. I know you the same way I know that every time I see the sun rise, I want to look over and see you next to me, in my arms, smiling."

Her fingers twitched within his. "It isn't true. What Rush wrote."

His heart wrenched. She wasn't going to make this easy. He didn't blame her. "I know."

"Not most of it anyway," she hurried on, as though needing to voice the truth as much as he needed to hear it. "There *was* a rich boy. Brad Worthington. He was a college sophomore here on summer vacation. I was a senior in high school and hopelessly, recklessly in love. There *was* a pregnancy. Unfortunately, a child didn't play into Brad's future, and neither did I. He made that clear when he sent me a 'Dear John' letter with a check and the name of a discreet doctor. I—" Her voice cracked.

Marcus lifted her hands and kissed her knuckles, his gaze steady and warm on hers.

He wasn't going anywhere, and he wanted her to know it.

She drew a deep breath. "I tore up the check and sent a

letter back to Brad informing him that I had every intention of keeping the baby. Then I did the hardest thing I've ever done in my life. I told my mother. She told Pop. They were so understanding, Marcus. So supportive."

"I'm not surprised."

"Then it got ugly. Brad's father offered Pop a huge sum of cash to sever all connections between the Malones and the Worthingtons. Baby included. Needless to say, Pop wanted to break more than ties. He told them to shove that money...well, you can guess where."

Marcus squeezed her hands as a lump lodged in his throat. Simply put, he wanted to find the no-good Brad Worthington and beat the living crap out him. His father, too.

"Contrary to Rush's story, I never gave up my child, Marcus. I miscarried."

Marcus pulled her against him and held her close, wanting to absorb her pain—all of it, past, present, and future. "I'm so sorry, sweetheart. So very sorry."

"Something inside me died the day I lost her. Or him." She sucked in a ragged breath. "To see those lies in print. To know you believed it..." She shook her head. "You breathed life back into a part of me I thought long dead. You don't know what it felt like to watch you walk away from that."

Tears stung his eyes. "Daisy..."

"Then I realized you weren't thinking clearly. I know the guilt of feeling responsible for someone's death. I know it very well. It makes you do stupid things."

"And say stupid things." He stroked his thumbs over her knuckles. "Daisy, I need you to know that I'd do anything in the world to take it back. Anything. You've given me more than I deserve by showing up here today, and for that I'm grateful." He took a shaky breath. "Maybe I'm asking too much, but please say you forgive me, even if you don't love me anymore."

She pulled her hand from his. Her eyes darkened with something unreadable. "I never said I loved you."

His breath strangled in his throat. He tried to assimilate her words. Before his heart died its slow, final death, she slipped her arms around his neck. "Like you never said you loved me."

For a second he stood dazed. Then he latched his arms around her and held on for dear life. "I love you, he said, unable to speak the words fast enough. "I love you, Daisy. With every beat of my heart."

"I love you, too," she said, her breath warmth and comfort in his ear.

A fat tear squeezed out of his eye. He didn't care if the whole world saw it. He didn't care if Joe Rush had twenty telephoto lenses cocked and aimed on him. He loved this woman, and he wanted everyone to know it.

She looked up at him. Her own eyes shimmered with tears, and he vowed the only tears she'd ever cry again would be happy ones. "You're not the only one who made a mistake. I need *you* to know that. I should have told you about Brad. About the baby. I'm sorry you learned it from Rush. I'm sorry about the article, Marcus."

"It's not your fault."

"Well, yes. Actually it is. Remember Missy Polanski?"

"The spiteful shrew with the bleached hair." He cocked a knowing brow. "Let me guess. She tipped off Rush on my whereabouts. Suggested that something was brewing between us then fed him a crock of half-truths about your past and laced it with jealous innuendoes. Rush filled in the rest."

"Good guess. The witch is more transparent than I thought." She swiped blowing hair from her eyes. "She'd hoped to marry Brad. She claims I stole him then scared him off, ruining her chances for the good life."

"Ambitious for a teenager."

"The day after graduation, she married Bernie Polanski. Heir to his ailing father's appliance store chain."

"From what I hear, a hell of a second choice."

"I'll say. I hate to be petty, Marcus, but she got hers."

"How's that?"

"I went to her house to confront her about the article, but she wasn't there. Bernie was being dragged away in handcuffs."

Marcus grinned. "So the police finally found evidence. It's about time. I filed that complaint days ago."

Daisy's eyes widened. "You filed a complaint against Bernie Polanski?"

"Damn right. Jill might laugh off Polanski as pathetic, but it made me sick to think of him trying to lure naïve girls into his car. Not to mention he's messing with my sister-in-law. I hope they toss that perverted son of a bitch in jail and throw away the key. On second thought, maybe I should've broken his—"

Daisy pressed her finger to his lips. "You're a good man, Marcus Van Buren. I knew that from the beginning. That's why I fell in love with you."

They both smiled at each other, amazed and glowing in each other's love.

"Goddammit," he whooped as he picked her up and twirled her around. "How'd I get so lucky to find you?"

She got that ornery gleam in her eye. "Rufus was the one who found me."

"Yeah, and he'd be the first one to tell you. But now you're mine, and I won't let you get away again." He spun her around once more.

"Wait a minute!"

"What?"

"Put me down."

"Why?"

"Sister-in-law?"

"What?"

"You called Jill your sister-in-law."

His mouth twitched. "I did, didn't I?"

"Yes."

Thank God he'd grabbed his jacket from the floor this morning. The same jacket he'd worn last night to the pub. The same jacket in which he'd tucked the little black box along with intentions that had gone awry.

He set her down as he fumbled anxious fingers in his pocket. He dropped to one knee, drawing the attention of passersby clutching purple dinosaurs and leather-jacketed bulldogs. He opened the box and looked straight into Daisy's misty eyes. "Miss Daisy Malone, will you marry this elephant-sized-balls SOB who loves you with all his heart?"

Tears trembled on her lashes as she gazed at the ring he held. "It's beautiful."

"Fashioned out of the Austrian crystal from Laguna Vista's chandelier." He grinned. "I wanted it to be something meaningful. But don't worry, we'll go shopping for the largest diamond we can find as soon as you agree to be my wife."

"I don't want another ring," she said as he slipped the glittering ring on her finger. "This is perfect. Just like you." She blinked at the ring then at him. "Wait a minute."

"Now what?"

"Not that I'm complaining, but I'm the second woman you've proposed to this year. Are you sure about this?"

He rose. "Ah, the Kimberly Langford fiasco rears its ugly head."

"I've seen her picture. She's very beautiful."

"I never loved Kimberly. Not really. That's why she left me. That and the fact that she found someone with a thicker wallet."

Daisy cocked her head. "If you didn't love her, why did you ask her to marry you?"

He smiled sheepishly, like a kid caught with his hand in the cookie jar. "She was smart, pretty, and sweet, or so I thought at the time, and frankly the 'America's Most Eligible Bachelor' title was wearing on my nerves. I didn't believe in true love before now, so she seemed as good a choice as any."

"As good a choice as any?" Daisy laughed. It was either that or whack him in the head. "And here I was worried that you were on the rebound."

"Kimberly dented my ego, not my heart. Now come here."

Daisy ducked his grasp. "Wait a minute."

"*Now* what?"

"Is that why you asked me to marry you? Because I'm as good a choice as any?"

Marcus grinned. "I can assure you, Daisy, marrying you is one of the worst choices I've ever made."

"Thanks a lot."

"It ranks right up there with hiring Rufus Sinclair two years ago."

She smirked. "Now I know you're kidding. Rufus is the best assistant you ever had. You said so yourself. *And* he's your best friend."

Marcus' eyes twinkled. "And the biggest pain in my—"

"Hey!"

He pulled her to him before she could get away again. "Before I met you, I enjoyed a calm and controlled life. Once we're married and living at Laguna Vista, where three of my dead relatives and several of your living ones will no doubt pop in whenever they feel like it, I can assure you my life will be anything but calm and controlled."

She sobered. "We're going to live at Laguna Vista? I thought you were set to sell?"

"I called the buyer this morning. I told him the house was infested with ghosts, and I can't seem to get rid of them." His teasing didn't ease the tension about her mouth so he elaborated. "I don't want to get rid of them, Daisy. They're my family. It's their home as much as mine. They're welcome to stay as long as they wish."

"It's about time you figured that out." A smile touched her lips, and his heart soared. "Thaddeus said Jonas had the chance to cross over, but he didn't take it. He didn't want to leave Izzy and James."

"I know the feeling," he said, recalling with a shudder the finality of those tall, green bays. It seemed he and Jonas had more in common than just wayward blood. They'd both known Daisy Malone, and they'd both known her love. Daisy, who'd taught them that, no matter the lure of Heaven and all its peace, no matter the walls shadowing a heart, family was the most important thing in life, and death. Jonas could've abandoned his brother and sister for greener pastures, or puffy clouds or whatever. Marcus could've run back to New York, as he'd started to do, and locked himself away in his office skyscraper, never to let himself feel again.

At one time, they both would've done just that. But not

now. Not after Daisy. Today he and his grandfather had chosen the path of uncertainty. The path fraught with hurt. Risk. Love.

It was worth every step.

Daisy cleared her throat for his attention. She wiggled her hips and cocked a saucy brow. "C-c-crazy for you-oo. Gotta have you-oo..." She stopped singing and winked. "I've got an itch, sugar lips. If you know what I mean."

Marcus pulled her to him. "I catch your meaning loud and clear, sweet cheeks."

They sealed their future with a kiss so full of devotion, it seeped into their very bones.

When the gathering crowd applauded, Daisy and Marcus began to laugh. It soon degraded into gut-clenching hysterics as the intensity of the day disappeared. Marcus grabbed her hand and pulled her along.

"Where are we going?" she asked, her eyes tearing from laughter this time.

He came to a jarring halt in front of the Skyride. Or the "love ride" as Rufus had begun to refer to it. Marcus looked down at his bruised-eyed bride-to-be with all the love in his heart. "To scratch that itch."

Daisy grinned at him then up at the amusement ride. "You're kidding, right?"

"Chicken?"

Her eyes glittered. "Never challenge a Malone, Van Buren." She tugged at his collar. "Come on, lover boy. Geez. No one can accuse you of being a dud."

"Tell that to Rufus, will you? Never mind. I'll tell him. You just concentrate on us."

She pressed her mouth to his as he bought two tickets. "Now and forever."